Dirty
Little
War

ALSO BY DIETRICH KALTEIS

Ride the Lightning
The Deadbeat Club
Triggerfish
House of Blazes
Zero Avenue
Poughkeepsie Shuffle
Call Down the Thunder
Cradle of the Deep
Under an Outlaw Moon
Nobody from Somewhere
The Get
Crooked

Dirty Little War

A CRIME NOVEL

Dietrich Kalteis

Copyright © Dietrich Kalteis, 2025

Published by ECW Press
665 Gerrard Street East
Toronto, Ontario, Canada M4M 1Y2
416-694-3348 / info@ecwpress.com

Cover design: David A. Gee

LIBRARY AND ARCHIVES CANADA CATALOGUING IN PUBLICATION

Title: Dirty little war : a crime novel / Dietrich Kalteis.

Names: Kalteis, Dietrich, 1954- author

Identifiers: Canadiana (print) 20240495993 | Canadiana (ebook) 20240496728

ISBN 978-1-77041-796-0 (softcover)
ISBN 978-1-77852-378-6 (PDF)
ISBN 978-1-77852-377-9 (ePub)

Subjects: LCGFT: Detective and mystery fiction. | LCGFT: Novels.

Classification: LCC PS8621.A474 D57 2025 | DDC C813/.6—dc23

This book is funded in part by the Government of Canada. *Ce livre est financé en partie par le gouvernement du Canada.* We acknowledge the support of the Canada Council for the Arts. *Nous remercions le Conseil des arts du Canada de son soutien.* We would like to acknowledge the funding support of the Ontario Arts Council (OAC) and the Government of Ontario for their support. We also acknowledge the support of the Government of Ontario through the Ontario Book Publishing Tax Credit, and through Ontario Creates.

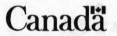

Canada Council
for the Arts

Conseil des arts
du Canada

Ontario

ONTARIO ARTS COUNCIL
CONSEIL DES ARTS DE L'ONTARIO
an Ontario government agency
un organisme du gouvernement de l'Ontario

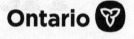

ONTARIO
CREATES

PRINTED AND BOUND IN CANADA   PRINTING: FRIESENS   5 4 3 2 1

Get the ebook free!*
*proof of purchase required

Purchase the print edition and receive the ebook free.
For details, go to ecwpress.com/ebook.

To Andie
Always

1

"**Y**ou go down in the first." Nails Morton said from the corner of his mouth, leaning close, the straw boater tilted low. A little taller with some size and about a decade on Huck, the man talking like he was imparting wisdom. Huck Waller taking a stab at why they called this guy Nails, one of Dean O'Banion's crew, built like a baby grand with the look of a scrapper about him.

"Taking a dive's not my style," Huck told him, shaking his head.

"You got no money, then you got no style, boyo." Nails giving him a slow poke to the ribs. "It's why you take your coat off, am I right? And make it look good, huh. These fellas ain't chumps."

"Just after the fiver." It's what Huck was promised for stripping down and stepping to the toe line, just another Hobo Joe stepping from a boxcar, a slab of meat for some man to beat on, the men in the crowd sizing him up, placing their wagers. This lean kid who didn't have the mean look or scars of a fighter.

Most of these men forming the circle were Irish, calling it fisticuffs or strap fighting, wanting to stick to the old ways they brought from the Isle, but leaving behind the famine and conflict, letting their troubles take another shape in this new land.

Huck was getting a sinking feeling about the whole set-up, no place for the Marquis of Queensbury rules here, that's for sure. No fancy dancing around a roped ring, just a good punch-up, two men going toe to toe till one went down. Taped hands and thirty seconds between rounds, the fight over when one fighter went down and stayed down past an eight count.

This city where pro fights had been banned along with the booze, where every man loved his sport as much as his drink. The sport living on in secret alleys and out behind boxcars like this, waiting for its comeback on this one-time swampland connecting to the city's rail lines, out of sight of the Exchange. The foul stench coming from the stockyards, stinging the eyes, the livestock pens holding hundreds of hogs.

Not a corner man or ring doctor — no corner and no ring, not even a spit bucket — and not a man in this crowd caring about the size or reach of either opponent, just a crowd fueled by booze, come to bet on the bare-knuckling. One or two of them giving the occasional look over at the man holding the bet money. The man with a smile on his face, and the bulge of a pistol under the coat.

Huck stepped to the line and showed his hands, Nails Morton pitting him against a rawboned Neanderthal now stepping to the line, giving Huck a hard look, a front tooth missing.

"I seen a hundred of you, and . . ." Grinding his hands together and growling.

Nails clapped Huck on the back like they were pals, saying, "You want some good advice, take the fall." Smiling over at his gangster pals, two of them working the crowd, taking

8

the bets, both with satchels holding the wagers slung over their shoulders, both with pistols shoved in their belts. Both scratching on notepads, taking bets on the rounds, giving odds on the prediction.

"Thanks just the same," Huck said, smelling booze on the guy facing him.

"Maybe I ain't being plain enough." Nails smiled, leaning in again, his jacket falling open enough for Huck to see the butt of the pistol.

"I get you fine," Huck said. "You say it nice and promise me more than the five, undo your coat and show me you ain't asking."

"You do catch on." Nails kept the smile.

Huck looked at the circle of men on the tear, some still placing bets, and this two-bit crook acting like that Rothstein, the gangster who put in the fix and got the Sox to throw the World Series a year back, eight players in on it, all taking payoffs, losing to the Reds and causing a scandal that got them banned for life for their troubles.

"It's more than advice," Nails said. "A show of friendship if you will."

"We friends now?"

"Could be."

"Well, friend, like I told you, I don't dive."

"Then here's my final number. Around here we call it a cut . . ." Looking eye to eye, Nails said, "A good show and it's ten points of what we pull in. This crowd, I'm guessing you make ten easy, could be more. How's that sound?"

"Sounds like you're not hearing the no part."

"Then, you could be looking at a different kind of cut." The smile was gone now.

Huck couldn't believe this guy. These North Side gangsters setting up this toe-to-toe, rolling a keg of cheap beer off the back of a truck, making money off a couple of pikers and a fixed

9

fight. From what he learned since hitting town, the Back of the Yards wasn't North Side turf, the gang pushing its boundaries, flexing its muscles since springing up from Little Hell.

Nails was back to smiling, stepping over to his well-dressed pals at the front of the circle, standing among the gathered men of little means, the other two with pockets stuffed with the wagers, making money in this hobo capital of the country.

More men coming around the boxcar cast shadows ahead of them on the frozen ground, taking a spot near the bonfire, eyeing Huck stripped down to his undershirt, reaching in their pockets, placing bets on the other scrapper. Fifty of them around the circle now, standing in the chill and dipping from the beer keg, the first tin warding off the autumn chill, the second getting a hand to drop deeper in a pocket, putting up wages, a chance to double up, the third tin helping them forget the hard times, this country reeling after sending its boys to die in those far-off trenches, giving its women the vote, getting caught in an economic downturn and putting up with the Senate pushing through its damned Eighteenth Amendment.

Stepping to the center, Huck faced this scratch fighter, an Irishman with a long scar angling across forehead to chin. Taller and longer of reach, dubbed Gypsy Doyle, calling himself a descendant of the great Yankee Sullivan himself, the last of the traveling Irish, a true gypsy.

Huck guessing he was one of O'Banion's crew, not a fighter at all but a street thug stepping into a rigged fight, standing flat-footed, glaring at Huck and smacking a wrapped fist into his open palm, putting on a show to get the men betting more.

Huck was feeling the old rush he got anytime he used to step into the ring back in Bogalusa, looking over his man, searching for signs of an Achilles' heel, even if it was imaginary. Telling himself there was no way this bum could beat him. Loosening his neck and shoulders, sketching Gypsy Doyle with a glass jaw and flab under the shirt. Flexing his fingers inside the wraps, Huck tried to will away the chill coming in off the lake.

Doyle toed the line and spat, thumped bare knuckles together, called to the men around the circle, winked at Nails Morton, then at the men done collecting their bets.

"A guy calls himself Gypsy means he's in the wrong place — just a guy putting on a show," Huck said.

Grinning, Doyle showed the missing tooth, making the man look rat-arsed, saying, "You even Irish, laddie?"

"You're about to find out." Raising his taped hands, Huck put a foot to the scrape the ref, Gorilla Al Weinshank, had heeled along the hard ground, the square-jawed man who ran a North Side speak called the Alcazar.

Standing between the fighters, Gorilla Al recited the rules loud enough for the crowd to hear: "I'll have no thumbs, no biting and no shite. Now knuckle up, boys, and say your prayers."

Doyle kept up the glower, trying to menace Huck, growling too — getting the crowd lathered up.

His own eyes on the man's ribcage, letting him see what was coming, Huck leaned back in the southpaw stance, something he had tried out at Finnegan's Gym back in the Quarter, on account of being blessed with a pretty good left and able to fight off either side. Figured to switch in round two, forgetting what Nails Morton whispered about diving, Huck having no intention of throwing it — any fighter with a heart in his chest was in it to win.

Gorilla Al raised his hand, getting the crowd to settle.

Doyle throwing one for Huck's chin before Gorilla Al even dropped the hand.

Slipping it, Huck countered with a left, taking the follow-up on the shoulder, blocked the next with his elbow, throwing a stinger into the opening, banging it against Doyle's ribcage, making it count. Backing the man up, showing who he was.

Doyle stepped back to the line, shaking it off, jabbing, dropping the shoulder, trying an uppercut.

Huck slipped that too, hammering a straight left for the ribs, and landing it.

Doyle putting on a show like it had no effect. Coming in again, fingers curled for a claw at the eyes, missing with it.

Gorilla Al stepped between them, giving Huck a sour look, pushing them apart.

"Sure you ain't Irish?" Doyle said, toeing the line, his smile supposed to mean he wasn't hurt, showing the gap between his teeth, licking blood off his lip.

Catcalls, cheers, waving arms, the circle of men slopping their tin mugs.

Doyle went to tie him up, trying to lock Huck's elbows, butting with his head. Lowering his chin, Huck gate-blocked and grabbed hold, Doyle smashing up his knee, going for the groin. Feeling the ache below, Huck broke the clinch, breathing through the pain, Doyle swinging an elbow, landing a solid blow, sending Huck to a knee.

Second round, Huck put his foot back to the line. Doyle nodding when Gorilla Al warned him about the knee, a thing not tolerated — more show for the crowd.

Huck's roundhouse caught the piker in the belly, lifting Doyle to his toes, sending him backward with whirling arms, looking staggered. But Doyle didn't quit, coming back to the line, feinting a lead hand, throwing a good right, catching Huck on the jaw, grunting and keeping to his feet, smirking like the fight was his. Throwing his lead arm, striking with the palm and raking with his nails, missing Huck's eyes, but clawing his forehead.

Feeling the sting, Huck ducked a roundhouse and came behind it with a chop to the ribs, catching Doyle swinging a wild overhand right. Huck feinted and stepped in with a looping uppercut, knocking Doyle back off the line, the man grunting, breathing hard, bloody mouth hanging open, showing the gap between his teeth.

The crowd catching Doyle from falling, shoving him back to the line, wanting a finish to it now.

Gorilla Al spread his hands, stepping between them, declaring the end of the second, ducking one from Doyle himself. Cursing him, then glaring at Huck, pointing a finger and speaking through his teeth, "You son of a bitch."

Nails Morton stood watching, unbothered by the spit and beer landing on his fine suit, his bet lost.

I can find you. That's what the man's look told Huck, meaning Huck could end up in the bottom of one of the hog pens after the fight, looking like he got rolled for his winnings.

But right then, the fighter in him figured to put Doyle down, ignoring the ringing in his ear, the sting of the gouges on his forehead, the ache in his groin. Running his tongue around his mouth, teeth all there, nose not busted, no cuts or swelling around the eyes, as far as he could tell. Fingers stiff with the cold, but no broken bones, Huck knowing not to throw bare knuckles at the man's thick skull, what he'd do in a proper bout with boxing gloves, putting the weight behind the punches without the risk of busting up his hands.

The half minute was over, and Huck stepped to where the toe line had been, now rubbed out, leaning back with his fists up, not looking in Doyle's eyes, but down at his chest to catch the man's moves.

Gorilla Al signaled, and Huck bobbed, looking for an opening. Ducking a right, he drove a left for the man's belly, Doyle letting out a whoosh of air. Huck throwing a follow-up right to the ribs. Doyle missing with a rocket to the head, and Huck hitting for the body — a one, two — taking the sting out of Doyle's punches.

Doyle connecting with a lucky punch, sounded like a bat cracking a baseball, Huck catching it full on the jaw. Spit flying from his mouth, his head snapped to the side, his neck and body following. Grabbing hold to keep from falling, catching Doyle's forearms, tying him up, giving himself a moment for the two Doyles to become one again.

Breaking the clinch, Doyle didn't let up, figuring he had him now, throwing uppercuts, twisting his weight behind them, trying to finish it.

Huck slipped, hitting back with rag hands, not much sting behind his punches now. Taking a shot to the belly.

Gypsy Doyle kept up the smug look, throwing a ham for Huck's head. Huck ducking his chin, the punch striking skull bone. Doyle shaking the hand from the stab of pain. Huck clinching again.

Gorilla Al breaking it up, saying something about no hugging, calling the round.

Huck feeling Doyle's sweat on his own face, the man's chest heaving.

Huck gave back the grin, showing Doyle he wasn't hurt, guessing from the taste his teeth were bloody. Losing track of the rounds, gasping, his arms feeling like sacks. Turning his head, letting the bile fly, Nails Morton catching it on his trousers.

"Can you go on?" Gorilla Al got close, taking hold of his wrist, looking in Huck's eyes.

Nodding, Huck sucked air, stepped to the new line Gorilla scraped on the ground. Doyle had to be hurting from the body blows. The crowd shouting, some calling him a bum.

Doyle throwing a right.

Huck ducking, snapping one back, getting a grip on his fight, measuring his breathing.

Doyle swung and grunted, missing again and stumbling off the line.

Fighting past what Huck's trainer at Finnegan's called the old lassitude, he pressed, not giving Doyle time to reset, firing a short snap, knocking him onto his ass.

Felt his right eye swelling shut, hornets buzzing in his ears, reminding himself the winner took the five bucks, the loser getting nothing.

Doyle clinched and clawed, driving Huck back, coming over the line and going for the knockout, his left dropping low, his right rolled back for a roundhouse, coming all the way from Cork.

Taking the blow on the forearm, Huck countered, getting enough hip behind it, landing it against Doyle's ribs. Doyle stumbled, trying to keep to his feet, Huck reeling back too, feeling the sweat in spite of the cold. Two of them standing flat-footed, their arms dropped, chests heaving, the crowd yelling.

Both stepping to the line for the last time, Huck waited, shifted, timed the counter and threw what he had left, connecting against Doyle's jaw.

Gypsy Doyle reeled back and fell into Nails Morton. The man shoving Doyle forward, but he was out on his feet and down he went.

A roar of shouts and boos as Gorilla Al waved his hand, the fight over, calling Doyle the winner, Huck disqualified for punching off the line.

Looking at him, Huck couldn't believe it — but guessing he'd have to knock out Gorilla Al, Nails Morton, and half the crowd of drunks to collect the five bucks. Not Jack Dempsey's kind of fight, the kind of purse the champ would consider tip money, but five bucks would've meant Huck would be eating for the next few days.

The crowd started to break up, a few of them scowling at him. He wanted to go after the gangsters, the sons of bitches cheating him out of five lousy bucks, but knew he best head along the tracks and get out of there, guessing they were more likely to come looking for him for not taking the dive.

2

As cross as two sticks, getting stiffed for the five bucks, his body aching from getting slugged, he was chewing over how he could have ended the fight sooner, a match that didn't allow for footwork, just standing toe to toe, with no gloves, slugging till one man hit the dirt. He'd been fighting Gypsy Doyle's fight, not using what he'd been taught. And if he stepped in again, he'd know better, and sure as hell he'd get the five bucks up front.

Walking the Northwestern track in a bearing for the Navy Pier, heading for the shitty room in Bughouse Square, somewhere past the tall buildings looming ahead, looking eerie, not many lights on this time of night. A seedy part of town the locals called Hobohemia, next to the goddamn Gold Coast, the haves rubbing it in the faces of the have-nots. This city being all divided up, and Huck getting to know when he was stepping over the turf of one gang and into the next's.

Coming to town with less than ten bucks of his coming-north money left, enough to cover the rent for a couple of weeks, that is if he only ate once a day, this city having a way of scooping out a man's pockets.

The wind chased in off the lake and it bit to the bone, but it was pushing back some of the reek from the Union Stockyards, its fetid ditch where the meat-packers dumped the eyeballs and bones that couldn't be stuffed into the ballpark franks, the bubbly sludge and sewage draining into the ugly river flowing its way through town. Recalling something the slumlord said about the river being the prettiest you'd ever see, a kaleidoscope of sight and smell: green at the sausage factory, blue at the soap factory, yellow at the tannery — a sight you wouldn't trade for anything on earth. Taking his hand from holding his collar closed against the wind, Huck covered his mouth and nose, moving faster along the tracks, the scraggly blades of grass wagging between the ties.

Ahead, a lamplight glowed on a billboard for MacLaren's Cheese, Huck thinking about the thirty varieties, his stomach doing a flip, making him bend and spit.

When he raised up, the lamplight showed them coming up onto the track ahead — three of them. Huck looking around, too sore to run. Bending for a stone from between the tracks. Then recognizing Nails Morton, flanked by Gypsy Doyle and Gorilla Al Weinshank.

"Easy now, boyo," Nails said, putting a hand to the boater to keep the wind from claiming it.

"You bring my fiver?" Huck hefted the stone, knowing these guys were armed with more than stones. On a good day he might outrun any one of them, but not after getting banged around by Doyle.

Nails's grin widened, and he looked to the others, then back to Huck. "The man's surely Irish."

"And dumb as that stone," Gypsy Doyle said, not smiling.

Huck guessing this was about not taking the dive, payback for what they lost on the fight.

"It ain't what you're thinking," Nails said.

"I think you owe me money."

"Cost us plenty more than five bucks," Gorilla Al said.

"Guess you asked the wrong guy."

"What we're asking, you want to make more?" Nails said.

"Only place I dive's in a lake."

"You wanna end in the lake — that's no problem," Gypsy Doyle said.

Gorilla Al kept the friendly look, shaking his head.

"You getting to the point?" Huck said, flipping the stone away.

"Point is we can use a good man," Nails said.

"Don't know a thing about me."

"Well, call me a good judge of character."

Gorilla Al nodded, saying, "Seen you can take care of yourself. Ain't that so, Doyle?"

"Got in a lucky shot, is all," Gypsy Doyle said.

Clapping Doyle on the back, Nails said, "If you don't count the rest of them."

Nails and Gorilla Al looked amused.

Taking out the crushed pack of Picayune, Pride of New Orleans, his last pack, Huck tapped one out, digging in a pocket, finding a match and scratching his thumb across it, lighting up, saying, "Use a good man, what, like a punching bag?"

"Different kind of work."

"What's the pay?"

"You get a cut."

"And this job, it within the law?"

The three of them looking at each other, grinning.

"Wait'll Deanie gets a load of this guy," Gorilla Al said.

"So what do we call you?" Nails said.

Huck said his name.

"Alright Huck Waller — step right this way, your future's waiting." Turning, Nails started walking, the others following.

Huck thinking a moment, then he followed, calling, "I still want that fiver."

3

Clearing out of New Orleans after killing the pimp folks called Bubbling-Over, three hundred pounds of gator-mean daddy. A set-to over a working gal Huck was chatting with at Flora Breaux's, a two-bit joint in Storyville, this being at the start of the Volstead.

Being young and dumb is what sent Huck shoving his belongings in a sack, having to leave, catching a ride in back of a rig, right out of Jefferson Parish, a Chinese truck-farmer making a weekly run up to Natchez. Huck sharing the ride with a load of pecans.

Spent the night in a shack-town, then caught another ride with a middle-aged couple heading for Memphis, doing it in their ailing Peerless, the couple visiting relations, making about sixty miles of bad road the first day, most of it in sight of the Mississippi River, and most of it upgrade. Ten miles along, a front tire blew out, Huck helping the man get it off and roll it to a Texaco in the next town, a couple of miles off, getting it patched up and helping him roll it back.

Having a lunch of eggs and biscuits, they got underway again by early afternoon, making another forty miles before the right hind tire blew. Getting out the map, the man guessed the next town was Vicksburg, less than twenty miles, opting to take off the punctured tire and drive in on the rim, bouncing and scraping along the rutted road, half of it hardpan, getting halfway by nightfall.

A night of sleeping under a willow outside a campground, the couple curling up in the Peerless, Huck swatting skeeters most of the night, getting up before the sun with a change of plan, walking on his own the last stretch, paying the fare and boarding a Ford TT bus, heading from Vicksburg to Memphis.

The next night he slept out back of the Union Station, opening his eyes when he heard them coming, railway bulls looking for hobos riding the rails — thugs hired to keep the tramps off. There were two of them doing a sweep, walking along the edge of the yard. Huck keeping his head down below the tall grass.

When they were gone, he stepped past the baggage car, along the line of boxcars, looking for a hop-on spot. An old Black hobo riding the blinds, the man telling him to shoo. Another man on the rails, lying across the trusses between the steel wheels. Keeping watch for the bulls, Huck climbed to the boxcar's deck, the locomotive hissing steam ahead of its tender, its whistle blowing, set to pull out of the Memphis Yard.

Two Chickasaw brothers named Jacobs — Johnny a little older, and Billy no more than shaving age. The three of them riding atop, the brothers glad for his company, hiding from what they called the 'bo chasers, the private cops that made sport of pitching hobos from moving cars, especially the ones that weren't white. Getting out of Shelby County ahead of whoever was chasing them, riding past Tennessee cotton fields, small towns and the fields of Kentucky, the brothers sharing what food and tobacco they had.

The train pulled into Effingham with dawn breaking, and the brothers climbed down, saying so long and hoofing west to Springfield, believing they had relations there, and hoping to find any kind of work.

Shaking from the morning cold, Huck got down for a stretch, taking his constitutional past a grove of cedar. Hitching up his britches and walking along the tracks, he made like he owned the place, but kept a watch for the bulls, passing loaded flatcars, finding an open door on a boxcar, riding the Illinois Central the rest of the way, huddling in a corner with his jacket over him, getting colder by the mile.

Stepping over the rail-yard ties that first time, just west of the Loop, he couldn't believe all the crisscrossing tracks, accented by the dusting of an early snow, a godforsaken time of year, the ground hard as cement and that hellhound wind whipping off Lake Michigan. Sticking to the shadows of the boxcars, Huck never felt a chill like that in his life. Nothing like the easy breezes back home, already getting homesick for that Canal Street jazz, the Creole women calling "Belles saucisses!" out front of their markets, the dances and parades at the drop of a hat. Huck thinking what he wouldn't give for a plate of red beans and rice.

Taking the iron road north after the mix-up with Bubbling-Over. The king pimp sticking out a thick hand with the five rings, wanting payment after Huck stepped into Flora Breaux's, talking to one of his ladies.

Huck had been moonshining, selling off the last batch and coming in to drink some decent Island rum, talking trash to a long-limbed gal calling herself Maxie — yellow hair that looked painted on — sitting next to her at the bar, a scent like prohibition in a bottle trying to mask her own ripe tang, calling Huck her good-looking boy, her top showing what she figured he came looking for. An old bloodhound lay in the corner, folds over its eyes, giving the world a worn-out and bored look, like it had seen this abandon of morals a hundred times too many. Maxie pointed out the sign on the wall, reading it aloud, "*Order of the Garter: Shame on Him Who Thinks Evil of It.*"

Huck was sipping rum and talking, Maxie's hand going from his knee to his thigh, when Bubbling-Over stepped up behind them, putting one hand on her, the other, the one with the rings, on Huck's shoulder, telling him, "Ya owe me two bills, my boy."

"You got the wrong picture, mister. We're just talking, that's it. Last time I checked, that part's free," Huck said, annoyed by the sweaty hand, looking over his shoulder at the ruddy-faced man, the hanging jowls that looked like he was kin to the bloodhound, greasy hair going thin and gray at the temples.

The pimp dug his fingers harder into Huck's shoulder, squeezing to the bone, saying, "Chatting or bouncing on Maxie, it's all the same how you spend time with my dove. 'Less you think she ain't dove 'nough for you?"

"You take your hand back, I'll go sit someplace else, finish my drink and blow," Huck said it calm, looking to the barman, getting no help there, the man in concentration, wiping a rag on a stubborn spot at the far end of his bar top.

"You figure this for some high-track joint?" Bubbling-Over said. "Come in here and you pay or it's pain you get — your choice."

"You got me mixed with a chump that pays to talk to . . . doves." Huck considered his drink, the Island rum that tasted like it had been watered with kerosene. Eyes on Bubbling-Over's refection in the mirror behind the shelves of bottles.

"You hear that tone of voice, cher?" Maxie was on her feet, one hand on her hip. "Can't let this egg talk at me like that — like I can't turn a sawbuck any time I want." Lifting her dress to her garter.

Huck seeing the hand reach the sheath strapped to her thick leg, the dove pulling a blade, the thing looking like a letter opener, but good enough for sticking in a man's belly, trying to hand it to the pimp, saying, "Stick him for me, daddy."

The pimp let go of the shoulder, ignored the blade, reaching for his convincer inside his own vest — a two-shot derringer. The thing looking ridiculous in his ham fist.

Huck came off the stool, turning and splashing his drink in the man's eyes, catching the wrist, turning it enough, the two-shot going off, a hell of a bang for a little gun.

Maxie screamed, dropping the knife and clutching her arm. Glass blew up behind the bar, the mirror and bottles smashing and bursting, the shelf collapsing.

Bubbling-Over sputtered, looking at the derringer in Huck's hand now.

Huck aiming the double barrels at him. Not sure it would even slow the big pimp down, Huck started talking loud through the ringing in his ears, "I come in for hell in a glass, that's it." Glancing at the howling woman, her arm bloody.

The bloodhound lay there, hadn't moved.

Bubbling-Over's wet face reddened, then he lunged, Huck pulling the trigger, the shot stopping the pimp, looking surprised down at his shirt turning red. And he slumped to one knee, doing it slow, fat fingers starfished on his chest, then he flopped sideways onto the floor, sucking for breath, sounding like a bellows, his mouth going like a beached carp's.

Maxie the dove screamed, throwing herself down next to him, "Oh, daddy, daddy." Looking up at Huck through tears — the tears streaking the paint on her face — yelling something in French.

Cracking the two-shot, Huck dropped the spent shells on the floor, tossing the tiny gun for what he figured was an open window, sending it smashing through the glass, the two-shot landing out on the banquette. Looking to the barman, saying, "Put it on his tab."

The barman was reaching for a bat behind the bar, Huck bending and snagging the pimp's watch-chain, hauling up a dandy gold watch, and he was out the door.

Running into an alley, thinking he should have taken the day's take from the barman's jar, the man likely in on the scam, the three of them laying for some young sap to come walking in.

The mess of it was Bubbling-Over was known to have ties to "Silver Dollar" Sam and the Matrangas, the crime family with a hand in just about everything shady down in the Quarter. Huck knew of them from selling his moonshine. The Italian immigrants seeing them as saints, on account of the money the Matrangas sometimes handed to the poor. Then there were the cops the big pimp paid off, and if Bubbling-Over croaked . . .

He'd been dumb to step in Flora Breaux's alone in the first place, but right then it was time to blow out of town. Going back to the shotgun house, his room in back, the one he shared with the cockroaches and bedbugs, already paid up for the week, the place just off Bourbon. Huck packed what he had in the old suitcase and got out of there. Couldn't get word to his old dad, let him know he had to go. Making his way north, planning to start fresh and find some kind of work. He'd get somebody to write when he got there, explain it in a letter.

Hopping on the mainline, the Illinois Central chugging its way north, taking him to the city of big shoulders and industry. Huck not afraid to sweat and lift heavy. Renting the nothing-fancy boarding room in Bughouse Square, that Hobohemia next to the Gold Coast that gave him a view of how the muckety-mucks lived.

4

It took about a week, and Huck had seen enough of the signs in shop windows, couldn't read most of them, but getting the meaning: *No Work* — newcomers keep going, we can't take care of our own. Notices posted at the factories: *No Work. No Irish. No Blacks.* Now he was down to working with the North Side Gang.

Ducking the seventy-cent tab, he hurried from the chop suey house, his belly full, the Chinese owner yelling after him, calling him a dirty son of a whore, then giving chase. Huck hoofed it along the icy street past a meat-cutting joint, heading for the no-man's land between North Side and South Side turf. Belching as he ran, turning and making the kind of taunting with his tongue and lips, a sound that kids made, Huck kept just ahead, hearing the old man's footfalls behind him along the tracks, calling and promising him a good thrashing. The old man was huffing like a locomotive, Huck leading him along the shadows of boxcars.

Looking over his shoulder, for a moment thinking he lost the old man, catching the flicker of flame coming off the trash can ahead, better than a dozen men standing close and holding their hands to the fire, gathering for the fights. Some laughing, all drinking and betting, Nails Morton walking among them, taking their bills, scratching with his pencil, taking down names and bets in his notepad. The barrel of beer already doing its job, getting the men worked up and loosening their purse strings.

Two fighters stood at the toe line, one white, one Black, stripped to the waists, Gorilla Al Weinshank refereeing, giving the signal, and they began pummeling the hell out of each other. The crowd not expecting to see Bold Mike McTigue or Tom Sharkey from Dundalk, or the great Dempsey of Curran stepping to the toe line, but they were fired up just the same, coming out in any kind of weather. This boxing tradition said to go back centuries, once a way of defending family honor and settling disputes. The crowd loving that the gang rolled out a keg, not charging for it, loving good sport and a chance to double their money, getting juiced and loosening the purse strings, most of them stumbling away with empty pockets. The gang coming away with just a few hundred on a good night, doing it for the good of community, the way Gorilla Al liked to put it.

Huck getting his five bucks up front this time, plus the cost of supper if he could keep it down. Stopping by the fire now, he put his hands out to the trash can's heat, not looking back, guessing at worst he might heave up the seventy-cent supper.

"Got you, you deadbeat!" the restaurant man came up behind him, grabbing for his collar.

Huck shook him off with, "Hey! You got the wrong guy."

"A deadbeat!" His eyes bulged, the man standing about five and a half feet, wiry and about fifty, sucking hard to catch his breath — looking over his shoulder like he might get jumped.

Behind Huck, the two fighters were banging on each other, the dull thump of fists as they toed the line, both ducking and weaving, one throwing a club of a punch, the other catching it full in the face — falling like a felled tree. Gorilla Al stepped between them, calling the round, pushing the standing man back, giving the downed man the eight count. The crowd whooping and clanging their tins.

Nails Morton stepped between Huck and the restaurant man, giving them both hard looks, his jacket open showing the revolver stuck in his pants, saying, "What's the rumpus?"

The restaurant man pointed a finger, wheezing. "Deadbeat ducked his tab. Owes me seventy cents, plus a tip."

Nails turned to Huck, scowling and saying, "What you got to say about it?"

"The man's no Oscar Mayer, charging for that hog slop — I can tell you that."

"Mama's recipe!" The restaurant man was shaking the finger, then bettering it to a fist.

"You admit to ducking, not paying up on account of slop?" Nails asked, saying it loud, drawing the crowd's attention, no longer interested in a fighter who wasn't getting up.

"Hell, yes I do."

"And you, sir, are insulted?"

"He's got to pay."

"Food the roaches won't touch," Huck said, glancing around, getting approving nods, the crowd growing, over twenty men now. "Ought to pay me if I make it."

"Whoa up!" Nails said, catching the restaurant man jumping at Huck, pressing a hand against his boney chest, easing him back, keeping his other hand raised like he was keeping the peace — at the fights.

The full attention of the crowd on them now, Nails raising his voice, "Well, we got one fella calling an injustice, the other claiming a cruelty." Turning to the gathered, calling out, "What do we do about it, boys?"

"FIGHT!" the crowd called out, some chanting the word.

"Well, now . . ." Nails said it like why didn't he think of that.

A few more picked up the chant.

Nails waved his arm to settle them, saying to Huck, "If you're willing . . ."

"Could toxify a man, ought to call it slop suey." Huck spat at the ground.

Giving a head-shake, Nails turned to the restaurant man, having to hold him back again, saying, "What do you say about it, mister?"

The Chinese man looked around, incredulous, not ready for this, saying, "I'm twice his age."

"Well, can't say you're in your prime, got to admit that. But this being no kind of courtroom . . ." Nails said, supposing it wouldn't be much of a fight, this boney old-timer. Somebody suggesting they tie one hand behind Huck's back, the crowd liking the idea, some giving odds on it.

Looking past the oldster, Nails turned to the footfalls coming, a look on his face like it could be railroad bulls again, or some coppers they weren't friendly with, meaning ones they didn't pay off, coming to bust up their good time. Not that he would mind, his pockets stuffed with the fight bets.

This new man was an easy six feet, not Chinese, a stained cook's apron around his middle, coming up behind the old man, saying, "What's going on, Pops?"

The old man aimed a finger at Huck, "Stiffed me for seventy cents and no tip. Says you cook up slop."

"That so?" The younger man looked around, quick putting it together, seeing the revolver in Nails's pants.

"What we got here's a dilemma," Nails said to him. "One accusing the other."

"And you want Pops punching it out, decide who's right? Is that it?" The young man was wiping hands on his apron and not looking bothered by the crowd or that Nails was armed.

"This being a boxing match-up, not a court of law," Nails said, shrugging, playing to the growing crowd.

"Guess you won't mind a swap then, me for Pops. Me being the one accused of cooking the so-called slop." Hard eyes on Huck.

The crowd was lapping it up, shouting, hands waving, men putting up more wagers, some calling it even, others thinking it ought to be two to one.

Nails feigned consideration, then looked at Huck, like what could he do about it.

Huck looked the man over, seeing the switch-up Nails pulled on him. Cursing himself for going along with ducking the tab, provoking a fight — his lack of good sense.

Gorilla Al turned to the two fighters from the previous bout, the white one still down on the ground, the other bloody and barely on his feet. Dismissing it as a draw, he waved for somebody to get them out of the circle, only a few in the crowd booing about the call. The rest of the men were looking over Huck and the young cook, placing their bets.

The cook untied the apron, taking off his shirt, handing them to Pops. The build of a slugger, no fat on him.

Gorilla Al moved into the middle of the circle, wagging his fingers, wanting the two men to step up, scratching his heel along the ground, and giving his usual line, "No biting, no kicking, and toe to the line at all —"

"Forget your rules. Just a sound whipping coming," the cook said, smacking his fist into an open palm — it made a good thump. "That good with you?" Looking at Huck.

Huck nodded.

The crowd was cheering and wanting it to get underway.

Gorilla Al shrugged, making no objection, looking to Huck like what could he do, helping him with the wraps. Asking the young man's name, finding out this was Denny O'Keefe, who just happened to be a ranked fighter. Pops helping to wrap the fighter's hands. Huck watched Denny move around, loosening up, pointing at Huck, like he had this coming.

Gorilla Al shrugged again to Huck, standing between them as Nails and Gypsy Doyle took the bets, writing in their books, and stuffing their pockets with cash. Forty or fifty men and the odds against Huck, word spreading through the crowd this Denny O'Keefe was a ranked welterweight.

Gorilla Al pointed to him, calling out, "Over here, we got Duking Denny O'Keefe." Some of the crowd cheering. Gorilla Al pointing to Huck. "And over here, Huck the Hammer." Then holding up both hands, he called out, declaring this a grudge match, so they were forgoing the Irish stand-down tradition, calling it, "No holds barred!"

Another cheer arose.

Huck felt his belly full of chop suey, not the best way to step into a fight. Getting the five bucks up front had dumbed him down, Huck risking the bashed knuckles and ribs, his ears and eyes still swollen from the scrap with Gypsy Doyle, this one showing the promise of a busted nose or getting his teeth knocked out. At the least, he'd be in for days of eating soup with a jaw too sore to chew — but with five bucks, at least he'd be eating.

Now he was peeling off his shirt, sizing up Denny O'Keefe, about the same weight, a little taller meaning more reach. Bouncing on his toes, Huck tried to get loose. Gorilla Al Weinshank making a show of patting both fighters down, checking the wrapped hands, giving the locals the idea this was on the up and up. Then leaning close to Huck, saying, "Not gonna ask this time."

"About what?"

"About going down in the first." He signaled and Huck stepped up, face to face with O'Keefe. Gorilla Al raised, then dropped the arm, and Huck ducked a hard right, coming up under it, banging one into O'Keefe's belly, knocking the man back a half step. Raising his fists and moving to his right, Huck starting in southpaw, feinting a jab, slamming home a good left hook, then changed it up, feinting right, tagging O'Keefe with another left.

O'Keefe threw a headshot, not a good idea in this kind of fighting, punching at Huck's skull. Hurting the bare hand meant you wouldn't be punching with it again, not with any power anyway. Something any bare-knuckler could tell you. Bobbing around, O'Keefe threw a feint, then a rocket, connecting with Huck's head again.

Slipping the next one, Huck threw a right and missed, getting tagged with another stinging right, feeling himself knocked back into the crowd. Arms pushing him right back, O'Keefe not letting up, bobbing and getting in a couple of body shots before going back upstairs, peppering Huck with shots, throwing a roundhouse that Huck took on the point of the elbow, a trick he learned from Gypsy Doyle. Huck taking some of the sting from O'Keefe's right hand. Feeling himself dropping his hands, already winded.

Gorilla Al got between them to break a clinch. O'Keefe bouncing on his toes. Pops egging him on.

Huck felt like sagging and throwing up, wanting to take a knee.

O'Keefe hit him with another head shot, then the pro was shaking his head, saying that was it, turning and walking away. Pops in tow, the crowd booing, not getting their money's worth.

Gorilla Al stood perplexed, then reached for Huck's wrist and hoisted it up.

When the crowd was gone, Nails Morton handed Huck an extra five bucks, calling it his cut, O'Keefe quitting on account of hurting his hand on Huck's thick melon. Telling Huck to come by on the weekend, Nails gave him the location of the next round of fights in the woods just west of Norwood Park, a chance for him to get to know the gang's boss, Dean O'Banion, Nails calling him Deanie. Saying they might have something better than slugging for him.

5

The swelling in his hands had gone down by the following Friday, Huck showing up behind the park at Norwood, a grove of trees, sheltered from view. A bonfire blazed and Gorilla Al rolled another keg of beer off the back of a truck. Men stood around drinking from tins, some giving him a nod, knowing who he was now, whispers going from man to man, calling him Hard-Bark Huck, a ringer looking to go pro.

Limbering up, he spotted a couple of men in suits standing with Nails Morton and Gypsy Doyle, guessing the one in the middle was Dean O'Banion, head of the outfit, short with a round boyish face, not the look Huck pictured for a gangster. The other two looked harder, their eyes darting around, Gorilla Al telling him the one on the left was Hymie Weiss, the other being Vincent "The Schemer" Drucci. Another guy, dressed up like a cowboy, was taking bets. Men at the fire and around the circle tipped their caps to Dean like he was the bishop.

Then Huck found himself standing across from a seaman called Mulligan, a two-hundred pounder off an ore-toting steamer out of Pittsburgh called the *Widlar*, the ship that struck the rocks off Pancake Shoals en route from Duluth to the Soo, the ship pounded to pieces, its crew in peril till they were rescued. Finding himself without a ship and out of work, Mulligan took to making money with his fists, same as Huck. The only difference being the weight class, that and the man was spitting hate like venom before the match-up, calling to the crowd, "I beat the lake, cheated an ice-and-water death, now I'm going to beat the pulp from this excuse of a man." Raking Huck with his eyes, getting more bets changing hands, the two-to-one odds swinging in the bigger man's favor.

Coming over to Huck, Nails looked over at Mulligan as he stripped out of his coat. Nails giving a soft whistle, lowering his newsboy.

"I ain't taking no dive," Huck said.

"I'm guessing you'll wish you did."

"And I'm guessing you boys got trouble telling weight divisions."

"Can step down if you want."

"Got a sister back home could whip this bum," Huck talking trash, loud enough for Mulligan to hear, flexing his shoulders, getting himself set.

"With you hiding behind her and running that mouth." Mulligan called back, nodding his head. "Yeah you, boy — gonna split some lightning. Beaming and holding up his hams, showing the wrapped fists, meaning he'd let them do his talking. Gorilla Al pointed to the line in the dirt, the crowd getting into it, shouting and drinking, sensing a good one coming, flames dancing from the bonfire. Fighters toeing the line, Gorilla Al going over the rules, the pistol showing under his jacket. "No biting or kicking. No bunking off the line. And give a listen-up when I say. Rules is rules." Then calling loud enough for the crowd, "Here we got Punchin' Patrick Mulligan, all the way from Dingle."

The Irish in the crowd cheering him.

Then Gorilla Al was pointing to Huck the Hammer.

Some of the crowd booing, the rest of them catcalling, most betting against Huck, some remembering the O'Keefe fight, thinking of him as a sneak-thief ducking a restaurant tab, catching a lucky break. Gypsy Doyle taking side bets on which round Huck would go down, most of the crowd not giving him a hope past the first.

"Five to one," is what Huck heard somebody call out now; the one dressed like a cowboy taking that bet.

Gorilla Al raised his arm, giving it a long moment, waiting on the crowd to settle.

"Hope you like hospital food." Mulligan was glaring at him, putting a big foot to the line. "Gonna feed it to you in a tube."

"God have mercy." Gorilla Al signaled and Mulligan threw a haymaker, Huck dodging it, snapping a right for the ribcage, chopping with a left, stepping back, avoiding a clinch.

Gorilla Al stepping between them, warning them about coming off the scratch. Huck slipped and countered, Mulligan stepping on Huck's foot, kept him from moving, throwing a good shot, Huck's nose exploding like a tomato. Staggering back, thinking he'd never been hit that hard. Shaking it off, stepping back, throwing jabs, blocking with elbows, and following with combinations, connecting and making it look good.

Mulligan got wild eyes and started punching like he was in a hurry, head tucked low, coming off the line, using his weight and bearing down.

Huck slipped and left Mulligan pawing at air.

Gorilla Al got between them again, warning Huck about coming off that line.

Forgetting what he picked up at that Bogalusa gym, this was an alley brawl, the big man grabbing for him, wanting to drag him to the ground, wanting to choke him.

Felt like he was punching bricks, slipping and rolling, Huck kept Mulligan from using his weight, the crowd shouting and booing him. Somebody threw a punch, catching Huck behind the ear, not liking the way Huck kept backing off the line, pissing in the face of Irish tradition.

Taking another warning from Gorilla Al, Huck stepped up, got caught with a good hook, Mulligan following it with an uppercut from center earth. Huck ducked another, staggering back into the crowd, getting pushed forward. Mulligan catching hold of his hair, hammering Huck's face. Huck bringing up his elbow, connecting with jawbone.

Gorilla Al got between them again, warning them both about grabbing, calling it round one.

Mulligan made a grab for Gorilla Al's pistol, but Al shoved him off. Huck was sucking air, needing to send his Sunday punch past the man's guard. Going to the line again, banging at the man's ribs, weaving and blocking with his forearms.

Mulligan tried to tie up his arms, bucking with his forehead, knocking Huck back again. The crowd shoving Huck forward. The big man swarming him, clouting and catching him in a bear hug, arching his back and lifting Huck off the ground, squeezing.

The crowd loving it.

Gritting his teeth, Huck felt the air crushed from him, bringing up a knee and breaking free.

Gorilla Al warning about low blows, then calling the round.

Huck's legs wanted to give out. Getting shoved from behind. Ramming back an elbow, he caught somebody, hearing a grunt, getting more boos and a tin cup bouncing off his back. Gorilla Al asking if he could go on.

Nodding, Huck aimed to make it through the round — that or there was no money. Changing from the southpaw, jabbing with the left, both hands aching through the tape, catching Mulligan with a solid blow, knocking him off the line. Fighting through the pain, striking with his palms meant closing the distance, going for the man's jaw, catching him with a good uppercut, then another.

Mulligan shook it off, stepping in and throwing a hammer, Huck ducking it and catching him on the temple with the back of his fist, then landed a big forearm. Mulligan throwing a hook, Huck taking it on top of his skull, Mulligan striking bone, shaking the hand as he reeled back. Huck not giving him time to set up, throwing open-handed uppercuts, catching him full on the chin, Mulligan staggering back, trying to focus on Huck, then he dropped like a stone.

Looking down at the man, he was aware of Gorilla Al stepping in and raising his arm. The crowd yelling and booing, beer splashing Huck.

Feeling his own knees go to jelly, thinking he was going to vomit, he let Nails lead him from the circle, Gorilla Al trying to revive Mulligan.

Mulligan lifting his head a few inches, looking around like he was wondering where he was, then winking at Huck.

6

They put Huck in back of a Franklin, Dean O'Banion and Bugs Moran on either side, Nails Morton, Gypsy Doyle and Gorilla Al up front. Nails getting behind the wheel.

"Hell of a fight," Dean O'Banion said, patting him on the back. "How you faring, Champ?"

"I been better."

"Appreciate if you don't throw up on my shoes."

The rest of them laughing.

Huck looked out as Nails drove them past Irving Park, turning left instead of right, not heading for their turf over on the Gold Coast, instead driving toward Cicero in the other direction. Getting a bad feeling, he was weighing his chances of jumping out. But to do it, he'd have to climb over either O'Banion or Bugs Moran to get out a door. Not good odds in the shape he was in.

Nails pulled up in front of an ordinary-looking building, three stories with a sign out front, Huck thinking it read Hawthorne Smoke Shop, the lights of the storefront out. All of them climbing out and going around the side. Gorilla Al tapping on the back door, a slot opening, and a bouncer letting them in, being very polite, treating them like visiting royalty, calling them Mr. O'Banion and Mr. Moran.

Turned out the smoke shop was a front for a casino called the Ship. Nails leading Huck past a line of Pace slot machines, a chalkboard with a man running a racing book, Huck getting cleaned up in a washroom in the back. Gorilla Al coming to the door, handing him a suit, then taking him to a table upstairs, chandeliers hanging from the ceiling, paintings in gold frames covering the walls, roulette wheels, a faro table with stacks of chips, craps, blackjack, and chuck-a-luck. The well-dressed standing around holding cocktail glasses, a playground for the wealthy, going against the law, drinking and gambling.

Nails introduced Huck to Hymie Weiss and Vincent "The Schemer" Drucci, both in suits, standing by the chuck-a-luck, Drucci jiggling dice in his hand.

"Hell of a fight, kid," Hymie said, holding out his hand, going easy on the shake, seeing Huck's hand was banged up. "Can tell you got miles of heart."

"Got lucky mostly," Huck said, then shaking Drucci's hand after he transferred the dice, trying not to wince when The Schemer squeezed the hand, not going easy on him, saying, "That's what I think too, you got lucky." Then saying he had fifty riding on the one where Huck was supposed to go down in the first. Huck guessing which way he'd bet.

"Got to admit, didn't see you going the distance, not with that ape," Nails said, talking about tonight's fight. "What do you say, Deanie?"

Dean had come from behind Huck, looking around for the waiter, snapping his fingers, saying, "The service in this joint . . ."

"But the crowd was eating it up," Gorilla Al said to Huck.

"How much we take?" Drucci asked.

"Three and a half," Nails said, giving a shrug.

"Not counting the keg," Drucci said. "You can feed chickens with what's left."

"But we roll out the barrel and we got pals for life, the kind that whistle when they see cops," Dean said, turning back to Huck. "Something good as gold in this town." Looking him over. "There's a high and low way of making it, kid . . . A guy like you can get his head banged around, or he puts his feet up, uses his noodle for more than ducking."

"Seemed like a good idea at the time," Huck said, running his tongue along inside his mouth, feeling a cut back of his lip.

"There's your trouble — that just-getting-by way of thinking," Dean said. "Let me ask you, what's the most important thing a fella's got in his pocket? And don't say your maypole."

"Money, I guess."

"Money you guess. Wrong — most important thing in your pocket's politicians."

"Guess I got things to learn."

"Pay attention, you'll do alright." Dean pointed to one of the huge chandeliers. "The mistake of life's thinking it's all out of reach. Not that you asked, but if you did, I'd tell you it don't have to be like that. A fella's got to be hard so life's not, you understand, but first he's got to see a thing clear . . ." Motioning around the room at the fine folk standing at the gambling tables. A waiter in a tux delivered drinks on a tray, another one near the entrance with a tray of deviled eggs and olives.

Looking at a chandelier, Dean saying, "It's all hanging there, like fruit."

A third waiter approached the table, smiling and speaking loudly, "Nice to see you again, Mr. O'Banion. How are you this fine evening, good sir?" Then, "Would you care for something?"

"A steak for my friend here — for his eye. And a bowl of soup on account he won't be chewing for a while." Dean giving Huck a light clap on the back.

Doyle and Drucci laughed. Huck aware some of the patrons were looking over at them.

"How about a bottle, something with bubbles," Dean told the waiter, saying it loud.

The waiter looked flummoxed, turning to the room, saying just as loud so all could hear, "Sorry my good sir, perhaps you haven't heard of the Volstead."

Dean looked startled, saying, "The river in Russia?"

"No sir, the Eighteenth Amendment — one that says we can't serve spirits."

O'Banion saying to the room, "The kid must be new, hasn't figured why we painted the door green."

Getting some laughs.

Gorilla Al leaned close to Huck, saying, "What some joints started doing after the Eighteenth, painting their doors green, meaning it's business as usual."

Huck nodded but didn't know what to make of the banter. Patrons looking over, some smiling.

"Volstead Act, now there's one for you." Dean was facing the room now.

Getting nods of agreement.

"Well, this Republican son of a bitch Volstead — we going to welcome him in this place?" Looking around.

Men and women calling back, "No!" Some shaking their heads.

Dean going on, "I abide by the First Amendment, one that says I can speak my mind."

A man at the faro table called, "Here, here."

"And the Second . . ." Dean pulled back his jacket, showing the pistol at his hip, pulled the other side, showing another, winking at a lady in a fine gown at the nearest table. "Got another one I can show you later, my dear."

The woman covered her mouth, but not offended.

"Second Amendment's about keeping the state free, and our right to defend it."

"That's right, Deanie," a man called from across the room.

"Third and Fourth don't make no difference . . ."

The waiter returned with a bottle on a tray, poorly hidden by a towel. Some of the patrons applauding.

"The Fifth says I can take the Fifth. Ain't that right, Judge?" Dean said to an elderly gent who nodded and smiled. Reaching for the bottle of Dom Pérignon from the waiter's tray, Dean saying, "And the Sixth says I'm owed a speedy trial, the Seventh gets me a jury of my peers, and the Eighth gets me bailed out."

From a couple of tables over, someone shouted, "You tell 'em, Deanie."

"Alright, I will." Dean stepped away from the table to the middle of the room now, all eyes on him as he easily uncorked the bottle with his thumbs, the cork popping and champagne flowing out, Dean careful not to get it on his suit.

"Let's skip to the Eighteenth, the one that says the demon's in the drink; to that, I say hogwash. You all with me?"

"YES!"

"You know the one thing I can't abide, is this Volstead fellow telling me I can't drink with my pals." Dean extended his arms, the bottle in one hand, still frothing bubbly. "I say let's reform the reform."

"YES!"

"Waiter — drinks for all my pals — on the lads of Kilgubbin."

Patrons were clapping, some hooting — all of them loving Dean O'Banion.

"Yes sir!" The waiter turned on his heels, heading off, the second waiter by the door following him.

Huck getting the picture, the gang was supplying the demand, keeping the cellar of the Ship well stocked, Dean playing Robin Hood, along with his merry band, bringing in the booze, and getting rich doing it.

Dean looked at the bottle, saying, "Fellow who invented this stuff was a monk or friar — guy right next to God. Now, the top brass says it ain't allowed."

One waiter coming with a tray of flutes, Dean pouring, keeping the champagne from foaming on his suit, and he went about filling and passing out glasses. Everybody in the place imbibing. The waiters hurrying around the room, bringing more bottles and glasses, corks popping, glasses being filled and refilled.

Then the head waiter stepped next to Dean again, holding a hand out to him, Dean getting applause, plenty of smiles from the ladies.

The head waiter saying, "The room thanks you, Mr. O'Banion."

The woman in the long gown, asking, "Would you kindly sing for us, Deanie?"

Dean put on a bashful look, smiling when others called and clapped.

"You folks don't want this old bird to sing, do you?"

Catcalls and more applause.

"Well, I ought to wait till you all drink up, sweetens the sour notes, but if you insist . . ."

And they did.

Leaning to Huck, Gorilla Al said, "Deanie used to sing at McGovern's Liberty, you know it, over on Clark? Sang like a bird alright, we lads rifling the pockets in the coatroom, lifting anything worth something. Did not too bad back in the day."

Huck guessed Gorilla Al was doing his best, making them sound like a fun-loving bunch, having some laughs while engaged in criminal activity. Between sips of champagne, Gorilla Al sketched out how they grew up together, the North Siders starting out, cutting their teeth on petty crime. Bugs Moran stealing cart horses when he was a lad of twelve, demanding ransom and selling the horses back to the owners. "Being a good Catholic boy, The Schemer liked dressing as a priest, standing outside some house of the holy, any faith, it didn't matter. The collar, the beads with the cross, the whole bit, liked telling some passing woman she had a nice can, and how he wanted to toss her a Hail Mary. Sometimes Deanie played along, putting on a show of coming along and beating up the priest for disrespecting the doll."

Now Dean stood up on a table, steadied himself and started singing "Prohibition Blues." The man possessing a strong tenor voice, delighting the room. Bowing to applause when he was done, stepping off the table, saying, "Okay, I sang for my supper, now where's that steak."

Getting more laughs.

Dean letting the waiter refill his glass. Toasting the room again, the man in his element.

Somebody calling for more, others applauding. Without too much coaxing, Dean got back up on the table and was singing again, doing justice to "Danny Boy."

43

7

A few inches shorter than Huck, small dark eyes and a slit for a mouth set in a wide face, Dean O'Banion swung an arm around him, part friendly, partly to keep him upright. The champagne on top of getting knocked silly in the night's fight taking its toll on Huck. The North Side boys got back in the Franklin, a zozzled Nails Morton behind the wheel, driving too fast toward the lake.

Feeling the drink, Huck told Dean he liked the way the man sang, thought he had a natural voice and ought to record a few numbers. He was thinking his old clothes could use a wash, wishing they had let him keep the suit, Huck taking it off before they left, getting into his old rags.

"So, how'd you come by boxing, get picked on as a snot-nose, the usual way?" Dean asked.

"Seen Dempsey one time. You know him?"

"The Mauler, everybody does. Gonna have a few bucks on the one coming up, Dempsey and Brennan, up in Madison Square Gardens. You hear about it?"

"Yeah, love to see it." Huck only dreamed of having the kind of money to catch the 20th Century Limited to New York, pay the pullman charge, get a room at the Plaza and watch the fight that promised to make history. "Seen him knock out Carl Morris, one they dubbed Oklahoma's White Hope."

"That right?"

"Saw that hope going down like a sack, right in the first. Something about the man's style, Dempsey, I mean. Soon as he got in the ring, had the look like he already won. Man, the power — could hear the thud of his punches all the way in the cheap seats. Heard long time back when he went by Kid Blackie, he walked in barrooms, calling out, 'I can't sing worth a dang and I can't dance neither, but I can lick any son of a bitch in the house.' Taking on all comers, mopping the floor with most of them. Making his name."

"And that's what did it for you?"

"Well, guess it helped some. But I was in it by then. Guess it started back in the parish. My old dad took me to the fights one time, seeing Fred Fulton and 'Porky' Dan Flynn go at it."

Dean shaking his head, didn't know the names.

"Right in the Tommy Burns Arena, that man Tommy Burns, a legend himself."

"Sure, Tommy Burns." Dean nodding, knowing that name.

"Tommy reffing the fight."

"That did it, huh?"

"Was out on the street after, and I see Porky Dan on the sidewalk, ranting at Tommy, claiming the man was blind, over the hill, calling a bad decision. Then threatens to teach old Tommy a lesson right then and there. So, Tommy just shrugs, keeps his cool and says, 'Not the first wrong move you made today, Porky.' And like that, Porky rushes in, and Tommy throws one good hook, just the one, and he turns around, leaving poor old Porky Dan lying on the sidewalk, counting canaries."

Dean nodded, asking, "So, besides getting knocked around, what else you good at, kid?"

"Well, ran some shine back in the Quarter."

"That so, huh?" Dean taking more interest, the rest of them grinning.

"Yes sir. Seems some of us were loath to give it up there as well. So, you might say I took a shine to it, got my hands on an old depot hack, put heavy-duties under her, modified the Model T engine, stripped her down, and got her zipping those back roads one jump ahead of the law."

The men in the car getting into it.

"So you can drive, huh?"

"Drove them back roads like a hellcat, left the local law breathing dust and scratching their heads." Huck recalling some advice from the *Times-Picayune*, retelling it to Dean, "We got told to dig out the sackcloth and ashes, get on the wagon, and welcome Old Man Gloom and pretend we liked it."

"Well, how about you heal up and come see me, and maybe you won't need to duck a seventy-cent check or a fist next time. How's that sound?"

"You mind if I soak these in ice first?" Huck said, showing his knuckles, asking them to stop four blocks from his place, embarrassed about the flop he was living in, not wanting to give the impression he was some loser.

"Can see you got bricks for fists, hope you got more up here," Dean said, tapping his temple. "You sure you ain't Irish?"

"Well sir, I'm sure feeling kinda Irish right now."

The rest of them laughing.

"Well, we can't all be." Dean laid a hand on his shoulder, saying not being Irish could be considered a misfortune of birth. Reaching in a pocket, peeling a few dollars from his roll, handing it to him. "What the boys likely owe you."

Not arguing, and not counting it, Huck tucked it away, thanking him.

"Mull over what I said." Dean added, "And watch for the Mustache Petes." What he called the Italian gangs roving the streets at night.

Getting out of the Franklin, Huck watched Nails bang a wheel into the curb, then drive off. And Huck was walking the four blocks hoping the night air would help to sober him a bit. Hadn't wanted them to see the dump he was living in, then wondering why he'd care what they thought. Walking west, thinking the bubbly was something he could get a taste for, easy going down — too easy — yet it had a way of sneaking into a man's head and kicking hell around inside his skull.

Having a few bucks in his pocket felt good — this town that at first didn't want him around, sent him searching for work that didn't exist. Crazy prices on everything he needed: nine bucks for the coat that doubled as his blanket, ten cents just for a loaf of bread, forty cents a dozen eggs. A picture show costing fifteen cents. Nobody was hiring, what shopkeepers called tough economic sledding. Huck had lined up in the November cold for day jobs, but never was culled out. Now, things could be looking up.

Glancing around at the shadows, he kept walking. The night air clearing his head, and moving was keeping him warm. Huck aware of the sore ribs and knuckles, thinking when his jaw stopped aching he'd find some joint and order up a steak with some of the money Dean O'Banion just gave him.

Walking past rooming houses, wondering how a guy like Dean lived, picturing a fine two-story house, a fireplace warming the front room, chandeliers like they had at the Ship lighting the place, likely had a woman in a feather bed, a blonde with some curves, could be more than one.

Thinking of Dean's offer through the booze fog. Not sure of the street name he was crossing when he heard the scrape of a shoe from behind. Glancing back at the shadows, not seeing anybody. Wondering if the champagne gods were playing tricks, thinking of what Dean said about Mustache Petes. Stopping again when he got to the next corner, taking another look back, sure a shadow ducked out of sight. Stopping once more out front of the Square-Deal Laundry, listening. Wondering if Dean and his lads were up to some trick, he ducked into the mouth of an alley, out of the streetlamp's light, putting his back to the bricks, waiting. Letting his eyes adjust to the dark, Huck searched around for something he could swing. Not finding anything. Going deeper into the piss-smell of the alley, he guessed he only had a block or so to go, thinking this alley led to another one, letting him cut around the back of his building.

Too dark to see much, he tried scanning the ground again, looking for something like a weapon. Hearing the steps behind him, coming closer now. Putting himself against the wall and crouching, feeling around for anything he could use, hearing his own heart pounding. His hand grasped a piece of brick, not very big, but good enough. Thinking he saw more movement, he threw it, hearing a thud and a yelp.

"Any closer and I start shooting." Huck waited and listened for a long minute. Feeling the chill, he started moving again, making his way out of there, going back toward the street, wanting to get to his flea-dive and flip the jerry-built lock, longing to sleep most of the next day.

No idea what struck him from behind, something colliding with his skull, sent him reeling, trying to keep to his feet as the world spun. Seeing shoes in front of him, he threw a punch and missed, losing his balance. Getting struck again as the ground rushed up. Huck feeling hands on him, going through his pockets, somebody saying, "Goddamn Irish — stay on your own goddamn side."

Huck wanting to say he wasn't Irish, but the dark swam in around him.

8

The sun overhead was bright behind his closed lids, its warmth on his face. He was lying under the willow, a favorite spot from a long time ago, back when he was a kid. He and his brother, Arlen, dangling their bare feet over the cut-bank of the Bogue Lusa, their backs against the willow trunk, having a youthful talk about what they were going to do with their lives, failing to agree on who was going to marry Eula Mae and who was going to get stuck with her sister Cora. And they talked about all the money they were going to make, all the triumphs coming their way, sure they'd end up in one kind of enterprise or another, the two of them working side by side. When the creek ran full, they dug up crawlers and grubs, bringing their cane poles and fishing off that cut-bank for chub and cats.

Those times before the trouble with Great Southern, the goddamn lumber company trying to own everything in sight, their daddy working at the sawmill, doing what he called labor discipline, active in keeping the unions out and the workers in line, telling his boys he expected more from them, expecting them to attend school, insisting there was nothing more important than book-learning, the reason he worked as hard as he did, so they wouldn't have to. Widowed and remarried to a run-off woman, he was often tight-lipped, Alfred "JonJon" Waller raising his boys the best way he saw fit, putting them in charge of the cooking and cleaning while he went off from dawn to dusk, coming home tired and expecting his supper. On the occasions when he sat and talked to his boys, he'd tell of what he saw brewing at the mill, the white and Black workers alike organizing themselves, wanting more pay and better conditions, something he worked hard against, but something he believed they had a right to want. Telling his boys they ought to be grateful to be living in a land that was free — at least at first sight.

Then the light of the sun paled, and the willow and the creek faded from his mind, and the image of Arlen was gone. His old dad was gone too, and their tin-roofed place washed into the past.

Rousing to voices and the smells around him, something like antiseptic masking something festering, Huck opened an eye like it might be too much to take in at once. The other eye still swollen shut. He was on his back in a hospital bed, an iron bedframe with a metal footboard. A chair next to the bed. Looking down at his feet, a thin blanket over him, he realized he had nothing on, and his clothes were gone. That bubbly drink was something else, bottled by French devils.

It was an open floor of a hospital with beds lining the wall, more of them under a bank of high windows across the aisle. Men lying in them. The guy across with his head wrapped in white bandage, just his eyes and nose showing, a tube running to a hanging glass bottle. Huck put his one eye on a nurse in uniform, the white cap on her head, pushing an elderly man in a wheelchair, hurrying along and not glancing over at him.

He put together how he got there, remembered getting jumped and somebody slugging him from behind. Remembered

Dean warning him about the Mustache Petes. Huck guessing his pockets had been turned out — goddamn pants stripped right off his body. Looking down at his feet sticking out from under the blanket, his socks with both his big toes poking through. Reaching a hand up to the side of his head, wincing as he touched the knot the size of a pecan. Looking around for his pants, he propped up, leaning to the side, groaning from a jab to the ribs.

Moving an arm, then the other, flexing his fingers, then his legs and toes, touching his body and counting up his injuries. Except for the knot, the rest of the bruises were likely from the match with Mulligan, his ribs feeling crushed, his knuckles scraped and raw like they'd been dragged behind a cart. He tried to sit up, doing it slow, not wanting to make the thumping in his skull worse. He was on the edge of getting the spins and his gut started churning its warning. Easing his head back on the pillow, feeling the throb keeping time with his heartbeat.

He must have dozed then and when he started coming around again he got a notion of being in Arlen's surgical ward, the base hospital at Saône-et-Loire, where his brother landed after being wounded overseas, his brother fighting somebody else's war, the one their old dad had warned them about.

Orderlies pushed a stretcher past him, an arm flopping down, a doctor and nurse alongside, trading looks of concern, hurrying past.

Holding up his hand, he tried to hail them, watching them go past, Huck looking up at his hand like it belonged on somebody else's arm. Then he was able to prop up, looking at the ailing men on the beds along the ward. The spinning and nausea came fast and the contents of his stomach rushed up. Leaning to the side, he threw up. Sleek with sweat, he lay back, wiping his mouth on the ratty blanket. Wanting to get out of there as soon as his head and stomach settled, and his pants showed up.

"Oh my." It was a nurse, pretty with her brown hair tied back, dark eyes looking concerned, standing next to the cot, looking down at him.

"You mind me asking what you did with my pants, miss?"

"That's what you want to ask me about, pants? Not, where am I? Or, how'd I get here? Or, sorry I barfed up on your floor."

"Sorry about that. Okay, so where am I?"

"Grant Hospital."

"Never heard of it."

"Right at Lincoln and Webster."

"Well, for the record, I didn't ask to get dropped here."

"It's free to the worthy poor, like the sign says, if that's your worry." She started to step to the side of the bed, looked at the puddle of vomit, thought better of it and stood at the foot, saying, "Police brought you in, and from the look, you took on half the town." Looking into his one eye, giving him more of that concerned and caring look. "And you have yourself a doozy of a concussion."

"Well, I got a hard bark." Past the antiseptic smell, he thought he caught a scent of something she was wearing, not perfume, but maybe a bath soap, something like that.

"Not hard enough."

"You're probably right."

Then she looked at her clipboard, saying, "I'll need a name for the file."

"Huckabee Waller, friends just call me Huck." Watching her write it on her chart, saying to her, "You got one, a name?"

"Nurse."

"That's it, nurse?"

"That's all you need." She looked serious, but the dark eyes were smiling.

"Okay, so Nurse, tell me why'd you take my pants?"

"Shouldn't we concern ourselves with your head, Mr. Waller?"

"Aw, it's alright, I just took a knock."

"One that landed you here for observation."

"How long's this observation?"

"Doctor Gillis would like to see the swelling go down before your release. And that eye."

"You take them off, my pants?"

"You're being perfectly awful, Mr. Waller." She tried to look stern, but her eyes wouldn't go along.

"What kind of bedside manner you call that, taking a man's pants?"

"I've seen it all before, Mr. Waller. Nothing so special about you, I'm sorry to say. Now lie back and be a good boy while I go get an orderly to clean up this mess you made."

"Guess I got no choice. Oh, one more thing . . ."

She turned back. "Yes, Mr. Waller?"

"I'm just wondering, why take my pants, I mean, when it's my head that got banged up?"

"It's just what I do." With that she walked off, smiling like she got the last word, her heels clicking on the floor of the ward.

Watching her one-eyed, thinking nothing had a right to look that good packed into a nurse's uniform. Craning his neck until she was out of sight, his head thumping and hurting from the effort, but he was thinking he wouldn't mind seeing her outside of this place, that or he could get beat up again and left in some alley, pin a note to his shirt, asking that they drop him at Grant Hospital, this place of antiseptic smells and being free to the worthy poor. Looking up, the ceiling staring back, a fan up there whirring, circulating the air. Then he was drifting to sleep again, going back to the time with Arlen, sitting under that willow by that bank of the Bogue Lusa.

Living with his old dad and stepmother, the damned company town that sprang from the pines growing around it, slapped up a couple of years before Huck entered his teens, his old dad moving them from their shotgun house on Wells, quitting one job, and moving his boys out of New Orleans to the new place. Bogalusa built from the pine forests around it in under a year: a hotel and a place of worship, with promises of a school and a hospital to come. The bossman of the sawmill turned out to be a hated man called Sullivan, dubbing the place the Magic City, electing himself mayor and heading up the mill on the north side, the workers and their families living on the south end. Since the day it got incorporated, Bogalusa had been slow in dying, started out poor and rough as hell and went downhill from inception. No school and no hospital ever built, the place of worship used for beano and a legion hall most nights.

Like everybody living there, the brothers were put to work as soon as they entered their teen years, around the time his stepmother ran off, the boys working shifts for Great Southern, making railway ties, clearing away the pines for miles around. In '17, Arlen got the call, couldn't get out of there fast enough and went and served overseas. Huck could still see his old dad sitting at the table praying over the couple of letters they got, finally weeping as the men in their pressed uniforms came and told how Arlen had fought brave, made the ultimate sacrifice defending his country. The allied counterattack of the second battle of the Marne, fighting the Huns. The uniformed men told his old dad he ought to be proud. His old dad, spitting, telling those men Arlen only signed up to prove his family's Austrian roots didn't run so deep, not wanting his family branded as alien enemies, getting sent to Fort Oglethorpe and interned till the Great War found an end.

9

If his hands didn't hurt, then his stomach would be growling. The bare-knuckle fights were putting some money in his pocket. And though tempting, getting in deeper with Dean O'Banion was something he best chew on before jumping in all the way. Thinking that those not wanting to be sufferers took it upon themselves, turning to one kind of cunning plan or another — always on the grab for some of that easy money. And Huck was quick to learn there were a hell of a lot of sufferers in this town, but not so much easy money.

And he was thinking back to that mob boss, Big Jim Colosimo, being gunned down in his own restaurant. The man just got married and was standing in his fancy place on Wabash, looking out at his South Side domain, maybe thinking he had the world by the tail, running the rackets, booze and broads — had himself his own rosy outlook until he caught one in back of his head and was left bleeding out on his fine rug. Leaving the other gangs to claw up the territory like hyenas grabbing for scraps.

Mornings when the snow wasn't piling up and shutting down the city, Huck went and stood in lines waiting on day work, sometimes coming up empty, sometimes hired on to load up boxcars for two bits an hour. Another time mopping up the killing floor of a meatpacking factory, that one paying twenty-eight cents an hour. He went knocking at factory and sweatshop doors. Some of the foremen looking him over, on the lookout for pro-union agitators and troublemakers, seeing the healing cuts and bruises on Huck's face, telling him to beat it.

End of the second week after the Mulligan fight, he was back at the boxcars, Gorilla Al putting him on the toe line again, paying a ten-percent cut, past asking him to take a dive.

Finding himself looking across the scratch at a retired copper called Manis, another Corkman with arms and shoulders carved from oak, a square jaw to match, a meanness honed in another faraway war with the Black and Tans, the man possessing an ugly punching style evolved from back alley beatdowns. Butting with his skull, clawing and stabbing thumbs for Huck's eyes, biting in a clinch, his elbows for clubbing, heels for stomping on his feet. Putting Huck on his ass and ending the first round.

Willing himself to stick to what he learned from Winston, the old Black trainer in that Bogalusa gym. At Gorilla Al's signal, he stepped back to the line, looking in the copper's eyes, letting the man know this fight would be going a different way.

Elbows tight to his ribs, Huck fired straight lefts, then reversed his stance to southpaw, jabbing with his right, putting enough sting behind the punches to keep the cop off balance, looking for an opening for the left, pivoting off the ball of the front foot, getting the hip and shoulder into it and putting weight into the punches. Firing rockets into the openings anytime the copper tried to throw a punch.

Sweat beaded on Manis's forehead, the extra weight turning on him halfway through the second round. Blocking one with his forearm, Huck connected with his elbow, ducking and coming under a swing, butting with his head, avoiding a clinch, letting Manis bang himself out, and waiting for that one big opening.

Puffing hard, Manis dropped his arms, and Huck threw a jab, a quick move inside and he snapped an uppercut, knocking Manis back. Blood dripping from the man's mouth, Manis turning to biting and poking for Huck's eyes.

In the third, Huck got his chance, ducking a haymaker, he came under it, banging one against the cop's nose, sending a splash of blood across his face. Manis staggered and Huck kept on him, clubbing as the man covered up, using his elbows like pikes, dropping to a knee, somehow surviving the round.

In the fourth, Huck landed a good hook, then a straight right, the copper dropping to a knee again, the man's face bloody, mouth hanging open and his breath coming in gasps. Gorilla Al stepped between them, the crowd wanting more.

At the eight count, Manis shook his head, rose up slow and limped off.

And Huck made forty bucks off that one, enough to stay in bed for two days, drinking coffee and clear broth. Paid for the one-room flop on West Madison by the week, what the slumlord called a furnished room: a stained mattress and musty blanket, a wobbly chair by the smeared window, rolled newspaper under one leg, a chest of drawers that looked like it had tumbled off a truck, a bucket on the floor to catch what looked like tobacco drips from the stained ceiling. Costing Huck two bucks a week, likely getting fleeced on account of being new to town, speaking in what the slumlord called a yat accent.

Then he was back to looking for work around the Loop, called that on account of the cable cars looping in the district streets, then making the return trip. Huck trying all the department stores and movie houses around State and Madison, hoping to get hired on as security.

With no luck, he was back to fighting the next week, this time against a tunnel-man off a Great Lakes freighter, working on board three months, then taking a month off, stepping to the toe line, making money on the side, dubbing himself Wrecking Bill. Gorilla Al giving even odds after Huck's fight against Manis. Thick arms and a bald skull that looked about an inch thick, and a nose like twisted tree root. Showing his wrapped hands, Wrecking Bill stepped to the line, standing flat-footed, smiling at Huck like it was a promise of doom. Gorilla Al giving his instructions, saying he wanted nothing dirty. Bill pursing his lips, blowing Huck a kiss, saying, "Nighty night."

At the signal, Wrecking Bill came straight across the line, an overhand right slicing air as it missed. Huck smashing at the ribs, Wrecking Bill smiling it off. Throwing again and getting the same. Then he chased Huck off the line, trying to catch him in a bear hug, the crowd yelling for it. Gorilla Al letting it go on account the crowd was loving it.

Backing around the circle, Huck threw shots to keep him off, Wrecking Bill getting in a lucky punch, grappling Huck to the ground, fingers going for his throat, trying to finish him. Gorilla Al got a hold, trying to pull him off, Wrecking Bill throwing a backfist at him. Gorilla Al pulling his revolver, putting it against the man's ear and started counting to eight.

Between the rounds, Gorilla Al warned Wrecking Bill he'd shoot him if there was a next time. Stirred up, the crowd did their part, drinking and betting even more, Wrecking Bill a five-to-one favorite, Nails Morton and Gypsy Doyle taking all bets.

Licking away blood, forgetting about the toe line, Huck went for the body. Wrecking Bill threw big slow punches, Huck getting out of the way of most, leaving Bill chopping at air. In the fourth, Huck changed up, standing toe to toe, thinking the sting was gone from Wrecking Bill's punches, his hands getting heavier and slower, the man's mouth hanging open.

Huck banged him with body shots but couldn't put him down. The final round, Huck caught somebody in the crowd slipping something into Bill's gauzed hand. Starting the round with wild swings, Wrecking Bill went for the knockout. Backing up again, Huck took a hard right and was driven into the crowd, somebody yelling for Wrecking Bill to end it. The big man stamping a foot down on Huck's to keep him from moving, hitting him again with what he had in his hand and that ended it, Huck going down.

Gorilla Al took Wrecking Bill by the wrist, yanking up his arm, declaring him winner.

Somebody shouted it was rigged, others calling for their money back, Huck on the ground, seeing the crowd turning ugly. Gorilla Al taking his pistol and showing it around, saying it was the final decision of the ref.

Gypsy Doyle got Huck up on his feet and led him out of there. Gorilla Al and Nails Morton staying back, settling the crowd down, rolling another barrel of beer off the back of Gorilla Al's truck. Doyle opening the door of a Tin Lizzie and helping Huck onto the front seat.

"Last time I let you boys pick my fights," Huck said, willing his vision into focus.

Doyle turned the key, pulling the brake back, the spark and gas levers down, starting the engine.

"The man had a pipe, something in his hand."

"Yeah, I saw it," Doyle said unconcerned, then got out, going to the front and giving it a crank, listening for the engine's putter, then getting back in. "Crowd was loving it, and you put up a good tussle."

"Crowd just loves blood."

"A man works all week, he wants his beer and skittles." Working the pedals, Doyle released the handle of the brake, the car moving. Doyle shifting gears, driving out of there.

"Yeah, well, it's my blood we're talking about," Huck said.

"Deanie told you he wants a word."

"I'm done with this."

"Well, just hear the man out."

"Truth be told, you people give me a bad feeling."

"Ought to work on that rosy outlook."

Turning his punched-up face to the side mirror, Huck wasn't seeing any rosy outlook.

10

They were sitting at a table in the Four Deuces, Huck across from Dean and Hymie Weiss, Gypsy Doyle standing and watching the door to the place.

"Not about being Mick, Italian or Pole. It's about territory and holding onto it," Dean said. "It's all about having the right guys."

"Look, I'm done fighting, and I can't shoot to save my life," Huck said.

"What I hear is you got heart — and you don't back down." Dean looked at Hymie, then back to Huck. "Top of that, you told me you ran shine one time, drove like a wild man, keeping ahead of the law. You remember?"

"I said that?"

Dean grinned and nodded.

"From the look, you got plenty of guys — no disrespect, but why me?" Huck thinking he ought to go back to knocking on doors, sure there had to be some kind of honest work in this town.

"It's not what you hold in your hand, it's what you can hang on to," Dean said.

Gypsy Doyle came with a cup of coffee, setting it in front of Huck, asking, "You want soup? Can get 'em to fix something."

Shaking his head, Huck thanked him, doubting he could hold much down.

Reaching in a pocket, taking a roll of bills, Dean counted off fifty, saying, "Make one run for me, see if it works out." The run being over the frozen river at Detroit, up to Waterloo on the Canadian side, bringing back a load of whiskey, Huck driving and Gypsy Doyle riding shotgun.

"Be another fifty when you get back."

Fifty being double what most jobs paid in a week, these guys throwing money around like they just printed it.

"This guy Torrio took over from Colosimo — got the South Side, and we got the North, the Gennas got theirs, Touhys with a patch, a bunch of others, all of 'em running booze, the stuff coming in every port. One thirsty town means plenty to go around, but here we are squabbling over turf." Dean slid the sugar bowl to him, saying, "This town's full of folks that got booze in the bloodlines, calling it tradition, their right to drink. Irish, Pole, dago, Jew, don't much matter. None of them letting some statesman wave his amendment in their face, telling them they can't have a drink. Telling you, it's a gold mine."

"'Less you got something against easy money," Hymie Weiss said.

Pointing to his own face, Huck said, "This look like easy money?" Picking up the cup in a shaking hand, wincing at the pain as it touched his lip, he sipped.

"We don't deal in rotgut or shine — we leave that to the dagos," Dean said. "We bring in the good stuff, sell it to the class joints and hotels — why the Gold Coast belongs to us."

"Just for taking a ride across the river, a hundred bucks," Hymie said, giving him a what-have-you-got-to-lose look.

"Crossing a border with illegal booze, how much time I get for that?" Huck said, thinking the Canadian border was four hours away, plenty of places to get ambushed or busted along the way.

"It comes down to it, you drive or you shoot, but mostly you cross without a hitch. Get loaded up and back you come. We grease the right palms and get the right tip-offs — meaning there's hardly a hitch." Hymie waved his hand like there was nothing to it.

"Heard about some guy, Bernaducci, something like that, tried bringing a load across and ended trading shots with the Mounties and got himself planted. Guess he was making that easy money."

"That was the South Side, and a dumb move," Hymie said. "Italians don't like parting with the green, so they don't make the payoffs, and they don't get the tip-offs. We got the Purples on side, Mounties looking the other way, finding out when they got a roadblock up."

"Hundred bucks just for driving?" Huck couldn't help thinking he could sure do with money like that.

Dean and Hymie looked at each other, telling him about making the run to Waterloo, a town just a few hours east of the border, with only two regular cops on foot patrol in its downtown core. Dean explaining to Huck that folks on the Canadian side were allowed to make hootch, but they couldn't sell it. Not seeing what sense that made. Dean striking a deal with Ephram, the manager of the Huether Hotel, hiding loads of Seagram's and barrels of Kuntz beer in a cold cellar big enough for a hundred cases and twenty barrels. The hotel employees and locals not abiding by Canada's Temperance Act, something that threatened to take away their jobs, the staff treating Dean like a modern-day Robin Hood. Dean and his North Side lads staying at the hotel free of charge, tipping big, and frequenting the local shops, laying their money down.

Dean saying, "It works out, maybe you get a slice."

"Yeah, how big's this slice?"

"Call it two points . . . twenty, thirty thousand a load. Means you get . . ." Dean said, doing the arithmetic in his head. "Means you're gonna need deeper pockets."

"And when I'm not driving?"

"That's up to you."

Huck thinking if he didn't make it back, then it's two points of nothing. But still . . .

"You rather go punch yourself out, or work yourself stiff, that's up to you."

"I got that now, sore and stiff." Huck thinking at least nobody was shooting at him, saying, "Look, I appreciate the offer, Dean, but you mind if I sit with it a while longer?"

Dean looked at him deadpan, and Hymie wished him luck, saying, "I say you're back in a week, hat in hand."

Thanking them for the coffee, Huck was slow getting up.

"Give him a ride to his place," Dean said to Doyle.

Doyle led the way and held the door for Huck.

"You don't mind, drop me at Grant Hospital instead." Huck following, moving slow.

The three of them looked at him.

"Nurse there, think she's taken a shine to me."

11

"**C**ome in here looking like a man turned inside out," Dex Ayres said, the supervisor of the Yellow Cab livery on Main, the guy in charge of hiring drivers. Half-rising from a velvet chair a kind of lilac color, he stretched his hand across the desk. His white sleeves rolled up, a big map of the city behind him, push pins stuck into it. Pinstripe jacket hanging on a coat hook behind the kidney-shaped desk, leather top with claw-foot legs. A big silver lighter on top.

"A boxing match." Huck tried not to flinch, shaking the hand. Fretting the middle knuckle of his right hand could be busted, his right ear still ringing, a week after the fight with Wrecking Bill.

"That mean you're a pugilist?"

"Not like Blackjack Davie — mostly club fights, lately bare-knuckling."

"You ever win one?" Dex Ayres grinned, a friendly manner about him. "No offense, Huck, is it?"

"That's right. Well, sir, half of them were bums, sure enough, but they're big and hit like they're chopping meat."

"Only matters who's standing at the end, the way I understand it," Dex said.

"Something like that."

"Well, your nose is straight enough, and your ears don't look scabbed too bad. I'm guessing you know when it's time to get out."

"One thing I picked up, ducking outshines hitting."

"Meaning you're good at ducking — like my question. So, I ask again, why'd I want an ex-fighter driving one of my fleet?"

"Well, I'm kind of a people person."

The two of them smiling, taking each other in.

"You mind if I ask your age?"

"Twenty-four." Huck guessed he looked older under the swelling.

"So, a pugilist comes in, wants to drive a cab. Has me wondering why?"

"Well, sir . . ." Scratching his head, Huck said, "The way I hear it, Yellow's got a heck of a fleet: balloon tires, windshield wipers, two-way radios, the whole bit. And your Mr. Hertz put in the city's first traffic light." Huck showing what he learned, getting set to make his pitch, his idea still taking shape.

"That's right, the first one the city's seen, right up on Wabash, something we're all proud of." Dex Ayres smiled, looked pleased that Huck had done some checking.

"The way I figure it, you could use a fellow knows his way around and doesn't run from a scrap either." Huck had overheard two drivers talking at a diner about the trouble between Yellow and Checker, a business rivalry turning to open warfare in the streets. And the idea started taking shape.

Dex thought a moment, then said, "From the accent, you're not from around here, Huck Walker?"

"It's Waller, and that's right — from Bogalusa in Washington Parish." Seeing that it didn't ring a bell, he said, "Down New Orleans way."

Dex Ayres frowned. "So you're new to town but looking to drive one of my fleet?"

Huck seeing his mistake, this dandy thinking he came in looking for a job driving a taxi, then admitting he was new to town. "Let's say I been getting the lay of the land."

"Okay, then how about you point me to Back of the Yards?" Dex swiveled his chair so he could take in the big map.

Huck looked from the map out the window, saying, "Well sir, for that I just got to follow my nose."

Dex smiled at that. "How about Cicero?"

"Cicero's the wettest spot on the map." Huck pointed west, remembered the North Siders driving him to the Ship.

"And the Loop? Show me on the map?"

"Loop's where Big Jim bought it, over on South Wabash," Huck said, wagged a finger at the map, remembering what Gypsy Doyle told him about Colosimo, the boss of the South Side, getting clipped Black Hand–style in his own joint, waiting on a whiskey shipment. Had a funeral for a king, a fancy silver coffin in a hearse followed by a throng of a thousand, laid to his just deserts in Oakwood. Hinky Dink and Bathhouse John, and a bunch of congressmen and judges mourning the crook like he was a saint.

"And I can tell you one of your drivers got in a punch-up over at Lakeside." Huck pointed to the map. "Another one got laid up in Garfield Park two days back. You want I can point out Cook County Hospital." Winging it from the scuttlebutt he heard from Moses, the Black mechanic working on a taxi downstairs, Huck getting here early and stopping to ask about the bullet hole in one of its fenders, getting some lowdown on the trouble between Yellow and Checker.

Dex considered a moment, saying, "You ever drive a Model J, Huck?"

"If it's got wheels, I can drive her. Back home, I ran spuds, sometimes corn." Not mentioning they were in the form of moonshine. "Drove a big old farm truck and kept her between the ditches just fine."

"I admit I've got a man or two laid up, and another one quit on me last night, so ordinarily I'd say I can't use you, but . . ."

"Just for fun, let me ask what's the pay?"

"Thirty a week with Sundays off."

"This fella that quit, got himself in a scuffle with this Checker outfit, did he?" Huck getting around to it now, the idea he'd been playing with since hearing about the taxi war going on in the streets.

"Let's say he's gone to answer a different call."

"You ask me, you need more'n another Joe that can hold a steering wheel and read a map. I'm talking about the knock-'em-downs at the taxi stands."

Dex hesitated before saying, "What are you getting at, Huck?"

"Well, sir. Way I see it, you need a man that does the running off, not the running from."

Dex bunched his eyebrows, then said, "Look, we don't hire muscle, if that's what this is . . ." Smiling, he said, "Maybe try a gin joint, a blind pig I believe they're calling them."

"Heard there's been a shooting too."

"Well, the papers do stretch it, their job being to sell papers."

"Sounds like you got customers running off instead of getting in."

"And you're the man to end our troubles, that it?"

"That's what I'm saying."

"Sounds like you could lead us deeper."

"The way I see it, when you're not being heard, you got to speak up. And I can help you with that." Huck gave him an even look, his one eye still half swollen, bruises on his face turning from brown to yellow. "But I'll tell you this, it's gonna take more than thirty a week."

Now Dex was grinning, leaning forward on the desk, saying, "Just for sport, let's say I'm listening."

"First off, I see it as a two-man job. Going around in one of your taxis, worrying the competition." Thinking of Gypsy Doyle as the second man, the man who didn't seem the type to back down from trouble. "That's for starters."

"Just how much more are you thinking?"

"Let's say a hundred a week and your problem goes away. Oh, and I'll need a taxi."

"A taxi?"

"It's how we get around."

"And just how long do you see this taking?"

"A month and you should see something, two and it'll be cleared up, three tops."

"And by cleared up . . ."

"Means your trouble with Checker's a thing of the past."

"A hundred a week?"

"Per man." Huck thinking he hit it a little hard, a hundred a week was likely double what Dex Ayres made for running the livery.

"Well now . . ." Dex looked to the ceiling like he couldn't believe it, or he was conferring with a higher power, then he looked back at Huck, saying, "It's something I'd have to run past Mr. Hertz, though I can't say he'll see the humor."

"I can't see where it's funny," Huck said.

"Ought to sit on this side of the desk, no offense intended." And he gave a forced smile.

"Well, could be I'm talking to the wrong man," Huck said, starting to rise.

"I'm afraid you can't see Mr. Hertz, out of the question, if that's where this is going."

"I'm talking about going to the other outfit. Fellow's name's Morris Markin, think I heard it right. Anyway, sorry to have taken your time, mister," Huck said, and he started for the door.

"Now just hold on. You can't just come in here then . . ."

"That's just it, I can."

"Goddamn, the brass balls on you." Dex Ayres leaned back in his lilac chair, collecting himself.

Huck stood and waited, trying to look agreeable.

"I can tell you straight off, a hundred a man won't fly." Dex waited till Huck sat back down, saying, "Let's call it fifty a week, and the second man's one of my choosing. We give it two weeks, then I'll gauge the results."

"I don't stick my neck out for fifty, and I don't go in with a man I don't know."

"We got some pretty tough boys here — the ones taking it to Checker."

"Two of 'em in hospital, and one just walked off. Look, Mr. Ayres, the kind of man I'm thinking trims the hedges with a Tommy gun. Any of your fellas do something like that?"

"I don't want anybody getting hurt. I'm sure Mr. Hertz would concur."

"What I got in mind's sending a message, one that's clear and loud enough."

Dex looked at him, still some doubt in his eyes.

"'Less I miss my guess, you're gonna have more than one or two boys jumping ship," Huck said. "Tell you what, how about we split the difference and call it eighty for starters — each, I mean." Huck giving a little ground, then saying, "And don't tell me you got to take it to the boss. I can see you're the man in charge." Huck looking past the kidney-shaped desk, the man in the velvet chair.

"Well . . ." Dex steepled his fingers, twisted his mouth into a smile, made like he was considering, finally nodding, saying, "Three things I'll need." Holding up his fingers, counting off. "I expect a report, end of the week. Two, it's over when I say. And three, you and me never had this talk."

Huck reached across the desk and stuck out his hand, ready to wince at the pain.

Instead of shaking hands, Dex pulled open his top drawer, took out a metal box, removed forty dollars from petty cash, counted it out and set it down. "I'll see you next week, hear about your results, then you get the rest. And bring this second man. I want to meet him."

12

Walking out of the men's shop, he was feeling like a top dog, the package of his old clothes under his arm. Getting in the Yellow taxi and driving to Lincoln and Webster — stopping at Grant Hospital, the end of Huck's first day on the new job, wanting to talk to one of the drivers.

Walter Yemich had been laid up after catching a beating on the day shift yesterday, right at a taxi stand two blocks from the livery, three Checker drivers pulling behind his cab, dragging him out and slugging him with pipes, leaving him busted and bleeding next to his taxi.

The father of six with bruised ribs and a fractured skull, a dozen stitches above one eye, likely to be out of work for a month or more. The Yellow drivers had taken up a collection at the livery to help with the hospital bills, sending bags of food to Yemich's family. Dex Ayres told Huck about it, asking him to take the collection money to the hospital and hand it to Yemich.

Stopping outside Grant Hospital after driving around in the Yellow taxi like bait all day, parking along the downtown stands, waiting for any Checker drivers wanting to give him a try. Huck putting the reserved sign in his window, meaning he wasn't taking any fares.

He took the stairs and went to intake, being directed to Yemich's ward, finding the man in a bed with his head and chest wrapped, the same ward Huck had been in. The man's wife sitting next to him, holding his hand. Telling them who he was, then saying, "How you feeling, Walt?"

"I'm just grand, brother, what do you think?" The man's voice somewhere between a whisper and a croak.

Passing the flowers and collection envelope to the wife, Huck said, "Sorry this happened."

"You the one they hired to watch his back?" It was the wife asking, the gaunt-looking woman kept her tone even, but the blame showed in her eyes.

"I came on after the fact, ma'am. But I'll be watching the stands from here on."

"Eighty bucks a week, that right, what they pay you?" the wife said, giving him a sharp look.

Huck looked at her, thinking word got around in a heck of a hurry, not sure how she found out about it.

"It's alright, Flo." Yemich winced through the pain, patting his wife's hand, saying, "He's not the one jumped me."

"Not the one who stopped it either."

"It's my first day on the job, ma'am," Huck reminded her. Then to Walt, "And Ayres wants you to know he's got your job waiting."

"Well, you go tell him what to do with it, then. Walt's gone packing," the wife said. "Got too much sense for taxi driving. You just go on and tell him." Making a shooing motion with her fingers.

"Guess I don't blame you," Huck said, standing there another dumb minute, not feeling like a top dog in his new outfit right then, wishing them both luck and getting out of there.

Walking the corridor, down a flight of stairs, going to the admin office and asking about Yemich's bill. The woman at the desk checked a chart, telling him it was five dollars a day for the bed, plus additional costs for pain medication. Huck thinking for that kind of money the bed ought to come with one of Bubbling-Over's soiled doves in it. Reaching in his pocket, he gave the intake nurse what he had left on him, told her he'd be back with the rest.

Walking from the office, he nearly knocked into the same nurse who had tended to him a month ago — those same dark eyes. Huck saying, "Hey, how're you doing, miss?" Wishing he had a name to tag on the end. The woman shorter than she appeared when she was standing over his hospital cot.

She looked at him, but it didn't register.

"Come on, you remember me?"

"And why'd that be?" Her look was of surprise. Edging around him and hardly slowing down.

"Was brought in after getting mugged — you got me back on my feet."

"You want you can thank the doctor. Me, I likely just changed your bedpan."

"Asked me about Bogalusa, where I'm from."

"Well, nice to see you again, Bogalusa. Anyway, I've got bedpans calling my name." She started stepping past him.

"Never caught your name," Huck said, trying again.

"Like I told you, it's Nurse."

"So you do remember."

"Nice try."

"Hold on a second. Just how's a fella, new to town, get to see a nice girl like you again?"

"I don't know, could try getting hit by a coach."

Huck watched her walk down the corridor, white shoes clanking on the polished floor, this place of misery and healing.

"Ouch." A Black orderly with graying hair was pushing a wheelchair past him along the hall, saying, "You got shot down in flames, brother. Come on, climb on." Chuckling to himself, shaking his head, and moving along the hall.

13

"**W**ant to know if you're better at throwing or shooting." Gypsy Doyle got in the passenger side, setting the butt of the shotgun on the floor, twin barrels pointing up, shutting the door and setting a bag on the floor, holding the shotgun between his knees.

"Depends what I'm throwing." Huck second-guessing his idea of bringing Gypsy Doyle into Yellow's taxi war, seeing the man had a way of taking over. The stiffness and swelling from fighting had eased. Huck making his first run with Doyle, getting to know him on the drive to Canada, crossing the frozen Detroit River at Belle Isle at night, hearing the cracking underneath, the tires slipping on the black ice, driving through Windsor, then on to Waterloo to the east, to the Seagram's distillery on Erb Street, loaded up the Bowman Dairy truck and drove back, crossing over the ice ahead of daybreak. Telling Doyle about the taxi trouble, Doyle saying sure he'd help out.

So, Huck took him to the livery, introduced him to Dex Ayres, seeing the fear in the superintendent's eyes at meeting Gypsy Doyle, this man with the knife scar angling down his face. Doyle seeing the fear too, smiling and showing Dex the gap where the tooth was missing.

"The way it'll go, I do the shooting if any, and you do the throwing." Opening the bag, Doyle showing the sticks, calling it the devil's porridge.

"A bit much, ain't it?" Huck said.

Reaching in a pocket, Doyle tossed him a lighter, Huck catching it. The silver one from Dex Ayres's desk.

"Checker shoots up Yellow's joint, so we blow up one of theirs."

"Got nothing against sending the fear of God, but . . ."

"Well now, Huck, it's right in the bible, an eye for an eye. And you want me coming along, earning my pay . . ."

Huck was looking at the sticks in the bag.

"Look, maybe you're good with your dukes," Doyle said. "But when it comes to blowing shit up . . ."

"Ask me, you're not so bad with your dukes," Huck said.

"Point is, we're keen old dogs, you and me, and we don't back down. It's what the man hired us to do. What makes us do it, I don't know — guess it's the dough."

Huck guessed Gypsy Doyle might be a little touched. And now he was driving along South Michigan, and in Doyle's mind there was no turning back.

Pulling up to the Checker livery, several Mogul cabs parked at an angle out front, Huck left the engine of the Yellow idling, Doyle getting out with the scattergun, walking around the cabs out front, kicked the door of one, leaving a good dent, then stepped to the livery's door and opened it, holding it with a foot, calling inside, "Howdy boys. I'm giving you fair warning. I count ten and then I'm coming in shooting." Racking the slide, he counted off, "One, two, three — God be with you." Stepping to the side, putting his back to the boards as a shot blasted through the door, wood splintering. Doyle grinning and nodding to Huck.

Eyeing the upper windows, Huck heard excited voices and footfalls from inside, the Checker crew making up their minds — to stand or run.

Leveling the barrels, Doyle drew a breath, like he was set to dive underwater. Shoving the door open wider with his foot, another gunshot ripping the morning, dust and bits of wood flying off the door frame. And Doyle leapt past the door — the boom of both barrels, more yelling and running inside, the scattering of men going out the back.

Stepping from the cab, Huck turtled his neck against the cold blowing in off the lake, biting through his clothes. Reaching in the bag, taking Dex Ayres's lighter.

The sound of scuffling inside stopped, Huck guessing Doyle had emptied the place. Taking a stick, then cupping a hand around the lighter's flame, holding it to the wick, letting it sizzle halfway. Stepping to the blasted door, he took a slow five count, not wanting the stick thrown back, then he lobbed it in, heard it bounce, putting his back to the outer wall. Crouching, both hands clapped over his ears.

The explosion blew out the front window, the ground shivering, debris blowing through the doorway. His ears were ringing, he took the next stick and lit it, counted again, then lobbed it inside, putting his back against the wall. After the blast, he was smelling smoke from inside.

Getting back in the Yellow, he heard a beam crash, then the staircase collapsing. The flicker of flames showing through the busted window.

Doyle was coming from around the back, the shotgun over his shoulder like he'd been bird hunting, climbing in the taxi, Huck driving them out of there, heading back down Michigan.

"Now, when it comes to bringing in whiskey . . ." Doyle said. "We run into Torrio's boys or the Gennas, they won't scare so easy." Doyle looked at him, getting out his cigarettes, offering the pack. "But the kind of money we're talking, kind of makes it worthwhile."

Huck looked out the windshield, driving to the North Side, something inside gnawing for him to drop Doyle off, then keep driving out of state and not stop till he got someplace warm.

14

Huck couldn't figure why the gang bothered with nickel-and-dime fight-fixing, other than it being for kicks or tradition. Since the Volstead reared its head, the cash cow was bootlegging, the North Side making money faster than they could count it, robbing liquor shipments belonging to competitors, mainly Torrio and the Gennas. Not to mention gaining the political connections to keep the South Side Italians in line. Doing it with the backing of the overriding Irish on the police force, more than half of them with the brogue in their voice, thick as pea soup.

That worked out on the U.S. side, but on the next run with Doyle, the two of them in the hopped-up Hupmobile were tailed on the Canadian side by a lone Mountie in a patrol car, who picked them up around midnight at a place called Maidstone, just a few miles out of Windsor.

"Guess you didn't pay this one off," Huck said.

"There's always one," Doyle said, checking the loads in the shotgun.

Huck gave it throttle and the chase was on, telling Doyle to hang tight, hitting top speed, toggling the switch to shut off the taillights. Running flat out a dozen miles, he couldn't lose the cop.

"Losing your touch," Doyle said, unconcerned.

"Hold on!" Huck said.

Doyle was hooting like a fool when Huck hit the binders, doing what he called a one-wheel brake, spinning the Hup around — their world going in a half circle, tires screeching. Huck clutching the wheel and shifting, Doyle still whooping as Huck gave her throttle, tires screeching, charging head on at the Mountie. The hundred yards between them disappearing — a game of chicken the Mountie hadn't reckoned on, veering his patrol car straight off the two-lane, jumping the ditch, losing control and rolling it in a fallow field.

Turning back around, Huck drove past the flipped patrol car, putting his headlights on the Mountie crawling from his wreck.

Doyle cranking down his window and calling out, "My granny can do better."

The two of them talking about it the rest of the way to Waterloo.

Doyle telling Huck, "Some Mounties ain't for sale, but lucky for us, they're better at riding horses."

He got to know Doyle on those long drives, the two of them getting along. Huck telling him about growing up on the Delta, about his family, his mixed roots, Austrian and French with a touch of Irish, and told about the food he missed and the carnivals along Bourbon. Told him of a time when they lived in a place called Cut Off, a big blow coming off the Gulf and smashing their place to sticks. Any joints lucky enough not to get knocked down stood crooked and crippled, many with their roofs knocked clean off. The family grabbing what they could carry, going to stay with his Teety Fleur in Orleans Parish, her place one of the few around undamaged. Huck recalled streets turned to rivers, the Presbyterian church in Lafayette Square collapsed, and most of the church steeples swatted off by an unseen hand. Young Huck thinking that God was plenty peeved at Presbyterians and Catholics alike, sending that hellish blow like it talked about in the Old Testament. All that a couple of years before moving to Bogalusa. And he told Doyle about leaving New Orleans in a hurry on account of shooting Bubbling-Over.

Doyle trading his own stories, claiming his grandad was a Civil War captain, involved in the First Battle of Memphis, not on the winning side, but a brave man just the same. Telling Huck about growing up to a family of cotton farmers, about crewing on a paddle steamer when he was in his teens, and the thrills of Beale Street when he had the jingle of coins in his pockets. Both jibing their home towns as the root of the blues, Huck talking about Buddy Bolden and Papa Jack Laine. Doyle talking about W.C. Handy and his Memphis Blues and the best horn player around called Satch. But Shelby County was too pokey for Doyle, saying there was no chance he was going to spend his days working cotton. Chicago, New York or Detroit were towns custom-made for a guy like him, and how he felt that way since he was a kid.

They rolled back into Chicago, dropped the load of Seagram's and the Hupmobile at a warehouse, Doyle wanting to get something to eat, directing Huck in his taxi to one of his favorite haunts, calling it Berghoff's Chuck Wagon. Doyle boasting how you got a free beer when you bought a sandwich or sausage, the North Side lads dropping off four kegs every week.

"They got this sandwich, *Leberkäse*, something like that," Gypsy Doyle mispronouncing it, but explaining the fare at this Austrian eatery, calling it the heinie diner. The two of them getting out of the taxi, heading for the door. Doyle going on, "Kinda like meatloaf, but on a bun, call it a *Kaiser*. Then they got this one made of raw beef, sounds like it'd give you the shits, don't it? But I'm telling you — *mmm mmm*."

A man in a ratty coat stepped from the alley next to Berghoff's. Stepping up to them, the man waved a long blade, the kind used for butchering meat, saying, "Okay ya bitches, empty them pockets."

Doyle looked at this rough-looking man, the coat looked like fleas held it together, dirty face and hair, the blade smeared and showing rust, seeing the second man coming from the shadows, stepping in front of Huck, showing a blade inside his coat.

Huck raised his hands to waist level, saying, "The food here any good?"

"I'll stick you and take it — all you got. Money, now!" the first man said, looking spooked.

"Man wants what we got," Doyle said to Huck, shrugging like there was no way around it.

"Tell you what, knock off this foolishness, fellas, and how about we buy you a sandwich?" Huck said.

"Gonna gut you."

"Do any good saying you come on the wrong fellas?"

The man looked past him to the Yellow taxi, saying, "Got your pocket full of taxi fare. Give it."

Doyle considered, twisting his mouth, saying to Huck, "Well, best give it then."

"I'm doing the telling here." The man waved the long blade like maybe Doyle hadn't seen it, stepping closer, glancing at his buddy to make sure he was with him.

Doyle patted his coat pocket, saying, "Come take it then."

"You from Dunning, the booby house?" The man zigzagged the knife in the air.

"This town's going to the dogs," Doyle said to Huck, holding his hands wide, taking a step closer to the man.

Not the way the man figured this ought to go. Hesitating, glancing over his shoulder again.

"You want what I got, then go on and take it." Doyle stood two feet from him, taking out his billfold, holding it out.

Backing up half a step, the man growled and raised his knife.

Tossing the billfold in a lazy flip — the man's eyes following it — Doyle stepped in and threw his fist into the man's middle, catching the knife hand with his left as the man doubled over, twisting the arm. The blade clattering to the walk next to the billfold. Clutching a handful of greasy hair, Doyle stood him upright and hit him again. Letting him fall, then sweeping the blade away with his foot. The man curled on the ground, his hand stretching out for the blade. Doyle turned, looking at the other man, then raised his heel, driving it down on the fallen man's hand — the snapping sound of bones.

The man on the ground screamed, clutching the hand.

The other one stared at the twisted hand, let his own knife drop, then he turned and ran into the alley, right into a pile of crates, falling headlong over them, scrambling along the ground on all fours, getting away.

Doyle stooped for his billfold, saying, "Then they got these dumplings called *Klöse*, serve 'em alongside this pork chop they call a *Kassler*, man, it's real good too." Doyle stepped past the fallen man, saying to Huck, "Think I'm going with that, but you ought to try this raw meat I told you about . . . Or, if you wanna play it safe, just go for the flapjacks, call it *Pfann* something or other, but you say flapjacks and Luka'll know what you mean." Doyle looked at his fingers as they entered. "Man, I gotta wash my hands."

Luka the owner came from in back, had been chopping onions, getting set for the lunch special. Luka recognizing

Huck from the rail-car fights, the Austrian loved putting money down, said he made a three-to-one jackpot on Huck after his fight with Manis the cop. Luka saying Huck ought to come in for soup after his next fight, something he wouldn't have to chew. Told him it would be on the house.

15

A dozen Yellow drivers sat around tables talking about getting some payback, avenging Walter Yemich, lining the bar of the blind pig called the Shores, up the block from the old Walden Shaw livery on Main, none of the drivers seeing a need for ringers like Huck Waller and Gypsy Doyle. They were tough men themselves stirred up by drink, ready and eager to handle any scrap Checker cared to dish up. Nobody needed to tell him how they felt, Huck standing there, drinking his beer alone.

He heard how a bunch of them got in their taxis and rode up to a meeting hall Checker used, throwing bricks and busting out some windows. Did a quick retreat when about fifty Checker drivers charged out, the men inside, come to listen to a salt talk about unionizing, some of them for it, some against it. All of them flooding out the door, all of the same mind — first time that evening — letting fists and rocks fly. Nobody knew which side fired the first shot, a bullet blasting out an office window across the street, more shots followed as the Yellow drivers piled back in their taxis and roared off, leaving a couple of Checker men on the ground by the time the coppers on patrol arrived.

Coming into the livery the day after, Dex Ayres gathered the drivers and mechanics at the double doors of the livery's garage. With Huck standing next to him, like he was his personal bodyguard, he got them settled by the time a ReVere-Duesenberg pulled up out front, the uniformed driver coming around and opening the rear door, John D. Hertz stepping out, dressed in a fine suit and overcoat, a silk scarf around his neck, a homburg on his head. His driver took a box from the trunk, setting it on the ground before the boss. Smiling, John D. Hertz stood before them, putting a shining shoe up on the box.

"Seems you boys took the law in your hands," Hertz started, looking around at the faces. Most of the men looking sheepish, or away, or down at their own shoes.

"Well, who am I to cast blame on you?" Hertz waited till some of those faces looked up, then going on, "Big Bill and his coppers have their hands full, busy searching for foot juice and not being able to tell a blind pig from a hush shop — all the while Checker's on the rampage, trying to put us out of business."

More of the men were glancing up now.

"Going around and poaching our fares, attacking honest men on the street, taking the food from our children's mouths. Our proud fleet being pocked with pistol and buckshot, headlights knocked out, tires slashed, and a couple of our boys laid up in hospital. Any of you men church-going?"

Getting some nodding heads and a few raised hands.

"Well, then you know your scriptures, and you heard the verse in King James about an eye for an eye."

The men were all looking at him now. The second time that week Huck heard the biblical reference.

"And you know what I say about it?" Hertz stopping for effect, stepping both feet up on the box, a head above them. "I say, they want to go hubcap to hubcap . . ." Hertz building them up, making a fist, raising it and shaking it. "By God, I say we oblige them."

That got the men nodding, some shouting.

"We'll oblige them alright, all the way from Evanston all the way down the Shore. I say we've been tolerant too long. They want a war on wheels, going from fare to fist to firearms, then I say we give it to 'em." Hertz sounding like he was set to send his troops over the trenches.

They were stirred up and they were with him. Many of them veterans of the Great War, plenty of them bringing back a Mauser or a Colt Hammerless, one of the ex-navy boys smuggling back a trench mortar, another saying he had a Mills bomb. To a man, they were ready to rain more hell on Checker, the numbers running in Yellow's favor, eleven hundred cabs nearly doubled the Checker fleet. And Checker's union trouble was causing dissension among its own ranks.

John D. Hertz promised to do his bit, going to his police ties to block and stall the sale of an extra two hundred and fifty new cabs ordered up by Checker's owner, Morris Markin. Hertz wound down his speech by telling his boys he'd been dealing with rivals since he bought up the Shaw Livery Company, before turning it into the Yellow empire six years back, doing whatever needed doing, and always ending on top. Holding his hand up for them to see, his fingers splayed, then making a fist again, a crushing gesture this time, getting them all whooping and shouting some more.

This taxi war that was making the front page of every daily around, the *Trib* running the headline: "Taxis Take a Stand and Shoot It Out." The Associated Press calling Chicago the Wild Midwest.

In spite of the taxi troubles, folks kept flagging Yellow and Checker down, climbing onto the back seats, needing to get across town, from Wilmette to Gary, passengers getting down between the seats anytime the fender scraping or shooting started. And they were taking those stories home for supper-table talk. In spite of the violence, nobody had been killed — yet.

Huck considered it could be safer stepping to the toe line, the only thing being thrown at him were wild punches. But he was making good money with Yellow, even had some left over by the end of each week, first time in his life. Then there was what he made from running whiskey with Doyle.

16

Gypsy Doyle was happy to let him drive the Hupmobile on the next run to Detroit, this rig with the hot engine and beefed-up springs, Bowman Dairy painted down both sides. And Huck showing he had driving skills. Riding shotgun, Doyle slept half of the way, nursing a hangover with the twin barrels between his knees, then telling Huck that since the Volstead every legal joint selling hootch in the country had pretty much packed it in. "More'n two hundred thousand speaks springing up to take their place, not one paying taxes, you believe it?"

"A dumb move for Harding."

"Got every quack in the country applying for a medicinal liquor license, and sacramental wine sales, man, going right through the steeple." Doyle shaking his head and laughing about it. "Just better than a year, and we're making more cabbage than the thieving mayor. Deanie's talking about just weighing the green instead of counting it."

Huck tried to picture that kind of money, thinking of the points the gang was paying him just for making this run, guessing he'd come away with two hundred just for driving to Detroit that night, waiting on the skiff to bring the load across the river at Belle Isle, now that the ice had thawed, the way they did it most of the year.

Pulling up to the pick-up spot, Huck saw the river ahead, the spotter waving an arm. Huck turning the truck on the road and backing in to make the loading easy, allowing for a quick getaway.

"Ought to throw in with us all the way, make the runs and jack some loads — forget about this taxi bullshit," Doyle said. "Just nickels and dimes when there's real dough for the taking."

"I like being my own man." Keeping an eye on the spotter, Huck said he'd think on it, making it about his independence, but the way they set him up at the fights never sat right, leaving him an uneasy feeling around Dean O'Banion and his lads of Kilgubbin, especially his enforcer Vincent Drucci, the one they called The Schemer. The man and his crazy burning eyes. And since meeting John D. Hertz, Huck had taken a shine to the man — sure he was a bit showy, but he liked the way the taxi boss had talked to his troops that day, seeing him as savvy.

"Just as likely to get shot either way, but with us you can afford the funeral."

"You see getting shot as a selling feature?"

"Think you get what I'm saying."

Huck pointed, seeing the signal man waving the "all clear," meaning the skiff was starting to make its run.

"Deanie sang in the church choir, Holy Name Cathedral," Doyle said. "I tell you that?"

"Somebody mentioned something like that."

"Back in school he got called Gimpy, on account one leg's shorter. But try calling him that, see what happens."

Huck nodded, believing the man had a short fuse, something that showed in his eyes.

"Him and Bugs, Hymie and Vince go all the way back to the Market Street Gang. Swiping anything they got their hands on, later signing on as sluggers for the *Trib*, going around to newsstands selling the *Examiner*, getting them to change their minds. What was called the Circulation Wars. All that long before I came on board."

"The *Trib*, huh?"

"Till they switched to the *Examiner*, working a better deal. Deanie going where the money was, the rest going along."

"A tight bunch."

"Like brothers."

Huck could see that, the way they were with each other.

"Guy called Charlie the Ox taught him safecracking. Leading to the only time Deanie got busted, well, one of the times. Only other time was for assault."

"Somebody call him Gimpy?"

"Think that's funny?" Gypsy Doyle serious now, maybe he was sorry he mentioned it. Shrugging it off and saying, "Only time he was ever in the joint, a reformatory on account of his age."

"You're telling me, why?"

"I'm painting you a picture."

"Just a fun-loving bunch, and the leader sings in the choir."

"Top of that he arranges bouquets like you can't believe."

"Flowers?"

"Yeah, flowers, what else? Taught himself after his mother passed, making flowers for her grave."

Taking his eyes off the skiff, Huck looked at him.

"He's a man of many talents, what can I say?"

"With the boyish looks . . ."

"And don't let 'em fool you." Doyle shook his head at some memory, saying, "His old man moved him and his brother to what they called Kilgubbin, nothing but squatters' shacks by Little Hell. Sang at this inn where Deanie waitered. He'd give them the Irish tenor while Bugs and Hymie went in the coat room, picking pockets. Sometimes, he'd fix folks drinks, give 'em the Mickey Finn, you know what that is?"

"Sure."

"He'd sing and put 'em out, then help himself to what they had in their pockets." Doyle was smiling, opening his door and getting out, laying the shotgun on the seat, seeing the skiff come to shore — laden down, the load of booze under a tarp. Reaching his pistol from under the seat, he stuck in in his belt, saying, "Let's go earn our keep."

17

Over five hundred bucks stashed behind the wall board of his one-room place, a flimsy lock on the door. Huck was looking out the livery's front window, wondering about going to the bank and setting up an account. Keeping that kind of money hidden in Hobohemia was asking for trouble, not forgetting the night he got jumped by the Mustache Petes. Lost in his thoughts, he was slow seeing the cab packed with Checker men roaring up, two men hanging out and shooting out the livery windows. Huck throwing himself to the floor, Moses the mechanic grabbing the shotgun leaning by the door, going to the busted window, set to return fire, but the wheelman pushed the pedal and the Checker was already racing away.

Huck brushed dirt off his pants as Moses handed him the shotgun, not saying a word about the paid watchman not seeing trouble coming and throwing himself on the floor.

Taking a glass jug, Huck went and filled it at the pony pump out back of the livery, got in his taxi and drove solo to the Checker garage on Hudson, stopping out front, getting out and stuffing a rag in the jug of petrol, set the rag to flame and tossed it, the jug smashing against the clapboard side. Taking the shotgun from behind the seat, Huck put two rounds through the front window, getting in and driving off before the Checker man with a Winchester rifle showed up late on the livery roof, returning fire like it was Fort Dearborn, giving nearby citizens some more of that Wild Midwest.

The police came by the Yellow livery asking questions about the taxi with the bullet hole through its roof-liner, but not making any arrests. Dex Ayres said hiring Huck might have been a mistake — their troubles not going away, in fact seemed to be escalating — but he was keeping him on for now.

The evening papers claimed Mayor "Big Bill" Thompson was losing his mind over taxi drivers shooting up his fair city, pacing a hole in his rug, unable to put an end to it.

John D. Hertz had been called to the mayor's office, and he came by the livery in his Duesenberg and told Huck to drive him to city hall. Told him on the way he just fired his driver, that he was clearing away some dead wood. Huck thinking he would be next.

Waiting in the mayor's outer office, Huck heard Big Bill rant at the Yellow boss, telling him all bets were off, friendship aside he wasn't having a taxi war on his streets, his council still sweeping up after the race riots that menaced his town, what the papers had called Red Summer, riots that took thirty-eight lives, mostly on the South Side. The mayor ranting about his scarred city. "Denizens uneasy, homicides on the rise with a less than one-in-four conviction rate I have to answer for. Gangs going at it, dozens of bootlegging operations, always some Italian feud or other, the Black Hand extorting from immigrants, the goddamn *Trib* calling it fertile ground for the criminal kind. Enough illegal whiskey to fill the goddamn river, and all of it set to give me a coronary."

Hertz agreed it was time to end it, but not in the way the good mayor was thinking. Hertz made it plain there would be no sit-down or shaking of hands with that Markin son of a bitch. Hertz developing a tumor-sized dislike for that man. On top of which he figured his pal with the Republican heart was going to lose to Dever come the '23 election. Told him that to his face and walked out of the office, then had Huck drive him back to the livery.

Calling his drivers and the reporters from the *Trib* and *Herald-Examiner*, John D. Hertz stood outside the former Shaw livery with its shot-out window, his foot up on the wood box, telling them of his meeting with the mayor, and how he was declaring open war on Checker, his men around him cheering. Huck watching the boss showboating the same way Dean O'Banion had done, doing it without the singing, but Hertz was in his element, sounding like he was talking to the men in those faraway trenches, getting ready to jump up and run at his command, following their bayonets, like his brother, Arlen, had done.

Huck coming away from Hertz's spiel wondering if he had less chance of getting hurt running whiskey with the gangsters, or even going back to stepping to the toe line against some ape with twenty pounds on him, still he was curious to see how this taxi war would play out.

18

He watched the same kid through the windshield, a skinny boy of about ten. If his hair was clean, maybe it'd be blond. In a ratty jacket that looked too big, the boy didn't seem bothered by the cold, earning pennies, helping the high-society types with bags and carrying them to the hotel steps, the doorman and porters leaving the boy to his trade, not chasing him off. Huck had the taxi parked across from the stand out front of the Drake, this new palace of galas and ballrooms, built a year back and opening just as the flames of the South Side riots burned out.

Dex Ayres had told him how old man Drake got into the hotel business back at the time of the Great Fire back in '71, standing outside the former Tremont House next to its owner as the fire closed in. Drake asking the owner if he cared to sell, the owner asking if he was daft seeing the hotel was about to go up in flames, Drake assured that he was sound of mind, and the owner was quick to shake on the deal, doing it before a crowd of witnesses. Drake having noted a change in the wind's direction before making the lowball offer, and holding the man to it afterwards.

Now the boy was helping an elderly couple from the Drake, a Yellow cab pulling up to the stand. Huck giving a wave to the driver, not sure of the man's name, looking around the intersection — no sign of Checker trouble, and no sign of Gypsy Doyle either, the man a hard-drinking and a card-gambling fool, supposed to meet him here and go on a run to Waterloo, likely to be the last one this year using the skiff and signal man, crossing at Detroit. Next time they'd be driving across once the ice formed.

The missed run would cost Huck a hundred on the night, meaning he wouldn't be adding to the twelve hundred sitting in the First National, this time of great thirst building him a tidy nest egg — the first time in his life he was more than flush.

When he got his pay from Yellow on Friday, he'd stuff half in an envelope and mail it to his old dad, writing as best he could that more was coming. His old dad back to living with Teety Fleur in her Creole cottage, the woman working a stall in the Quarter, serving up crawdad boil and po-boys in both heads and tails season. Huck could almost taste it, the bowls of mudbugs, the gumbo, and étouffée.

The blond boy crossed the street and went past a market cart, nicking an apple off the back end, doing it with a practiced hand. Then walking across Walton, bumping into a well-dressed man crossing the other way, not watching where he was going, nearly getting knocked over. The gent scowled at him, telling the boy to watch his step. The boy saying he was sorry, kept eating his apple and walking along.

Huck was grinning, shaking his head, knowing the play.

Then the man was shouting, "Hey! You, boy. Somebody grab him. He's a thief!" Yelling about his watch and chain, calling for a policeman, then giving foot chase.

The boy tossed the half-eaten apple and easily darted across Michigan on his young legs, nearly getting clipped by a delivery truck. Dodging the wheels, then he was gone around the next corner.

Getting his taxi started, Huck drove from the hotel, across Walton, rolling along a couple of side streets before seeing the boy walking along Michigan Avenue, heading south. Pulling along the curb, he reached across, cranking down the passenger window, calling out, "How much you want for it?"

The boy kept walking along, eyeing him like he was deciding whether to bolt again.

"Want to buy that watch from you." Huck rolled along, an intersection coming up at the end of the block.

"Get away, ya dirty old sicko."

"Just going to pawn it anyhow. So let me save you the trouble."

"Don't talk to nobody in a yellow car."

"Something wrong with my car?"

"It's yellow."

"On account it's a taxi, but I expect you figured that out. And likely know a taxi man's got to be on time. And to be on time, a taxi man needs a good watch."

"Go away, cuckoo man."

"Was gonna offer you top dollar, but you go on calling me names . . ." Huck stopped at the intersection.

The boy turned the corner, walking faster, Huck having to wait on a couple of cars, finally swinging around the corner, the boy halfway up the block, still hustling along, taking one look over his shoulder.

Huck was feeling the chill, the passenger window rolled down, slowing along the curb, and calling to the boy again, "How's ten bucks sound?"

The boy slowed, looked in at him, then onto the back seat like a copper might be hiding there. Saying, "You ain't even seen it."

"I figure if it's worth stealing . . ."

"Well, I seen it, and it's worth more'n that, a damned sight more."

"How much you asking?"

"Well, if I had a watch, and I ain't saying I do —"

It was the shouting that had them both looking back. The man he robbed, bringing a big copper, hailing for the boy to halt.

"Get in!" Huck told him.

The boy wavered, the man he robbed and the cop running from a half block back.

Jumping in back, the boy slammed the door, looking out the back, the cop and man nearly on them.

"Where to, son?" Rolling slow, Huck ignored the two men as they ran alongside, the cop banging on the trunk lid, yelling for him to stop. Leaning across, Huck cranked up the passenger window.

"Just drive, will ya." Panic in the boy's voice.

And Huck did, turning at the next corner so he nearly clipped the two men — the copper still banging on the trunk lid — then Huck gave it some throttle, driving south on North Michigan, easily losing the pursuers.

"Why'd you do that?" the boy said.

"Could be I'm cuckoo."

"Sorry I said it."

"Well, you could be right." Huck looked over the seat at him. "So, if you're done assessing the watch, I'd still like to buy her, then let me know where can I drop you."

The boy shrugged like it didn't matter.

"You mind a word of advice, you ought to lay low a while," Huck said, stopping at the curb.

The boy opened the back door.

Huck saying, "Hey, the watch."

The boy reached in his jacket, pulling it by the chain, offering it to Huck.

Leaning to the side, Huck reached in a pocket and took out his roll, counting off ten dollars and offered it.

The boy's look went from surprised to doubtful to suspicious — slow reaching for it.

Neither wanting to be the first to let go, then they did at the same time, Huck taking the watch, giving it a heft like he knew gold from tin, putting it to his ear, saying, "I can see by this, it's time to eat. Seeing you didn't finish that apple, maybe you're of the same mind."

Still looking doubtful, the boy hesitated.

"You do eat, right?"

"Course I eat."

Huck betting breakfast didn't come regular to the boy, saying, "I know this place makes pretty good flapjacks, only they call it something else."

"What's that?"

"Maybe you call 'em hotcakes."

"You talking about pancakes?"

"I'm talking about eating them — with syrup dripping down — and butter."

"Best way to have 'em, that's for sure." The boy was looking at the bills in his hand. "How much they charge?"

"Let's make it part of the deal." Huck having to reach across and help him with shutting the door. Guessing he was right about the boy being about ten, but betting some of them were big years.

The boy was looking around the block as Huck rolled on, driving down Michigan, heading to the Loop, to Berghoff's Chuck Wagon.

Looking over at the boy, Huck wasn't sure the best way to talk to him, saying, "The name's Huck, by the way."

The boy nodded.

Huck giving some brake, letting a Ford T cross in front of him. Then saying, "So you know who I am . . ."

"Like in the book," the boy said.

"The book?"

"Huckleberry Finn."

"Only huckleberry I know's in a pie."

"Don't know about that, but the book's pretty good."

"You telling me you read, huh?"

"Sure I do. Who can't?"

"Guess you're in school then." Huck wondering where he learned to pickpocket.

"Well, you'd be wrong."

"Just come by it naturally, a born reader?"

"That's more of that cuckoo talk," the boy giving it back to him.

"They teach you to chit-chat like that, this school you didn't go to?"

The boy giving him an odd look, scrunching his nose like he was considering, then he said, "I like your name."

"Well, I've grown attached to it."

"You ain't from around here," the boy said.

"What makes you say so?"

"You talk funny."

"It's how we talk in Bogalusa."

"You're making that up."

"Nope. It's down around New Orleans. You heard of that?"

"Sure, it's down south. Saw it on a map."

Making a turn, Huck drove behind a Schulze bread truck, swinging into the opposing lane, getting around it, the fumes from the truck strong, blue smoke puffing from its tailpipe. "How about you?"

"How about me what?"

"Well, for starters, I bet you got a name?"

Looking like he wasn't sure about giving it up, then the boy said, "Izzy."

Huck nodded, guessing it was short for something, but now wasn't the time to ask.

"It's short for Isaac." Like the boy was reading his thoughts.

Huck repeated it, then said, "A good name, like in the bible."

"Haven't read it, but heard plenty the times I been to church."

"What faith, if it's okay to ask?"

"Not decided yet, but I'm not so much for the Catholics on account of passing the plate and all the rules like when to eat fish. Guess I'm partial to Kingdom Hall so far, you know it?"

"Can't say so."

"Well, it's a good one, but mostly any one that's open, especially when it's cold and raining. I just go in back and sit."

"Sure." Huck nodded like that made sense, saying, "So, you come by reading natural. How d'you do that?"

"Well, I've always been keen on a good tale, and since nobody's been around to read to me, I guess I just picked it up."

"Just like that, you picked it up?" Huck thinking he had trouble getting past a headline.

"Got taught my letters, the sound they make. Momma left magazines she was reading around, so I picked them up, put my finger to a word, sounded it out and went to the next one, putting it together."

Huck coming up with a hundred questions, but knowing better than to ask them, driving across the river, then State and heading down to Adams, one of the few places he knew without a map. The same bunch of men out front of the nickel joint across from Berghoff's, some looking full of daytime drink, others looking out from the doorway. A few men eyeing the taxi, likely remembering the trouble when Huck and Gypsy Doyle pulled up the last time, taking care of the two hobos pulling knives on them.

Holding the door to Berghoff's for Izzy, Huck nodded to Luka and took the table by the front, Izzy sitting with his back to the window, Huck positioned so he could see out. An elderly couple sitting down toward the kitchen, looked like they were having strudel.

Luka came over, putting a hand on Huck's shoulder, "How you doing, champ? Still got your teeth, huh?"

"Still got 'em, and me and my friend here'd sure like to sink them into a stack of flapjacks, all the fixings too."

Luka nodded, saying, "Pfannkuchen. And coffee?"

"Sure thing." Huck looking at Izzy, saying, "And a milk for my friend here." Huck guessing it was too early for the free beer.

"Coffee's good," Izzy said.

Luka nodded, like why not, and off he went.

"So, what are you reading now?" Huck guessing it was a safe topic.

"Got started on *Moby Dick*, you know it?"

"*Moby Dick*, that a fella?"

"It's a fish — a whale, a great big white one."

"Never got around to much reading, but I figure to take it up sometime," Huck said. "And one about a whale sounds good."

Izzy looked thoughtful a moment, like he was wondering how it was that a grown-up didn't read much. "Well, if you do, *Moby Dick*'s a good one alright. And the one with your name, well, almost your name."

"This Huckleberry?"

"Right."

"I'll keep 'em both in mind."

"You don't, then you're missing out." This boy sounding like he'd skipped a few decades.

Coming with the coffees, Luka glanced out the window at the drunkards milling outside the speakeasy across the street, then went back to his kitchen.

Picking up his tin cup in both hands, Izzy warmed his fingers, blowing across the top, sipping it black, the nod of his head meaning it was good. Huck trying his own cup, leaning back as Luka came and set the plates down, each with a piled stack, thick pads of butter melting on top and sliding down, a bottle of Log Cabin. Asking, "You gents like some jam? It's homemade."

"What kind of jam?" Huck asked.

"We got strawberry, and got some huckleberry too."

Izzy lighting up.

"Guess we'll go with the huckleberry," Huck said, smiling, catching the movement out the window, a couple of the men from the speak were crossing the street, eyes on his taxi. One of them walked along the side of it, stopping at the front, looking at it. Huck wondering if it was the same drunk Gypsy Doyle had laid out, filthy long hair and stubbled face, a long coat too big on him.

Thanking Luka when he came back, setting a jam jar down, Izzy got busy, spooning some over his stack, pouring on the syrup, then digging in. Huck taking a bite. The two of them looking at each other, nodding approval, eating and enjoying in silence.

Luka going for the coffee pot, refilling their tins, glancing out the window again, then to Huck, asking if they wanted anything else.

"Don't know about you," Huck said to Izzy, "but I'm stuffed as a holiday bird."

Izzy nodded, his cheek full, reaching for his tin, saying, "Best thing I ate in a while. Don't matter what you call 'em." Finishing his coffee.

Huck called thanks to Luka, setting down a couple of bucks, thinking a meal like that was worth the fat tip.

"Those men looking for a ride?" Izzy pushed in his chair, looking out and seeing the men around the taxi.

Slipping his fork in his jacket pocket, Huck went to the door, holding it open, telling Izzy, "Get in while I talk to these fellas and find out."

Izzy doing like he was told, going to the passenger door and getting in.

The lanky fellow was leaning on the hood, chewing something, a shoe up on the bumper. Three other men with him all looked drunk, but standing to the side, Huck making them for spectators. The lanky one showed no sign of moving, no sign of recognizing Huck either.

"You got one in mind, friend?" Huck stopped and asked him.

"What one's that?"

"Hospital you want a lift to."

The man's cackle came out as a snort, snot blasting from his nose, landing in his stubble. "Wouldn't go no place in this yellow heap." The man wiping his nose, smearing it on the taxi, the hand going in the pocket, Huck guessing he was going to pull the same grimy blade.

Taking a couple of easy steps, his hand coming from the pocket, Huck stuck him with the fork, right in his top of his thigh, let go, looking at it sticking in.

The man looked down like he didn't believe it, then let go a gurgling wail through clenched jaws.

His pals froze, the three of them looking at the blood forming around the tines, blood staining down the man's trouser leg.

"How 'bout you boys. You looking for a lift?"

All three backing into the street. A klaxon horn *aooghaed*, making them jump, the three men scattering.

The man with the fork hopped for the sidewalk, setting himself down, looking to Luka stepping from his door, a big rolling pin in his mitt.

Stepping over to the man, Huck said to him, "You still got snot hanging from your nose." Pulled the fork from his leg, wiped it on the man's coat as the man howled. Handing the fork to Luka, Huck said, "Nearly walked off with your cutlery." Thanking him again for the fine eats and for the intention, meaning coming to their aid with his rolling pin. Getting in the taxi, he busied himself with getting it started.

Izzy's eyes were round, the boy speechless.

"Looks like it wants to rain," Huck said off the cuff and started driving. Turning the taxi around and heading back up Michigan before saying, "Got no excuse behaving like that." Thinking of how he might explain it, knowing he likely scared the bejesus from the boy, guessing he might jump out again first chance he got.

"You kidding — that's the best thing I seen in my whole life."

Huck looked at him, the boy not scared, more like flabbergasted.

It hit Huck he didn't know where to drop him, reaching across and getting the wiper to work. "Where d'you want to go?"

The boy shrugged, saying, "Anyplace uptown's fine. I can walk the rest."

"In the rain?"

"I'm just around the hotel."

Huck looked at him, saying, "Not one to tell you your business, but it's best you don't loot where you live. And if I were you, I'd work on them fingers — just a word to the wise."

Izzy looked at him. "What kind of thing's that to say to a kid?"

"I just stuck a fork in a fella's leg."

"Well, you're supposed to say not to do it."

"You see any point in me telling you that?"

The boy thought about it, then said, "Guess not."

"What I'm saying is you do a thing, it's best to get good at it."

"You never have an off day?" Izzy said.

"That what that was — an off day?"

"Sure."

"Well, I had plenty of them — fact is, had more than I can count. It's how I come to know what I know. And it don't make me smart. Just means I likely banged my head on the wall more'n you."

"It's not a thing a fella can practice, but I run a lot."

"Makes sense."

"That guy back there, one you forked . . . how'd you know?"

"Saw it in his eyes." Not mentioning he was pretty sure he recognized him from the other time.

"Could be he was all talk."

"Guys like that . . . they're never much on talking." Huck shook his head. "And you never give them the jump. See?"

"Need to get me a fork, I guess." Izzy jabbed his curled fingers in the air.

Huck looked at him, and the two of them were grinning.

19

Turned out Izzy had been on his own since his mother went missing during the riots over a year and a half back, the Red Summer riots that hit like chain lightning. She went out one evening, never coming back. That's how much Izzy told him, not saying whether she died or just ran off, the boy not wanting to talk more on it. Huck putting the rest together, with no family, the boy had been living on the street, getting by on the scraps of life, holing up in the basement of Old St. Pat's, the Catholics not yet in wont of locking up doors at night. Alternating between the church basement and a covered delivery port behind the Drake, Izzy stashed an old burlap tarp he found behind some crates, using it as a blanket. The boy working for tips and on his light fingers, practicing on the elite coming for afternoon tea at the Drake.

After letting the boy off a block from the Drake, Huck got onto an idea, going to Dex Ayres the next morning, telling him Yellow ought to have a lookout at the livery, somebody spending nights and keeping an eye on the place, on account of the war with Checker. This on the heels of another Yellow driver getting attacked at one of the stands, three Checker taxis pulling up and a half dozen men jumping out with ball bats and chasing the man off, flipping his taxi in the Loop at Madison, right out front of the La Salle, sending a message to Hertz and company, showing how they felt about the mayor granting permits to his pal John D. Hertz for most of the prime taxi stands, then taking his sweet time handing the leftovers to Checker.

By Dex Ayres's account, John D. Hertz came in and pitched a fit of epic proportions right in Dex's office, tossing the desk ledger against his wall, gouging plaster and busting the lath. Moses the mechanic patching the wall.

Moses telling Huck how John D. went storming down to city hall again, giving Big Bill the mayor an earful, demanding he get the chief of police on the horn, get some justice on the streets, starting with the arrest of that Ruskie Morris Markin.

"So a night watchman's just the thing you need," Huck said to Dex.

Shaking his head, Dex likely chalking it up as another one of Huck's bright ideas, something that was going to cost the company more money that he'd have trouble explaining to Hertz. Dex making it plain he wasn't all that happy with Huck's lack of gain, though he did get wind of him stabbing a ne'er-do-well with a fork, finding out the chump had been a strike breaker working off and on for Checker. Still, Dex had doubts about Gypsy Doyle, a guy he only met the one time, paying him through Huck. Two hard men working for the company off the books, another thing he wouldn't care to explain to John D.

"The way I figure it, it won't cost you much," Huck said.

"By not much . . ."

"Look, you need night eyes on the place, can we agree on that?"

"I'm listening."

"This fellow, Hawkeye, we set him up out of the way, and he watches the place at night." Huck trying to come up with a way to work in three squares a day.

"This fella some rummy?"

"Never touched a drop in his life."

"Been in jail?"

"Nope."

"Hawkeye the watchman."

"That's right."

"Why's he need a cot if he's supposed to be watching? This Hawkeye's up on the roof, or looking out windows, patrolling the grounds."

"For when he needs to go dead quiet middle of the place, listening for sounds that ain't mice — can't be walking and listening — 'less you want him in your fancy chair at those quiet times."

"This is a place of business, Huck, not some flop, understand that. And where've we got room for something like that, a cot?"

"I got that figured out. The old closet under the stairs — just got to clear some brooms and pails, and we put it in there. Good central spot to do his watching and detecting, hear just about anything creeping from there."

"This a pygmy we're talking about?" Dex held his hands apart, showing the width of the staircase.

"He's not a big fella, but not so fussy either. You'll see when you meet him." Huck not seeing a way around that part. "Main thing, he's got eyes that can spot a Checker a mile off."

Dex made a face, like he was working against common sense. Then he had his hands full after another of the drivers, Pikey, had his taxi wrecked, a brick chucked through his windshield from an overpass causing him to crash, ending with a dozen stitches in Pikey's head, and another of the fleet was written off, something else he'd have to explain to John D.

Leaving it alone for a couple of days, Huck kept on him, getting around to admitting the watchman was on the young side. And when Dex got past the idea of recruiting children and complaining how he wasn't running an orphanage, he conceded to pay Izzy the two bucks a week Huck demanded and gave up the closet under the stairs, but not agreeing to feed the boy, leaving that up to Huck. Again, calling it a trial basis.

Clearing the space, Huck swept it out — the space on the drafty side, but guessing it beat the cellar of the old church. Driving up and down Michigan and the Boulevard Link, along the waterfront past the Drake, he found Izzy trailing a rich couple along Lake Shore, pulling his cab along the curb and inviting him for some of Luka's flapjacks and putting the idea forward. Talking through the details over an extra stack and coffee, Izzy agreed to try it out, taking the job to heart, taking up position by the front window, watching for enemy taxis, ready to sing out if a Checker rolled past. The boy quick to get along with Moses the mechanic and Snooky the apprentice. Huck seeing to a bedroll and a lantern, loaning Izzy the watch and chain, saying he'd need it to be punctual.

Coming by and making sure the boy was treated right. Moses and Snooky not wanting to get on the wrong side of Huck, on top of which the two were quick to see the worth of a keen set of eyes on the place at night. It meant they could get on with their work, and not worry about their tools still being there the next day.

Dex Ayres loosened to the idea of having somebody in the place at night, not entirely sure what a boy of ten could do in case of attack, but he'd give it a try — though he remained nervous about John D. finding out.

20

On the fourth night on watch, a cinder block was chucked through the livery's window, Izzy cutting his foot on the busted glass when he ran out shouting after the fleeing car.

When Huck got to the livery the next morning, he sat with him, bandaged the foot, brushing glass from the boy's hair. Izzy saying it was a black sedan, saw it through the busted window, speeding away, marked the time as two a.m. sharp, but he couldn't make out who was inside.

When Dex Ayres came in, he asked if the boy was sleeping on the job, Huck telling him Izzy was patrolling out back when he heard the smash of glass.

"Some watchman," is all Ayres said about it.

Huck started taking Izzy along on days when he patrolled the taxi stands, running off Checkers trying to poach Yellow fares, driving past the Drake, then down to the Loop, a couple of the drivers warning him about driving too far onto the South Side, some of that Black fury from the riots hanging on from well over a year ago. Though Moses told a different story about it, how mobs of whites went after any Blacks they saw on the streets, including Moses himself — the riots that kicked off after a Black teen swam into a 'whites only' part of the beach at 29th, some white knucklehead throwing a rock, hitting the teen and drowning him. Nothing new to Huck, remembering the Robert Charles riots back home when he was a kid. Charles being a Black activist who shot a couple of cops, sparking a manhunt for Charles and a white riot that went on for three days, claiming twenty-eight lives, including Charles himself.

Parking the taxi in the treed spot near the Oak Street Beach, Huck settled on the seat and leaned his head back. Izzy kept a sharp eye for Checkers while Huck took his cat nap, catching some Zs after a long night of bringing a load of Seagram's into town with Doyle.

Taking Huck's Thermos and a book from under his coat, Izzy read and kept watch.

"What you reading today?"

"It's called *Sky Island*." Izzy showed him the cover. "It's about Trot and Cap'n Bill, see? Telling of their capers."

"A captain, huh?" Huck took it in, wondering if Izzy was putting some of it together from looking at the pictures. "You really come by it on your own?"

"Mama taught the sounds the letters make." Taking the book back, Izzy opened to a page, saying, "See, Cap'n Bill's a sailor with a wood leg." Pointing to the drawing, Huck looking and following the boy's finger, nodding, thinking of the stack of well-worn books on a wood crate next to the boy's cot. Wondering if the boy nicked them from someplace.

Izzy was proud of his stack of books. *The Dutch Twins* about Kit and Kat, living in a place called Holland, where they got the windmills. And *The Secret Garden*, then *Maya the Bee*, and *Red Chief*, *Land of Oz* and *King Arthur*. Izzy loved showing them to him, telling him, "Soon's I read 'em, I sell 'em or trade 'em, then I get more. A whole world in there, Huck. Reading's the best thing I ever did. No offense. I mean if you want, maybe I could teach you some."

"Figure you can teach me to read?"

"Does seem funny." Izzy grinned just thinking about it, a kid teaching a grown-up.

Smiling, Huck swallowed the lump, thinking he needed to do a better job tending to this boy. Sharp as a tack, a street urchin teaching himself to read, but still not wanting to open up much about how he came to living on the street. Izzy uncapping the Thermos, sipping the coffee.

"Sure you don't want milk?" Huck watched him, remembered seeing the Bowman trucks making deliveries over by the Loop, the ones Dean and the North Side Gang were using to deliver their booze, thinking he could flag one down and get a bottle of milk from the driver.

"I'm best with coffee," Izzy said.

"Boys like milk."

"Who says so?"

"One of those known facts."

"Can splash some in my coffee, that make you feel better?"

Huck was thinking of the pump handle out back of the livery, likely frozen, the only water fit for drinking and washing. Telling himself again he had to do better for the boy, making note to stop at Berghoff's for some free beer, get one of Luka's liver sandwiches. Having a hunch Moses and the apprentice brought in extra food — enough to keep Izzy from feeling the need to swipe fruit from the market stalls, the boy knowing how to look out for himself.

Not his kin, but Huck felt something — like a kind of worry, Huck never having to look out for anybody else before. And adding a thicker blanket to the mental list — the pot stove off at night and plenty of drafts in the old livery. The boy rolling his coat under his head for a pillow.

"You're like me, Huck, two of us are about the same." Izzy looked up from his book.

"How you figure that?" Huck opened an eye, looking at him.

"Well, neither of us got a home to speak about, we want to see the world and find the best spot in it, doing what we got to along the way, and top of which we see eye to eye on most things."

"Like flapjacks?"

"You mean pancakes." Izzy laughed, huddled in the jacket Huck got him, his legs folded under him on the car seat. When Huck dozed, Izzy picked up the book again, opening it to his marked page. Huck thinking of the boy as ten but going on thirty.

After his nap, Izzy informing him it was twenty-two minutes exactly, Huck drove along the taxi stands along North Michigan. Seeing a Checker pull up to the one out front of the Drake. Waving to get the cabbie's attention, pointing to the sign, meaning it belonged to Yellow. John D. Hertz sticking his taxi stands in the best spots all over town, some of the drivers at the livery joking how the boss was like a big dog, greasing official palms and lifting his leg and marking his ground.

The Checker man held up his middle finger.

Izzy telling Huck how French soldiers waved middle fingers at their English enemies, on account the redcoats promised to cut off the fingers of any captured French archers, back before the French started ramming balles down their muzzle loaders.

"That so, huh?" Turning his taxi around in the street, Huck pulled up in front of the Checker, backing up and clanging against its bumper, saying, "Oops."

Ignoring him, the Checker man leaned across his front seat, giving a wave to an elderly woman coming from the hotel's main door, meaning his taxi was free. The woman moved slow on her cane, a porter in tow, carrying her luggage under his arms, both heading for the Checker.

"Son of a bitch," Huck said, rolling down his window, leaning his head out and calling back to the driver, "Hey! You blind?" Being ignored, he turned to Izzy, telling him to sit tight.

"You bring a fork?" Izzy brightened, pulling one he nicked from Berghoff's from his pocket, closing the book and offering it to him.

"Just gonna put this fella straight." Getting out, wishing he'd left the boy at the livery this time.

"Just hold up, ma'am," he called to the woman on her cane, the porter stopping, that man knowing trouble when he saw it coming, not the first bit of it at this stand, right out front of the this fine new hotel. "Got to clear up a couple things." Looking at the Checker driver, keeping his temper from rising like a tide.

But the woman had a train to catch, bound for New York, negotiating the stone walk out front of the Drake, still aiming for the Checker, not caring which cab she got in. Paid for her stay, sleeping on her bed of roses, now she was wrapped in her yellow fur, her matching hat, the kind of woman used to getting things the way she wanted.

"Go small if I say so," Huck called to Izzy, meaning for him to duck down if it went past words.

Izzy nodded, but kept on watching, fork in hand.

Huck stepped to the back of his taxi, feeling the cold knifing through his coat, the wind whipping off the lake.

The Checker man made no move to get out of his rig, not looking at Huck, just waiting.

Huck tried one more time, pointing to the tin badge atop the post marking the cab stand — Yellow Cab, dependable and fast. "If you can't read, you can tell by the color."

"No inglese." The guy sitting with both hands on the wheel, acting like Huck wasn't there.

The elderly woman was coming along the walk.

"Over here, lady." Izzy called out his window, pointing to their rig, saying, "First in line's how it works, ma'am."

Ignoring him with her suck-lemon look, the woman kept moving.

The porter stood fast, looked to be freezing in his flimsy uniform, glancing back to the doorman at the top of the steps, the grand entrance, the two of them likely guessing how this would go, Yellow versus Checker right out front of the Drake.

The woman stopped, considering a moment, asking Huck, "How much?"

"Forty-five a mile, ma'am — standard fare." Huck who had never taken a fare, but his was the only Yellow in sight.

Turning to the Checker man, her cane in her left hand to keep her steady, her handbag strap over the shoulder of her fur coat.

The man called out, "Forty cents, lady." The Italian accent gone.

And she started to shuffle his way. The porter inching behind her with two suitcases, shrugging at Huck. The doorman waved a gloved hand inside to the concierge, seeing the trouble about to boil, the kind of trouble that could leave stains on the new walk out front, along with bad press sure to land on the front page of tomorrow's *Trib*. The Drake not tolerating drivers beating on each other right outside the doors of their fine marble lobby.

Guessing hotel security was on the way, maybe the cops getting a call too, Huck frowned.

"Thirty-five," Izzy called to her, getting into it, helping Huck out.

The woman stopped again, turning from one taxi to the other, like she was considering. "Thirty," the Checker man called, locking his door and sliding across the seat, rolling down the passenger window for better haggling.

"Standard's forty-five a mile, ma'am, so you're getting a bargain." Izzy got out, speaking to her. "And you take the first in line. It's just how it's done in this town."

Huck stood looking to the porter for some kind of help, not getting any, the man just standing with luggage in each hand, a bag across his shoulder.

The woman held up a hand, looking from Izzy to the other driver, ignoring Huck.

"Twenty-five," the Checker man said, out-bidding himself, advising her to watch her step.

"He's poaching from an honest man, trying to feed his family," Izzy said. Pointing to the sign, saying, "Sure you can tell color, ma'am. This being a Yellow stand, and this being a Yellow." His arms wrapped round himself showing the cold, Izzy took a step toward her, saying, "You got a heart, don't you lady? I'm only ten, you know."

"Money talks louder than pity, boy." The old woman stood her ground, leaning on her cane, looked to be enjoying the haggling, for a moment forgetting about catching her train.

"Twenty a mile," the Checker man blurted, again negotiating against himself. "You want to tip, that's okay."

Huck held back from going around and grabbing the man by the scruff, a sure way to get the Drake management to haul away the Yellow sign, something Huck didn't want to explain to Dex Ayres. Taking another tact, he called, "Don't mind me asking, where are you headed, ma'am?"

"I told you, the train station."

"Best ask this fella if he knows the way then? See, the trouble with these Checker fellas, they get their release from Old Joliet, or they get plucked fresh off some boat, and Checker sticks 'em behind the wheel and sends them out poaching fares, easy as stealing chickens where they come from, taking work from honest men."

"Fifteen cents," the Checker man called.

"They hear train station and they figure there's just the one. Then take you on a goose chase and get you lost, maybe strand you on the South Side, a good guarantee of losing that fine fur hat, likely the coat to boot."

Putting a white-gloved hand to her throat, the woman giving the Checker man a doubtful look.

"Train station, sure, sure, I know it," the man said, waving a hand, pointing to the lake.

"That be the Chesapeake/Ohio, or the Western Indiana out of the Dearborn terminal?" Huck gave the man a moment, then said, "Or that be the New York Central at LaSalle? Or could be the Pittsburgh/Cincinnatti out of Union." Huck twisted his mouth like he was thinking, making use of what he remembered from hopping the freight cars coming north, getting to know some of the trains, all those criss-crossing tracks, knowing others from the bare-knuckling out behind the boxcars. Pointing a finger, going on, "Or we got the Minneapolis/St. Paul out of Central. Come to think of it, there's the Lake Shore/South Bend at Randolph running today. You know it? From the dumb look, I guess not. Then we got the Grand Trunk. Ever hear of it? Or the Wabash and the Baltimore and Ohio. Any ring a bell?" Huck thinking what he didn't make up he got mixed up, but he was on a roll.

The woman narrowed her eyes at the Checker man.

"You tell me, I drive, sure, sure." The man repeating, "Ten cents a mile, okee-dokey. I'll take you."

"And miss the all-aboard," Huck said, shaking his head like it was a pity. "These trains run like your mantle clock, ma'am."

Izzy took out his watch, looking at it, frowning and shaking his head.

The woman leaned harder on her cane, looking pale, running out of steam. The porter standing behind her with the luggage, looked like he was wilting too, his teeth chattering.

"That ten cents a mile's gonna cost you a missed fare, maybe another night at the Drake, if they got a room. Yuh, this fella's bound to take you round the Loop and head out to Cicero and points beyond, and you miss your train, it's practically guaranteed."

That was it, the old woman turned for the Yellow. Huck cinching it, saying, "That's right, you take a Yellow at a Yellow stand, and you got the John D. Hertz guarantee to catch your train on time — 'less of course, it's already departed."

Izzy went to help her, pointing the porter to the back of the taxi. Going to the trunk, reaching past the butting bumpers, the porter opened the trunk and dropped the bags in, hurrying back to the hotel, not waiting on a tip. Izzy was holding the back door open for her.

"Five cents!" the Checker man cried out, a last-ditch attempt, holding up the fingers of one hand.

Huck returned the finger gesture, turned and left the man cursing Huck's ancestors. Could be he'd be driving the woman around looking for some train station himself, but Huck felt it was a win for Yellow. A story he could take back to the livery, tell Dex Ayres how Izzy the night-watch helped him out of a jam.

Huck shut the trunk lid and started for his door, one eye on the Checker man who got out of his rig, leaving his door hanging open, calling to Huck, "Think you got all the stands, you Yellow bastards got nothing — just a bunch of sons of bitches." Spitting in his direction.

"That all you got, spit?"

"Make a living same as you." The Checker man stayed by his open door, muttering something more that wasn't English, the man crossed himself, giving a glance across his shoulder, folded his arms like he wasn't going anywhere, staying parked by the stand.

"My train leaves at nine sharp," the woman called from Huck's back seat, checking her own timepiece, tapping a boney finger on the window.

Huck stood looking at the driver a moment longer, saying, "Another time . . ."

The driver glanced back over his shoulder again, like he was waiting on somebody, then he reached under his front seat, coming out holding a lug wrench.

Huck seeing past the man's shoulder, a black sedan speeding along North Michigan.

The Checker man was smiling — setting Huck up, stalling to keep him there. He spat again, holding the lug wrench along his leg.

Izzy was pointing at the onrushing sedan, calling to Huck, sure it was the same one that had attacked the livery, then the boy was telling the old woman to get set for the ride of her life. Sliding across the seat, he got behind the steering, working the levers the way he'd seen Huck do it.

The woman swatted at him across the seat, yelling something about this company allowing children to drive, waving her boney hand for the porter to come back and do something, swearing nobody was getting a tip on this day.

The black Stutz bore down and screeched its brakes, two men in front, one in back, stopping in the street.

The Checker man gave a yell and ran at Huck, swinging the lug wrench.

Stepping in, Huck got his forearm up, not blocking but going with it, his body turning with the swing, using his hip and arm-dragging the man over his shoulder, twisting, and he had him in the air. The Checker man grunted surprise, letting go of the wrench, his world turning, body going over and landing hard on the pavement. The air punched out of him, but he was reaching for the lug wrench, Huck stomping on the arm, bending for the wrench as two of the men jumped from the sedan. Stopping them as he lobbed the heavy wrench at the taxi's windshield, the glass spidering and falling in.

The man on the ground got his feet under him, pulling a blade with his good hand, trying to poke at Huck's leg. Stepping back, Huck felt its sting, the blade cutting through trousers, slicing his calf.

The driver of the Stutz drew a pistol from his coat, and Huck moved. Izzy had his door open, the engine running.

The woman in back yelped for help, the porter and doorman gone from the hotel doors.

Behind the wheel, Huck roared them out of there, the two men jumping back in the Stutz, the taxi driver dog-crawling for the Checker, both cars giving chase.

Heads were poking out the front of the Drake, men and women on both sides of North Michigan watching the spectacle.

"I won't pay a goddamn cent!" The woman croaked, her hands locked across her handbag like they might snatch it. "And this rude bo—" She was tossed across the back seat as Huck swerved to avoid a pair of pedestrians.

Seeing the Stutz gaining, Huck pulled around a stopped car, the Shaw taxi being no match against the black sedan. Giving it throttle, as fast as the Rochester-Duesenberg engine would take them. His bad luck, Moses the mechanic had been working on a new rig that morning, one with the Weidely twelve-cylinder under the hood, an engine that would leave the Stutz in the dust.

"Told me you know the statio—" She was tossed against the door, Huck swinging a hard turn, doing what he could to shake the Stutz. Thinking he heard a gunshot. Telling Izzy to get on the floor and hang onto something, racing them out of there, as fast as the engine would take them, tires slipping on the iced-over street, Huck wheeling a turn at Michigan, losing sight of the Stutz and Checker for a block.

Southbound traffic becoming thick as they zoomed by the Water Tower, tires screeching in a two-wheel turn at Chicago, Huck hitting a slick patch, tires sliding on the asphalt, the Yellow spanking the curb. Huck straightening it out, the chassis swaying as they got onto State, the old woman in back mumbling a prayer.

"I'll get you to Union, that the one, lady?" Huck not getting an answer, cranking around a rail car, its trolley pole touching the wires above. Heading for the river bridge, passing a Blatz truck, the brewer pushing malt extract these days. Dodging an oncoming Ford, then swinging back into his own lane, their mirrors tapping and sparks flashing. The Stutz showed a half a block back, coming past the Blatz truck. The Checker getting caught behind the truck.

A horse-drawn hearse and funeral possession was causing the jam, Huck driving in the opposite lane, getting around it. The old woman in back was slapping at the back of Huck's seat like she was flogging a nag.

He was going the wrong way — should be going north, a chance to run into the North Side Gang, thinking they might help out. Huck pushing on the accelerator, the engine lagging as he turned at Illinois, the tires sliding. Taking his chances on the drawbridge being down, he drove over it, getting them onto Wacker, weaving around an accident, two cars locking horns.

Both hands gripping the wheel, he sped along the dirty river. Another pedestrian jumping for the sidewalk, dropping a folder, pages fluttering out, the man cursing.

Going to be complaint calls made to the livery, citizens irate and demanding to speak to John D. Hertz about this flying maniac, giving the Yellow boss a piece of their minds.

Any luck Huck would see a patrol car, this kind of driving getting the coppers' attention.

Still clutching the bag with one hand, the old woman was hanging on to the rear door, trying to stop from being tossed around.

"Union. She wants Union," Izzy said, getting back up on the seat, his feet pressed to the dash, one hand gripping the seat, the other on the door handle. Looking out back.

"This here's what haggling a fare gets you." Fighting the steering, nothing Huck could do about the Stutz gaining.

The woman just stared, mumbling to her God.

He blew past a stop tower, klaxon horns blatting, the traffic copper working the signal, blasting his whistle.

Huck chanced another look behind him, not sure what street he was on, the Stutz coming up on his bumper, nothing Huck could do about it.

Pushing aside the urge to pull over and do it face to face. Would have except for Izzy and the old woman. He kept racing, the Stutz banging his bumper, jolting the taxi. Huck fighting the steering, making another hard turn, feeling the right side lift, rushing the wrong way down a one-way, another streetcar coming at them, clanging its bell. Pulling to the right, his wheels scraped the curb, more klaxons honking. Felt like he got dropped in a boiling pot.

The Stutz bucked them from behind again. Huck swerving from one curb to the other, driving head on into traffic, then back into his lane.

"Need my Bromo!" the old woman croaked, jabbing a finger, pointing to a Walgreen sign blurring past.

"Not sure you got the full picture here, ma'am," Huck called. "Stop!"

Huck took the bridge, not sure which one it was, then he was roaring past Union Station, seeing one of the flying squad parked out front, a number written on its door, but no copper in sight.

"Stop!" The old woman had hold of her cane, trying to swat him, seeing the train station blur past.

Gripping it, Izzy tried to wrestle it from her, keeping her from striking Huck.

"Use your fist if you got to," Huck said, hearing another gunshot over his shrieking engine. Felt the bullet thunk into the back end. "Get down. Now!"

Izzy got as low on the seat as he could, his arm over the seat-back, still hanging onto the cane, the woman hanging on too, neither giving up.

"Those fellas are serious, lady." Huck swerved again. The woman losing her grip on the cane, getting tossed against the passenger side, the door flying open, the woman starting to fall out, Huck dodging a lamppost, the post slamming the door back shut. Zigzagging up Canal, Huck saw the thug on the passenger side leaning out of the Stutz's window. His shot missing, striking the bricks of Fannie Mae's, Huck cranked the wheel hard, smashing into the quarter panel, trying to keep the Stutz back, the Yellow taxi swaying on jelly springs. Thinking he had a chance of making the livery, Moses keeping a scattergun by the door.

A tin drum sounded from under the hood, something smelling like it was smoldering, the rear wheel on his side was wobbling. The woman was clawing at the back of the seat, begging him to stop.

The Stutz rammed them again, the woman falling to the cab's rear floor, Huck fighting the wheel, the goddamn Commonwealth Mogul like the runt of the road, the worst thing John D. could have put on the road, the boss man buying out the company that built them. The drivers dubbing them street crawlers. Gripping the wheel, he felt another impact, telling Izzy to get back on the floor.

Seeing the passenger lean out, aiming a pistol for his front tire, Huck cranked the steering, bashing their door, knocking the pistol away.

The passenger cursed, hanging out the window now, trying to grab hold of the Mogul.

Huck swerved again, trying to press the man between the vehicles.

The driver of the Stutz cranked his wheel too, fenders grinding, Huck's wheels scraping the curb, the sound like a ripping saw. Locking his hands on the wheel, he felt himself being plowed up onto the curb. Stomping the pedal, he felt his brakes go to dust.

The Yellow bounced the curb, Huck yelling, seeing the Stutz veer away, dodging a street pole, driving into the opposing lane, the driver missed sideswiping a delivery van, trading paint, leaving the side mirror spinning in the road. The Checker coming next, tearing past, the driver yelling something.

That was all in a blink — the Yellow lifting, tipping, and sliding on its passenger side, metal grinding along the sidewalk, the taxi plowing into a grocer's cart, cantaloupes, tomatoes, and splinters flying, the proprietor throwing himself clear of fruit, shrapnel, and exploding cart. Huck's taxi propelled through the storefront, glass and debris raining down, a board smashing the windshield, a beam toppling, crushing sheet metal. Dust rising like a fog.

The two cars sped off, the bumper of the Stutz crumpled, its fender dragging and sparking on the road. The passenger waving an arm out the window like "have a nice day."

21

Coughing dust, not sure if he made it for a moment, then Huck opened his eyes and he was looking at the world sideways. Moving his fingers, then his arm and legs, ribs hurting from being twisted around, then slammed against the steering, but nothing felt broken.

Putting it together, the Stutz ramming them off the road, his cab flipping, crashing through the fruit stand and ending on its passenger side in the storefront. The ripped awning claimed this was Umberto's — well, it used to be Umberto's.

Izzy was next to him, arms and legs tangled together with his own, the boy coughing dust.

Huck seeing the gash across the boy's forehead, saying, "Can you move?"

Izzy nodded, putting his arms around Huck's neck, and he started to sob, putting his hand over his eyes like he was embarrassed to do it. Huck held him a moment, then brushed glass and dust from his clothes. Couldn't believe how small the boy felt.

Looking to the back, feeling a stab in his neck, asking, "How about you, lady? You alright?"

"I'm suing."

"Yeah, but can you move?"

"When I find my cane, you're going to find out. Then I'm going to find a lawyer."

"That's just fine, ma'am." He couldn't blame her.

The metal of the door was crumpled, Huck letting go of the boy, getting on his knees and hoisting himself out the window opening. Working around the fallen beam, he scaled down the side of the tipped taxi, got his feet to the ground, then reaching back up, took hold of Izzy's outstretched hands and hauled him up and out. He was looking around the street at the people gawking, no sign of the three men in the Stutz, or the Checker driver.

Umberto the grocer rose off the sidewalk, brushed off his apron, his face scraped, looking at the spoils, vegetables and fruit squashed or bruised all over the ground. Then looking to Huck.

"You okay, mister?" Huck said.

The grocer held his hands wide, stumbling forward, sputtering what had to be a curse — Italian or Greek — looking like he wanted to tear a piece off Huck.

"You not see them cars?" Huck pointed to the street, the Stutz and Checker gone now, more folks gathering, looking at the scene.

"I see you." Umberto was looking at the spoils, picking a splintered board from the ruined stand, saying. "Who's gonna pay — you?"

"Get to a call box, or take your swipe, either one." Huck figuring everybody in town wanted to take a swipe at him, and maybe this guy had a right.

The grocer swung the board, smacking the dead eye of the Mogul's headlight, shattering its glass.

Smelling the petrol, Huck climbed up the underside of the tipped taxi. The back door's window glass was intact, forcing him to hold onto the wheel, stepping on the linkage, careful of the hot exhaust, grabbing hold of the running board and pulling himself up, standing on the side, the beam had crushed the rear panel, the taxi rocking as he tugged to get the back door open, the hinges and springs creaking. He leaned in, offering to help the woman out. She reached for his hand, still clutching her bag with her other hand, like he still might snatch it.

Asking her again, "You hurt?"

"I'm just peachy."

"I need to move you."

She righted herself, moving her legs, then nodded to him.

Taking hold of her arm, moving slow, feeling the stab in his ribs, the pain in his calf from the knife wound, his pant leg soaked with blood below the knee, he stepped onto the side of the rear seat, helping her up and out. Kept her from falling off as the car rocked more, stepping down the underside, moving ahead of her.

One of the peddlers along the block called to Umberto, saying the coppers were on the way.

Taking his board, Umberto swept at the debris as Huck got her down, easing her from the wreck. Izzy helped guide her alongside the busted shop.

Cars slowed, everybody getting a good look, taking in the latest battle scene of the taxi war. The grocer standing among his ruined produce.

Huck watched Izzy help the woman step clear of the wreck, leading her along the brick wall to what he guessed to be a safe distance, easing her down against the wall, offering a bite of the apple.

Looking at him, she shook her head. "Apples and age don't get along, boy." Showing her poor teeth, she gave his hand a squeeze. "But thank you." Offering the spot next to her.

Izzy sat, biting into the apple.

"Suppose I missed my train," the woman said.

"I'd say so, yup." Izzy nodded.

"And that man's not getting a tip." Looking over at Huck.

"Said you're going to sue?" Izzy said, not sure what that meant.

"Here." She reached in her bag, came up with a coin, offering it to Izzy.

Huck turned, looking at the wreck, fuel leaking like it was bleeding.

"Where the hell you learn to drive?" the grocer said, seeing it too, understanding what was left of his livelihood was likely to go up in flames. Untying his apron, making a sling from it, he went and gathered any fruit worth saving.

The Yellow caught fire then, lazy flames licking up its underside. The fire brigade would be sliding down the pole invented right here in Old Windy, and they'd be coming with their pumper, its bell clanging.

Huck watched a man pull up and set his press camera on a wooden tripod, capturing the scene.

Watching the flames grow, Izzy was telling the old woman he read about the conflagration that devoured this whole town fifty years back, Mrs. O'Leary's cow tipping a lantern, describing the strong wind pushing its sparks from the southwest. "Everything made of wood went up like a campfire, the Water Tower and pumping station at Michigan was all that got spared. Even the grease floating in the goddamn river burned that day."

"Don't use the Lord's name in vain, boy."

"Sorry, ma'am."

22

"**G**uess you proved the man hired his own muscle," Dex Ayres said, meaning Checker's boss, Morris Markin. He was looking out the office window, his own muscle being outmuscled and run off the road, with a young boy in front and a frail, elderly but well-to-do passenger in back, the widow of a wealthy industrialist, laid up in the hospital, talking to reporters, telling her side of it, blaming Huck for instigating trouble out front of the Drake. When she wasn't talking to reporters, she was talking to her pack of lawyers, putting together a suit of epic proportions, what the papers were calling it. To top it off, the one-year-old taxi was a total wreck, the second one lost in a week.

Something else Dex would have to explain to John D. Hertz, the boss driving down from his Trout Lake ranch, wanting to have a word with his supervisor, likely to go up one side of Dex and down the other. Good chance there would be a job ad posted in the same papers for a new supervisor before this day was done. And Dex wasn't sure he wanted it anyhow after some Checker wacko took a potshot at him yesterday, driving past his house and shooting out his front window, Dex inside having supper with his wife.

"Like I said, there were three of them," Huck said. "Well, four if you count the Checker driver."

"They had a car, you had a car."

"They had two cars, and maybe I'd a stood a chance in something other than a lame Mogul — that damned Stutz is in a different weight class." Huck's knee and calf hurt like hell, Dex not offering him the seat across from the kidney-shaped desk, making him pay for coming out on the losing end. No point telling the supervisor it cost twenty bucks, fifteen for him, five for the boy, and who knew how much for the old woman once they released her from her private room at Grant Hospital. Huck thinking he ought to go pay her bill too, but it would likely be covered in settlement with Yellow.

The sawbones sewed the stitches above Huck's ear and a dozen more for the knife cut in his calf, told him nothing was busted, and to put ice on his bruised ribs and keep off the leg a few days. Something Izzy could have told him for free. The sawbones told him the boy was alright, just had some bruising. Gave the boy a lollypop — and likely put it on Huck's bill. Top of that, when Huck went to admin to pay the bill, the woman in the office told him the pretty nurse wasn't working at Grant any longer, something about cutbacks. She did leak that her name was Karla and told him it was against policy to give any personal information on staff, past or present.

"Sewed you up, huh?" Dex said, pointing to the shaved spot above Huck's ear.

"Cost me a buck a stitch." Lightly touching the shaved patch, the line of stitches across the eggplant bruise. Huck hoping Dex would reimburse him for the hospital bill, on account the attack happened on company time. The man more concerned with the wrecked cab and the old woman suing, getting shot at himself, and what John D. Hertz would have to say about the whole mess, the muscle his supervisor hired behind his back on the losing end. And a photo of Huck at the crash scene, the caption calling it "Not Yellow's finest hour."

"Where'd they patch you up?"

"Grant."

"Should've gone to Cook County."

"What's wrong with Grant?"

"Looks like they got vets." Dex pointed to the stitches.

"I'll keep it in mind next time."

"And speaking of muscle, where was this Gypsy what's his name?"

"Was scouting the other stands," Huck lied, then said something about needing to hire on a few more toughs.

"I got men all around. Still, I got my window shot out and a wife who likely won't sleep without the light on, and I got you in the middle of this mess."

"I'm talking about the right kind of men."

"So far, I got you run off the road, the other one I hire's a no-show, the third one's a kid."

"I'm talking about Dean O'Banion."

"The man's a gangster."

"A serious fellow alright, but one that runs this part of town."

"John D.'s going to have a bird as it is."

"Well, you're getting your windows shot out, your cabs knocked all over in the street — think he's having more'n a bird already." And Huck leaned on the desk, partly for effect, but mainly to take weight off his throbbing leg, saying, "And it's an idea you sure don't want Morris Markin thinking of first."

"What's that mean?" Dex looked ill at ease all of a sudden, leaning back in the lilac chair.

"Let's say he goes to O'Banion first, or to the Italians . . ."

Getting a haunted look, Dex took a glance out the window, feeling the weight of that, finally saying, "So, go see him then, this O'Banion, but keep it under your hat. I mean around here it stays between me and you."

Huck nodded, another idea coming to him, one that promised to show a profit, something he'd ponder and work out later.

23

"So what, now we're in the taxi business?" Dean O'Banion said, standing at the corner of 48th and Ogden in Cicero, right across from Eddie's Tavern, the joint not making any pretense about what it was, signs in the window Huck guessed were about cabaret and dancing.

They were there to hijack one of the Gennas' loads, doing it in broad daylight to send a strong message, and Dean didn't want to hear about making a deal with Yellow, looking at the gawdy taxi Huck had pulled up in. He'd heard how Huck got rammed off the road by a Stutz, Huck driving one of these Commonwealth Moguls at the time — a flimsy build with an excuse for an engine, not something that could haul loads of hootch, not without a lot of modification.

Huck went around to the back, opening the trunk, showing the size. His idea was hidden compartments could be built in, the taxis used to make the city runs, replacing the milk trucks they'd been using, the other gangs all knowing about the milk trucks, making them targets.

"Hear him out, Deanie," Gypsy Doyle said, following behind. "Taxis drive all over town, day or night, nobody thinking nothing about it."

Dean looked over the taxi, shaking his head, not liking the idea of using taxis that were already warring with each other. He'd been talking about buying an interest in Schofield's in North River, the flower shop across from the Holy Name Cathedral where he attended mass. Using the place as headquarters and a legit business to launder their money, having more of it than they could get clean already, and definitely more than any of them could spend in a lifetime. He was looking to the future, taking life easy, making the rounds at the supper clubs at night, singing "Danny Boy." Joking with his guys that he'd be making flower arrangements by day for all the gangster funerals that were happening like clockwork, another growth industry.

"We get compartments put in — here and here." Huck pointing to the wheel wells. "You make all the runs you want, all over town, and nobody's the wiser."

"The damn thing's yellow," Dean said, stepping away from the taxi, leaving the two of them looking at each other. Walking to the side of the warehouse, he stood waiting on the truck, looking at his pocket watch — done with talking about taxis.

Doyle shrugged at Huck, then followed Dean. Huck shutting the trunk.

"It's like a beacon — here comes the booze," Dean said to Doyle.

"That's the thing, who'd suspect something yellow?" Doyle said. "Just saying maybe it's time for a change."

"You telling me now, huh Doyle?"

"We been using the Bowmans since the start."

"The start," Dean looked at Huck. "Know how I got into this, the booze?"

Huck shook his head.

"Swiped my first truckload long before the Eighteenth Amendment — and did it solo." Looking at Doyle, then back. "Come up on the driver, man stopped at the side of the road taking a leak, give him a tap on back of the head. The man falls, his blind meat in hand, never got a look at me. Me, I drove off and sold the load back to the same owner." Dean gave a laugh. "Made fifteen grand for a couple hours of work. Go beat that."

"Then Torrio got in," Doyle said, still trying to make his point. "And the Gennas, the Touhys, Maddox, Circus Cafe, Klondike O'Donnell. Everybody and his mother."

"Call for booze went off the charts," Dean admitted. "A city that guzzles down twenty thousand barrels a week, thirty million bucks in beer alone in a month — a month! You believe it?"

"Jesus," Huck said, giving a head shake.

"A million of it goes straight into the pockets of the politicos, you know, officials and anybody with a badge. Still, do the math and see the future. Beer costing five bucks a barrel to brew and selling for north of fifty. Know what it means? Means there's plenty to be made."

"Still, greed being what it is . . ." Doyle said.

"Why we show a firm hand, anybody stepping on our turf," Dean said. "And why we dole out and grease palms — the right palms. It's a growth industry, pure and simple. Everybody wanting a piece. So, we look out for what's ours, and it's why we use the milk trucks."

"Still, three of the Bowmans been hit in what, a couple of months?" Doyle said.

"Fuckin' Gennas," Dean said, looking annoyed, then glancing out past the corner.

Doyle had told Huck of the six brothers setting up their own action down by the Loop, rubbing up against the edge of the North Side turf, the brothers building a name for being hard and not afraid to cross lines. Bugs and Hymie thinking it was Torrio's right hand Capone stirring the pot, causing rivalry between the North Side and the Gennas, this Scarface not caring who he crossed.

The reason Dean was lashing back now, hitting a South Side shipment, making it look like the Gennas did it, getting Johnny Torrio's attention, setting Italian against Italian. Meantime, his lads were looking for new routes to bring their loads in from Canada, keeping them from getting hijacked.

"We take care of this Hertz guy's war —" Doyle started to say.

Dean cut him off. "And what, we get to ride around in his taxis, meantime they're getting shot at by this Checker outfit? You ever see booze go up in flames?"

Huck tried again, saying, "How about if we —"

"Who's we?"

"Okay, you — put Checker out of the game. Yellow puts up the taxis, and you get a piece."

"What's a piece?"

"I'm thinking ten percent."

"Why not think twenty-five, or better," Dean said. "Ten's a slice, twenty-five's a piece."

"Well, I don't know . . ." Huck started.

"'Course you don't." Dean gave him a sharp look, then to Gypsy Doyle, seeing these guys weren't letting up. "Okay, you go see about it."

"I'll set it up with Dex Ayres," Huck said.

"Who's this guy?"

"Supervisor of the —"

Dean put up a hand, shaking his head, saying to Doyle, "You talk to the top man, this Hertz — the guy that owns it." Looking to Huck, saying, "You set it up and Doyle does the sit-down." Dean kept the hand up, stopped Huck from saying any more. Hearing an engine coming, Dean peeked from the side of the building again, seeing the Bromes and Earlrick truck coming, the shipment of Bloody Angelo Genna's booze in back. Pulling the kerchief up over his face, saying, "Time to get to work."

Doyle and Huck pulling their kerchiefs up.

24

Walking into the livery, Huck went looking for Izzy under the stairs in back. Hearing angry voices up in Dex Ayres's office. Two of the cabbies, Vito and Tony, sat at a card table, a game of checkers set up, both with elbows on the table, Vito taking a red and hopping two blacks. One of the taxis on blocks with a back wheel off, a couple of bullet holes through its body panels, Moses lying under it on a creeper. Snooky at a bench patching a tire.

Huck starting for the back when he heard the first pop, knowing what it was, the two checker players looking around, jumping from the table. Huck was ducking and running for the front, yelling, "Gun!"

Footfalls coming down the stairs, John D. Hertz grabbing the shotgun Moses kept at the door. A couple more shots rang out in the street. A window shattered above his head, John D. hurrying outside. The sound of a roaring engine and screeching tires. John D. standing at the door, aiming at the disappearing sedan, but too late to pepper it with buckshot.

Huck had grabbed a lug wrench off the mechanic's bench, running outside after him. The two of them standing and watching the sedan speed off.

"You see the make?" Huck said.

"Stutz, a black one." Hertz looked at him.

Moses followed them out, pistol in his hand.

"The hell you going to do with that?" John D. looked at the lug wrench in Huck's hand.

"How come you didn't shoot?

The two of them looking at each other, then both turning to the shot-up front of the place, the smashed glass at their feet.

It was Snooky calling from the side of the building, "We got a man down."

One of the drivers lay on the ground. Moses ran over, saying it was Tony, had just been inside playing checkers.

Dex Ayres poked his head out the front door, looking over at the fallen man, Vito running to call for an ambulance, Huck going over and seeing the man lying there was dying, blood pooling under him.

John D. shook his head, told Dex to stay by the door and keep watch, handing him the shotgun. Then he was heading back for the office, taking the stairs.

Huck dropped the wrench and went to the back, finding Izzy under his cot, telling him, "It's alright now." Grabbing a box and telling him to pack what he owned.

"Where we going, Huck?"

"Place I should've taken you."

"I'm not staying with the nuns."

"You're gonna stay with me."

"Going to let them sons of bitches know it's a bad idea, shooting up my place." John D. came back down and stood behind him. "And where in hell you going?"

"Getting him safe."

"We're in a war here. One of our guys on the ground."

"What's his name?" Huck said.

"What?"

"The one who got shot — what's his name?" Bending for a comic book, guessing Izzy dropped it when the shots rang out. Standing, looking eye to eye, saying to John D. Hertz, "The man works for you, and you don't know his name."

"And you're Huck, the hundred-dollar man hired to keep this from happening." John D. stared back.

"You gonna step aside?" Huck asked him, thinking the man was pretty sharp, finding out Dex had upped the pay from eighty.

A car drove up out front, Huck guessing this was the police, hearing car doors closing.

"Guess you got plenty of guns now."

"Go get Dex. I want you both in the office." And Hertz turned and went back up the stairs.

Ignoring him, Huck said to the boy, "You all set?"

Izzy stood with a box in hand, books, clothes filling it, his blanket on top. And Huck took it from him and led the way out the back door, not wanting him to see the man on the ground, and wanting to avoid the police and their questions, getting Izzy into the front of one of the taxis out back, saying to him, "What do you say to flapjacks?"

Izzy always up for flapjacks.

25

"**S**hot out my front window and scared my wife half to hell." Dex looked across his desk, filling their glasses, sliding two across, retelling how his house had been targeted, talking to Gypsy Doyle, saying, "But let me start by asking why I'm not talking to Dean O'Banion, no offense." Giving Huck a sideways glance. The superintendent acting like his own shadow could get the best of him since the dressing down he took from John D.

"And I'm asking why a dandy figures he can talk down his nose at me," Doyle said, then looked at Huck.

Huck shook his head, this meeting that should be between O'Banion and Hertz, both leaving it to flunkeys.

"You run it by me, and if it sounds right, then I take it to Mr. Hertz," Dex said. "The only way he wants it." Leaning back in the lilac chair.

"Guess you figure me for the errand boy," Doyle said, looking across the fancy desk.

"Hardly that. Fact I know about you, Mr. Doyle. You were a Market Streeter, used to run with Charlie Reiser, one they called the Ox, I believe. Now, you're hired muscle, if that's the term." Dex's eyes going to the knife scar running from the top of Doyle's skull to his chin, right past the left eye. "You run bootleg, with this one riding along." Dex glanced at Huck. "And now you want to run it around town in our fleet. That about the size of it?"

"Told him all that, did you?" Gypsy Doyle giving Huck an annoyed look.

"I did my own checking, Mr. Doyle," Dex said, lifting his glass. "While my own muscle here was being run off the road, crashing up one of our cabs."

"Heard something about that." Doyle grinned like it was funny.

Huck letting the supervisor in his navy vest, cufflinks and bow tie talk like that.

"With a fare in the back too. The woman's still laid up in Cook County, having every kind of brace put on her body, meantime posing for the shutterbugs the newspapers send over, then talking to lawyers at her bedside, plotting to sue us. What do you think of that?"

"Think if you keep talking about him like that, you ought to look how close you're sitting to that window." Doyle looked from Dex to Huck again. "Could end up in the hospital bed next to the little old lady." Doyle took a first sip from his glass, twisting his face, holding it away, looking at it. "The hell is this?"

"Gin," Dex said. "Hendrick's — the finest."

"Why's it taste like . . . Goddamn, you got a cat in here?"

"An acquired taste, I suppose," Dex said, a smile forming. "Likely the juniper." Giving a wave of his hand, turning in his chair, reaching another bottle from his credenza. "Gautier, flown in from France. That suit you better?"

Dex poured cognac into a fresh glass, set it in front of him, offering Huck one.

Huck waved it off, reaching in a pocket and looking at the watch he took from Bubbling-Over. Goddamn, ten in the morning. Leaving the glass of gin alone, recalling the smell of the swill that passed for gin back in Bogalusa, brewed up in some back-room basement or bathtub. Right after the Eighteenth was passed, Huck had stood watching sheriff's deputies pour gallons of the stuff in a drainage ditch after a raid they'd been tipped on, catching an old moonshiner selling jugs of it off the back of his cart out behind Rougelot's. Huck had been arrested too, driving the cart at the time, thinking he'd never forget that smell.

Dex tried a different tact, saying to Doyle, "You want to take care of our little taxi war, and I've got no doubt that you fellows can, but understand, we run a legitimate business with a need to keep up appearances."

"Legitimate, listen to you." Doyle picked up the glass, slapping back the cognac. "You got a problem, one we can fix, and I'm talking to you, not to this Hertz."

"I'm afraid Mr. Hertz was otherwise enga—"

Doyle held up a finger, stopping him, saying, "This close to the window — going to end up with your man Hertz calling up my man, Dean, and making arrangements to send you flowers. You get what I'm saying?"

Huck leaned forward, saying, "The question here's how Yellow keeps a distance from what happens next. Can we agree on that?"

"Mr. Hertz prefers to conduct business through official channels, legal and legitimate — his words, not mine." Dex watching Doyle as he spoke. "No offense to you or Mr. O'Banion, but we're considering bringing in the Pinkertons. Perhaps you're familiar."

"Sure, robbed them a bunch of times. Nice fellas, and obliging too. Quick to put up their hands." Doyle finished his drink and started to get up, done wasting his time.

"Whatever it takes, is how you put it," Huck said to Dex.

The superintendent nodded, gave a thoughtful look, turned his empty glass around on the desk, saying to Huck, "I did say that, but going forward I am obliged to discuss all matters with Mr. Hertz. But I'm afraid after reading about you crashing one of his fleet, getting us into a lawsuit and the papers making a meal of it, Mr. Hertz feels strongly about handling this another way."

"Meaning you could've saved me the drive over," Doyle said, standing.

"And I apologize for that," Dex said, then looked to Huck as he started to rise. "Though you and I need to discuss our arrangement . . ." He put out his hand to Doyle.

"Gonna tell me my services aren't needed." Huck got up too.

"Afraid that's Mr. Hertz's view on it, yes," Dex said.

"Well, I'll leave you fellas to it." Doyle ignored the hand and started for the door.

"Although . . ." Dex said.

Doyle slowed at the door.

"I suppose if things were set in motion."

"What kind of motion?"

"Let's say something goes Yellow's way, perhaps makes the papers . . ."

"Didn't you just can me?" Huck said.

"I'm saying Mr. Hertz is fond of reading the dailies — and if he likes what he reads . . ." Dex shrugged.

"You expect us to audition for him?" Doyle said, shaking his head like couldn't believe this gin-drinking pansy.

"A thing that would get your Mr. O'Banion and my Mr. Hertz sitting down, perhaps seeing eye to eye." Dex picked up his empty glass, studied it, then set it back down.

"Meaning you put off calling in the Pinkertons, not have them write you a report, give you a receipt, nice and official."

Doyle looked at him a moment more, then stepped up close, hovering over the desk.

Reaching behind for the decanter, Dex poured more cognac, and slid it across, then poured himself more gin, saying, "Mr. Hertz paid a carpenter to fix a stall, ninety cents an hour. New yearling was being a hot-head and liked kicking out the back. And anytime it did it, Mr. Hertz called back the carpenter. I asked him why he put up with it, and he says to me a good racehorse does a high-strung thing like that, means he's likely going to win."

"We talking horseflesh now?"

"My point is, the boss sees the promise in a thing . . ."

"On account of it kicking."

"A man can put up with a lot if he sees the promise." Dex sat and leaned back, teepeeing his fingers on the desk.

"Still wondering if we're getting someplace or just taking up a good morning." Doyle tipped back his glass and set it down. "You're talking about a man with a hammer, this ninety-cent man. Me, I got a gun."

"It's the bang that gets the man's attention," Dex said. "And if it gets him and your Mr. O'Banion to the table . . ."

Doyle looked at him, unimpressed.

"And while I can't promise more than that, I can tell you we've got friends at city hall, plenty of them, and some beyond that."

"The kind that talk from both sides of their mouth — bought a few myself. Who knows, maybe the same ones."

"Men with a keen sense of self-betterment," Dex said. "And you can't have too many friends like that, am I right, Mr. Doyle?"

"Let's say Hertz reads something in his dailies, what's that worth?"

"Always liked the way you Irish haggle," Dex said, smiling.

Looked to Huck like he was feeling the gin.

"It's you Scots that haggle. Irish, we got the luck," Doyle said. Looking to Huck, saying, "Waller — what's that, heinie or something, right?" Didn't wait for an answer, looking back at Dex, saying, "You want the thing done, put a grand on Markin's head, and the man's a stain on the street. There it is, plain English." And Doyle turned and left.

"What in hell was that?" Huck said to Dex after Doyle was down the stairs.

"That man likes kicking the stall."

Huck shook his head, couldn't believe this guy, saying, "You mentioned Charlie the Ox?"

"Did my homework, that's right."

"Didn't find out the guy owed Dean ten G's in card money one time, did you? Not quick in making a repayment on a loan, joking in the Wigwam one night, telling Dean he was gonna keep right on waiting. Dean laughed and went along like it was alright — like Doyle just did . . ."

"Your point?"

"The Ox ended in hospital after what looked like a botched robbery, his jaw wired shut — had to be placed under police guard. His woman came to see him next morning and found him croaked, what the coroner declared as death by suicide. Man had ten bullet holes in his chest. The cop on watch claimed he was in the water closet when it happened, only way anybody could've got in that room."

"I had my window shot out, my wife scared half to death, but I'm still here — was with Mr. Hertz from the start and saw this place built from the ground, three cabs turned into eleven hundred, stamped out plenty of competition through some tough times. Stood next to the man and the mayor when that first traffic light went in, right on Michigan." Dex picked up the empty glass again, turned it in his hand. Squaring up his shoulders, sitting back in his lilac chair.

There was no point talking to him, so Huck got set to leave, not sure he'd been canned or not.

"Markin and his independents want to muscle in." Dex smacked the glass on the desk. "And I want an end to it." Reaching in his drawer, he took an envelope and pushed it across the desk. "You and Doyle want to keep eating at Brando's while the rest of town's at some chili parlor or getting in a soup line, then I need something big to happen. And soon." There it was.

Huck shrugged, taking it and tapping the envelope next to the spilled gin. "Going to need a fresh cab." Not wanting to drive the same one they used for hijacking the Bromes and Earlrick truck in Cicero, running the load to Nails Morton's garage up on Maxwell.

"Tell me you didn't crack up another one?"

"I just like them fresh."

Huck heard footsteps coming up the stairs, could see a flash of fear in Dex's eyes, the man likely figuring it was Doyle coming back, maybe changed his mind about pitching him out the window.

26

Clement, one of the drivers, stood at the door, and Huck and Dex both reeled, catching a hell of a stench coming off the man.

"Goddamn it!" Dex threw a hand over his nose with one hand, waving him back with the other.

"Goddamn is right," Clement said in a croak, walking in, the awful smell filling the room.

"Jesus!" Huck had a hand over his mouth and nose, eyes watering.

Dex was out of his chair, waving for Clement to get out.

"Fuckers tossed a polecat in my rig. Goddamn I smell, naw, I reek." Clement looking like he wanted to jump out of his own skin.

"Get out!" Dex kept waving.

"Just come to say I quit."

"Fine, fine, just get out."

"Not till I get what you sons of bitches owe me."

"I'm in a goddamn meeting."

"I can wait." Clement folded his arms, standing in the middle of the room, letting the unholy stink do the talking.

"Please!" Dex croaked, fingers pinching his nose, waving the other hand like it might get the smell out. "Get paid Fridays, you know that. Get — get — God . . ." Motioning for Huck to do something.

Huck went to the window, twisting the latch and pushing up the pane. Seeing the black Stutz below, the same three guys inside, the one on the passenger side looking up at him, making a finger gun, dropping his thumb like the hammer. All of them laughing.

"Ought to wear off by Christmas." Clement stood there, blocking the door, saying, "Them sons of bitches tossed a sack in my window. Goddamn. I can't go in my house like this."

Dex just groaned and gagged.

"What's God pack up the ass end of them buggers?" Clement's voice was hoarse, but he was talking like he was passing the time of day. "There I was, picked up a crosstown, having a chat with the rider, talking about the Sox's chances," Clement spat on the floor, then went on. "Goddamn black rig roars up around Wallace by the stockyards. One on the passenger side hails me to crank my window. Thinking an out-of-towner wanting directions to Comiskey, so I slow and wind it down. And he lobs in the sack. Nearly wrecked my rig pulling over, throwing up on myself. The rider jumps out and runs up Wallace. No fare, no tip, nothing. And the black rig tears off, the guys inside laughing their heads off."

"Get out." Dex was wheezing and gagging.

"I got all day — an honest man out of work. You want, we can talk about them traffic lights and taxi stands you like boasting about. Can tell me about all the new bangtails Hertz got himself, having himself a nice country life."

Dex reached in his drawer for his pocket pistol, aiming it at Clement.

Not budging, Clement went on. "You called this fight, you and Hertz. You pay up, including the two-buck fare plus tip, top of what I got coming. I figure it sums to say, forty, and we'll call it square. That, or I go to the damn *Trib* and tell them what's really been going on — soon as I stop stinking." He spat again.

Watching the Stutz till it was out of sight, Huck took the envelope and pulled some bills from it and handed them to Clement.

Doing slow arithmetic, Clement said, "Plus a half dollar for the bath house, no way I'm going home like this. And the double-up on the lye soap," Clement said. "Wife won't let me in smelling like hell's doo-doo."

Huck held out another bill. "Don't come back, Clem, even when you smell pretty."

Clement nodded, and he left.

Dex tossed the pistol in the drawer, cursing, then grabbed his wastebasket, doubled over it and spewed his breakfast and the morning's gin into it.

Huck thinking he might join him, the worst stench on earth, one that would likely cling to the office walls for a month — likely to embed itself in that velvet chair longer than that.

"Goddamn it," Dex croaked and teetered for the door.

"You owe me another fifty," Huck said, the money he just gave to Clement, following him out.

Dex nodded, wiping his mouth with his sleeve, leaving the office and going down the steps.

"And about that other cab?" Huck said, reminding him about the new wheels.

"Just follow the stink, cab's at the end of it." Dex got that out, meaning Clement's rig, then he was throwing up at the base of the stairs.

27

That stench was sure to stick to the fibers, so Huck ditched his new clothes, bought another pair of trousers and a chambray shirt, costing him three bucks. Walter's Bath House and a bottle of English Lavender set him back another half dollar.

When he figured he got enough of the stench off, he took Izzy to supper at Luka's Chuck Wagon, then back to his nothing-fancy boarding room in Bughouse Square, gave him the bed and blanket, emptied the top drawer of the dresser for him, put the wobbly chair under the bulb hanging from the stained ceiling, told him he'd be back in an hour and left him to read. Then Huck went to a nickel joint he'd been to a couple of times, feeling the need for a drink and a spin on the floor with a nickel gal.

Walking in past Declan, the doorman in the overalls, more of a sentry than a bouncer, there to call a warning if he saw the coppers coming on a raid. Declan pointed to a hand-painted sign tacked to a wall, boasting they had the Jimmy Joy Orchestra, there for one night only. Huck stepped into the dim of the cellar club, the locals calling the joint the Alley Cat, with no sign out front on account of the Eighteenth.

The air was thick with smoke, sweat and perfume gone sour, hanging like a stratosphere. Far from the worst thing Huck had breathed in that day. A door on sawhorses passed as the bar top, a bucket nailed to the floor for spitting and cigarette butts, most of the butts ground out on the floor. A line of crates and boards made shelves. Bottles and jars lined the top, Henry the barman, wearing a stained butcher's apron, perched on a stool on the business side, a fat hand on the bar top. A roll of ticket stubs and a tin box for collecting money by his feet. A blackjack on its lid in case any of the drunks got any ideas. Selling tickets, a dime a dance with the nickel hoppers sitting at the opposite side of the dance floor, six of them working this time of night. Reaching for a bottle, Henry refilled a couple of glasses, pawing up coins and tucking them in the apron.

Men perched on the row of stools along the bar, others stood behind them, reaching across, exchanging coins for drinks. Huck recognizing a handful of Yellow drivers, this being their joint, a block north of the livery. Dex Ayres advising the drivers start going in joints in pairs or groups until the trouble with Checker got settled.

A white-haired oldster looked like he was set to pass out and slide to the floor, his head wagging, the man done for the night. Two others stood and looked ready to jump for the stool.

Men drinking and doing a bunk on their miseries, forgetting about fed-up wives and unfed kids, their livelihoods that never measured up. Couples were cutting a rug to what the Jimmy Joy Orchestra was pumping out, the four-man band on a stage made of nailed-together crates.

The white-haired drunk tumbled off the stool, and two drivers pushed at each other to get to it. While they shoved,

Huck sat on the stool, glad it wasn't wet. The drivers thinking better than to challenge him, knowing who he was. Trying to catch the barman's eye, Huck half-turned, looking past the standing men, guessing the hoofers from the heelers, the ones who came to dance from the ones who came to paw at the women. The Jimmy Joy boys were murdering a Carl Fenton number, Huck thinking it was called "Cuban Moon." Remembered hearing it on a flattop one time, what folks back home called porch music.

The tune ended and Jimmy Joy thanked the sole clapping drunk, looked to the dancers, then to his bandmates and called for something new, calling it the Charleston, signaling a break was coming up after that, a chance for the men to grab a smoke or water their horses, reminding them to buy more dance tickets. A couple of the men on the floor traded partners, handing over their stubs, the hoppers tucking them away, smiling like they couldn't wait to speed the tempo and dodge those flying feet.

Jimmy Joy put his fiddle to his chin, wagged his bow through the smoke, counted down, and the band erupted, the hoppers adding percussion with their heels, the drunken men pounding their feet and swinging their arms, Turkey Trotting into each other. One of the nickel gals was knocked to the floor. The man who banged into her hadn't noticed, his eyes closed, all his joints flying. The woman crawled for the wall to keep from being stomped. The other hoppers were ducking more than dancing, dodging the untied work boots.

"A dangerous night," Huck said to Henry, the barman coming along the bar, Huck not liking the greasy man, a huckster for the women dancing.

"What you want?" Henry asked.

"Lemme try a highball."

"A what the fuck?"

"Whiskey and a hit of soda, called a highball — and you make it in a clean glass."

Henry muttered something, spitting at the straw floor, reached and held up the roll of tickets. "How many you want?"

Huck held up a finger meaning one, still aching from the crash, guessing one dance was going to do it.

Reaching into a crate beneath the bar, Henry lifted a jug, splashing booze in a jar, called it Thunderbird and slid it across, saying, "Two bits and a dime. You want it plain?"

"Told you to hit it with soda. And why you call 'em nickel dancers if you charge a dime?" Having fun with the son of a bitch.

Henry shook his head, reaching for another bottle and pouring the fizz on top.

Fishing out the coins, Huck set them down. Lifting the jar, ignoring the grease marks, taking a sip and gritting his teeth. A bathtub batch likely from the Genna brothers, a hint of beets, potato peels, and juniper, the soda helping him get it down — swill costing fifty cents a jug to make, being sold to these nickel joints and speaks for six bucks, Henry charging two bits a shot. Everybody making money. Only other way for folks to get a drink was to brew a basement batch, or find a sawbones prescribing wine for ailments, or get on their knees on Sunday and get the sacramental wine from ministers of the gospel.

Looking across at the hoppers, two sitting in chairs, a long-legged negress next to a brunette with a pretty face. Both painted up. Something familiar about the brunette. Huck stared at her through the cloud of smoke as he sipped, and it came to him — the nurse from Grant Hospital, the one who didn't give him her name or the time of day. Recalling the woman at the admin office called her Karla. Huck knowing a lot of these women were moonlighting, making extra scratch, some of them straight off a boat in need of work, making what they could.

The nurse sat talking to the dancer next to her, the two of them watching the couples on the floor, the nurse saying something, both of them laughing. The band finishing the number, getting off the stage and taking a break.

"Looks lonesome with no tip." Henry looked at the coins.

Huck turned back to Henry, the man taking the coins off the bar top, looking at them in his palm, working the sum, deciding it was close enough, dropping them in his apron, the apron heavy with coins, looking down the line of men along the bar.

"Ought to be hangdog serving this toilet water," Huck said to him, guessing the service would go downhill from there, but he just wanted the one drink and to take a twirl on the floor, then head back to his flat, lie down on the bedroll on the floor having given Izzy the bed. Thinking with Izzy staying at his place, and with the money he was now making, he ought to get a better place, some flat with an extra room.

Huck set the glass down, saying, "Not to put too fine a point on her, Henry, but what you got in here, tater peels?" Frowning at the glass, the man next to him laughing.

"Rest of the room laps it up. You don't like it, there's the door," Henry told him.

"I'll find it as long as I don't go blind first." He pushed the glass away, thinking of a batch he brewed with his brother, Arlen, one time, Huck getting the copper while Arlen found a tucked-away spot behind a copse of trees in back of a cow pasture. A creek running by gave them water for cooling and draining the used mash. Moving their mash barrels and jugs at night by mule and wagon. They wrapped the wheels and mules' feet in burlap to keep the clip-clop noise down on the back roads. And they sold their shine at the back of the Elmer Candy Company, the rest they kept in quart bottles, some hidden in the old piano their stepmother, Bladie Mae, used to play in the parlor, the rest in the back of the barn or in the cold cellar. Might've made a good business of it if Arlen hadn't gone one-way into that damned war.

The dance stub between his fingers, he got off the stool and weaved his way past the men waiting for a turn at the bar, then past the ones on the floor waiting to dance as the Jimmy Joy Orchestra took to the stage for a next set.

Walking up to the brunette, Huck got a close look — the hair in a bob, not tied back like she wore it at Grant's — but he was sure it was the same nurse. The white uniform swapped for a Paris look, gams showing, hose gartered below the knee, a cloche hat, the negress next to her in a turban, both smiling at him. Catching a hint of perfume through the sweat and smoke filling the room, he stepped close enough and said, "How about we put on the ritz?" Feeling dumb for saying it.

She smiled, saying, "This your idea of the Ritz?"

He smiled and held out the stub.

Looking at him a moment, she took the stub, getting to her feet, tucking it in a little purse hanging from a thin leather strap around her neck, smoothing the frilly dress, saying, "Just the dance, so we're clear." Her eyes meeting his.

"What it says, good for one dance." Shrugging like what else, he stepped to the floor and offered his hand, Jimmy Joy announcing the boys were getting set to dig into one they learned from the Harmony Kings, calling it "Ain't It a Shame."

Turning to him on the floor, she gave him a practiced smile.

"You don't remember me?" Huck said, hoping for a foxtrot, thinking he could fake the moves.

"Sure, we danced before."

"Naw. Was at Grant's, you're the nurse. Got me patched up and back on my feet." Pointing to his head where the stitches had been, seeing she didn't remember him, but there was something like worry behind the pretty eyes. Huck feeling even dumber now for dropping that on her.

"You got me mixed up, mister. I dance, it's why you came, right?"

The music started, too loud for talking.

Huck held up his hands.

She looked at him, then to her friend on the chair like she was looking to the safe shore, saying close enough to his ear, "No touching."

"How you foxtrot with no touching?"

And she pushed back a smile, shaking her head. And she showed him how, started the step and bounce to the music, swinging her arms, adding the kicks, then the twists — showed him how to do it without touching. Huck started moving, mimicking her moves, feeling like he was rooted to the floor, could barely do a box step. Dancers around him moved like they were on a frying pan. Huck aped her moves and kicked his feet, off the beat, but trying to keep up, stepping and swinging his arms, banging into another fellow. Main thing, he told himself was don't tromp on her toes.

"How about we get out of here?" he said to her after, felt the sweat under his shirt, hoping that polecat smell had no linger.

"Can see I'm working, but if you want to dance, why not get another ticket?"

"Sure we met — at the Grant that time."

"Like I told you, you've got me mixed up."

Another man pushed past him, holding out a ticket stub to her, "If you ain't dancing, bub, then make some room."

Wanting to deck the man for shoving, Huck nodded to her and left.

28

"**H**ow do I know that? Like I told you, I had eyes on the place, nobody coming in or going out." Gypsy Doyle shrugged. "You want to send a message, then let's send it." Insisting they make a big enough bang to have Hertz see that getting in bed with the North Side was the way to end the taxi war that had dragged on over two years now. Doyle thinking firebombing Morris Markin's house ought to do the trick.

"Not a Checker driver going to feel safe. Not in their taxis, and not in their own places. I mean, if we can get at their boss . . ."

"How about if he's got his wife and kids in there?" Huck not wanting to strike the match if there was a chance of somebody being inside, saying, "The last thing anybody needs, make a martyr of the guy, the kind of thing that ends with us swinging from a rope in back of the Cook County jail."

"Told you, I put eyes on the place," Doyle said, sounding tired of Huck dragging his feet. "And there's nobody in there."

"I heard what you said."

"You want, go wait by the car." Doyle started to turn, then turned back again, saying, "And . . ."

Huck looked at him, saying, "I know, I best be waiting."

His grin showing the space where the tooth had been, Doyle said, "And you see something, you give a holler. I know you can whine, but can you holler?"

Huck was starting to see Doyle as plain dumb, a vacant man, thinking he shouldn't have gone along with this. Thinking of a rumor he heard, how it was Ragen's Colts that got things stirred up in the Black Belt back in '19, setting a couple of Packingtown shacks afire back before the riots, getting the Irish and Lugans stirred up and blaming the Blacks. Didn't take much more than striking a match, same as Doyle was doing now.

Huck having the feeling the North Side figured him for some stockyard fighter, thick enough to stand toe to toe, throwing punches till the last man was standing, but not seeing him as much more than that. A guy they let drive their whiskey in from Canada.

Standing by the door of the stolen sedan, the one Doyle got for the job, Huck watched him go past the hedge, disappearing a moment, then reappearing by the front window.

Feeling the cold of night, he watched Doyle take a bottle from inside his coat, then uncork it, balling and shoving in a rag, leaving some trailing out. He turned the bottle upside down, the petrol soaking the rag. Fishing in a pocket, looking from one black window to the next, he fumbled with the tin of matches, got one out and struck it, holding it to the trailing sleeve. A whoosh of flame.

Counting five, holding it out from his side, Doyle lobbed it through the front window, glass exploding and the bottle smashing on the floor inside, a whoosh of flame taking hold of the planks, roaring up the drapes and the near wall. The room coming to light, furniture inside catching. In the time it took Doyle to come at a run, flames were licking to the ceiling.

Ducking past the hedge, Doyle hurried and kept to the shadows. The crackling coming to life behind him, the glow lighting up the street.

Huck was in the sedan, revving the engine, already rolling when Doyle came running, grabbing for the door handle, throwing himself into the moving car, whooping.

29

The number ended, Jimmy Joy holding his fiddle, thanking the ladies and gents on the dance floor for keeping them on an extra week, by popular demand he called it, then announced they were taking a break. Taking a bow like there was applause, he stepped off the nailed crates, past the three drunken men and their nickel steppers, the women all eager to get off the floor. Other men were pushing through the crowded room for the bar, Henry the bartender reaching a jug and setting jars on the bar top, started filling them, trading them for coins, hands reaching in.

"How about it?" Huck asked Karla the nurse, third time he'd come in this week, seeking her out, handing her his dance stubs.

"You know there's no music, right?" she said.

"I'll settle for a coffee then."

"It's a dime a dance, a nickel I get to keep, and there's no coffee in this joint — even if there was, would you drink it?" Giving him a tired look.

"Just want to get to know you."

"They got the word N-O where you come from?" She gave him a look like maybe he lacked a few marbles, saying, "Talking leads to dipping a beak, then to something else. That what you're thinking?" The look changed, her eyes going back to tired. "Look, I don't know you . . . I just dance, okay?"

"Where I come from, talking's a good way to fix the not-knowing part."

"Why me? There's lots of gals here."

"None that helped get me stitched up, took my clothes and left me buck naked on that cot."

She frowned, trying to hide the amusement, then said, "And just where do you find coffee this time of night?"

"I know a place."

"Let me guess — yours?"

"Place called the Chuck Wagon — makes a good cup, plus the best flapjacks around. Over on . . ." Couldn't think of the name of the street, saying, "You like flapjacks? I bet you do."

"You even got a car?"

"Got lots of them, drive a different one every week."

"A tycoon, huh?" Giving a tired smile.

"Work for a taxi outfit, the yellow ones." Curious about this nurse Karla from Grant Hospital, now dancing for nickels. He was wanting to get to know her, saying, "Sometimes I drive a truck, but that's another job."

"Yellow — you're one of the fellas waging war on the street?"

"If you rather, we can walk."

"You get tired of it?"

"What's that?"

"Driving, after doing it all day?"

"I guess so."

"So you ask a dancer to ankle it, me being on my feet all day."

"So, we're back to driving then."

"You understand beat it?"

Watching her turn to the chairs along the wall, sitting between a couple of dancers, one of them with a shoe off, rubbing her foot. The nurse started talking to her, not looking his way again.

Pocketing the dance stub, he turned for the back door. Standing outside in the cold air, making and lighting a smoke. Been a lousy day — the old woman from the wreck had kept up her lawsuit, the company finally settling and covering her doctor and legal bills. Dex Ayres cast the blame on him for it, calling Huck to his office, having his guts for garters, saying John D. Hertz wanted to see him too — something that would likely end with both of them getting canned. The story and the photo of that crash site was still showing up in the dailies. The *Trib*, the *Daily News* and the *Evening Post* blaming the wreck on the escalation of trouble between Yellow and Checker. Dex showing him the story of the firebombing of Morris Markin's place in the *Herald-Examiner*, the paper once distributed by Dean O'Banion's crew, back when the North Side put pressure on local merchants and newsstands to peddle the right papers. The same story running in the *Journal*, the clean paper for clean-thinking people.

If it wasn't for the money he was making, Huck told himself he'd leave and head back to Bogalusa, stay with his old dad and Teety Fleur, go lay flowers by Bladie Mae's grave, his stepmother who ran off with a crew boss from Lawo Coal up in Tennessee someplace. Huck had looked her up, found her bedridden at the Home of the Friendless. There was no crew boss, only the sick behind her eyes, skin as pale as sand, and a cough that didn't quit. Just didn't want to burden them all with what she knew was coming. Never had been another man, his daddy being double any man she ever met, and she told him Huck would be one too. Huck figuring himself double the fool, and that was for sure.

Taking her hand, he sat by her bed, Bladie Mae coughing into her fist. Huck seeing the blood streaks, wanting to take her to a proper hospital. Bladie telling him it was too late for that. Had a doctor tell her the tuberculosis would take her, and there was nothing more to be done about it.

Wasn't long and she was under the Elmwood ground, and Huck stood with his old dad, both of them quiet as the preacher said the words. The two of them picking up handfuls of dirt and tossing it, same way they had done for Arlen.

And he did feel the pull to go back home, but Huck knew he wasn't leaving, he was making real money, and soon he'd be living an easy life, a big house, dining in the finest places, a motor car like the ReVere-Duesenberg John D. rolled around in.

"You far off, huh?"

It was Karla the nurse, pulling him from his thoughts. Stepping out from the doorway, she stood next to him, taking the cigarette from his fingers, putting it to her own lips and dragging on it.

"Didn't mean to come off so starchy," she said.

"Likely get that all day, fellas coming up with lines."

"That coffee just coffee?"

"'Less you want to eat."

"What did you call them, flapjacks?"

"Or chop suey, oysters, whatever you like."

"Coffee's just fine."

And he pointed to the Yellow taxi, going and opening the passenger door.

"Flapjacks, that like batter cakes?"

"Call 'em what you like, but they're good any time — butter and syrup, anything you like." Huck trying to keep his tongue from tripping on the words.

"Admit you do make them sound good." She looked up at the stars, letting him get the passenger door for her. She was smiling, but she was looking unsure about it too.

"I'm Huck by the way," Huck said, getting in the driver's side, going about getting the engine fired up.

"It's Lizzy."

"That the one you had growing up or just the one for dancing?"

"How about it's Lizzy for now."

"Lizzy it is."

"Huck — that like in the book?"

"That'd be Huckleberry Finn — me, I'm a Huckabee, Huckabee Waller."

"Huckabee Waller — you don't just make that up."

"No, I guess not."

"Well, I think it suits you." She dragged on the smoke again and gave it back to him. "So what else do you do, Huckabee Waller, I mean besides drive this taxi and pester working girls?"

"I'm in safety consulting for Yellow, plus I do a little importing on the side, driving a truck."

"Safety consulting and importing."

"Uh huh."

"You know you just said nothing — I mean about yourself."

"Well, I'm not so interesting."

"Well, let's hope you're wrong." She stifled a yawn, then smiled.

"I didn't mean it like that."

"Good to hold back some, and a bit of mystery's a nice touch," she said. "Your momma must've expected something from you, giving you a handle like that."

"For that, you'd have to ask my old dad, living down in New Orleans with my Teety Fleur." Never wondered much about his real momma, Huck growing up and thinking of Bladie Mae that way.

"Well, I just bet there's a story behind it."

He smiled, driving south of the Loop, guessing Luka might have locked up for the night, but hoping the old Austrian wouldn't mind too much, coming downstairs, opening up and putting on a pot of coffee. Hoping he wouldn't have to stab any bums with a fork, Huck was fishing for something more to say, part of him feeling he was clodhopping through getting to know her, but feeling easy with her at the same time.

"You come north, and you get yourself mixed up in what the papers call a war of fists and fenders."

"Papers make headlines out of anything."

"And why do they paint them yellow, the taxis?"

"Supposed to stick out to catch the fares, the way John D. Hertz figures it."

"Well, I can tell you there's nothing fair about what that man's charging." She was smiling, making this easy.

"Forty-five a mile, I don't know, it ain't so —" And he stopped himself, seeing she was smiling. "You're having fun with me, huh?"

"I am, but I will say I have to dance a mile to make forty-five cents — feels like that anyway."

"Company takes most of it," Huck said. "The drivers are lucky they get a tip." Thinking the only fare he ever took ended in a crash, the old woman ending up in the Grant and suing Hertz for ten grand, where he met this nurse Karla, calling herself Lizzy. Saying to her, "Bet you get tips. Sorry, I don't mean —"

"Some dew-dropper offers me a tip, he expects something more than a twirl on the dance floor."

"Sounds like you ladies ought to join the Wobblies, demand a fair day's pay and all that." Huck was picturing nickel dancers joining the industrial workers, sure those union fellas wouldn't mind.

"Now who's poking fun?" She smiled her perfect teeth at him.

"Guess it's tough getting by, every place you go."

"Heard a cab got tipped on Michigan. Don't know if it was yellow. *Post* called both outfits a bunch of reds and radicals, calling on the mayor to do something about it. You ask me, it's all like telling it to Sweeney."

"Who's —"

"Means half of what you read's hokum."

"Bet you're right about that." Huck not saying he could only make out about half of what he tried to read anyway, and that with Izzy helping him to learn.

"You ask me, this town's been loco since the cow kicked the lantern." She was still smiling, saying, "Guess I got a lot to say on it."

"Well, we got past the names, and talk of sore feet and the feud Yellow's got going on, and we ain't even there yet."

"It's what they call small talk."

"Here we go," Huck said, pointing to the storefront sign declaring Berghoff's Chuck Wagon, Austrian Specialties — and chop suey. The lights still on inside.

"That wreck some time back, a lady coming out of the Drake, catching a cab and ending up in the Grant . . ." She was looking at him, smiling again. "Was you, think I recognized your picture from the paper."

"So it was you, the nurse, that time they brought me in?" He stepped to the door, pulling it open for her.

And she nodded, saying, "With my hair up and under the cap, the white uniform and sensible shoes. Figured it gave me a different look."

"I could tell those eyes anyplace." Huck embarrassed as soon as he said it, quickly saying, "So it's nursing by day and nickel hopping at night." Waving to Luka, showing her to his usual spot by the window. Looking across at the speak, glad it was too cold a night for the drunks to be outside milling around. Seeing it was boarded up, likely been raided and shut down.

"Started dancing when the Grant let us know they were laying off staff. I figured I hadn't been there long and had no seniority, so I better find something else quick, that or I wouldn't make the rent."

"Laying off staff — with all the business us cabbies keep sending their way?" He pushed in her chair, then took his own.

"They called it a sign of the times, how they put it."

And he nodded to Luka and ordered coffee, saying to her, "You try Cook County or St. Joseph's?"

"Same story all around."

Said he was sorry to hear it, then asked how she came to nursing, asked if it was like a calling.

"Rolled bandages for the Red Cross and stuck pins in a map, showing troop movement to the wounded, showed them what they were missing out on."

"You didn't get sent over?"

"They never sent immigrants. Had no trust in what Wilson called a muddy heritage. Some others saying it was no place for women."

"Was no place for nobody," Huck said.

"You get sent over?"

"Naw, was too young." Telling her how brother Arlen had a mind to sign up even before the war, wanting to get deployed to Mexico and hunt for Pancho Villa. Arlen raring for action the whole time Wilson was sitting on his thumbs in his White House and making up his mind. When the boys were finally sent, and Wilson lowered the draft age, Arlen jumped at the chance and got put in Pershing's expeditionary force, sent over to make the world safe.

"I'm glad you were too young."

"Stayed home with the sin and weight of it, being on the wrong side of eighteen. Got a job at Sam's Grocery and bought their bonds, though, and did my bit. Got a couple of letters, Arlen telling about driving a Quad and getting stuck in French mud, moving supplies. Telling me how it was different than our mud — guess you don't want to hear all this."

"Go on."

"Second letter told how he got sent to a front-line place called Cantigny, under some French command, couldn't understand a word they said to him." Huck not saying how he had to get Teety Fleur to read the letters to him.

"Last letter told how he got assigned to the First Battalion, sent in with the Sixth Marines at some place called Belleau Wood. Got handed a rifle with a pig-sticker, made to live in a trench, praying the mustard gas and mortars and pounding MG o8s missed them. A whistle telling him when to run blind over the top, machine-gun nests waiting to oblige. The Huns called them devil dogs, what it said in the *Herald*, the paper back home. Got no more letters after that." Huck realizing he was putting a damper on things, saying, "Sorry to go on about it."

"Don't be. It's honest and shows you got feelings."

Luka came with the coffee, setting the cups down, asking if they wanted anything else. Thanking him, Huck felt like something crawled down his throat, stopping him from telling how the French awarded Arlen the Croix de Guerre, that damned red-and-green ribbon. His old dad keeping the box with the ribbon in a drawer. What Huck wouldn't give to set those images free, ones that kept him from sleeping nights — nightmares of Arlen running into that hellfire. Half of the Sixth gone after the first charge on those damn machine-gun nests. Huck living with the weight of not being there — not like he could have saved Arlen. Likely would have done his bit, dying alongside him in that damned French mud. Now he realized he best change the topic as he spooned sugar in his coffee, not sure if that was one or two spoons.

"I never bought their bonds," she said, looking at him like she could read the pain. Setting her spoon down, her hand reaching for his. "Remember them saying if you don't buy 'em, they ought to put you down for the water cure, whatever that is."

Feeling the smooth and warmth of her hand, he said, "You stayed back then you were too young or a slacker. Patriots signed and cowards whined — the war to end all wars, they called it."

"Just hope nobody's dumb enough to do it again."

He remembered his old man practically begging Arlen to go on the lam, take his chances on ending in the big tank at the Parish Prison. But Arlen had his head full of being a hero, Pershing calling a marine with a rifle the deadliest thing on Earth, and his Uncle Sam pointing that damned finger, the only thing keeping the world free, Arlen feeling it was his duty.

"Ouch, you know I'm a girl, right?" She pulled her hand free, shaking it.

"Sorry." He realized he'd taken her hand and had been squeezing it.

She took his hand again, her face softened and she said, "You'll get it right."

"Guess I got some ghosts."

"We all have ghosts."

30

Luka came with the coffee pot, saying, "Where's the boy tonight?" Topping up her tin, setting it in front of her, maybe thinking she was the boy's mother. Looking at Huck like he realized maybe he shouldn't have asked.

"Likely got his nose in a book," Huck told him. Then to her, "This street kid I brought in, got him fed."

"Two times," Luka said, filling Huck's tin, and he started to leave with the pot.

Huck asked him to pack up a sandwich, whatever he had on the go.

Luka nodded and went in the back.

"Looks like there's more to Huckabee Waller than meets the eye," she said.

He gave a shrug, glancing out the window, the gas lamp casting yellow light along the deserted street.

"So far, I got a fella who chases nurses, dances on two left feet, likes going for coffee middle of the night, and feeds kids on the street. I got it right so far?"

"Well, one thing, I'm good at digging myself a hole."

"Like how?"

"Like if I was to ask if that's your real name, Lizzy? I mean, I got told dancers don't give the real ones, names, I mean."

"What you really want, you want to know if I'm starting to trust you?"

"Guess we all hold something back."

"What's yours — your hold-back?"

Luka poked his head past the curtain, looking apologetic, asking if they wanted anything else before he cleaned up in the kitchen.

"How about it?" Huck asked Lizzy, not wanting this to end.

"Just coffee's good." She smiled, looked at a handwritten sign on the wall, maybe wondering what chop suey was doing in an Austrian joint, along with the head cheese, what Luka called his house specialties.

Lifting his cup, he blew across it, sipping. "So, think you might go back to nursing sometime?"

"That really what you want to talk about?" She flicked her hand, meaning it was alright. "Used to think it picked me, like a calling. They needed nurses on account of all the ones they sent overseas, so I signed up. When they got done with their war, head nurse at the Grant wanted me to stay on, so I stayed. Guess I liked feeling I was doing some good. And did plenty of it when the riots ran hot, the hospital short-staffed the whole time, had me working double shifts. Now, they're cutting back . . ." She shrugged.

"Hard times."

"I got no complaints. And the dancing's not so bad, except for some of the gents coming in, thinking pawing a woman is dancing, hoping it'll go someplace more. Some gals oblige, needing the money for feeding their kids. I don't know, but that's not me — in case I gave out the wrong idea."

"I got it — just coffee."

"Just coffee."

"Happy just getting to know you . . ."

"All dogs got ideas, even the lame ones come sniffing."

"Meaning men are dogs?"

"More like open books, except half the ones coming in can't read."

Huck glanced around, saying, "How about we cut a rug sometime? I mean, someplace nice with a decent band."

"When I'm off the floor, it feels like time served — and I got the sore feet to prove it."

"Was thinking a church dance, a dine-and-dance, cabaret, something like that."

"Like a date?"

"Like a date."

"Mostly, I'm wore out and no kind of company. Happy to be home soaking my feet, dropping in bed — alone, you understand?"

"Then how about just the eating part. I bet you do that. Then I'll get you home, and you can soak or drop in bed, either one."

"And you're not going to try and come inside?"

"Only if you ask."

"Could turn out we're like chalk and cheese."

"One way to find out." He took his tobacco and papers, rolling one, offering it to her.

Taking a pack of Cameos from her pocket, she let him light her up. "And if I did ask you in for a nightcap? What would you say?"

"I'd say a thing like that's not even legal." Huck smiled.

"Even what the druggist sells?"

"Any of it beats the poison at your dance joint." Huck glad she wasn't sounding like the temperance type, nothing like that Hatchet Granny who used to go around busting up all the blind pigs and gin joints someplace in Kentucky. That old granny would get no rest in this town, everybody nipping on the sly, everybody making money on it, and every back-door politician and city official picking at the bones. All of them likely to string that granny up from a lamppost.

"Went with the girls to the Four Deuces one time after work, safety in numbers on account of the seedy area. You ever been?"

Huck shook his head, dragging on his smoke. That place being one of Torrio's joints.

"Had a Bee's Knees. Admit it was kinda nice."

"Bee's Knees, huh?" Huck looked at her fingers wrapping the cup — nice thin fingers.

"It's a drink. You know drinks got names, right?" Gave another shrug and she sipped. "The girls going for gin rickeys and sidecars, one ordered a Mary Pickford. You know who that is?"

"The one from the picture shows?"

"The waiter called her America's Sweetheart, told how she was in Havana with her new hubby, you know, Douglas Fairbanks, and Charlie Chaplin was there. Bartender takes one look at her and mixes up a drink on the spot and names it for her, saying her name with that cute accent." Her eyes flashed for a moment, then she looked back at him. "Guess that sounds loopy."

"You try it, the Mary drink?" Huck thinking he could barely tell bathtub gin from petrol. Picking up his cup, drinking the bitter coffee, wondering how long since Luka had brewed it.

"Told us Mary wasn't her real name, Pickford either. I forget what the real one was. Don't know why I'm even talking about it."

"Must feel funny, changing your name, like you're gonna be somebody else," he said.

"Maybe on the screen, it's like that, being somebody else. We got told to come up with names for dancing. Something supposed to sound alluring, the way Henry told us."

"Henry's a pimp."

She was nodding. "Calls it one of his house rules, if you can imagine a shady joint with house rules."

"Funny, you don't look like the house-rule kind."

"You're back to wondering if Lizzy's my real name . . ."

"Maybe I'll find out."

Looking at him like she was wondering how far to trust him, then saying, "The whole thing's Karla Mae Eliza Bow — used to be Bono till they shortened it. There, you happy?"

"Your folks have trouble picking just one?"

"Karla from the old world, Mae for the new one, and Eliza's after my nagymama, one that passed before I was born." She waited a moment, saying, "This is where you tell me about yours."

"Huck's short for Huckabee, Huckabee Waller, like I told you."

"It's a good one, but you mind me yawning while I drink this? Two of us talking about Bee's Knees and the history of names."

"Just getting to know each other. What say I stop by the Alley Cat sometime, we'll have that dance, then go and talk some more."

"No chinning on company time. I step off the floor, and Henry puts on another gal, then I'm done for the night — another of his house rules." She tugged up the collar of her coat, warding off the chill.

"The man ought to learn about fair play."

"He makes the rules."

"Well, I'd like to see you again."

"Should tell you I'm not on my own."

"You're hitched?" Now he looked surprised.

"Not that, no." The look on his face made her smile.

"A jealous cat?"

"A nagymama."

"A what?"

"It's my grandma." She was smiling again. "In Hungarian."

"The one that passed?"

"The other one, you know we all got two, right?"

"How'd you get away with no accent?"

"I was born and raised in Burnside."

"South of the tracks?"

"A place called the Triangle. Home to the Hunkies coming off the boats, the poppas working the Nickel Plate, Pullman, Burnside Steel, one yard or another. Schooled at Our Lady of Hungary, the playground with the chimney stacks blowing soot. Place I grew up's between a barroom and boarding-house. The way it was, the way it still is. There you go, now you know more."

He liked hearing it, getting to know her. "You moved out, making your own way, took your naggy mamma with you."

"Nagymama. And what I did, I went from nursing to big-time entertainer." Her eyes smiling again. "That's all you get till I hear more of your story."

"Well, I'm mick on the old man's side, what he called it. My momma was from the Alps someplace — slide down one side you're saying, 'Grüezi,' take another slope and you say, 'Ciao.' He told us boys to keep mum about the bosch roots, 'less we end up in one of them camps. The old man liked joking about her being gone, guess to lighten it up. Used to cook the only German dish he knew, called it *Grießbrei* or something like that — the most awful slop — used to joke we could eat it or set bricks with it."

She made a face, saying it sounded awful.

"Only time he didn't joke was when Wilson lined with the Brits. Used to tell us boys it's why his folks came here way back, to get away from the English, that and going hungry back where they came from — getting called the Famine Irish, that and a lot worse."

"You said 'us,' you and your brother?"

"Yeah, Arlen. When Wilson blew the charge, the old man spoke against us signing with Uncle Sam, thinking it better to get labeled of low morale."

"This the brother that died?"

Huck nodded, recalled the push to buy bonds again — you didn't buy them, somebody took down your name. Somebody was always watching and taking down names. His old man refusing to support the war effort.

"Had an uncle got put in one of them blimps they sent over the channel, think they were spying and dropping bombs. Remember my momma crying when she got the letter, you know the one?"

"Yeah, with the black. Sorry to hear it." Huck shook his head, catching himself from talking more about Arlen. Pushing those thoughts away, saying, "The old man got on with the sheriffs during wartime. Made sergeant after a shootout in the courthouse, some guy avenging on a prisoner awaiting trial, accused of killing the shooter's brother, something like that. The old man made sergeant, could've made lieutenant, even had notions of running for sheriff when he was in his cups. Figured there were enough Irish around to get him the vote."

"He run?"

"He got shot — in the leg. Some drugstore robbery in the Quarter gone wrong. Wasn't even on duty, just coming out of the hardware next door — a bag of roofing nails. Walked with a hitch after that, guess he lost the urge for running." Told her after that they moved to Bogalusa, his dad taking a job with the sawmill, busting up union meetings.

"I've got to stop asking all these questions."

"All that's a long time back." Thinking he was being a wet blanket.

After a while, she said, "Think he would've got the vote, your old dad?"

"Remember him saying, 'A Lugan won't vote for a Pole, and a Pole won't vote Lugan. The Bosch won't vote for either one, but all three'll vote Irish.' Figured if he did run, he'd be alderman by now."

"So, do you offer me a lift back or make me hoof it?" Her smile was magic.

"Gent sees a lady home where I come from — especially this time of night, in a town like this."

"Except I let you drive me back, then you'll know where I live."

"Can't see no other way."

"I could blindfold you."

"Drive with my eyes covered?"

"Have to trust me to be your eyes."

"I can't tell if you're kidding."

"You expect me to trust you." She was playing again, and he liked that. She picked up her cup, looking thoughtful, then she reached across the table, ran her fingertip along his scarred knuckles. "You hold the steering kinda tight, huh?"

"Did some boxing. Well, I used to. Retired from it now."

"Ever do anything easy?"

"Tried to play some flattop back home, but turned out I was all thumbs."

"So, you went around hitting people instead?"

"But did it with a song in my heart." He matched her smile, saying, "I could tell you there's a science to it."

"That what happened to your nose, science?"

"I'm not a thug, nothing like that."

"I wasn't thinking that, like you're not thinking I'm some hoofer on the low track."

"Maybe I could take you to the fights sometime, and you can see for yourself — the science of it."

"And watch grown men go down swinging? That, or stay home and soak my feet. Hmm." Looking thoughtful, that playful look in her eyes. "Tell me about this music you didn't play on a flattop?"

"Porch music." Seeing she didn't know what that was, he explained it, then said, "Plan on getting back to it someday."

"So, you gave up the strumming for punching?"

"Something like that."

She finished her cup, reached into her bag, pulled out a scarf, smiling, saying, "You ready?"

"You really want to blindfold me?"

Her smile widened. "You trust me, or not?"

31

Shrinking into her coat to keep warm, Karla was opening the taxi's door, now looking like she wasn't sure, saying, "This is fine, I'm just around the corner."

"You going to keep me blindfolded?" Huck couldn't peek past the blindfold, thinking he had to be crazy driving Chicago streets, letting this woman hold the steering wheel, correcting, guiding and telling him, "Left, a bit more left, now right . . . oh, you've got traffic coming." Huck seeing headlight glare through her scarf. Thinking he could die right now, catching the scent on that scarf, something she was wearing, that soap smell he remembered from Grant Hospital, the first time he put eyes on her. And he had kept it on, giving it gas when she told him, turning the wheel left or right at her say-so. Driving a dozen frozen blocks, going slow with wool before his eyes, letting her keep him to the center of his side of the road. Only jolted against the curb twice, or maybe it was a parked car.

"This neighborhood, how'd that look, bringing home a blindfolded man?" And she pulled it off him in a single tug.

"Look like you're taking a hostage." He was rapid-blinking his eyes, taking in the surroundings.

That got her giggling, not the woman who had been on guard. Saying, "I can look out for myself, you know?"

"I can see that, and I see there's plenty more I want to know."

"Like what?"

"What I got so far's a nurse that likes to dance, goes by Lizzy, then turns out to be Karla Mae Eliza Bow. Goes for a coffee and ends up taking a chance."

"And I've got a fellow who's part security, part fighter playing Boy Scout."

"With a musical side."

"Well, the jury's out on that."

"How come?"

"You wouldn't know you got rhythm, I mean, the way you dance."

"Thought you were kidding about the two left feet." Huck acting like he was surprised.

She stopped herself from getting out, leaning back across the seat, her lips brushing his cheek, the way you might kiss an uncle. Halfway out of the cab, she said, "Seeing you're in security, guess it'd be alright, you can escort me to the door."

Huck making a three-finger salute, the way he'd seen it done somewhere. They got out and went around the next corner, Huck looking up at a brick tenement, four stories tall.

At the steps, she stifled a yawn, saying, "Got to warn you I'm a bit of a flat tire, all night on the dance floor's catching up."

"And how about your nagymama?"

"I made her up, at least the living with me part — come on," she said, taking his arm, leading him up the steps to the door.

"No more blindfold?"

"'Less you think we need it?"

32

Walking into the Alley Cat — the joint hopping tonight, thick with smoke and funky smells — Huck nodded to bouncer Declan. Edging his way to the makeshift bar, he squeezed between bookend drunks and sat on a stool, Huck nodded to Husky, one of the Yellow drivers down the line, the man looking bent, grinning and hoisting a glass to Huck, spilling some down his shirt front, downing the rest before he spilled more.

Glancing over the heads to the far wall, he was looking for Karla. They'd been seeing each other regular for a while, and he liked coming in to pick her up, but he couldn't see much past the bodies milling and crowding the dance floor. Snooky and Curtis were doing some kind of dance that looked halfway between a barn dance and a waltz, hoofing it with a couple of the nickel gals. The song ended and the two of them made their way to the bar.

"So, you still the watchdog, huh?" Snooky edged toward him, his hair wet from whatever he'd been doing on the dance floor — looked like he'd been swimming — reaching an empty jar off the bar.

"Something like that."

"Remember that time, getting the stink out of Clement's rig, goddamn stink hanging on for dear life. The man quit on account of it, and Moses made me scrub the stink out, must've used a pound of that lye soap. You remember? Ended ripping the seats out."

"Yeah." Huck looked at him, the apprentice in his cups, his head bobbing, skinny body swaying, words getting caught on his tongue.

"Them Checker fuckers still got some payday coming on that score, I'd say." Snooky looking at him like he was hoping Huck had more to say on it.

"Sure thing." Leaning on the bar top, Huck was taking in the number the band was murdering, trying to get Henry the barman's attention.

Keeping up the chinwag while waving the empty jar, Snooky went on, "Hear they laid for you too, and with your boy on board."

"Not my boy, but yeah, Izzy was there — and an old woman riding in back. Was a while back now."

"The one sued the outfit."

"That's right."

Snooky looked into the empty jar like he was disappointed, then slammed it on the bar, saying, "Goddamn Checker!"

Got a "hear hear" from Curtis, the man on the far side. Signaling Henry the barman for a refill, Snooky said to Huck, "You pretty flush these days, brother — old man Hertz sure taking a shine to you." Then his eyes lit like an idea came to him. "Say, it ought to be me buying, but seeing it's two days off'n payday, and you keeping in reg'lar work, making a pile more'n what any of us are making . . ."

Huck looked to Henry, who was serving drinks, taking his time coming down the bar, Huck wanting to find Karla and get her out of this hotbox of a place after she was done, feeling his suit start to stick to him. Looking across the floor again, but not seeing her.

"Yeah, ought to be me buying, sure enough 'cept . . ." Snooky wasn't giving up, then he gave a start and hopped off the stool with a jolt, looking down where the seat had been unscrewed, realizing he'd been sitting on the round of the metal post sticking up. "Well, God almighty, ain't that a fine howdy-do. Who stole the sitting part?" Putting a hand to his backside, feeling the tear in his britches, it set him off cursing.

Curtis took in his predicament, laughing and pointing.

Giving a pitiful look, Snooky pulled out his pant's pocket, showing he had nothing but lint, saying to Huck, "Like I been saying, brother, ought'a be me buying . . ."

Huck nodded to Henry, held up two fingers in a V, thinking here was the real crime, what these speaks were charging for a drink of this watered liquor. But the barman didn't see him, or was ignoring him.

"Hear ol' Clem ended on some job line," Snooky said, nodding his thanks, standing over the post now. "But good to see you're doin' alright."

"I'm getting by," Huck said, getting annoyed with Henry for taking his sweet time, Huck here to deliver three crates of whiskey, had them in the trunk of the taxi out front, doing a favor for Gorilla Al. Glad to make the stop on account it meant catching a dance with Karla, hoping to get her out of there after.

"That man's solid gold in my book — was with the company from the get-go," Snooky said, catching hold of Huck's sleeve. "And pay it no mind, what the fellas are saying 'round the place."

"Saying about what — me?" Huck pulled his arm away.

"Ah, you know how they talk, like old hens. How they got rid of Clem, making room for you. But hey, it don't mean beans to me, brother." The grimy hand back on Huck's sleeve.

Annoyed by the hand, this suit costing him ten bucks, Huck watched Henry splash whiskey from a jug into two jars, then slid them across to the men along the bar, coming this way now.

"Didn't ask my pleasure," Huck said to Henry.

"Whiskey and wimmen. One's here, the other's there." Henry glanced to the dance floor, then to the jug in his hand, saying, "It's this or nothing — your boys being slow bringing it in." Meaning he usually served the good stuff to O'Banion's lads that made the deliveries, not the watered stuff he served to the patrons.

"Got three cases in my trunk."

"Then bring 'em in the back."

Snooky slid his glass forward, Henry telling him, "No credit."

"It's on me," Huck said, indicating with his finger a round for Snooky and Curtis, fishing coins from his pocket, setting fifty cents down, waiting till Henry poured.

Tasting from his glass, Snooky winced, saying, "Tapped from the pump handle fixed to an ethyl barrel out back."

"Don't like it, go drink someplace else," Henry said.

"Like I said, I got three crates in my trunk. You want it, send Declan to fetch it."

"That's right, you're getting that top-dog look, standing here in your dandy suit. Say, what does something like that set you back?"

Huck just looked at him, this barman not going to get a rise out of him, his big bouncer at the door, looking this way.

"And that hoofer, the one you took out of here, how's she faring?"

"Lizzy," Snooky said, blinking his eyes like something just flew into one. "That's a fine dish alright."

"Best we leave her out of it," Huck said. "Now, you want the crates, or I can take 'em back."

"Can see me and Declan are busy, but go on and grab a gal, have a spin while you wait, just don't run off with this one. Fella might take them for Sisters of St. Francis, on account of the pretty smiles, but they're just happy not getting their feet tromped." Nothing friendly in the way Henry said it. "Anything more'n a dance, and you got to talk 'em up, or go see their man out back." Meaning one of the pimps hanging around the alley behind the place. "Bet you remember how it goes."

"Not trying to steal your dancer, Henry. If she leaves, then she's got good sense and does it on her own." Huck figured there was no point reaching over the bar and socking Henry, doing what would likely get a couple of these drunks and Declan jumping at him.

Snooky said he'd bring the crates in, do it as a favor, and Huck set a couple more coins down, watching Henry pour another splash of juice into the glass, Snooky tipping it up, the man's mouth open like a carp's, his Adam's apple bobbing. Emptying it in a swallow, he slapped the jar down on the bar, saying, "Like mother's milk." Making a satisfied smack of the lips, reaching in the empty pocket like he forgot. Looking at Huck again, ever hopeful.

Huck turned to go — thinking he'd go back and tell Gorilla Al to deliver it himself — catching sight of them coming in past Declan, the three men from the Stutz, plus a couple more, all wearing long coats. Remembering the way the red-haired one laughed on the passenger side when they bounced Huck over the curb, just before they sent him crashing through the produce cart and into the shop front.

They stood now, eyeing the room, the tall one pointing to the dance floor. Vito and Buzz and a couple of Yellow drivers were dancing with the nickel gals. The boys galumphing like they were heel-pounding nails, unaware trouble just walked in. The three men from the Stutz moved to the dance floor, the others going toward the bar.

They made their way through the crowded place, pushing folks aside, getting to the dance floor, the Jimmy Joy Orchestra, the sign still saying *For One Night Only*. The leader scratching a bow across a fiddle, sounding like he was mimicking a cat on a back fence, the band making a mess of "Ain't We Got Fun."

Huck looked along the bar for any more Yellow drivers down the line from Snooky and Curtis. Then he was pushing his way through, past swinging elbows and dancing feet. A couple more men walked in the front of the place, Huck getting set for what was coming. Shoving his way onto the floor, past a dancing couple, grabbing for Vito's sleeve.

"Well, if it ain't the old ass kisser." Puckering his mouth, Vito made a kissing sound, kept on clomping his feet.

Wasn't what Huck expected, the first guy to hit him was one of his own. Not much of a punch that landed square on his jaw, but it knocked him back, into another man dancing, and that sparked what came next. The place erupting.

Knuckles flew out of nowhere, crashed into Vito's kissing mouth, sending him sputtering and reeling into his dance partner, knocking the nickel hopper backward into Buzz. Sending that man into another man standing by the make-shift stage, spilling the man's whiskey, knocking over the *For One Night Only* sign. The place was in full motion. The man shaking off his spilled whiskey, shoving Buzz, then going after him, grabbing for his throat.

Huck seeing the red-haired Stutz man coming at him, his fist cocked back.

Huck got slammed from behind, the blow to the ear sending him reeling sideways, the redhead's fist going past his eyes, landing against Vito's jaw. The fight going like fire in a cornfield, the whole place jumping.

Ducking another punch, Huck stumbled right, keeping to his feet, turning and facing off with Snooky, just bought the man a drink, now the drunk was swinging at him, calling him a son of a bitch. Huck shoved him aside, trying to get to the back door.

Spotting the wheelman of the Stutz, a giant of a man, at the same time the giant saw him, coming for him now, shoving men out of his way, throwing a haymaker that Huck ducked. Buzz threw himself into the fray, trying to drag the giant to the floor. The big man shook him off and hit Buzz, knocking him down, the man flopping out cold.

The whole place had gone from drinking and dancing to punching, clawing, and biting. The bar-top door got pushed over, the sound of crashing glass, yelling and screams of pain.

The band had halted like a heart attack after the first punch, the Jimmy Joy boys fleeing the stage, cradling their instruments and trying for the back way out.

Huck threw an elbow at the driver of the Stutz, then caught one on the jaw. A jug shattering against Vito's skull, the man dropping again to the floor. The Stutz man catching Huck with a solid blow, sending him down too. Huck balling his fingers into fists, saving them from getting stomped. One of the hoppers landed next to him, a cut on her forehead. Recognizing Karla's Black friend, Huck got his feet under him, pulling the woman up, and making for the exit, all around them men were grabbing and punching, another man crashing into him, out cold before he hit the floor, his sweaty head bleeding at the scalp.

Yelling and more grunts and fists flying. His vision blurred and his ears were ringing, Huck had hold of the woman, shoving her ahead of him for the exit. No helping Buzz, Vito or Snooky, the other Yellow men lost in the fray behind him.

Someone grabbed hold of Jimmy Joy's fiddle, raising it up and smashing it over the giant's head, the Stutz man forgetting about Huck and clutching hold of the man, lifting him in the air by the neck, smashing his face with his free hand.

Huck pushed the woman forward, the woman crying, her hands over her mouth. Then Buddy the red-haired man found him and came at him again, Huck cocking his head back, the fist missing him and catching the crying woman full in the face, her nose crushed, a wash of blood erupting behind a look of shock, the woman dropping back, Huck trying to catch her, taking a blow to the back for it. Turning for Buddy, but he was gone, disappearing in the sea of grunting and groaning. Huck moved the woman forward, in sight of the door now.

Then Snooky was there next to him, face bloody with a big welt forming at his temple, and Huck caught hold of his shirtfront and had him moving for the door, herding the two of them through the mob, wary of getting hit from all sides. No sign of the Stutz men now, swallowed in the free-for-all. Shoving the two for the open door, feeling the press of bodies and the fresh cold of the night, stepping over a man sprawled on the floor, Huck thinking it looked like Henry the barman.

Ducking a raised stool, Huck pressed them into the mass milling at the door, all of them trying to get out at once. Stage crates were tossed behind him, smashing glass and splashing whiskey. Now he was smelling smoke, chancing a glance back, seeing the glimmer of fire where the bar had stood.

Vito was with them now, pushing from behind to get out. Struck across the back, Huck didn't turn, just kept going. A hand clutched at his collar, Huck heel-kicking and the man let go with a yelp. Snooky had hold of the nickel dancer's arm, helping her to the door. A crate was flung, smashing against the wall to their right.

All around, the dance floor was fists flying and kicking feet, some bodies out on the floor, the fight a living thing — the fire glowing.

Ahead of him, the Black woman moved past two men punching hell out of each other, and she was running as soon as she got past the door. Somebody on the floor tugged at Huck's pant leg, trying to pull himself up. Huck shaking him off. A bottle crashed across a skull to his right, glass and booze spraying.

Somebody yelling, "Po-leece!"

A body collided into him and toppled through the doorway. Huck pressing Snooky through, stepping on somebody's fingers. Hearing the coppers inside, breaking up the fight with nightsticks, yelling and blowing whistles for order. Huck wondering if he could get to the taxi out front.

A fist caught the side of his face, Huck getting knocked sideways, tasting blood. Turning on a big-boned man, the man trying to headbutt him. Lowering his chin, Huck grabbed hold, bringing his knee up hard, catching the man square in the groin, the man crumbling. Losing sight of Snooky and the nickel hopper, seeing Vito being thrown through the doorway by Declan. Others rushing out and scattering.

A whistle blew inside, then a pistol shot, the cops trying to clear out the burning place. Huck wanting to avoid a night in a city tank of puke and piss, waiting on his appearance before some judge, happy to hand out thirty days in the hole.

Somebody yelling, "Stop!" from out in the lot, a copper coming around the side of the next building, sidestepping a row of trash cans.

The folks out back scattered like ants, going in all directions. The cop was coming straight at Huck, with his billy in the air.

Going with the swing of it, Huck grabbed the wrist and pulled the cop forward, twisting his hip and throwing them both, Huck landing hard on the man, knocking away the night stick. Getting up, Huck started to back away, the cop clearing his head, clawing to unholster his revolver, calling him a son of a bitch.

Huck seeing the trashcan go up, wet trash sloshing out. The cop turned as Snooky brought the inverted can down over the cop's head and shoulders, pinning him, the cop's yells echoing inside, his pistol going off, firing into the air.

Bending for the billy, Snooky knocked the pistol away, then bashed at the can, the cop unable to push it off. Snooky chopping a blow at the cop's knee, the lawman's cry echoing inside the trash can as he tumbled back, writhing on the ground. Tossing away the stick, Snooky picked up the pistol, and hurried alongside Huck, getting out of there, following the nickel hopper's steps and drops of blood in the snow, the woman out of sight as they got out to the street.

Snooky saying, sounding sober now, "How about them bottles you brung?"

Huck just looked at him, feeling scraped and bruised, the pocket of his suit nearly torn off. Feeling the knot at the side of his head, the throbbing inside his skull, not sure how many times he'd been hit. He led the way around the building, knowing he'd never hear the end of it around the depot, how Snooky saved the guy who was supposed to be watching out for them, their now hundred-bucks-a-week man needing help from the apprentice.

From a distance, they watched a paddy wagon roar up, racing past them, Snooky tossing the copper's pistol away, and the two making their way to the front of the building, getting in the Yellow, Huck driving the hell out of there, dropping Snooky off, giving him one of the cases for his trouble.

He made his way to the block where Karla lived, in spite of being blindfolded he pieced together the route. Remembering the corner of the tenement, parking the taxi, taking a bottle from the remaining crates and going up the stairs, standing in front of her door, his suit ripped in a couple of other places, hoping it could be sewn.

She asked who it was before cracking the door open, seeing it was him, taking the chain off, pulling the door open, taking a look at his condition, saying, "Let me guess . . . the noble art?"

"I understand you're a nurse."

33

"**I** was hoping you had some liniment on hand." Standing and looking along the drafty hallway, a single bulb on a cord halfway down. Not wanting to wake the neighbors, not a sound coming from these walls looking thin as pasteboard.

"That's what you come for, liniment?"

Handing her the bottle, reaching in his pocket, he held up a bent ticket stub. "And a dance?"

"Never should've let you take off the blindfold." Holding the door as far as the chain allowed and looking at him like she was unsure.

"Didn't see you tonight, the Alley Cat — missed my dance."

"That's your line?"

"I wanted to see you."

"Better."

"Wild horses couldn't keep me away."

"Looks like they tried." Looking at him a moment longer, saying, "So, you going to tell me what happened, or just stand there while you heal?" She motioned him in, wanting him out of the hall. Turned and set the bottle on the counter, gave him a kiss, then was checking the fresh bruises on his face.

He told her what happened at the Alley Cat, about the Checker men coming in spoiling for a fight, tearing up the place. "The whole place broke out, all trying to go out the door at one time, thinking it's better to get trampled than busted."

"The place still standing?"

"Was on fire last time I looked."

"A hundred places around, and you pick mine to burn down."

"Was just making a delivery."

"Landing right in the middle of it."

"Right place, wrong time." He flipped up his hands in surrender.

"Think it follows you like you got it on a leash." Going to the door, she flipped the lock out of habit, slipping the chain on. Taking hold of his sleeve, she eased him over to the lamp, getting a better look at the swelling on his face, running her fingers along his cheek. There was a book lying face down on the table, the table lamp the only light in the room.

He caught the soap smell again, thinking he could get used to it, saying, "If I turned and walked away every time, what'd that make me?"

"Quick on the uptake." She said he could do with some ice, then asked, "Any place you don't hurt?"

"Lucky I'm good at healing up." Trying not to groan as he sat in the chair.

"From the sound, I'm out of work — again."

"Be glad to drive you, look around for something else." Huck looked around the room, small and dark, the bed, the chair he was in, a chest of drawers, a cooktop on a table, dishes and cups in two neat stacks, a shelf next to the table with a row of books. "You been reading, huh?" Reaching for the shelf, stopping and asking, "You mind?"

"Be my guest." She watched him, saying, "Didn't see you as the reading kind."

"That young fella, Izzy, he goes for it, just sits and reads."
Huck flipped the pages, not saying he could hardly read his
own name till Izzy started teaching him, no pictures helping
him out in this one, saying, "All of ten and he teaches himself
to do it."

"Didn't learn it in school?"

"Told me his mom, maybe it was the nuns helped him
too, but mostly, he took it up on his own."

"Sounds like quite the fellow."

"You ought to meet him."

She nodded, looking at him like she guessed there was
more coming.

"Told me about some of the books he's got. One about a
captain going out on the sea after a whale that run off with
his leg."

"Moby Dick."

"That's it. And another one about a fellow called Huck,
same as me, and some of his capers."

"Huckleberry Finn."

"Sounds like you two got the same books." He picked up
the one she'd been reading.

She stepped close, pointing to the cover, saying, *"Main
Street* by Sinclair Lewis."

"Any good?"

"About a young woman with dreams of redesigning towns.
Not one your young friend's likely to read." She reached along
the shelf, pulling another one out, saying, "This one's about an
orphan who falls into the criminal life, but it's not as grim as
all that, and it's filled with the most delightful characters. Why
don't you take it along and see if your young friend likes it?"

"I can't just take your book."

"Why not?"

"Well, it wouldn't be —"

"Yes?"

198

He didn't have an answer.

"That's what books are for, to be read."

He thanked her, holding it, saying, "Sure, he'll like it. Orphans, huh?"

"If he likes Twain and Melville, I think he might go for Dickens."

"Well, I'll let you know what he says." Huck nodded again, promising to return it. Noticing the sleeved 78s next to the lined books, but no Victrola, thinking he'd ask about that another time.

"Penny for your thoughts."

"Just so I got it right, you live on your own, not with your nanny . . ."

"Nagymama — grandmother. I told you that, didn't know you then."

"But you trust me now."

"Let's say I'm getting closer." She glanced around the room, went and took a framed photo, showing it to him, saying, "My nagy had me believing shining knights are like unicorns — meaning mostly make-believe. Taught me to trust slow."

"Well, I can't say I measure up to unicorns."

"But you don't put on the chichi — what you see's what you get, the way I'm seeing you."

Setting the book down, he took her hand, drawing her to him, saying, "I heard all kinds of things growing up, how to be in the world. Maybe some's true, but you wouldn't know it by looking at most of the folks saying it."

"Don't think you and I need to worry about the too-perfect part, me dancing for nickels, and you showing up with your bruises, middle of the night."

This close, the light was shining in her eyes, the nicest eyes he'd ever seen.

"About that dance?" she said, holding the ticket between two fingers.

"You mean here?" Hardly any room to move in the place.

"Why not? I mean you paid the dime."

"No music, I mean I see you got records, but no Victrola, but still, I guess if the mood's right . . ."

"Let's see, I just found out I got no work to go to, it's late, and here I am standing with a banged-up fellow, and I've got no music. Got a bottle of temptation, or I got tea — you like tea?"

"I like tea, love temptation."

"Tea it is." And she took the kettle from a shelf, poured water from a pitcher and set the kettle on the burner and lit the pilot.

"We start stepping around in here, we're bound to knock something over and likely wake the whole place," he said.

"I wasn't thinking the Charleston." She came over to him. "And if I get turned out, we can dance in the street." And she started swaying, saying, "Maybe best if you kick off your shoes." She took his hand, and she let him lead, the floorboards creaking under their feet, and they danced slow as the kettle started whistling its tune.

"Still wondering, why me? Lots of gals in that place, all of them good looking."

"I only saw you." Feeling his cheeks go red in the dim light. "That scare you?"

"Just a little."

34

"**H**ow you feel about getting hitched?" Huck sat up in bed, his head against the wall, Karla under the covers, looking up at him surprised. How long had it been? They'd been together a dozen times by his count, taking her to the Chuck Wagon, tapping on her door after a run to Canada, or the time he showed up after the Alley Cat burned down, all beat up, his clothes ripped, letting her apply the antiseptic, the two of them dancing to no music, always ending up in her bed.

"You sure got your romantic notions, Huckabee Waller." Looking at him like he might be kidding, or gone goofy, coming to her place late again, the unexpected becoming expected.

"Let's say you got me thinking about it."

"My nagy said every girl ought to get herself hitched and have kids, that or risk turning spinster. I don't know, maybe it was more of a warning."

"Are you ducking the question?"

"You asked how I felt about it."

"Well?"

"I'm wondering if you're serious."

"Why wouldn't I be?"

"Just give me a minute, nobody's ever not asked me, not like that." She fanned herself with her fingers, like it was suddenly hot.

"By not like that — meaning you been asked before?"

"Had a fella one time, let's say we . . . never mind."

"Were going to say you came close. How close?"

"You asking if he popped the question or something else?"

Huck shook his head, saying, "Suppose I got no right to ask that."

"You want to know if I ever think about us like that? Well, I guess I have, seeing where it goes."

"You're tangling me all up."

"Maybe if you ask me straight and stop pawing the ground."

"You don't want to talk about it, that's okay." He turned to the window, hiding the smile. "How's the weather, snowing again?"

"Start over and do it proper." She play-slapped his arm.

"Who was this fella that didn't ask you before?"

She sighed, saying, "Jimmy turned out to be a wet blanket, back when I was wet behind the ears once upon a time, talked about having a house and filling it with babies. Folks always telling me that's what I ought to do. Now out with it."

"Why this Jimmy, I mean —"

"Like I said, I didn't know better." She sat up, pulling the blanket over her breasts, sighing and saying, "Don't ask how, but I found out there was this waitress, some breakfast joint he went to, getting his eggs over easy."

"Two-timing, you mean?"

"Didn't come out and say so, but dewy-eyed as I was, I smelled it on him — her smell."

"You sent him packing?"

"Not thinking straight, I went to this breakfast joint, mostly to see what she looked like, maybe to mess up her looks."

"You clobbered her?" Huck lifting his brows.

"Wanted to know what it was she had — only she wasn't on shift that day. Can't believe I was that naïve."

"So, no cat fight?"

"Found out where she lived and went banging on her door. Hoping for a bug-eyed Betty, but she was hardly that, tall and pretty. Said who I was and her jaw drops like she's seen a ghost. Woman was Elouise — turned out, what he told her, I was his dearly departed, lost to him in childbirth, at the start of the riots. Doctors at the hospital had their hands full of dead and dying, and couldn't tend to me right."

"Jimmy, the lying sack of flop."

"Anyway, this Elouise got fed the same lies, the creep worming his way into her heart and her bed, and cheating on her too."

"Don't need to talk about it," Huck said, feeling bad for asking.

"Know what she told me? I wasn't what she expected."

"You mean being alive?"

"Told me he wrote her a poem. I said I never got one and asked to see it, and she got it from a scrapbook and read it, the two of us laughing at something that corny, something like, 'Every time I look in your eyes, it reminds me of you. Those eyes are like sapphires painted blue.' If you can believe it, a mug writing something like that. Anyway, we had a good laugh, the two of us taking it and tearing it up, burning the bits on her stove."

"And you left him?"

"Uh uhn. I had Elouise to supper. Told Jimmy I made a friend at the market and invited her over, hoping it was alright with him, after all, him about to become the man of the house. Before he started up, acting all lord and master, going on about the food he worked skin and teeth for, she was knocking at the door. Should've seen him go colors like he wasn't getting air — thought he was gonna keel right there on the rug." Karla grinned. "Asked him, 'What's the matter, Jimmy? You see a ghost?'"

Huck was laughing, "You got the devil in you, girl."

"Two of us got him sitting at the table, serving him chops, cabbage and beans. He looks at me, then her, maybe he figures it could work out, two women and one bed, who knows what went on in Jimmy's belfry. Stuck his fork in his mouth, chewing like he had a cloth tongue. I asked him if his pork was toothsome.

"Tell the truth, I was having a time. Elouise says we ought to do it again sometime, her place next time, that is if he pulled through. He gives her this look, then me, then down at his pork, his eyes going round, then he gets scared, then he gets mean, tells me if I was any kind of dame it wouldn't have happened, him needing more. Looks at her and asks what kind of hussy does a thing like that, cheats on a man's wife-to-be — then folds his arms and says he's not the one leaving. So I told him for sure he was leaving, likely on a gurney, and he starts to get up like he's gonna take his belt to me, and I tell him the more he jumps around, the faster the borax'll work. He gives me his sheep look, and I point at his plate and ask if I got to spell it out, then he starts grabbing his neck. Told him I'd been spilling it in his food, tablespoon at a time, since I found out about the cheating, about two weeks' worth. I couldn't believe it, he starts gagging for real, getting this look like he's really seen a ghost — maybe his own ghost."

"You really do it?"

"He figured I did, what doctors call a placebo."

"He still with us, on this mortal plane?" Huck asked, guessing he should tell her about Izzy living in his flat, instead of saving it for the right time.

"The man's dead to me, him and all his secrets — that's all I'm going to say."

"You know, that's the best duck-around I ever heard."

"I'm sure I don't know what you mean." Her eyes were dancing, her cheeks flushed, Karla playing with him again.

"You gonna marry me or not?"

"Not going to say one way or the other till you do it on one knee and proper."

"You know I had a late night, cramped in a truck, all the way from Canada, you really want me —"

She pointed to the floor.

35

"**I**t's the fine points of strike breaking, now pay attention." Getting out of the passenger side, Gypsy Doyle checked the load in the revolver, snapping the cylinder shut, tucking it in a pocket. Taking the fire axe from the back seat. He turned to the Druggan-Lake boys' sedan pulling up behind, there to join them. Four big men getting out with bats and clubs, following Doyle around the side.

Huck reached the shotgun from behind the seat, getting out as the others went around the back. Facing the livery, the lettering with icicles hanging from it like teeth, declaring the brick two-story livery was home to Checker Taxi Co. — Hack and Livery Stable. He fumbled over the words but made out the sign under the letters: *Lowest rate of fare*, and underneath that *The Thinking Fellow Calls a Checker*. Patting his pocket for the extra shells, he crossed to the center of the street, having a look around. The rest of them gone around back, Huck waiting to hear the clamor coming from inside — shouting and smashing, then the rushing of feet.

Pointing the barrels at the Checker sign, he fired at the letters, taking out the *C*, then firing again, blowing away the

ER. The sign pocked with holes, now reading *HECK*. Past the ringing in his ears, more yelling and crashing sounded from inside, another gunshot, a window bursting, the union meeting cancelled, men running out a side door, one scrambling out an upstairs window, diving to a flat roof.

Reloading, he aimed the barrels, the double-ought buck loads, stepping in front of the entrance and firing both barrels, punching the door off its hinges. Moving in as he popped the gun open, ejecting the spent shells and sliding in fresh ones, hearing more yelling out back, a car engine revving as it raced away. Snapping it shut, he went in, his ears ringing and his eyes adjusting to the dark of the place. Watching for movement, stepping over the busted door. The sound of another car speeding off.

Druggan's boys were swinging axes and bats, busting up the place, Doyle coming in from the back, the livery cleared out.

The two of them getting out of there, Huck tossing the shotgun on the back seat, Doyle dropping the fire axe on the floor, then driving off and heading up North Michigan, crossing the river, past Grand and the new construction going on, the once industrial and bohemian neighborhood giving way to retail shops, office buildings and hotels.

"Not gonna end the man's union troubles," Doyle said.

"Markin sees he's getting what he's paying for," Huck said, looking out at the construction, more tall buildings going up all the time. Having gone to Morris Markin, telling the man who he was and that he could end the man's union troubles. The Checker boss looked dumbstruck, this Yellow slugger coming into his office, the man hired by Hertz to put him out of business, offering to end his union troubles. Huck making it plain that he wouldn't lift a finger against Yellow, just against the union agitators — for a hundred a week. Oh, and he had a partner, also a hundred a week. He could have had Huck thrown out, but Markin saw that any man with the brass balls to walk in his office and offer to work both sides was likely a man to get the job done. Markin paying the two hundred a week, calling it a trial basis, also wanting a weekly report.

"That a Yellow stand?" Doyle pointed as they crossed Chicago Avenue, the stand out front of the Drake, a Checker cab pulled into the spot. "That just ain't right." Doyle saying, "Except, tell me if I'm wrong, ain't we working for Checker today?"

"Well now, that's a fine line, I suppose. The man's only paying us to ease his union troubles."

"And we done that."

"Right."

"And that there's a poacher, what Yellow hired you to take care of. You alone, and not me."

"But seeing how we're pals . . ."

"Right."

"Top of which, nothing says we can't have some kicks," Huck said, turning at Oak and finding a space to park.

Going in the Oak Street door, Huck came out the front entrance, the doorman recognizing him. Huck tipping the man, then skipped down the steps, waving to the cabbie, recognizing him as the same driver that set him up with the three men in the Stutz that time.

The Checker driver gave a friendly wave, no sign of recognition.

Huck getting in the back, saying, "This a Yellow stand, ain't it?"

"That outfit's got trouble keeping up, so Checker's helping out. You from out of town, mister?"

"Akron, just in on business." Huck nodded, telling the cabbie he was waiting on an associate, just checking out.

"Your lucky day," the Checker man said.

"How's that?"

"Yellow's jacked their fare to sixty cents a mile. At Checker, we just charge fifty."

"My lucky day then," Huck agreed, knowing they all charged the same, but he was playing the hayseed just in town on business.

"This world goes up by the minute, ain't that so?" The cabbie checked his pocket watch.

"That's the gospel," Huck settled on the back seat.

"Where you gents heading?"

"Train station." Huck looking at the front of the hotel. Doyle stopping in the lobby, chatting with a pretty woman waiting on her husband to settle with the desk. Huck hoping Doyle wasn't getting himself sidetracked.

"Got to add a nickel after five minutes," the cabbie said, happy to wait.

"You charge for waiting?"

"Well sir, time's money as they say." The cabbie gave a sympathetic smile.

"They do say that." Huck nodded.

"Akron, huh? That the one in Ohio?"

"That's the one."

"Got a twang to your voice, like you're from someplace that don't freeze in winter."

"Bogalusa originally, down New Orleans way."

"That right? A nice place?"

"Nice enough in winter, but lots of bugs and heat rest of the time."

"Oh, should let you know, Union's a five-mile ride, just so you know up front."

"At fifty a mile, huh?" Huck low-whistling like he was figuring the fare, knowing it wasn't half that far, the cabbie fleecing him like a pilgrim before he even put it in gear.

"What line you fellas in?"

"Sell conveyor belts to the auto industry."

"That right? Guess it's a good line, Ford charging better than nine hundred for one of their boilers these days."

"We sell to Hupp, Kissel, and General Motors, bunch of others. We're not choosy." Huck watched Doyle coming from the front, tipping the doorman, then coming to the taxi, getting in the front seat.

"You fellows traveling light, huh?" The cabbie noting they had no luggage, looking at Doyle's scarred face.

"Well, in our line, it pays to pack light," Doyle said, giving his missing-tooth smile. "Being in security, you got to be quick on your feet."

"Security?" The cabbie looked at Huck confused.

"Not like the Pinkertons," Huck said. "In our line we got patents to look out for, lots of breach going on."

"Conveyor belts you said?"

"That's right, security with less badge and more intervention."

"Invention, huh?"

"A fancy way of saying we get paid to spot meddlers," Doyle said.

"Meddlers, huh?"

"Ones looking to knock off our innovations," Huck said.

"Conveyor belts, who'd of thought it." And the cabbie pulled from the stand, making the turn at Oak.

"Wouldn't believe that Hudson outfit — the lengths they'll go, the dirty bag of tricks they got."

"That right, huh? Well, I'm a Ford man to the bone."

"Good old Model T," Doyle said. "No finer auto, and that fella Henry says, 'No use passing one of his, there's another Ford up ahead.'"

The cabbie smiled at that, then said, "You want the one at Union on Canal?" Meaning the station. Huck guessing it was something he learned from their previous encounter, that time Huck recited the stations and trains.

"That's right," Huck said, seeing the man heading for State, going west instead of south, where the station was.

"Good money in that, security on the conveyors?" The cabbie slowed for the heavy traffic, a bread truck stopped ahead, a line of autos trying to get around it.

"Like you wouldn't believe," Huck said, throwing in, "just got a pay hike, ten more a week."

That got the cabbie whistling again, saying, "Heck I could do with pay like that. Sorry about the traffic fellas, feel bad having to charge you the extra."

"Don't give it a thought," Huck said.

"Where'd you say, Akron?"

"Akron?" Doyle raised a brow, looking at Huck.

"One place you freeze your tail's same as the next," Huck said.

The cabbie nodded, looking at his watch again, slipping it back in his pocket. "Bet you got some fine Akron gals to keep you warm, huh?"

"Loose as a goose and so many you can't believe," Doyle said.

"Well, you boys keep talking, you're gonna get me pulling stakes. Supposing they got cabs?"

"And none of them shooting at each other."

"Can see you read about our taxi war, huh?" The cab coming to a stop, a gridlock up ahead.

"Heard something about it," Huck said.

"Truth be told, it's that Yellow outfit — they want it all for themselves." The cabbie pointed to another Yellow stand, a Yellow cab in the spot, saying, "Go around busting up our places, tipping our cabs in the street, dumping them in the river too. One with the driver still inside. Half our fleet's got bullet holes."

The Yellow driver was Vito, looking over and seeing Huck

in the back of a Checker, saluting the Checker driver and blowing him a kiss.

"How they get away with something like that?" Gypsy Doyle said.

"Wish I knew, but I can tell you it's hard for an honest man to make a living." The cabbie threw up his hand, looking at the traffic jam and sighed, saying, "Hate to do it, fellas, but I got to charge you a nickel extra every five minutes. Company rules." Taking out his watch again, looking at the dial. "Like to be up front about all the charges. Not my doing, you understand."

"Don't give it a thought, pal," Gypsy Doyle said. "We got the expense account."

"So, this security work, you say it's like the Pinkertons?"

"Only with less paperwork. Just takes a cool lid and the knack for walking in instead of running out."

"You got to be a tough son of gun then, I bet?"

"If it comes to it, but a cool head goes a long way."

"There much call for it, I mean, the meddling part?"

"The reason why we're in your fair town, matter of fact," Doyle said. "In this chillin' place, freezing our tails."

"So cold I saw a dog stuck to a fireplug this morning," the cabbie said, rubbing his hands together. "Ought to see this place in a couple months, middle of winter, no truer hell."

"Thought hell's the hot place," Doyle said.

"Till it freezes over," the cabbie said. "Open your front door, and you got snow piled to here. Takes a better part of an hour digging out and scraping ice just to find my rig. Then pray it'll start up."

The traffic started moving, and the cabbie was pointing out some skyscrapers like it was something to see. The Home Insurance Building, the site of the new Temple Building. Talking like they were taking a tour, giving them their money's worth.

"City gets bigger every time I look at it," Huck said, knowing the man got both buildings wrong.

"Got its fill of dirt labor, the ones can't speak plain English coming in by the boatloads." Swinging around a parked delivery truck, two guys offloading furniture. "If it ain't the eyeties, it's the Pomaks, yiftos, and darkies, crawling from every corner."

"That can't be good," Huck said.

"Snapping up jobs, taking work from honest men. Don't matter they can't read a map. Only thing they ever rode had a mule out front."

"Figure this weather'd scare 'em off," Doyle said.

"You'd think that, but they stick. More coming all the time. Getting themselves an old hack and getting fares lost on the wrong side of town."

Gypsy Doyle turned in the seat, looking at Huck. "Where'd you say your kin hailed from?"

"Dublin, a long way back," Huck said.

"That the boot part, what they call it on the map?"

"You're thinking Italy."

"Italy, right. What am I thinking?" Doyle clapped his own forehead, saying, "I got some of that, eyetie, you call it — Sicily on my mama's side, you heard of it?"

"That the boot part?" Huck said.

"Naw, the part that looks like the boot's kicking it. Folks came for a better life, keep from getting kicked by all the rednecks they got here."

"How d'you get here, Huck?" Doyle said.

"Rode in on a rail."

"First-class cabin — like the blue bloods?"

"Rode on top, my fingers and toes the only thing blue from the cold. Couple of dark fellows up there with me, sharing their grub and smokes, all of us getting along. Them fellas were brothers, run off by the boll weevil they said, coming north to see about this better life they been promised."

"Picked cotton back in Memphis for a while," Doyle said. "Was young enough, but I tell you, bending in the hot sun, man oh man. You fellas ever pick cotton?"

"Me, I got an aversion to back-bending," Huck said.

"We all washed up from some place, off one boat or another, ones who got here first feeling of the first water. My old man's kin running from rot and rain and the Brits," Doyle said, then to the cabbie, "Let me guess — your kin still puts sheets on their heads, ones with the holes cut out. Hold a rope and yell, 'There's one, get him.'"

"Nothing like that."

"Then like what?"

"Giving you fair warning 'bout Packingtown, is all," the cabbie said, frowning. "I seen this town get tore up, streets so you can't walk, day or night. Still plenty bad feeling about it." Sweat beading on the man's forehead in spite of the cold. "Look, I meant nothing by it."

Huck leaned forward, saying to him, "You figure his kind's been taking your jobs?"

"Didn't mean you fellas," the cabbie said, glancing back, putting his hands on the wheel.

"You taking us around town, getting stuck in traffic, making five out of a three-mile fare, overcharging every inch of the way," Huck said.

"What's this about then?" The man glanced over his shoulder.

"That train you're taking us to?"

"Yeah."

"You're getting on it," Doyle said. "Passenger or baggage, it's your choice."

"Look, I meant nothing by it, it's what they call small talk — the way folks do."

"You can get on, or we drive you to Skokie, and we bury you someplace."

"Be hard to bury him in this hard ground," Huck said.

"That's true, then we'll cover him with leaves, let the buzzards sort it out," Doyle said.

The cabbie frowned, pulling up to the front of the station, looking for a cop or a guard. Saying, "Let's call it four miles even. Forty-five cents per, that makes it a buck eighty, and forget the tip."

"Man doesn't want a tip," Doyle said, not moving to get out.

"From the hotel to here, it's three miles, tops," Huck said. "And forty-five's right, but I heard you dicker it down to a nickel that time, waiting on your pals in the Stutz to show."

The man turned in his seat, recognition flooding in now.

"Let me give you a tip . . ." Doyle reached in his coat pocket, taking a couple of dollars and holding them out, saying, "I were you, I'd hop a southbound. You rednecks ain't good at freezing."

"You can't just —" the driver said, his hand on the door handle, set to jump.

"I count five and you're still sitting there, then I start shooting." Doyle started counting. "One . . ."

"How about my cab?"

"Two . . ."

Huck watched the man grab the bills and get out, turned up his collar and hurried for the station, likely looking for a copper.

Sliding across the seat, Doyle watched the man disappear past the doors. He put it in gear and started driving. "Where to, mister?"

"Take me to the river, my good man."

36

Karla opened the door, Huck standing there with the boy, figuring most men came courting bringing a bouquet, here he was standing with his hand on the shoulder of a ten-year-old boy, the *Oliver Twist* book in his small hand.

Huck saying this was Izzy, putting an easy hand on his back, guiding him in. "The one I told you about."

"Yes, Huck's told me all about you," she said, leaning down, giving him warm and friendly.

Izzy looked at Huck, surprised, like he was wondering how much Huck had told her.

Huck winked, giving him a smile.

Izzy quick to thank her for the loan of the book, holding it out to her.

"You finish it so soon?"

"Just about, ma'am."

"Then you hang onto to it until you do — 'less you don't like it."

"Oh no, I like it just fine, ma'am."

"Well, I can see you're a fine fellow," she said, guiding him in, letting him sit on the only chair, Karla sitting on the end of the bed, Huck leaning by the alcove to the kitchen area.

"I bet you could go for a glass of milk," she said.

"He's not partial to it, but if you put on a pot of joe . . ." Huck said.

"Oh." She looked surprised just for a second, then broadened the smile, saying, "Coffee it is. What a fine idea."

"And eat, wait'll you see him eat," Huck said, feeling bad for saying it, seeing Izzy go red. Trying to save it by saying, "Speaking of that, I could go for something myself. How about I take me and my big mouth and duck out and fetch us something. Make us a fine picnic."

Karla looked paralyzed, Izzy sitting like he was frozen to the chair, saying, "I'll go with — and help, I mean."

"You stay here, you two get familiar. I'll put on the pot, then me and my big mouth'll be back before it's done boiling." And Huck got to work making coffee.

"How you take it again?" he asked Izzy, hoping he didn't say with a shot.

"Black's fine, you know how I take it." Izzy looked for a place to set the book down, putting it on the edge of the bed. "This alright, ma'am?"

"Yes, and you can call me Karla if you please."

"I was taught about respecting folks, though lately I've been forgetting some of it."

"I can see that, the respecting part, and I'd like us to get past the formalities, if that's alright with you, Izzy."

"That'd be fine, ma'am."

"Okay then," Karla looking at Huck, then back at Izzy, saying, "So, you like to read?"

"Yes, ma'am. And thank you again for the book. It's sure a fine one."

"Do you have a favorite part?"

"Soon as I read the first part about the woman dying, the mother, it drew me right in. And this boy, Oliver, being an orphan, I warmed up to him."

"Dickens was a fine author. And the book's based in part on his own childhood growing up in London, did you know that?"

"No, ma'am."

"Yes, his own father ended in debtor's prison, if you can imagine such a thing, and young Dickens was forced to leave school and take a job in a blacking factory. That's a place that makes boot polish."

"That's something, and he sure wrote a fine tale. I get stuck on some of the words, but I took a liking to it, but I'm not so sure I'm keen on Mr. Bumble though."

"Didn't care for him myself."

"You read when you were a kid?"

"About as young as you, and I do think it's one of the finest books ever written."

"Why'd you pass it on then?"

"So somebody else could enjoy it. A book's not much good collecting dust."

"No, ma'am."

"Karla," she said, getting up, taking the only two cups from a shelf above Huck's head, setting them next to the hot plate. Going back and sitting on the edge of the bed.

"Huck figures you and me'll get along," Izzy said, glancing over at Huck.

"Is that so? And what do you think about it?"

"I'd say so."

"Always like something to go along with coffee." Reaching a cookie tin, snapping off its lid and offering the ginger wafers to him. "Best we don't fill up too much, Huck going to get a picnic and all." Talking as if Huck wasn't there, making a game of it.

Izzy glanced at her, making sure it was alright, then reached and took one.

"This picnic — you think he means it in spirit?" Karla glanced to the window like she hadn't noticed, the wind howling against the glass.

Izzy gave her a look, like he wasn't sure what she meant, then he smiled, getting in on the game, saying, "Huck likes to make believe — likely wants you to toss a blanket on the floor and make like it's grass, pretending it's a spot by a lake, middle of summertime, then he'll tell us about this place, Bogalusa, where he grew up. That right, Huck?"

"You want to hear it, then I'll tell it," Huck said.

"Take two." She held out the tin again.

And he did.

Karla looked like she was feeling good sitting with him, the two of them nibbling on wafers, waiting for Huck to ruin the coffee.

They talked some more of Dickens, and of Jack London, and L. Frank Baum, and books that she likely thought a young boy might like, then she said again, "Best not spoil our appetite." This after the fourth or fifth wafer, Izzy showing no sign of slowing down.

"Suppose not." Izzy finishing the wafer.

She winked, thinking better of it, reached the tin and held it out again. "I won't tell if you won't."

And Izzy smiled and reached again.

Then she helped Huck with the coffee, taking the pot and filling the cups, setting one next to Izzy, saying, "I've got a feeling we both have plenty of room. That is, if Huck gets on with this picnic."

And Huck was pleased, the two of them getting along, guessing it was safe to leave them alone.

"Huck's not much on the cold," Izzy said. "Tells me where

he comes from, it don't get cold like here. Hot as a bear in summer and stays like that most of the time, right Huck?"

"Swear to God."

"And they got lots of bugs, spiders and fire ants. Huck says it's practically infested with roaches, though I don't see the problem with that. And they got swamps with garfish and gators too. 'Course I've never seen any of them, except the roaches, so he said he'd take me sometime if I want. Maybe he'll take you too."

"That would be nice," Karla said. "Though I'm not so sure about roaches and gators."

Huck stood watching, all of them quiet a minute, then Izzy picked up the book again, opening it to a spot and started to read.

"Sure have a want for reading," she said, watching him with the book in his lap, dunking a wafer in his cup this time and nibbling at it.

"Hardly nothing better," he said.

Never thought of her as the mothering kind, Huck had heard it was something that was supposed to come natural, and seeing her sitting with Izzy, he could see it in her.

The boy's lips moved over the words, sounding each one out, reading about Oliver and the Artful Dodger. And quietly as he could, Huck slipped out the door.

Tapping snow against the jamb when he stepped back in, tugging his shoes off, Karla coming and brushing snow from his shoulders, going up on her toes and kissing him. "Your nose is cold."

Shrugging off his coat, he gave a look back down the hall, closing the door, switching the lock and fastening the chain, saying to her, "Not a day for man or beast, that's for sure."

"Good thing we're indoors then." Her eyes searching his, like she was making sure that's where this picnic would be.

"What did you get, Huck?" Izzy closed the book, seeing the bag he handed Karla, likely guessing it was from the Chuck Wagon, not too far away from here.

"Never mind what I got, you stir up that appetite?"

"Never a doubt about that," Izzy said.

Karla took the bag over by the hob, unwrapped it, said she was glad to see the wrapped sandwiches, nothing she had to cook up. Asking when they wanted to eat.

"No time's better than when the bread's fresh," Huck said, winking at Izzy.

Izzy smiled and nodded.

Then she was looking at Huck, narrowing her eyes, "There's something else . . ."

"All that's in the bag." Huck narrowing his own eyes, like he didn't want her seeing into his dark corners.

"Not talking about your sandwiches — and skip the playing around. Out with it." Looking at him like she was measuring if he was being playful or serious.

"How d'you do that, like you know what's coming next?" he said.

"It's written all across your face. Don't know what it is, just know it's there."

"There's no fooling you, lady. Well, I think I found us a new place." Something the two of them had joked about since agreeing to marry, a place big enough to dance without bumping into something.

"You're moving?" Izzy looked alarmed.

"A nice two-bedroom place over by the Loop," Huck said.

She glanced around the tiny flat, raised her brows, and couldn't hide the smile. "It have running water?"

"That and a stove, an icebox, and big enough to swing a cat." He smiled, relieved that she still seemed of the same mind, that what they had talked about wasn't just pillow talk.

"Even got a washing machine." He took her hand in his and kissed her fingers.

"You got ice for fingers." But she didn't pull away.

"What's all that mean?" Izzy clapped *Oliver Twist* closed.

"Huck's got us a nest, for all of us," she said, looking from Izzy, back to Huck, not letting up, saying, "When are we going to see it?"

"Figured we'd eat first." He took a key from his pocket and showed it to them.

"Today?"

"The place is ours."

"You keep telling me half, the way you do, and we're getting off to a bad start." But she was all smiles, taking the key from him.

"Figure if I tell you half, you'll just guess the rest."

"You sure like playing."

"I like making you happy." And he kissed her again, his hands going around the small of her back, drawing her close.

"Oh, brother," Izzy said, calling this the mushy part.

"One day you'll be working to get to that part, boy." Huck winked at him.

"Said we were going to eat first," Izzy said, looking at the sandwiches she set on the table.

"Go wash up." Huck nicked his head at the basin by the window.

"I haven't been out."

"Wash up anyhow."

And Izzy stepped to the basin, pushing up his sleeves. "You get the liver or ham?"

"Got both kinds, just the way you like."

37

An oak-paneled office with the Tiffany lamp glowing yellow against the wood, the top desk drawer hanging open. Abe Lomberg's eyes were on the Colt next to the quill pens, an ugly thing meant to take life with the squeeze of a finger, the pen able to ruin a life even faster, just with a scrawl, something he came to know all too well.

Picking up the glass, he downed the drink, reaching the bottle and pouring another. Letting that sweet burn slide down his throat. Taking the revolver, he held it, the cold of the steel, snapping the cylinder and checking the load, clicking it shut again, understanding there were two ways to point it. Not taking the easier of the two, he aimed it at the back of the door, his hand sweating, but the barrel was steady enough. Then he turned it again, aiming it at the portrait of the man in the union uniform, the sardine-box shoulder bars, the Jeff Davis hat, the man's fine-trimmed mustache and sour expression held in time. That old man who never laughed a day in his life, disapproving of Abe every inch of his own life, now doing his disapproving from the beyond. His old man's voice locked in his head, telling him he was being namby-pamby, and how he could never get things right. The old man telling him why not stick the barrel in his own mouth and be done with it.

And Abe fired, put the bullet between the old man's eyes, the half bottle of Dutch courage helping him do it. Setting the revolver on the desk blotter, he looked at the ruined canvas as he forced up the cork with his thumb, the bottle making a popping sound lost to the ringing in his ears. Going for the other kind of shot, one that always led to the next.

Glancing out the window at the dawn glowing yellow above the rooftops to the east, making the usual promises. Too early for anybody else to be in the office, nobody alarmed by the pistol shot. The night had slipped off, leaving him worn out and half in the bag, and he dozed off like that in his chair, the glass in front of him, the shot-up portrait, one of the old man's eyes still staring and judging, and the pistol in easy reach.

It was the footfalls down the hall sometime later that woke him, then the rap of knuckles as the door opened.

"Abe, good to see you're up bright and early." Morris Markin stepped in, seeing the pistol and the bottle, looking at the ruined portrait on the wall opposite, putting it together, then stretching his hand over the desk, making like he was dropping in on a long-lost friend.

Coming in behind him, Huck stood inside, closing the door, not liking the look of the weapon by the man's hand. The one he was carrying was holstered under his jacket. Huck still being on Morris Markin's payroll, first helping him out with his union troubles, now as a troubleshooter while Markin made this business acquisition, meaning if there was any trouble, Huck would be the one shooting.

"Don't sleep so good these days," Abe Lomberg said, tossing the pistol in the drawer, but leaving it open, the smile meant to say he had things under control, shaking the offered hand. Nodding to Huck, not asking who he was or what he was doing there.

"How's the better half?" Morris set his homburg on the desk, the man already taking over.

"Suppose she's dandy," Abe said.

"Give her my regards, will you?"

"Next time I see her."

"A lucky man, Abe, yes sir, a wife like that, and great gams, if you don't mind me saying so."

"Think you're getting my goat?" Abe started reaching for the glass, then thought better of it.

Huck kept his eyes on the open drawer, Morris Markin acting like he hadn't noticed.

"Me, I never felt the need for getting hitched, at least to the wrong kind of woman," Morris said.

"It's sailors and Vaseline for you, then?" Abe trying not to sound angry.

"You've been drinking, Abe?" Morris smiled, that lofty look.

"Sound just like the wife."

"Once again, I'm afraid you've misread the situation, Abe. And while I do love the ladies, I fear wedlock agrees with you like a boiled cabbage, a tasteless thing with a linger of gas, by my guess. Now, shall we get to business . . ."

Abe picked up the near empty glass and drained it, then realized he was the only one drinking, offering with a gesture.

"Thanks just the same," Morris said, turning his eyes to the portrait, seeing the hole between the eyes.

"All of us are going to die someday," Abe said, pouring another shot and sliding it across the desk, not offering Huck anything.

Abe Lomberg pointed to the chair across the desk — a look on his face like he was inviting Genghis Khan into his tent, a look of hate for this man looming over his desk, the goddamn homburg hat on his desk. Looking at it like he wanted to stamp his fist down on it. Morris Markin coming to buy him out, to take over his auto body company, the one building the Mogul, the goddamn Checker taxis Markin had been ordering for the past few years, forcing Abe to expand his own operations. Then Markin cut back, blaming the times, causing the over-leveraged company to falter, the years following the war coming as lean ones. Abe didn't see it coming, and sure didn't pay heed to the warning signs. And this Morris Markin was hungry for acquisition, not losing any sleep on account of the carnage he left in the wake of doing business, showing up here with his checkbook and a bodyguard.

"Well, it works out for both of us then," Morris said, taking out his pen and opening the checkbook, leaning on the desk and scribbling an amount, holding the installment check up and blowing on the ink, then sliding it across.

Abe was working the cork out again, having to struggle. Lifting the bottle and splashing a couple more fingers in his glass, sloshing some over the side, looking sorry it didn't hit the hat, raising the glass in a toast, saying it in Russian, "Za zda-ró-vye." Draining it, looking like he wished pestilence and death on this man, the effects of the booze showing, likely the best he was going to feel that day.

"Not gonna find it in there, whatever it is," Morris said, looking at the bottle.

"Sound just like the wife alright," Abe said, taking the check and tucking it in a pocket.

"You took the loan, *gospodin*." Putting up a hand to stop him from arguing. "Maybe it was the wrong move, but you made it — so don't lay it at my feet."

Abe glanced at the open drawer, then back at Morris, letting him wonder if he was going to grab for the Colt.

Huck was unbuttoning his jacket, knowing he wouldn't make it.

"I reached out to you, trusted you," Abe said.

"You showed me your books — a grown man asking for a loan — with both eyes open," Morris said. Two years back, he was buying Mogul Checkers from Abe's company, Lomberg Auto Body. Abe securing the loan to make it happen. Morris Markin obliging — making the same kind of deals buying out Luxor and the Ascot Company before this one. Morris with a knack for thriving as competitors went to ruin, the man seeing it simply as doing business.

"You knew exactly when to recall the loan," Abe accused him.

"Your poor head for business is hardly my fault, Abe."

"Business, that what you call it?" Abe calling him a name in Russian. "Showing up with your muscle, shaking my hand, calling me gospodin, asking after my wife — like you're dropping in on a comrade — you and me getting off the same boat at Ellis."

"I got nothing against you, Abe. You want to think I'm the wolf, okay, I'm the wolf. But what's that make you — the sheep?"

Abe thumped a fist on the desk. "I know what I am, and what you did — you set me up."

"I were you, you know what I'd do . . ."

"A couple years off the boat and you think you can tell me — just look at you, what you've become." Abe shook his head, reached for the bottle again, then waved it off.

Morris picked up the man's glass, set it back down and pushed it toward Abe, saying, "Za zda-ró-vye — to you and your leaking boat."

"You took advantage."

"Tell it to the rabbi."

Abe Lomberg looked deflated, then said, "You going to rename it?"

Morris shrugged like he hadn't thought about it.

Huck betting the man had been thinking about the sign over the building, likely kept him up nights, seeing a new one with his name on it — big red letters on the wood — *M-A-R-K-I-N* — with a white outline. Likely had sketches made of how he wanted it to look.

"Something else you want to say?" Abe said.

"I'm waiting for you to get your ass out of my chair," Morris said.

Looking baffled, Abe took a final look at the open drawer, shoving it closed, taking the bottle, getting up and walking out of there, saying something else in Russian.

Huck betting it was along the lines of "Go fuck yourself."

When he was gone, Morris stepped around and tried the chair, leaning back in it and looking around, his eyes stopping on the spoiled portrait, saying, "Take that down, would you?"

Watching Huck take it down and lean it against the wall, Morris said, "Got my sights on Commonwealth Motors, another flounder. Take another sinking ship through a public stock offering, generate funds to clean up the balance sheet, secure the right loans, and grow the empire. Soon I'll push out your man Hertz too. What do you think of that?"

"Good to have ambitions, I guess," Huck said, unimpressed.

Morris Markin went on about passing the taxi empire down to his son, then his grandkids. Huck nodding and letting him talk.

"They got this fish in South America, bites anything that steps in the water. About like this . . ." Morris showed the length with his hands. "But a school'll take down an ox, get it stripped to the bone in less than a minute." Morris reached the revolver in the drawer, holding it like he was admiring it, saying, "You started out with Yellow, working against me."

"Uh huh." Huck aware of him holding the pistol, practically aiming it at him.

"How about coming around to the winning side?"

"At gunpoint?"

"I respect that — that and loyalty." Turning the pistol in a lazy fashion, still loosely aiming at Huck, saying, "But I think you get me?"

"Get you better when you put that away." Huck pulled his jacket back, the handle of his Colt showing. Watching this yutz with the Colt in his hand.

"I got no pity for a man like that," Morris said, setting the pistol in the drawer and closing it. "I'm just the bigger fish, that's all."

Huck looked at the shot-up portrait leaning by the wall, saying, "Just doing business, that it?"

"You got a point to make?" Morris looked at him.

"That cab of yours that went in the river. You remember?"

"Sure, was in the papers."

"Was me." Huck aimed a thumb at himself with his left, his right hand still at the butt of the pistol.

Morris half-rose from the chair, anger in his eyes.

"Wanted you to hear it from me."

"You forgetting you work for me?"

Taking a backward step to the door, Huck said, "Going back to Yellow, and gonna push more of yours in the river."

"What the —"

"And so you know, Hertz, that man's the bigger fish." With that, he turned and left, glad he'd been paid the week in advance.

38

"**B** road daylight killing of P.A. Skirven, father of two, shot through the heart." Huck read it slow, the headline in block letters across the top of the *Tribune*. Finding his way through the words since Izzy started showing him how, teaching him to sound them out. Looking across at Gypsy Doyle, the two sitting in the Chuck Wagon, finishing their coffee, set to make another run to the Canadian side.

"Man had've kept me on, it would've been over by now. Checker'd be a thing of the past," Doyle said, dropping coins on the table, wanting to get going, looking out the window, first at the roughs hanging outside the speak across the street, then up at the darkening sky.

Huck was drinking his free beer. Below the fold was another report on a cabbie taking a bullet in the foot at Logan Square, page six giving an account of a Checker man dragged to jail after a brawl at a taxi stand out front of the Hotel Sherman. Scanning past them, he stopped at a quote by the mayor, reading it aloud and stumbling over the words. "We'll see if the taxi men control and own the streets or the people." The mayor stating his outrage. Followed by a quote from Hertz himself, promising there would be no more mister nice guy. Putting up five grand of his own money as reward for bringing the killers of P.A. Skirven to justice, calling them a bunch of rogues.

"The man's just showing off," Doyle said, scraping back his chair.

Huck not hurrying, tipping back his glass. Reading more of the article: "Promises to take care of the widow and her young ones. Hoping the good folks of our fair city'll demand the killers get brought to justice."

"He called it that, our fair city?"

Huck nodded, saying, "Recounting the horror of that long line of Checker cabs roaring past the Shaw livery, unloading hundreds of rounds in broad daylight, destroying much of the place, along with half a dozen of his fleet parked out front."

"Like he's the white sheep." Doyle started for the door, saying, "Come on, looks like shit weather."

Thanking Luka, Huck went out the door and got behind the wheel of the Hupmobile, the engine and springs beefed up, likely could outrun any cop car on either side of the border. Looking at the line of drunks outside the speak — the place reopened, business as usual — thinking he spotted the one he stuck with the fork, the man looking over, then going inside the door.

"Like I said, Hertz's paper pusher should'a just paid me the reward."

"Took you off the books on account of your . . . past."

"He say that, my past?"

"No, called you a crook, and heavy handed."

"That little piker. I ought to go see him, straighten him out. But hell, hundred's pocket change." Doyle shrugged, saying, "Plus, I got to work for a guy like that, a little gin drinker in a purple chair, I'd just end up tossing him out the window."

"Told Checker's man I quit," Huck said.

"Changing sides again?"

"Gonna stick with Yellow, but I'm still thinking Dean could use taxis for the drops."

Doyle shook his head. "I were you, I'd forget it — put your mind on doubling up on the runs. I mean, while we got this truce."

The last sit-down with O'Banion and Torrio meant a shaky peace, both sides focused on expanding their turf, the North Side running more and more booze across from Canada.

"As long as it lasts," Huck said, thinking the tension between the Irish and Italians wasn't going away on account of a treaty. O'Banion having a dislike for Torrio that ran deep, and he didn't mind letting it show every chance he got. Hymie Weiss sat in on that meeting at the Four Deuces, telling the whole room he just came along on account the wops need watching. Torrio bringing along Capone, because he didn't trust the micks. Weiss and Capone eye-fucking each other the whole meeting. A dicey peace at best, but one that promised a share of profits and political connections, the North Side crew giving up a small piece of what they made from leasing the Sieben brewery, going partners with Torrio on it, calling the new operation the George Frank Brewery, supposedly making non-alcoholic beer. And they gave up some of the gambling they controlled, in turn gaining territory north of the Loop, including all the waterfront they weren't already dominating. Torrio promising to stop the Gennas from tramping onto North Side toes, getting all the independents in line. But Huck felt it wouldn't last, and keeping a foot in the door with Yellow Cab seemed a good move.

"What's that mean, long as it lasts?" Doyle looked at him from the passenger side.

"Not my place to say."

"First thing you got right." Doyle's fuse seemed short these days. He said, "You know mumblety-peg?"

"What's that?"

"A kid's game, you know — two players, a knife, and a patch of ground."

"Chicken, sure. You toss the knife, closest to the foot."

"It's what Deanie and Torrio are doing."

"I meant no disrespect."

"Look, we got a good thing. You make more'n you make with the taxis by a long sight, am I right?"

"So you keep reminding me." Couldn't argue that, Huck making more off one haul across the border than he made in a month working for Yellow.

"Ours is a business of sticking to shadows. And this taxi war keeps getting the headlines . . . why Deanie doesn't want anything yellow delivering the loads."

"And you figure I'm sticking my neck out."

"Not just yours."

"I'll think on it."

"You'll leave it alone?"

"Said I'll think on it."

And they were quiet, Huck driving the Lincoln Highway past Valparaiso, aiming for LaPorte, then South Bend, swinging north at Elkhart, then east at Mottville, taking the 12 into Detroit. Huck thinking O'Banion and his crew would never get along with Johnny Torrio's outfit, anymore than the trouble between Yellow and Checker would just blow away. In fact, the taxi war was bound to kick up after Skirven had been gunned down middle of the day, the family man waiting on a fare, the Yellow stand at Roosevelt and Kedzie, leaning against his taxi, having a smoke, talking to a couple of other drivers. A black car sped past, three men inside pouring over two dozen rounds into the taxis, killing Skirven. Another Yellow driver catching a round in the foot that same night at Logan and Milwaukee. And that had Hertz declaring what had come before was a comic opera up till now, swearing it would be a fight to the finish, getting the city council threatening to pull the licenses of both companies. Huck thinking he'd stay on with Yellow and see what happened, still needing to settle with the three mutts in the Stutz who ran him off the road that time, thinking they could be Skirven's shooters.

39

One of Druggan's boys had spotted the Stutz, getting word to Gypsy Doyle. Huck heard about the three fellows fitting the bill, hanging out at a place called the Oakland Room, down in the Levee District, south of the Loop, an after-hours hangout by the river. Happened to be a union rabble-rouse for Checker taking place that night, so Doyle went along with Huck, pulling into the dirt lot out back, having a look at the autos parked there. About a dozen Checker cabs among the vehicles filling the lot, parked in a row along the river. Doyle rolling his Ford in slow, spotting the Stutz near the end, flanked by a couple of Checker Marathons.

Rolling the window down to let the cigarette smoke waft out, they could hear the meeting coming to an end inside, a union motivator working up a lather, calling them a brother-hood. A couple of the drivers stepped out back, looking like they had their fill of speeches. The way they were swaying, it looked like they had their fill of the jag juice too, this part of town known to ignore the Eighteenth, boasting its gambling and bookie joints, the sporting houses coming to life when the sun tipped down, like a hive every night. The two men stood and smoked, leaning their backs to the clapboard, facing the lot as the cars started to clear out, the union meeting over. Huck recognized them, and he and Doyle sat there smoking and waiting, the Checker men not paying notice as they filed out and got in their cars.

The voices carried over the near empty lot, the two by the door talking about the Cubs' chances against the Cards in tomorrow's game, Sweetbread Bailey to open. The big bouncer stepping out with them was Flynn, Huck recognizing him as the driver that time he was run off the road. Flynn was saying it ought to be Lefty Tyler, no doubt in his mind. The lanky man leaning against the wall was called Cricket, saying Flynn was full of feathers. Buddy, the third man, red-haired and Irish as it gets, laughed at that, then stopped, finally spotting Doyle's Ford past the Stutz at the end of the lot, Huck looking at them as Buddy tapped Cricket's arm. The three men stopped talking, watching them.

The one called Flynn stepped into the lot, looking ready to engage.

"Show time." Huck got out, looking to the black river like he was taking in the sights, reaching in a pocket for his tobacco bag and papers.

"You boys lost your way or just your minds?" Flynn grinned, stopping halfway, Huck looking up like he just noticed him.

"You corn fed, huh?" Huck looked him up and down.

"I get by."

"How tall, you figure?"

"Six five."

"And you carry what — about two-twenty?"

"You aiming to measure my blind meat next?"

"That your heap?" Huck glanced back at the Stutz.

"The way you're talking, I'm guessing you want to get tossed in the river."

"I want you to try." Huck watched the other two coming off the wall now. He twisted up the smoke and stuck it between his lips. The red-haired man had been the one in back of the Stutz when they ran him off the road, the other one the passenger. Huck taking his time, this being a long time coming.

Flynn the bouncer frowned and started to move toward him. Doyle picked then to step from the driver's side, taking a pack of ready-mades from his coat, patting his pockets for a match, finding a box, lighting up and tossing the matches. Huck catching it one-handed, fishing one out and striking it off a thumb, looking back at the river as Doyle stepped around the back.

"Two fools going for a swim," Flynn said, standing easy like he'd done this a hundred times.

"Come looking for you." Huck dragged on the smoke, throwing a thumb toward the Stutz, saying, "The Touring model, that right?"

Doyle went over to the Stutz, taking lazy steps, unbuttoning his trousers. "Next time, go for the Bearcat — it's sportier." Pissing against it as he walked along its side.

"The fuck . . ." Cricket said, not believing this, Doyle relieving himself against the fender and wheel, like the man was marking territory.

Turning back, Doyle leaned against the door of the Stutz, smiling as he buttoned up, saying, "I'm a Ford man."

The two men moved now, Cricket going left, Buddy stepping right.

"A while back . . ." Huck said, holding up a hand to slow them. "You run a fellow off the road. Had a kid up front and an old lady in back. And you tore up the Alley Cat. You recall that?" Again, getting the idea they shot P.A. Skirven too.

"See who we got here, Flynn?" Cricket said, smiling. "Cabbie we sent off the road that time." Then to Huck, "Next time, let the granny do the driving."

Cricket took knucks from his pocket, putting them on like he was trying on gloves.

Buddy pulled a sap, making a show of it.

Still holding up the hand, Huck said, "One thing before we get to it . . . need two of you fit enough for pushing . . ." Aiming a finger at the Stutz. "That's going in the river."

"You expect us to . . ." Cricket laughed, shaking his head, not believing it.

Dragging on his smoke, Doyle pulled his jacket back, letting them see the butt of the pistol, exhaling, saying, "That'll be you two."

Huck looked to Flynn the bouncer, the one driving that day.

Cricket kept the smile, saying, "You hear that Flynn?" Then to Huck, "You got a taste for hospital food, huh, brother?"

"The man's lost his mind," Buddy said.

And like that, Cricket came in a rush, the knucks on his fist.

Slipping the swing, Huck hit him midships, grabbing him by the coat lapels as the air whooshed out of him, spinning him into Buddy, then kicking out Cricket's knee, headbutting him, busting his nose as the man jerked forward. Sent him sputtering and stumbling to the ground, losing his knucks. Taking a step, his eyes stayed on the big man as he stomped Cricket's leg, the man yelping and clutching his dislocated knee. Looking to Buddy, Huck said, "Guess you're pushing on your own."

Buddy stood helpless, holding his sap. Looking at Doyle holding the pistol.

Looking at the broken cigarette, Huck tossed it away, then to Flynn, saying, "You know me now?"

Flynn thumped a fist into his palm, a loud smack, saying, "How you doing?" And he lunged in.

Huck slipped and moved, kept from being grabbed, sending an elbow into the man's ribs. Ducking a haymaker and slamming home a right, moving away to keep him from clinching.

Buddy made no move, Doyle's pistol keeping him in place. Leaning on the Stutz, Doyle watched the fight, enjoying the smoke.

Flynn rushed again, Huck moving and hammering at his ribs. A left, then a cross.

The bouncer brushing it off, coming again and clamping both arms around Huck, lifting him off the ground and squeezing.

Freeing a hand, Huck clapped it against the man's ear, butting with his head, bringing his knee up between the man's legs.

Flynn groaned and regained the hold, spun Huck and rushed him backward, plowing him against the side of Doyle's Ford. Huck's head snapping back.

Buddy backed up and was calling to the back door. Faces showing from inside, a couple more men coming out.

Flynn had Huck by the scruff, dragging him and tossing him, sending him stumbling. Swiping at the blood on his face, Flynn spat and kept after him.

Huck shot out a jab, getting knocked to the ground, dodging the bouncer's shoe, Flynn stomping at him. Grabbing Cricket's knucks as he rolled, Huck got back on his feet. Backing from the cars, he put the black river behind him. Ducking another wild swing, he jabbed at the big man's ribs, getting in a good right with the knucks. Ducking, Huck hit him again, slowing him, putting weight into the punches, catching Flynn on the jaw, snapping his head, knocking out a couple of teeth, then ducking under another wild swing. Huck turning it around, jabbing with the leadened right, backing him up and chopping away.

Flynn's arms hung low, Huck catching him with a straight right, sending an uppercut to the chin, the bouncer reeling back and landing flat on the ground.

Gulping air as he stood swaying, Huck looked at Gypsy Doyle holding his pistol on Buddy and the men coming out the door.

Dropping the knucks in a pocket, Huck leaned to the side and threw up, wiping at a string of spit hanging from his chin. His fingers shook, taking the smoke Doyle held out to him, dragging on it a couple of times, dropping it in the gravel, twisting his shoe on it. Looking at the men by the door, he nodded to the Stutz and the Checkers on either side, saying, "Appreciate if you boys help push." Nodding to the river behind him.

40

Walking into the livery, Huck hailed to Moses, the mechanic getting an early start, taking in Huck's beat-up appearance, asking how he was faring. Then telling how a couple of Checker rigs ended in the river last night, pointing to the photo in the *Herald-Examiner*, smiling as he said, "Made the front page."

"Them Checker boys can't drive for diddly."

"Says somebody give 'em a push."

"That so?"

"And if that somebody'd give the word, I'd a been there." Moses looked serious, his hand around the wrench.

"Know I can count on you, Mo." Going to the back, Huck checked the back door was locked and bolted, looking at the closet under the stairs, back to being a home to brooms and shovels. Huck seeing a shriveled apple core on the floor.

Taking the stairs to the office, he was thinking about Izzy's mother, wondering if he'd open up about her sometime. Moses had told him he suspected she went missing during the riots, lots of people just disappearing back then, could be she'd been killed or run off, never heard from again. Told Huck from the start he ought to give thought to leaving the young fella with the nuns at St. Patrick's, how they'd look out for him proper and find him a fitting home. But then admitted Huck and his woman were giving the boy that.

Finding the office door closed, Huck pushed it and just walked in, but the man behind the desk wasn't Dex Ayres, looking up from the daily *Trib* spilled across the desk, a mug sitting like it was anchoring the pages.

John D. looked up, his suit jacket off, hanging on Dex's rack, his white shirt and vest with gold at the cuffs, a cravat as yellow as the taxis outside, the man looking like some Savile Row dandy, looking at Huck like he just swallowed something bitter when he was expecting sweet. "Well, what've you got to say?"

"Came to say it to Dex," Huck said.

"I'm the one pays the freight."

"You like reminding folks of that, huh?"

"Came to clear some dead wood, right now trying to figure what kind of man thinks he's worth a hundred a week." John D. Hertz looked amused.

"The kind that ends up looking like this." Huck pointing to the cuts and bruises on his face. Didn't look as bad after Karla took the antiseptic and swabs to him, but the fight still showed. He stepped to the kidney-shaped desk, reminding Hertz of his name and sticking out his hand.

"I know who you are." John D. eyed him, ignoring the hand. Sizing him up, then saying, "You have any idea why a man would have a chair like this?" Running a finger along the lilac arm.

"Velvet, I think he called it."

"Question's why, not what."

"And how'd I know a thing like that?"

"Well, in your opinion, would you say it's a fitting thing?"

"Me, I'd'a gone for leather."

"Leather," John D. repeated like he considered it.

"You asking me about fancying-up tips?" Huck looked around, taking in the changes that Hertz had made, stepping to where the city map had hung, a gun case against that wall. A Marlin repeater, a couple of carbines Huck didn't recognize, engravings on their stocks, a Colt Patterson revolving shotgun about a hundred years old, some Italian-looking bird gun, a lever-action pocket pistol, and a pair of flintlock saddle pistols that could have belonged to George Washington; on the front of the case was a brass plaquette: *In case of sinners.*

"You a collector, huh?" Huck asked.

"I tended to some business with Dex, then went looking for you. Well, looking was a half hour back, rest of the time I've been reading the daily," Hertz said, like he wasn't happy about it. "While you're off feeding your lost bird?"

"Guess you mean Izzy, used to be the night watchman."

"Just a boy is what I hear."

"Young fella with the eyes of a hawk. That what you want to talk about?"

"Want to talk about what a hundred a week gets me."

"You read about the taxis going in the river?" Huck nodded to the open paper.

"You're on the books for months now, and I've got one headline."

"I'm not a boastful man."

"I've got a war on my hands, and my hundred bucks gets me a couple of wet taxis."

"I could go on about a couple of Checker joints and meetings that got busted up, all the Checkers I run from your stands, ran one right out of town, another cab in the river. Actually been meaning to talk to Dex about all that, the hundred a week seems light. Fact, had Morris Markin paying me double that."

Hertz narrowed his eyes, took a moment before saying, "I can't tell if you've got brass balls or you've been struck dumb — Irish boxing, is it?"

"Well sir, I been hit plenty as you can see, that's true enough, but if I don't look out for myself, then who does? You?"

With that Hertz softened, saying, "Used to practice the noble art myself."

"That right?"

"Fought a time as Dan Donnelly."

Huck trying to picture this dandy Dan Donnelly stripped out of his fancy suit and in a pair of satin trunks — yellow, no doubt.

"Took what I learned, started sportswriting for the *Morning Herald*," John D. said. "Went on to manage a couple of fighters — you heard of the Tipton Slasher?"

"Can't say so, no."

"Well, I did plenty of looking out for myself, I can tell you that." He smiled now, saying, "How about you go out, come in and we try it again." Leaning back against the velvet, John D. considered, then went on, "Then you can tell me that part — working for that son of a bitch Markin."

"The son of a bitch wanted me bedeviling your outfit."

Hertz raised his brows. "And you're telling me this?"

"Helped him with some union troubles, is all."

"Not working both sides of the street?"

"He wanted me working for him, but we stopped seeing eye to eye, and I bet once he finds I dumped another of his taxis in the river, relations would've soured anyhow."

"You played him?"

"Maybe some." Huck pinched his thumb and forefinger together.

"Goddamn son, if you don't have brass balls."

"Bet you'd've paid a hundred just to see it."

"Goddamn right." And John D. Hertz stood and offered his hand. "Maybe you are worth it."

"It's going up twenty."

"Goddamn." John D. pumped his hand, Huck figuring the man was getting a new sense of this bumpkin across the desk.

"But the boy stays home."

"He ain't been on night watch for some time."

"'Cause I'm not running an orphanage."

"Just want me bedeviling old Morris?"

Stabbing a finger at the newspaper, Hertz said, "Give the snoops more of this, and I'll double the hundred. How's that sound?"

"Sounds like I won't be going to Markin for a counter-offer." Huck sat in the chair opposite.

"Goddamn brass balls alright." Hertz was nodding like he approved.

"Let's just say I got skin in the game." Lifting his hair in front, Huck showed the gash at his hairline, where the stitches had been.

"Crash that cost me a cab, the old woman taking legal action. You hear we settled out of court?"

"Reminds me, I paid some hospital bills that time, mine, some of the woman's, and the boy's too."

"Her lawyer was throwing around words like negligence and intoxication. She went to the *Trib*, claiming our driver was on the booze. Still going to see some quack about the vertebrae in her neck, pains in her knee and hip."

"Just saying I wouldn't mind getting reimbursed."

"What?"

"For the hospital bills." Huck recalling the amount to the penny, this captain of industry looking like he was set to make a big deal out of it. Part of him liking the man, another part wanting to climb over the kidney desk and see if he was any good — this man looking like he was born in a silk suit with a silver spoon in his mouth.

"This eagle-eyed lad — he yours by chance?"

"Just a kid nobody wanted." Huck guessing the man was distracted with his war on the streets, not knowing that Izzy hadn't been here in long time. Saying, "What I came in for's to see Dex about a fresh taxi."

"Well, as you can see Dex is no longer with us."

Huck nodded, looking to the gun cabinet, then saying, "Still need a new cab."

Swiveling the chair, Hertz looked out the window. "Do I want to know why?"

"Let's say the one I'm driving's kinda shot."

"By shot, you mean . . ."

Huck made a finger gun, dropping his thumb like a hammer. The Yellow shot at when they drove from the Oakland Room after getting the Stutz and two Checker taxis shoved in the river. A shooter getting up on the roof of the tavern, hitting the back end and putting a second round through the rear window, smashing the glass and tearing a swath through the upholstery as they sped off.

John D. closed his eyes, like maybe his head hurt.

"Mind me asking what the *D*'s for?" Huck asked, thinking Dandy, looking at the man across the desk, the captain of industry in his yellow ascot.

"I could say Dollars, some might say Damnation," John D. said, putting on a grin, then admitted it was Daniel, saying, "You really want to know or just passing time?"

"Paints a picture of who's paying me."

"Got six Johns or Jans working here, so they started sticking on the extras, so we've got Long John, Little John, Johnny Boy, and a couple more . . . you get the point. Other than that, you call John and half the heads turn."

"Why not Big John?"

"Where's the flair in that?" John D. pulled the top drawer and reached a box of hand-rolled cigars, offered Huck one, told him they were Cuban by way of Tampa. Huck waving no thanks. John D. taking one and running it under his nose, clipping the end, taking a silver lighter off the desk, what he called his torch, and fired it up, puffing a thick cloud.

Leaning back in the chair, Huck took out his makings from his jacket, making an equal show of rolling one, taking a match and scratching it on the side of the gaudy desk, and puffing it to life.

"You think I'm some fancy man? Let's clear that up. Was born in the poorest shithole you ever saw, a place called Sklabiňa."

"That sounds east of Jersey?"

"A mighty way east. Dirt floors and folks with a fondness for fists, me at ten getting the runt's end as the old man beat discipline in me till I ran off, selling newspapers and ending in some waif's home, shivered myself to sleep most nights, stealing bread to survive, eating potatoes raw from the ground. The old man came for me, I don't know how he found me, but he took me back — the closest we ever got to a bond. Couple years later he put us on a liner, sailed us here, stuck me in a school to learn the lingo. What I got was the nuns beating the lessons into me. At home, Papa was hitting Momma, Momma was hitting back, rolling pins, once a skillet, both of them back to hitting me. Once I got close to man-size, I took to swinging back, taught them hitting me came at a price. Learned to box at the Y and got myself in a club, fought amateur as Dan Donnelly."

"Said that already."

"Guess I did."

"You any good?"

John D. clapped his hands, saying, "One time, maybe. Won a couple championships. Moved to New York as soon as I got some size, fought under my own name a while, called

Kid Hertz, as in going to put the hurts on you. Found myself on the canvas a time too many and got out of it, used my head for something more than a bag, managed a while, then moved back here and started reporting."

"Trying to picture you as a hack."

"And a legman after the paper merged. Turned to selling cars on account I liked being around them, then got to renting them out. Scratched enough for a fleet of seven, old hacks going to rust mostly. Long story short, I climbed my way up." John D. gesturing with his hands, taking in the office, his domain — a lilac velvet chair under his seat.

"Guess you're doing alright," Huck said, bored with this, but nodding like he was impressed, wondering what the hell was keeping Gypsy Doyle, supposed to meet him here, then go on an early run to Canada. Guessing it was some woman.

"You can do anything, you have the right tools." John D. put the cigar between his teeth and tapped a finger to his temple.

"You mean money?"

"Money's what you make."

"Well, from the look you made plenty."

"On account of the tools," tapping his temple again. "And taking the right chances." Then he started talking about his ranch, and all the fine racehorses he'd acquired.

Huck trying not to yawn, saying, "Lost some dough on the ponies, maybe some of 'em were yours," tapping his smoke in the man's ashtray.

Walking into the office, a tin of coffee in hand, Gypsy Doyle said, "Don't go calling them ponies, Huck — gonna insult the man. There's pride at stake."

John D. asked who he was, then glanced at his watch, making a show of it, saying, "That's right, thoroughbreds, the blue bloods of racehorses."

"No cows? I like cows," Doyle said, smiling enough to show the missing tooth.

"Just thoroughbreds."

"Where the money goes, not into fixing the drafts and leaks in this old place," Doyle said. "Sure not putting it in the pockets of your drivers."

"Let me ask you one, Doyle — why am I sitting here taking shit from the hired help?" John D. said, not smiling now.

"Let's get it straight, I ain't the hired help. Fact, if I punch something, it won't be your clock."

"Then how about you tell me why you're here? I believe Dex expressed I wasn't interested, getting in bed with gangsters."

Doyle sipped from the tin, leaning on the threshold, giving Hertz an even look. "Stuck my neck out while your boy here was busting heads — putting three rigs in the river."

"Well, I thank you for that." John D. leaned back, saying, "Let's say, but I'm going in a different direction."

"Going with somebody else?"

"This is Chicago, gents. Toughs are a dime a dozen, no offense, but that's not the way."

"How about in English?" Doyle said.

John D. reached his billfold, took out a couple of bills and slid them over the desk, looking at Doyle. "For your time and any misunderstanding. To put it plain, I can't be seen associating."

Doyle narrowed his eyes.

John D. waiting through the silence.

Doyle's eyes stayed locked on his as he ignored the money, told Huck he'd be down in the car, then turned and left.

Huck started to get up, John D. holding up a hand, wanting him to stay. Waiting until Doyle had gone.

"How would it look — me associating with a criminal gang?" John D. said.

"So why am I here?"

"Don't see you the same way."

Huck looked at him a moment, then said, "How many horses you got?"

"Forty or so at Trout Valley, give or take — and nearly that at Amarillo Ranch and Stoner Creek. It's not how many, it's about finding that one in a million, like my Reigh Count, horse royalty sired from pedigree stock going back to the time of the Romans, one that blows past the others like they're tied to the fence. Up at Hawthorne right now with a trainer."

"Getting set to win a stakes race."

"That's the idea."

"There good money in it?"

John D. just smiled. "My Fannie manages the yearlings and two-year-olds. The woman works magic — has this bond with them. You don't have that, well then, there's not much point putting a saddle on them. Got this yearling coming up, should see it — runs like the wind."

"Spend the money and hope you know that one sure thing when you see it."

"Something like that."

"So, you mind telling me what I'm doing here?"

"Dex hired you as a thug in the shadows, and you got me sued and put a waif under the stairs. Wrecked about half the fleet. All off the books — something he tried to deny."

"So you canned him."

"Did that on account the man's got no vision." John D. looking at the chair he was sitting in, saying, "Still like someone to explain this desk and chair to me."

"Afraid I can't help you there."

And they were grinning at each other.

"What I'd like to do is offer you a position."

"A position?"

"Head of security."

"This being on the books?"

"That's right."

"Mind me asking why?"

"You just said something about looking for a sure thing."

"What do I have to do?"

"What you're doing now, except without your man Doyle, and no more moonlighting for Markin. Want you looking out for trouble, not causing it. Lately I've been getting threats. Fannie insisting I get somebody to watch my back."

"Position like that sounds like it ought to come with a raise."

John D. shook his head, not believing this guy, then reaching in the drawer, took a Remington pistol out and laid it on the desk, saying, "You know which end to point?"

"This in case the horse don't win?"

41

"We got something on tonight, Deanie wants you there," Gypsy Doyle said out the window of his Ford coupe, the cocky look as usual, pulling alongside Hertz's Duesenberg, Huck sitting behind the wheel, parked alongside a stand on North Michigan, playing chauffeur to Hertz, the man in the office tower across the street.

"Come by Schofield's, you know it?" Doyle was eying the car, shaking his head.

"On North State — sure." Huck had never set foot inside the flower shop, but he knew where it was, the North Side headquarters and hangout up a set of stairs. Looking past Doyle, he saw a Checker cab driving the opposite way, the driver making a finger gun, pointing it at him as he rolled on. Huck watched the cab in his side view, disappearing around the next corner.

"Whatever Yellow's paying you, it ain't enough." Doyle shook his head, telling Huck, "Eight o'clock — and wear something dark." And he drove off.

No arguing that, even with the pay hike, what Hertz paid him was still peanuts compared to running hootch over from Windsor. Doyle seeing that Huck was paid what was due, telling Dean and Hymie Weiss how Huck drove at the Mountie head on and put him off the road — a driver like that was just what the gang needed. Dean and Weiss agreeing. There was more than plenty to go around, these guys chalking it up to the cost of doing business.

Still, Huck planned to keep Yellow on the side, working for both outfits, his account at First National growing by the week, Huck thinking of buying shares in General Motors and U.S. Steel, looking to diversify his investments, something that John D. had offered to advise him on. They'd been in their apartment for about a year now, and since he was making plenty of money and planning to walk Karla up the courthouse steps, he was playing with thoughts of getting a fancier place for them and Izzy, some place on the Gold Coast. And he was thinking about getting himself a head-turner of an auto like this, some sleek coupe.

The idea was to take Karla to the Biograph that night, Karla wanting to see *Beyond the Rocks*, fond of Valentino's looks if not his acting, having a feeling that Gloria Swanson was apt to pull up Rudy's socks in this one, the woman a true talent. Huck going to slip the ring box in the Cracker Jack box and knock her socks off. Thinking if they caught the early show, he'd have her back home and be at the flower shop in time for whatever the gang was planning tonight.

Sitting on North Michigan, waiting on Hertz to finish his meeting, the pistol he gave him under the seat, Huck considered the Checker driver might circle around. Keeping his eye in the rearview mirror, not needing trouble to spoil his plans. But the Checker didn't roll back around, Hertz finishing the meeting earlier than expected.

Huck taking Karla for dinner before the show, her fingers going into the Cracker Jack, the scene where Valentino saves Gloria Swanson from a snowy mountain ledge. Huck glanced at Karla as she reached in the box, frowning as she touched something that wasn't caramel corn, taking it out and gasping. Theater goers turning for a look, Karla holding up the diamond and platinum ring, her mouth falling open, staring at what the jeweler called a floral motive, the man selling Huck on karats and clarity. Karla gave a whoop, more moviegoers turning, at first disturbed by the interruption, then giving a round of applause as she slipped it on, announcing she was to be married. Huck doing it proper.

Still on top of the world when he went up the stairs at Schofield's, replaying her saying "Yes." Walking in on a heated talk between Doyle and Vincent Drucci. Doyle saying they ought to stick to the treaty with Torrio, that it was good for business.

Drucci saying, "Get in bed with the dagos, and in no time we're taking it up the ass. Deanie's right going against them."

"Like swatting a hive with a stick, you ask me," Gypsy Doyle said, keeping his cool.

"You afraid of a few guineas now, Doyle?"

"Just don't see the need to push it."

Getting a beer from the icebox, Huck sat, putting together pieces of the argument. Turned out two of Torrio's guys had been nabbed with a load of shine in back of a hearse, hauling it across North Side turf. Suspicious cops on the payroll pulled the hearse over, finding the load of booze and demanding three hundred bucks from Torrio for its release. Torrio calling up Dean for a favor, asking him to call off his police dogs. Dean telling Torrio these particular dogs weren't his, and nothing he could do about it. Torrio asking him to take care of it anyway — as a friend. Dean getting hot under the collar, saying the only way to take care of it was for Torrio to pay the three hundred. The Gennas crossed into the same turf laid out in Torrio's very own treaty — not something Dean was going to fix. Telling Torrio he could have the two Genna men clipped for half that much, but simply put, it wasn't his problem. Dean hanging up the phone.

Drucci saying, "Would've done the same myself, told him off."

"After that, maybe you'll get your chance." Doyle looking over at Huck, saying, "What do you think?"

Huck just shrugged, seeing Dean step into the room.

"What are we talking about, the dagos?" Dean said, looking from man to man.

"Telling them about Torrio wanting you to pay the three hundred," Drucci said, now laughing.

"That's the trouble with that guy, he likes to sweat the nickels."

"Love to see his mug, he ever figures out the other thing," Drucci said, slapping his knee.

"What thing?" Doyle said.

"A couple more of their trucks didn't make it." Dean shrugged.

"You hit him?" Doyle said.

"Not so much hit, let's say misplaced," Dean said, looking around, seeing he had the floor. "Got them in a barn out of town, asking a ransom, making it look like the greaser brothers got a hand in it." Meaning the Gennas. "The Fox getting outfoxed, so to speak." Dean clapped his hands. "So, what're we drinking?"

"Be no more snuggling up, greaser to greaser," Drucci said.

"But why we splashing on the gasoline?" Doyle said.

"What, you got a problem?" Dean said, looking pissed at him.

Doyle flipped up his hands like he was conceding. "Ah, fuck it. You're the boss."

Going past the icebox to the table set up like a bar, Dean poured a shot, knocking it back, then looking at Huck.

"You wanna be a cabbie, then act like one. Let's go." Dean waving his hand, leading the way downstairs, going out the door and getting in the passenger side of the Yellow Huck had driven up in.

Drucci and Doyle followed behind in Drucci's Plymouth. Dean telling Huck to drive to a warehouse past Garfield Park, had him pull the taxi inside, not saying much to him on the drive. An International panel truck sat parked, two rows of fifty-gallon water barrels strapped in back.

Telling him the barrels were full of water, Dean had him leave the taxi in the warehouse and drive the truck.

Not asking why they were hauling water, Huck got in the truck with Dean and followed Drucci's Plymouth. The two of them still not saying much, Huck drove past the racetrack in Cicero, pulling past woods and fields. He spotted a police cruiser parked at the side of the dirt road ahead, Dean telling him to roll up behind and flash his lights.

The cop was a lieutenant called Grady, waving to Dean, driving on and leading the way. Dean telling Huck to follow. Two miles of eating the cop's dust, two more cruisers fell in line behind the Plymouth, Dean unbothered by it.

The lieutenant pulled onto a dirt road, Huck following for another half mile, turning onto a narrow dirt track, the truck hopping over the rough ground, raising enough dust to block out the Plymouth and cruisers following, the springs of the truck riding heavy with the weight of the full barrels. They pulled up out front of a barn, red-painted boards and a rusted roof. Huck was told to back up to the double doors.

Getting out and following Dean inside, working with Doyle and Drucci pulling tarps off, revealing cases of Kentucky whiskey, Huck guessing there were about a hundred and fifty cases, making it about eighteen hundred bottles. The two cops with Lieutenant Grady got up in back of the truck, shoved two barrels to the edge of the tailgate, one was filled and heavy to move, the other was empty.

Dean and Drucci carried the cases to the truck. Doyle and Huck took the bottles and poured the whiskey contents into the empty barrel, working as fast as they could. The three cops refilling the whiskey bottles with the water from the full barrel.

"Thought you were kidding about the water," Huck said.

Dean laughed, having a good time now.

The lieutenant lit a smoke and kept watch for dust clouds coming down the road, an eye out for the Gennas. The six men took better than half the night switching the whiskey for water, all of them sweating and tired. Re-corking and placing the bottles in the cases, they got them back under the tarps. Then they rolled the vehicles out to the road, swiping away their tire tracks with branches, leaving the Gennas' barn like they found it, driving the load of whiskey to a warehouse in Cicero, right in Al Capone's backyard.

Back at Schofield's, Dean estimated they just made a hundred-grand switcheroo, laughing till he cried, saying he'd give his share along with his right nut to see the look on Bloody Ang Genna's face when he found out they got water instead of whiskey in their barn.

Then Huck got a chance to share his good news, getting congratulations all around, Drucci wanting to know if the girl was blind. Doyle set up glasses and poured a round, Dean telling Huck to take his gal out on the town, take her to the Balaban and Katz, dubbed as "the wonder theater of the world," better than the Biograph any day of the week, then to the Drake for steaks and champagne, reserve a suite for the night, told Huck it was all on him. Then there was the envelope with the cash — a lot of cash.

42

The man had been talking his ear off, Huck wondering how the taxi boss was able to breathe at the same time. John D. invited Huck to take a look at his horses, his pride and joy, having him drive his Duesenberg the forty miles from the city. The Model A with the straight-eight engine, a buggy that could go like a rocket in spite of its weight, not a rig Checker thugs were going to muscle off the road — and nothing like the mules Mogul put out.

Insisting on sitting in back, Hertz played the man about town, leaving Huck to feel like part chauffeur, part bodyguard, slipping the pistol under the seat.

"Picture Michigan Avenue without the light I put in, paid out of my own pocket," John D. said. "There'd be a heap of crumpled steel. Cars piling into each other all the way from East Randolph to East 33rd. All that civic spirit on my dime."

Huck hearing about the traffic light for the third time that week — how John D. was saving lives. Claimed that putting in that light was what inspired the city council to put on a five-hundred-man traffic squad and the traffic towers along Michigan, and again at State and Madison.

Passing the sign for the village of Schaumburg, then getting to Trout Valley, rolling past gentle hills to the stone gate and up the long drive, to a place like Huck had never seen, John D. calling the architecture of the manor house Georgian, his little place in the country.

Then John D. went on blowing how he and a long-ago partner, Shaw, got the first auto agency on its feet back in '05. Grew the business, buying up Thomas Cabs and having meters built in. Went through different builds before settling on the Model J. "Huck, you listening?"

"Yeah, yeah, Thomas Cabs."

"No point in me talking if nobody's listening — not doing it for my health."

"Hearing every word," Huck lied. "Well, now and then a thought of my own does try to squeeze in, but don't you worry, I chase 'em off."

John D. laughed, saying, "Guess I'm passionate about it."

"Just a bit."

"You got any questions, how I made it?"

Huck thought a moment, saying, "Maybe one."

"Go on."

"How come yellow?" Huck turned and smiled, knowing the answer.

"You're playing with me."

"Guess I am, but I mean it kinda sticks out."

"There's the difference between you and me, Huck. Let me know when you see it."

"Main difference, I'd say, is about a million bucks."

"Well, you're more than a little short-sighted there, but it's not the money, it's having a vision, then going after it, sinking your teeth in." John D. waved his arm through the air, like he was trying to catch a thought, saying, "You know of P.T. Barnum?"

"He in taxis?"

"The greatest showman who ever lived, that's who. Man who said, 'Fortune doesn't favor a man who won't help himself.'"

Huck taking that in, mulling it over.

"Had that in my mind when I got in with Shaw and got things started, going on and pioneering an industry."

Huck was wondering what happened to that partner, getting an image of a push out the door, or could be a window.

"I put money in balloon tires, wipers on windows, drivers in uniform, two-way radios, meters to cut out the guess work — what nobody else was doing. Some thinking I was crazy. But I held that vision of Yellow cabs rolling up Michigan, down South State, getting folks home every day of the week, picking them up from the La Salle, the Bismarck, the Rialto, any point, any depot, Union League, the Hamilton Club, Marshall Field, Mandel Brothers, Lamb's Cafe — getting all of Chicago home safe and sound, riding in back of a Yellow with that limousine feeling."

"All this before the shooting in the street?" Huck looked at him in the mirror, meeting his eyes.

"Still think you're missing the point." John D. shook his head, going on, "Hired on this research institute, one that came up with the color, calling yellow distinct, folks seeing it coming a half mile away. The next one's coming right behind it. Oh, there goes another one."

"And makes a heck of a target."

"Well now, what color'd you suggest?" John D. kept shaking his head.

"Thinking camouflage, with thick plates on the side, and maybe a guy riding shotgun — better yet, a turret."

John D. laughed. "You ever see things on the bright side?"

"Tried it once, just wasn't for me."

John D. went on, "Under the thick skull, I think there could be a head for business."

"Good at surviving, that's for sure."

"I came up on the streets," John D. said. "Ran from home after a beating, one I likely had coming, scratched and scraped for pennies, went hungry and got sick —"

"Heard all this before, you know?"

"Point is, you and me came up on the same streets."

"And you turned it into all this," Huck said, looking up at the fine house.

The two of them getting out of the Dues, and John D. showed him the house, taking him out past the fine gardens, the treed grounds, then out to the fenced riding pens and stables.

Huck taking it all in, impressed with it, picturing something like this for himself, could practically taste it.

43

Parked along South Michigan, Huck had his eyes on the stand across the street, not his job anymore, but he kept watch for poachers anyway, a force of habit. Hertz was inside, meeting with one of his lawyers, working again to settle with the old woman from last year's car wreck, the woman coming up with new aches, a slipped disc that had gone undetected, along with blurred vision, a sawbones ready to swear on a bible it was on account of the accident.

Told to wait in the car, Huck was driving a Yellow today, John D.'s Duesenberg back at the livery, Moses giving it an oil change and once-over.

Huck saw them coming in the mirror, three of them walking to his taxi, Hymie Weiss sliding in up front, not saying a word, Vincent Drucci pushing a dark-haired man ahead of him, onto the back seat, getting in and slapping the door shut.

"Hey fellas. I already got a fare." A dumb thing to say. Huck looking from one to the other, getting a bad feeling right off.

"Drive," Drucci told him.

Huck looked at him over the seat, knowing it wasn't a time to argue, saying, "Drive where?"

The third man was hanging his head down like he was bent or half asleep.

"Along the lake, out of town."

Hymie kept looking straight ahead.

So Huck drove, knowing better than to ask more questions, getting them onto North Clark, past Rogers Park, the lake peeking past buildings to the east, looking gray in the afternoon light, a light chop with whitecaps showing. Guessing Hertz would come out of the office building, stand dumbfounded a minute, hail a different Yellow, cursing him all the way back to the office. Sure to be some explaining later on.

The tall buildings gave way to houses, then to woodland, then to pastures, Vincent Drucci finally saying, "Where's my manners . . ." Saying to the third man, "How you say it, Widnowski?"

"Widnuski — Stefan."

"Stefan here's a lying, thieving Polack," Drucci said. "Helped himself to one of our trucks."

"It was a mistake. If I knew it was your —"

Drucci slapped him across the top of his head. "Knew it was ours 'cause the Gennas put you up to it. How much they pay you?"

Widnuski groaned, started sobbing into his hands.

Hymie took a pack of smokes, calm like he was in a library, offering the pack to Huck. "Smoke?"

Huck took one, not looking to the back. Hymie found a match and scratched it to life, holding it across to Huck, then lighting his own. Huck still wondering where they were going, guessing they wanted him to put a beating on this Widnuski.

"Let me go, and I spit on the Gennas. Never, never again. *Phew.*" Winuski with a pleading tone. "It's the money, they promise me."

"Now you got regrets," Drucci said. "You make your bed, and you lie in it. You ever hear of that?"

"I got kids."

"Sure, the reason you did it," Drucci said. "Heard that a hundred times already."

"And a wife — a good woman — oh, such a good woman. Oh, what I put her through . . ." Widnuski shaking his head, full of regrets.

Hymie looked at Huck, like it was a pathetic show. They passed a sign marking the city limits, Hymie telling him to take the next right, Huck pulling the Yellow onto a farm road, took it for a half mile, getting close to the water, then was told to make another turn, the dirt road taking them along the shore, a spot behind Calvary Cemetery. The springs bouncing them, stones pinging against the undercarriage. A thick copse of birch before the land opened to the cemetery, Huck seeing stones and some crosses.

"This is good," Hymie said.

Huck stopped the taxi, getting set for whatever was coming next.

Drucci getting out on the passenger side, waving for Widnuski to get out.

"I'm sorry. No! No! Look —" The man resisted, hands clawing at the seats, feet scraping the metal floor, trying not to get pulled out.

Cursing, Drucci grabbed hold, dragging the man out, catching a fistful of black hair, Widnuski calling to the others for mercy, swearing he wouldn't do it again. Pleading it was a mistake. His children. His wife — pregnant again.

Hymie looked at Huck, passive, saying, "The man misread a situation, Bloody Angelo being a convincing guy . . . so Widnuski robs one of our trucks, pulls a piece on our guy and clips him over the ear. Mope who pulled it with him peached on him. Saving his own keester, so to speak. So, let me ask, what would you do?"

"With this guy?"

"Yeah, what do you do?"

"Guy says he won't do it again."

And Hymie shrugged and dragged on the smoke, took another from the pack, lit it off the butt of the other, rolled the window down and tossed out the butt, rolled the window back up, taking a look out toward the lake. Saying, "Nice view."

"It's all lies, it was —"

Drucci threw a punch, subduing Widnuski, dragging him from under his arms, past the trees, the heels of the man's shoes scraping the rough ground. Hauling him out of view.

"Going to iron the man's shoelaces, you heard it called that?" Hymie said, sitting there smoking and looking out at the lake.

"Don't know it, no," Huck said, seeing it was Drucci who was going to knock sense into Widnuski. Wondering why they got in his cab.

"Used to drop a line . . ." Hymie looking out at the water, then turned to Huck. "I mean I fished near here when I was a kid, some point of land jutting out, brings the fish in when they feed."

"That right?"

"You ever fish?"

"Sure."

"Walleye like you wouldn't believe. Or you call 'em pickerel?"

"Got nothing like that back home. Bass and cats in Pontchartrain, snapper and triple-tail out in the Gulf."

"That in the south, huh?"

"New Orleans."

"Why you talk like that. What do they call it, a gat accent?"

"Yat."

"Yat, huh?" Hymie nodded, then said, "Anyhow, walleye make good eaters, don't matter what you call them."

Huck heard the *bang bang* — making him jump. The echo rolling and fading out over the water.

Hymie puffed on the cigarette like he didn't hear anything, saying "You hear about Nails?"

"What?"

"Nails Morton, you know him — sure you two met."

"Yeah, at the fights, an okay guy."

"Was as in past tense, yeah. The man's pushing daisies."

"Dead?" Huck thinking it had something to do with Dean poking at the Italian hive, all the trouble catching up with them. Saying, "Sorry to hear about it."

"Yeah, a damn shame. Man was a soldier in the war, got some medal, French name."

"Croix de Guerre."

Hymie looked at Huck like he was wondering how he knew it, but didn't ask. Saying, "The man's riding a horse through Lincoln Park, don't ask me how come. Anyhow, some hack backfires and the damn beast rears and throws him. One of them rental nags too — got the spirit of porridge. Something Nails liked to do — ride and play cowboy, maybe thinking he was in the cavalry or something, I don't know."

"It threw him?"

"Witness says something could've stung it, spooked it, you know how they get. Anyway, coroner figures he hit his head — but this witness says Nails tried to get up, and the damn nag rears again and stomps him, not just once or twice, but went all Bojangles on him. A swayback nag that can barely walk, you believe something like that?"

"Jesus . . ."

"Yeah, well, The Schemer came to me, and we rounded a couple of the boys, Bugs and Louis 'Two Gun' — and we went finding this horse."

"You find it?"

"Drinking water at the duck pond, acting like nothing happened. Who knows, maybe Nails should've brought it a carrot once in a while. Anyhow, we evened things up."

"By evened . . ."

"Brought it to the spot where it did Nails, and gave it four to the head. Pow, pow, pow, and pow. What else you gonna do?"

Opening the back door, Drucci got back in, stamping his feet, saying, "Goddamn colder than a witch's tit. Let's go, I got a date."

44

After they married, they bought a five-room place by Lincoln Park, a better neighborhood, Huck feeling they were moving up. And there was no more talk of Karla having to dance for nickels, Huck making enough to fix the place up, with enough left to enroll Izzy in a proper school. The three of them living like a real family, telling about their days around the supper table. Karla doing a fine job of giving the place that woman's touch, flowers in a vase, pictures in frames on the walls Huck had patched up. And she was already talking of getting an even a bigger place, one with another washing machine and a fireplace, calling it an investment, their money making money.

Karla hooked her arm in his, looked at the ring on her finger, smiled, and they crossed Oak, the Drake up ahead — looked like a thousand lights were on, the uniformed man holding the door. Huck bringing her here for her twenty-fourth birthday, wondering if it was the same doorman, standing here the day he got in the fight out front at the Yellow stand, seemed like a long time ago now. The taxi skirmishes continuing yet.

He glanced to the street, the Yellow stand right where it had been. Behind it, the block was showing fresh signs of construction, the new Allerton Hotel going up two blocks to the south. Millions being poured into revitalizing this part of town since they put in the bridge, the one over Michigan Avenue, turning this part of town into the ritz.

"What's so funny?" Karla asked.

"Thinking back to when you danced at the Alley Cat, telling me your name's Lizzy."

"Was glad you didn't tramp my toes, all the while thinking I'd have to give you the brush-off."

"Well, I'm glad you took pity." He nodded to the hostess and walked with Karla across the marble, the two of them a well-to-do married couple coming for afternoon tea, him in the tailor-made pinstripes, the two-tone wingtips, Huck learning to stir without touching the sides of his cup, then placing the spoon on the saucer next to it. Karla in what she called her Fifth Avenue style, the white linen dress and hat. Karla falling in love with the Fountain Court — the high ceiling and lines of columns, the chandeliers and potted palm trees, the amazing trays of pastries and petit fours. The two of them treated like royalty, the hostess showing them to a table.

"How about it?" Huck asked after tea, reaching for her hand over the tablecloth. "Care to dance?"

"You know there's no music, right?" Letting him take her hand.

"Anytime I'm with you, there's music."

"Getting fancy with the words, Mr. Huckabee Waller, but I don't see no dance stub. Take me to this fancy place and get me wondering what you really have in mind."

"Just talking to you is more than fine."

"Talk that leads to dipping a beak, then to dipping something more. Think I don't know your tricks, mister?"

269

"Call me Huck, and where I come from, talking's a good way to fix that suspicious nature."

"But why me? Lots of pretty girls here." Karla glanced around the room, smiling as he got up, came around and got her chair.

"Well, on account it's your birthday, not to mention you got my ring on your finger. But even that first time at the Grant Hospital, I got filled with wonder."

"Wonder, huh?"

"Had me wondering what you looked like out of that uniform, without the little cap on." With that he led her from the Fountain Court, thanking the hostess on the way out.

The two of them bumping into Jack McGurn in the hallway. This gangster known as "Machine Gun," running with the Circus Cafe gang, a bunch of hoods into nickel-and-dime crime, pickpocketing and breaking into places. Dean and the boys calling on them anytime they needed a hand bringing loads of hootch across. Huck introducing him, McGurn taking Karla's hand and kissing it, asking what a fine-looking lady was doing with a mug like this, finding out it was her birthday, wishing her a happy one, trying for a glance down the front of her dress, not caring that Huck was watching him do it — like he was tempting him to do something about it.

"Kind of a creep," she said when they walked on.

"Well, you meet all kinds," is all Huck said.

Then she was back to playing, pretending to frown, saying, "And just where you taking me this time of night?"

"Oh, I got a place in mind." He hooked his arm.

"Let me guess, yours?" She put a hand on his arm.

"Sure, my car's right outside." He led her along the marble floor, taking her to the ballroom.

"Want to get me in your car, huh? How do I know you even got a car?"

"Got lots of them," Huck said.

"Telling me you're a tycoon, that it?" Karla turned down her lip, giving him doubtful.

"I drive a taxi, a different one anytime I want."

"You mean anytime you get one shot up."

"Well, we'll just walk then — it's not so far." They walked into the ballroom, the head waiter nodding, escorting them to a table in the front, a reserved sign on the linen.

"You ever get tired of it?" she said after the waiter pulled out her chair.

"The fighting?" Huck sat across from her.

"Driving, doing it all day?"

"Well sure, I guess so."

"So you ask a dancer to ankle it, me being on my dogs all day. I think you're out of luck as far as the dancing tonight, mister."

"Well, we'll just sit here and listen to the music, then," Huck said, smiling and holding her hand across the table, his one-in-a-million girl. Showing her a good time, taking her to the Fountain Court for tea every week, the two of them using the same lines, trying a few new ones.

They caught a set by the Bucktown Five, the front man with the horn introduced the band and they played a couple of numbers. Taking a bow to the applause, thanking the ladies and gents. Seemed a million years ago to Huck, Karla nickel-dancing with drunken men on the sawdust floor of the Alley Cat. The Jimmy Joy Orchestra with their *For One Night Only* sign. Henry the bartender filling glasses from a jug of watered swill, setting them on the bar top. And back then, he only saw this place from the taxi stand out front.

Later they'd go up to the suite he reserved, Karla liking the view of the Magnificent Mile.

The Bucktown Five got into an Isham Jones number "Swinging Down the Lane," then the violin player stepped to the microphone and informed the audience that before he introduced Vera Vaughn, the chanteuse for the evening, they had a special guest he was pleased to welcome to the stage.

Huck seeing Dean O'Banion getting up from a table on the opposite side of the stage, sitting with Hymie Weiss, Vincent Drucci, Bugs Moran, another man he didn't recognize, plus their ladies. Stepping to the stage, Dean got himself a nice round of applause from the room, taking a bow, the killer bootlegger giving a broad smile, then nodding to the band. Seeing Huck, he pointed a finger at him, taking his spot at the condenser microphone as the violinist counted down, Dean began singing "The One I Love (Belongs to Somebody Else)." Doing a fine job and getting a hearty round of applause after, and a few calls for more, mostly from his own table. Dean obliging and giving them "Danny Boy."

45

Huck was parked in a Yellow across from the stand out front of the Drake when Gypsy Doyle pulled alongside in his Ford, waiting for Huck to lean across and roll down his passenger-side window, told him to pick The Schemer up at his place down in the Loop and bring him to Schofield's.

"You figure me for a chauffeur, huh?" Huck was supposed to pick Hertz up from the livery in a half hour.

"You understand you're sitting in a taxi, right?" Doyle telling him Drucci was joining them on the run that night. Dean wanting an extra man along after getting a tip from one of the Circus Cafe crew, Machine Gun McGurn or Screwy Moore, one of them, warning Dean he heard a rumor that his boys might get hijacked tonight.

The word was Bloody Ang Genna was planning to hit back at the North Side, getting even for the water heist and the hijackings pulled on Genna crews, six of their trucks ripped off since Easter — with no payback, the kind of thing that made the Gennas look weak in Sicilian circles. Dean finding out the Gennas got wind they were bringing loads across the Detroit River on a skiff this time of year, a signal man on the

Detroit side waving a lantern when the driver in the boat got the all-clear to cross. The patrol cops were greased and paid to look the other way, but somebody leaked it.

Dean careful to keep on the right side of the Purples, paying for the privilege of crossing over the Bernstein brothers' turf, a bunch of well-organized Jews working out of Little Jerusalem, Dean paying the Purple toll before sending his guys to the pick-up spots they changed every time they brought a load across, switching from LaSalle, Sandwich, Walkerville and Riverside, then back, using the Purples' signal men and boat crews.

Huck knew about the Purples, but outside of the signal men and boat crews, he'd never run into any of them on the crossings he'd made with Doyle. McGurn and the Circus boys showing up sometimes, heavily armed and running escort, seeing that the good Canadian hootch made it into the hands of the waiting scofflaws in Old Windy.

Dean told Huck that night at the Drake ballroom that McGurn was basically a greaser, fair-complected and trying hard to put on the mick, changing his name from Vincenzo something or other, and that Dean suspected him of working both sides of the street, meaning McGurn was likely the one feeding intel to Torrio or the Gennas. Dean feeding McGurn a load of malarkey, seeing if the man was a rat or not. If he was, then he'd let Doyle and Drucci take him for one of those one-way drives and do a little exterminating. Huck wondering why Dean told him a thing like that. Could be they were watching to see if he'd keep it to himself, how far Huck could be trusted — the guy that was working for Yellow Cab on the side.

Picking up Drucci at his place, a nice walk-up apartment on Monroe, Huck headed back up South Michigan, driving to meet Doyle at Schofield's, listening to Drucci in back talking as the traffic slowed. Guessing the man had been drinking, Huck nodded and looked amused when he figured he should.

"So, me and Deanie, we blow this safe one time — let's see — back in June sometime." Drucci telling a story, Huck figuring the man, like Hertz, loved the sound of his own voice.

What Huck knew about him: Vincent "The Schemer" Drucci was a practical joker, a clown basically — him and Dean known to do anything for a laugh going back to the days when the two of them were growing up in Little Hell. Dean and Hymie finding Drucci back when they were kids, Drucci breaking into a phone box, reaching in for a handful of coins — Drucci ready to take them both on — young Dean telling him they could use a fellow with his talents, invited him into the gang, basically just the three of them at the time, adding Bugs a short time later, and the bunch of them had been tight since then.

"So this tea shop . . ." Drucci was looking at him.

"Sorry, go on."

"According to our Circus guy, tipping us they had a cash box stuffed full of more than Earl Grey, you understand, this joint being a front for one of Torrio's set-ups. So, Deanie and me figure to blow it, see, then hang it on the Gennas — why he brings me along, on account of my dago looks, plus I know a few words, see?"

"Sure."

"You figure I got dago looks?" Drucci not smiling.

"Your words, not mine." Huck giving him a bored look.

"Yeah, but you figure I got 'em, dago looks?"

"What I figure's you want to push, see how far I'll bend — maybe try me out."

"Just having fun with you, kid." Drucci was grinning now, throwing a tap of a punch at Huck's shoulder, a little harder than it needed to be, then he went on, "Little Englishman running the place's got this safe in back, see — one of them Wild West kind, the thing sitting on wheels with the big dial on the front, you know the one?"

"Sure."

"So, I ask why he don't trust his neighbors, typical English, am I right? Then I show him my piece and tell him to spin the dial and let's see him open it. 'Course the guy won't do it, so out comes the nitro, an old rock-man showing Deanie how to set it. So, Deanie's setting it up, telling the guy the step-by-step of it, getting set to blow the door or us to Kingdom Come, the guy ain't sure which. All of a sudden the cops kick in the door, the thing flying off the hinges, everybody yelling and pistols pointing at us. Turns out the tea-drinker's trouble-and-strife was up the stairs, not the trusting kind neither. Must'a gone out the fire escape and run for a call box."

"And they nabbed you?"

"Dead to rights, a bunch of blue boys rushing in, two in the front, three in the back. Dean raising the jam shot in his hand, calm as you please, saying he was getting butter fingers, all these coppers around, set to drop the tiny bottle, blow all of us to bits, telling them to back out the door. And fuck me, Deanie actually drops it, I mean by accident, and nothing, the thing doesn't blow, a fuckin' dud. You believe it?" Drucci barked a laugh, slapping his knees in back, going on, "Both of us locked up, then making bail, Deanie pulling down six months on account of it being his first time. Me . . ." Drucci held up three fingers, saying, "I skipped, I mean I had no choice."

"You skipped bail?"

"Technically still on the dodge." Drucci waved a hand, like what did he care. "I say let 'em come and look." Drucci pointing to a parked patrol car at the curb up ahead, just at Madison, one cop behind the wheel. Saying to Huck, "Pull up."

"What?"

"Gonna turn myself in."

"You're fucking with me?"

"Sure I am, guilty as hell too — been weighing on my conscience. Go on, pull up!" Drucci's look told him he wasn't kidding.

So, Huck pulled alongside, the copper glancing over, giving a tired look from behind the wheel. Huck hoping it was a cop on Dean's payroll.

Drucci rolled his window down, saying to the cop, "Officer fuck-am-a-bob, you got any idea who I am?"

The copper raised his brows, slow to shake his head. Drucci telling him his name, then saying, "And I skipped bail." Giving him a moment, then, "So, what are you gonna do about it?"

The copper's partner was coming from a cart up the block, a bag of peanuts in hand, taking in the situation, dropping the bag and reaching for his sidearm, coming on the double.

Drucci turned to Huck, saying, "So, you're the driver — you any good?"

Huck gave it gas, somebody else honking, the second cop jumping into the patrol car, Huck seeing their headlights in the rearview, the cop on the passenger side using the hand crank, getting the siren to howl.

"Okay, let's see it, hotshot," Drucci said, folding his arms and looking forward, not bothered by the pursuing patrol car, sitting back like he was going to enjoy this.

Huck hit the gas, the Mogul taxi not much for racing up Michigan, steering around another car with the patrol car gaining. No way he could outrun them, best he could hope for was dodging and losing them. His hands clamped to the wheel, bouncing his tires off the curb, the taxi rocking, and that got Drucci whooping like he was having the time of his life. The coppers right on Huck's bumper.

Then he saw it — the bridge tower and gray of the Wrigley Building looming ahead, the tender raising the bridge from the tower, the damn thing going up. Huck seeing the steam ship's stack.

"You fucking crazy!" Drucci was yelling or whooping, Huck couldn't tell as he hit the gas, getting everything he could out of it, rushing and hoping to beat the opening maw of the bridge, the deck lifting like a wall before his eyes. Cars waiting in a line ahead, Huck switched into the oncoming lane that was empty, passing the line, the coppers still gaining behind him.

And he roared up the bridge — funny thing, what he remembered most was the time — six on the nose on the Wrigley clock in front of him as the Yellow, the big tin canary going airborne — that moment when the wheels left the ground, the dirty river under them — nothing for a moment, then bottoming hard on the other half of the bridge deck, Huck smashed into the steering wheel, Drucci into the dash. Drucci still whooping or screaming, sparks flying from the undercarriage. One of the wheels rolling on ahead of them, the axle grinding on the asphalt like an anchor, Huck fighting the steering as the Mogul scraped to a halt. And like that Huck was out, his ribs sore from slamming against the steering, and he hobbled past the incoming line of cars waiting for the passing steamer, amazed looks from inside the line of cars. Last he saw of Drucci, the drunk gangster was slow getting out, limping off the other way, calling him a crazy son of a bitch.

Huck was moving like a granny when he heard the cop car's engine scream, rushing the ramp, and the coppers came flying across too, the patrol car crashing down hard, skidding and slamming into the tail end of the Yellow, sending the Mogul spinning into the first car in the waiting line.

Huck willed himself past the line of cars, taking one look back, Drucci and the cops nowhere in sight. No time to wonder if he got away. Not slowing for three blocks, long out of breath, before he was looking behind him again. Still no sign of Drucci or the coppers. And now he was hobbling along, taking inventory of his body, no broken bones or serious injuries as far as he could tell, building a story in his mind, figuring how he'd explain to John D. and likely the cops about the Yellow getting swiped from the stand out front of the Drake while he went to use the water closet. Huck acting out the scene, laying the blame on some sneak-thieving swine of a Checker driver.

46

"**Y**ou forgetting who landed you in that chair, Big Bill?" John D. said it like he was kidding, sitting across the desk, the brass nameplate declaring William Hale Thompson the mayor, like maybe you might forget who you're talking to, the mayor nearing the end of his second term. Having earned the nickname Kaiser Bill due to his stand against conscription and not in favor of sending their boys over to Europe. Earning condemnation among some of the populace, but gaining favor among the city's German and Irish who only saw Big Bill taking an anti-British stand.

Ten minutes before walking in here John D. had been going up one side of Huck and down the other on account of another destroyed taxi. Huck explaining he was in the Drake using the water closet, some filthy dog swiping the taxi right in front of the stand, likely one of Markin's madmen. The same story he told the cops. John D. didn't buy it, but backed him up at the Chicagoland station, claiming it had to be Checker who stole it, on account it was the type of dirty tricks they used to interfere in Yellow's business, doing it right under the noses of Chicago's finest.

As penance, John D. promised Huck would be driving him around even more like a chauffeur, calling it beefed-up security. John D. wanting to keep an eye on him. Not leaving Huck waiting out in the car, bringing him into meetings, Huck sitting and waiting in some outer office.

"Can't forget it when you keep bringing it up," Big Bill said. "Look, John, we're old friends, I grant you that — the reason I granted you the prime stands, if you recall. Now I've got you pissing in my ear. And I've got Markin whining in the other, threatening me with lawyers and running to the press."

"It's what the man does best, whining and running. Any fool can see the man's got union troubles coming out his own ears. That union slugger getting killed, shot by one of Markin's own boys."

Huck remembered reading in the *Trib* how the union's man Frank Sexton had been gunned down in a poolroom over on West Division, a joint where Yellow drivers hung around, shooting eight ball. A dozen Checker men were questioned before charges were laid against Jack Rose. First day of his trial, a handcuffed Rose was led from the courtroom when he was cut down by Sexton's weeping father raising his revolver and firing point blank. The entire city demanding something be done about this spiraling taxi war. The cops supposed to be cranking things down tight in the city.

"Alleged, alleged," Big Bill practically shouted. "Look, what I'm proposing here's a sit-down, get the two of you in a room, leave your guns and muscle outside and hash out a peace." The mayor took a quick glance at Huck by the door, not happy about Hertz insisting he be there, claiming the need for a bodyguard at all times now, what with Morris Markin acting like an avenging crackpot, letting his out-of-control goons loose on the street.

Big Bill kept talking, "The two of you hash this thing

out, once and for all. A city as grand as ours, there's got to be enough pie to divvy up."

Huck thinking of the trouble between O'Banion and Torrio and knowing there was never enough pie. And he was thinking of Drucci getting arrested two blocks from where they jumped the Michigan Avenue bridge. Drucci trying to escape on a twisted ankle, arrested for evasion and wanton endangerment, adding to the charge of skipping bail. Drucci blaming it on Huck's poor judgment.

"Spoken with diplomatic flair, Big Bill," John D. said. "But Markin won't sit down, damn coward wants his boys to do it in the street, it's what the man understands, his Ruskie nature."

"And I'm saying, do it, go on and choke the Jesus out of each other, just not on my streets." The mayor's face going red. "John, look here now, I won't have constituents getting run off the road, put in danger, and left to go limping to the papers — the same folks I'm supposed to be protecting, the ones who cast their ballots. Way things sit I couldn't beat that wet blanket Sweitzer another term."

"This thing's gone long enough, I grant you, Big Bill, but asking us to a sit-down . . ." John D. twisted his mouth in that way of his. He didn't bring up that it was common knowledge that Big Bill wasn't tossing his hat in the ring again for the upcoming mayoral race, so why do his bidding.

"I've got every kind of bootlegger and outlaw coming like the plagues of Egypt, meantime council's still sweeping up from the riots. And I've got you with your taxi war."

"Well, I'm sorry for it, Big Bill, I truly am, but surely you can see that whole Sexton mess gets pinned on Markin."

"You saying the man firebombed his own place? Wife and kids at the table having supper."

"Well, not so fast now, I wouldn't put it past him, but I tell you what, revoke his license, call back his stands, pending an investigation, and you spare all this grief and —"

"What you're doing, John, you're putting your hand down my pants and giving a big old squeeze." Big Bill's face went sour. "And smiling like you're doing me a favor."

"Man turns your city upside down, and you're acting like I'm asking too much."

"And how'd I even spin a thing like that?"

"The man's a stain — his drivers sent a voter and I lost count how many of my men to the hospital, a couple to the morgue, and never had to answer for any of it." Hertz turned in his chair. "Isn't that so, Huck — you being a victim yourself? Still walking with a limp."

"Was right in the thick of it, yes sir."

"See there."

"And somehow you're clean in this," Big Bill said, ignoring Huck.

"There you go, forgetting who put in that first traffic light, paid for it out of my own pocket —"

"Oh, for goodness sake!"

"Yes, for the goodness of our fair city, that's right. Working together for a better future, you remember that speech, one you made with me standing right next to you?"

"Quit blowing smoke, John. Of course I'm grateful to you, hell, we're all grateful. But I can't have you duking it out with Markin. I've got council calling for an investigation on both of you, some even accusing me of graft, claiming I've shown favoritism. Headlines screaming scandal and corruption — all that poison ink. Remember working at the *Herald*? You know what those people are like. You have no idea the swamp of sharp teeth I'm wading in."

"That reminds me . . ." John D. took an envelope from his inside pocket, glancing to see the door was shut, making a show of sliding it across the oak. "For the swamp fund."

"Very funny." Big Bill glanced over at Huck as he opened his drawer, dropped the envelope in and shut it.

"When they come with the torches, I'll come knocking at your door, John, my hat in hand."

"I'm not one to forget a friend, Big Bill. I think you know that, and I'd like to think you feel the same."

"Like I haven't done enough."

"And I was just hoping you'd put in a call to Collins, put some of that sway to good use." John D. rose from the chair, Huck guessing the man sensed he got what he came for.

"John, sometimes I'm not sure if you're asking or telling." The mayor furrowed his brow, so much that it looked knit together, but he stood and shook the offered hand.

"I'll leave you to it then, Big Bill — go and make those appointments," John D. said it like it was on the sly, yet being good-natured about it. "You get the right kind of fellows on board, and I'll see their tea gets sweetened."

"Can't buy all of us, John."

"Who says so?" John D. smiled, then after a moment, "A three-man committee ought to do it — the right men."

"Funny, you talking about sweetening my tea, and I'm thinking of scraping the flop off my shoe."

"It's what you people understand, the way things get done. And when there's a licensing issue, and a special edict or decree comes of it, an investigation into Checker . . ."

"That's going to take a lot of sweetening, John."

"The cost of doing business." Sighing, John D. got up, stepping to the door, saying, "Long time since we got together with the wives, Bill. Fannie's been asking after you. What say to dinner at Brando's?"

"You want the public seeing us being all chummy?"

"That hurts, Bill." John D. winced.

"I'm sorry. Of course I'll talk to Kate about it."

"We'll look forward to it then, and please give her my best." John D. saying it was good to see him as always, turning for the door, looking at Huck and rolling his eyes.

47

"**H**ow'd I do?"

"Sounded like a man who can live with looking at his own reflection," Huck said.

"First thing I learned, you stay a step ahead, or you'll get stepped on." John D. sat in back of his Dues, Huck getting behind the wheel.

John D. saying he'd heard through the grapevine that Huck had some driving skills, in spite of the trail of wrecked yellow sheet metal. Then he prattled on how Big Bill best pick the right men for this committee, facts that needed to be steered around, others nudged in the right direction, the way of the politicos. Telling Huck to drive him to see Cora Strayer, where he planned to talk with the woman detective about leading a different kind of investigation, digging up more dirt on Morris Markin, enough to send that son-of-a-bitch packing back to Kalamazoo.

Telling Huck a Russian Jew from Smolensk's bound to have a stinking fish somewhere in the back of the cupboard, and Cora Strayer's just the woman to find it.

"Press needs to see who's right and who's wrong in this," John D. said. "Got run off the road yourself — broad daylight, with a boy and old woman on board, putting everybody in hospital. That old woman ought to have sued Markin and not me."

Huck was tired of hearing that old business, been a long time since that crash. John D. settling the suit out of court over a year ago now, paying her lawyers off a second time — and still going on about it.

"Should've got our own witnesses. That Dex Ayres not known for thinking on his feet. Too much hand-holding with that man. Was the right move, letting him go." John D. sat back and mumbled to himself, watching the tall buildings flash by, Huck driving to the office of Cora Strayer.

"Checker runs honest men off the road, puts seniors in hospital, some to the morgue, wrecks a man's livelihood, citizens outraged — the headlines just write themselves. Have Big Bill's phone blowing off the ringer." Grinning at the thought of it, John D. saying, "I'm a businessman, Huck, not a thug, you understand that?"

"The pen's mightier than the sword, they say."

"And don't you ever forget it." Looking at him as Huck pulled up out front.

Bored, Huck walked in with him and waited in Cora Strayer's outer office, smoking cigarettes. After the meeting, they walked back to the Duesenberg, John D. waiting for Huck to open the back door like a chauffeur. Huck thinking he wouldn't mind shutting it on the man's foot, get him to shut up about his troubles for a while. Then he went around and got behind the wheel.

"Want you driving me for a while longer," John D. said.

"What do you call this?"

"From the ranch to town, I mean every day — till this Markin business blows over."

"That's what, forty miles?"

"Trout Valley, glad you remember the way — west of Des Plaines, Schaumburg, West Dundee, Carpentersville. A good driver knows his way around."

"What happened to head of security?"

"It's called job flexibility, Huck. Besides, you got the gun under the seat, right?"

"Yeah, and I know my way around town, but you're talking the whole state. I think there ought to be another raise coming."

"You want to talk about the taxis you wrecked up?"

"No sir, I don't." Huck smiled back.

"Got a new crop of yearlings I want to show you. Fannie picked them up at auction, a lot of promise."

"That right."

"If you're serious, maybe you want to buy in, but we'll talk more on that later." John D. saying, "Now, how about you give me your impression how one of my cabs went flying over the Michigan Avenue bridge while you were watering your horses." John D. still sounding like he was having doubt about the story Huck laid on the cops about answering nature's call.

Huck repeated the story, how he phoned from the call box down the block, phoning about the stolen taxi. Didn't tell him he flagged another Yellow and went to Schofield's, telling Gypsy Doyle what happened, the two of them waiting on Drucci, who didn't show. Not happy about it, Doyle helped with his alibi, tipping one of the waiters at the Drake enough to recollect he saw Huck coming from the water closet, same time the taxi disappeared from right out front. Doyle telling Huck the tip for the waiter was coming out of his end. Then the two of them made the drive to Detroit, taking along Gorilla Al Weinshank and Louis "Two Gun" Alterie, that man sticking out in his ten-gallon cowboy hat, the four of them bringing back a truckload, ready for an ambush that didn't come.

After they made the run, Dean had called Huck to the flower shop, Huck feeling like a chastised schoolboy, being told to keep his nose out of what Dean called the Yellow business, not wanting any more undue attention spilling on the North Side. Not in his usual good spirits, O'Banion was dealing with Torrio's outfit and the Gennas again, the gangs back to poaching each other's shipments. A couple of times they ended in shootouts, two of the North Side crew sent to hospital with gunshot wounds. On top of that, Torrio's man Capone had taken control of Cicero, just west of the North Side territory, the North Side giving up a warehouse where they had been stashing the liquor shipments coming from Canada, having to relocate it to another building Dean leased around the Loop.

John D. heard the concocted story once more as they pulled out front of the Cook County building, going in to see his accountant, then left Huck waiting by the Duesenberg. Huck having a fondness for the big car but a dislike for standing around like a chauffeur, having to wait for another of John D.'s meetings to end, last one of the day.

Then he had to hear the boss man carp on about the day's meetings, recapping them all the way to the Trout Valley ranch. Huck putting his mind on something else, uh-huhing and nodding at the right places, letting John D. think he had an audience. All the while Huck having plenty of his own to think about, like Karla wanting him to leave the rough stuff, having her own foreboding since running into Jack McGurn, reading about the recent killings, thinking they could start up a business of their own, something safe. And she was talking about sending Izzy to college in a couple more years, the boy as sharp as a whip, nearly as tall as Huck now. And she was talking more and more about having a baby of their own, reminding him her clock was ticking.

Seemed like a long time since Huck came hoboing into town, standing at the toe line, the Irish stand-down fights out back of the freight cars, with Gorilla Al collecting bets and Gypsy Doyle throwing wild punches. Huck fighting till he looked like he'd been beaten against a rock.

That's what rolled around in his head on the drive up to Trout Valley, John D. in back, the man's conversation more like a monologue, jawing on about meeting with the mayor and the woman detective, how Morris Markin's days were numbered, going to be run out of town, how John D. might consider buying the Checker interests for pennies on the dollar.

Huck barely heard a word all the way to the ranch, dropping the boss off, nodding when he was told to be back by nine sharp, knowing it would be more like ten by the time he dropped Izzy at school and made it back up here, something he'd blame on the traffic, it getting worse all the time. Then he'd drive the man back to town, take him to more meetings, bored out of his mind while having to keep a sharp eye out.

"Let me ask you, Huck . . ."

Huck looked at him.

"I buy that outfit, there's going to be some changes."

"How so?"

"Understand Markin's hired on Blacks to drive, picking up fares and driving the South Side. How you feel about that?"

"Feel about what?"

"Hiring on Blacks, drivers of color."

Huck shrugged. "Surprised you let Markin do it first, but in the end guess a fare's a fare."

"You suppose they tip?"

"The Blacks? Guess so."

"Telling me you'd pick them up if I make it company policy?"

"That what you're doing?"

"Let's say it is."

"Then that's the way it is."

"Meaning you'd abide?"

"I do like I'm told, you know that."

John D. shook his head. "You leave New Orleans free-willed, or you get run out on a rail? Come on now."

"You kidding, they love me back home." Huck thinking of that pimp Bubbling-Over, and how he'd handle the situation now. Thinking he could go back to the Quarter and look up the fat man if he was still alive after recovering from his wound, see what he had to say.

"Think the only color you care about's the green of money."

"Speaking of money — that horse you mentioned . . ."

"Reigh Count?"

"Right — horse royalty, you called him. Make all kinds of money with him, that right?"

"Well, I don't wish to . . . wait, why you asking?"

"How much to buy in on something like that?"

"You don't beat around the bush, do you?"

"No, sir."

"He's my finest, and he's not for sale, and I don't need a partner, just so we're clear. But if you want to start out, I can get Fannie to keep an eye out for a yearling."

"How much we talking?"

"Well, that depends. You take a winner like Man o' War — you ever hear the name?"

"Can't say so." Huck thinking here we go again.

"Freight train of a horse, won twenty of twenty-one, three world records. Took the wife to see him take the Travers in Saratoga — goddamn took our breath away. A horse like that, with total wins over a quarter million . . . why, the stud fees alone . . ." John D. was whistling. "Man who bought him as a yearling paid five thousand."

Now Huck whistled. "You're saying it's a game of chance. You get a yearling, but you don't know what you got."

"It's more than a game of chance, it's a passion, Huck. Take Reigh Count, we got our sights on the Kentucky Derby. Some in the game say he's the horse to do it."

"This Reigh Count, you got him back at the ranch?"

"Sure do. Would you like to meet him?"

"Think I might."

48

Letting the cylinders hum, Huck blew past a Bowman truck, his mind going to a time when he'd pulled up to one of their fleet and paid thirty cents for a bottle of milk, stopping at the A&P for an apple and a wedge of cheese, then to Jake's Economy for a dime novel, one about Buffalo Bill, and driving to the livery and finding Izzy on the cot under the stairs, coming to know the boy didn't like milk. Remembered how small he was back then, and how he looked up from his reading when Huck came in — relieved seeing him. Huck taking him to the Chuck Wagon every chance he got, gaining the boy's trust.

Huck on his way to pick up John D. at his place in Trout Valley now, Hertz getting a death threat in the post early in the week and taking it to heart, having his chief of security pick him up, pistol under the seat, shotgun on the rear floor. Since Morris Markin's house had been firebombed back in early June, John D. wasn't taking any chances, hearing through the grapevine that Markin had him pegged as being behind it.

The Duesenberg blew through early morning Des Plaines, then the dirt roads of Schaumburg, steep ditches on either side of these farm roads, fields fallow now and some already streaked with snow, here and there a drift against a fence line.

A wagon pulled up between the library and a soft-drink parlor, two men unpacking crates, giving uneasy looks his way as the big car rolled past. The Duesenberg drawing attention, maybe its share of suspicion too. Half the folks in the county too poor for the bus, the rest in the business of running liquor, meaning they were watching for fed agents and rival bootleggers. Or maybe they knew who the car belonged to, John D. Hertz being an acquired taste.

Karla kept on him to get out of the booze business, and didn't much care for him being armed and driving Hertz around — not wanting to find out he wasn't coming home one day. Feeling they had enough money for a store or a farm or some kind of business someplace. Huck telling her the taxi war couldn't go on forever, and there was rumbling about the Eighteenth being repealed. Meaning he'd be out of both soon enough, but meantime, there was money to be made — a lot of money.

Dean O'Banion's operation had doubled since the Eighteenth, the boss buying Schofield's flower shop lock, stock and barrel. Schofield's making a decent trade, and Dean making arrangements for any gangster laid to rest, that proving a steady line of work in its own right.

Since those early days, when Torrio had tried to map out territories to avoid the bloodshed, Dean's crew continued to control the North Side, meaning all of the Gold Coast was theirs. And until repeal came, there would be supply and demand. And with the latest treaty among the gangs, sharing in the payoffs with the politicos and police, the risks were trivial. Huck telling Karla the worst thing that could happen while driving the boss of the taxis to his ranch was the chance of falling asleep from the boredom, listening to the old windbag in back, not a bad fellow, but the man sure could talk.

But he knew she was right, and they had socked money away, putting it to work, investing twenty grand in yearlings in the past year, letting Fannie Hertz make her picks at auction, and he put more into half ownership of a two-year-old called Cyclone, and double that into its training. Huck feeling his inner equestrian, taking Karla and Izzy to Aurora Downs, hoping to get them enthused in the sport of kings.

And they sold the house and moved into the Drake until they could find a piece of land to build on, renting a suite on the top floor, liking the increased security of a doorman and concierge on duty. And Huck shelled out for his own Dues, a Model X, in short production, but with a reworked straight-eight, giving it a hundred horses, faster than John D.'s ReVere model.

Quick to point that out to the boss, and John D. quicker to challenge him to a friendly race, setting it up at the Washington Park track one Sunday, a single lap, each of them putting up a thousand bucks. Hertz letting the press in on it, the stands full of the city's muckety-mucks, watching the racers don the gloves and goggles. Winning by a bumper, Huck made a show of donating his winnings, folks in the stands reaching for their wallets, John D. donating another five grand to Relief and Aid, not to be outdone — getting some good publicity on the day, offsetting the headlines Yellow and Checker were making, going for the throat better than five years now, neither Hertz or Markin giving ground.

Now Huck was driving his Model X back from dropping the boss at Trout Valley, through the stretch of town run by the Touhys, then the Guilfoyle turf up at the top end of town. The Maddox turf came after that, the Klondike crew working North and Western, under the eyes of Torrio's madman lieutenant, Capone. Then came the Irish, the Klondike O'Donnells and the Druggan-Lake boys. Then more Italians, and the Gennas over by the Loop. All them getting rich — whiskey, gin and beer flowing with a pulse, midnight money changing hands, half the politicos and lawmen with their own hands out, and their eyes looking the other way.

Despite Karla's bidding, Huck agreed to stay on with John D., the boss fearing an attack on his life, getting word from a cop there could be reprisal for the firebombing at Markin's house, swearing he had nothing to do with it and blaming it on that man's union troubles.

Huck altered the route every few days in case somebody tried, telling John D. it would be a shame to get his Dues shot up driving into an ambush, the car standing out like a beacon. Not sure if Markin could resist entertaining the idea — with every contract killer in town looking to make a buck. Huck wanted to ask Gypsy Doyle to get a couple of boys to watch the ranch, but knew how Hertz felt about bringing gangsters into his business.

It was a hack stopped at Oakley that caught his eye, pulled up behind a cart, west side of the stockyards. The middle-aged driver climbed off his rig, cursing and waving his whip in the swayback's face, the nag in its traces, eyes wild, flanks shuddering in fear, having no place to go, eliminating and stepping in its own flop. The man cursing and letting the whip crack, first in the air, then striking in a blind fury, hitting the nag over and over.

Stopping in the road, Huck was out and crossing, a truck stopped short behind him, blasting its horn, unable to pass.

"Hey!" Huck called out.

The driver of the hack stopped and watched him come.

"You got something to say?" The hack driver turned, coiled the whip, getting his breathing under control as Huck came toward him.

The trucker stood on his running board, his door open, yelling at Huck, unable to get around the Dues.

"That ain't how it's done," Huck said, smiling like he was trying to help out.

Holding up his hand, the hack man let him see the whip, not wanting him coming any closer, the man not sure of Huck's intent. Seeing the driver get out of his truck, a broad-shouldered fellow with a boulder-size paunch, coming around the car in the road, cursing to get Huck's attention.

"Be with you in a jiffy," Huck called back, but the trucker kept coming.

"You best roll on, fancy man, you got trouble coming from both ends." The hack man turned, raised his arm to strike the mare again, the mare crying, the traces keeping her from sidestepping.

"You're gonna run out of horse," Huck said, turning enough to keep the truck driver in view.

"You're past getting on my nerves, boy." The hack man raised the whip.

The truck driver stopped behind Huck, eyes on the whip, keeping his distance.

Huck thought of the Colt under the seat, the hack man flicking the whip, cracking the tip just past Huck's ear. Getting set to do it again when Huck moved in and snatched it from his hand, shoving the man back, coiling up the whip, turning enough to see the trucker, saying, "Seen fine racehorses, all groomed and shining, and I can tell you, friend, there's no need to take a whip to 'em."

"This sorry hunk of glue on legs," the hack man said, showing stained teeth in a grin, then he came in a rush, Huck ducking under the swing, and he swatted him with the coiled whip.

The hack man sputtered, and Huck hit him again, driving him to his knees, then took his foot and shoved him over, the hack man ending in the horse flop, twisting out of the way

296

to keep from getting stepped on, the nag moving nervously, trying to look around, still fearing for its life.

Turning to the trucker, Huck said, "How about you, you figure I'm holding you up?"

"Guess I can wait." The driver started to turn, not wanting any part of it.

Tossing the crop away, Huck clutched a fistful of collar and stood the hack man up, catching the stink of horse shit on the man's coat. "Ought to get that looked at." He pointed to the welt showing on the man's face.

The hack man touched a hand to the side of his face, seeing blood on his fingers. Anger flashing, saying, "You got any idea who I work for? The Genna brothers, that's who. How you like them apples?"

"That right?" Huck said, looking at the back of the wagon, a tarp pulled over the back, Huck shoved the man aside, went and pulled the tarp aside, a dozen crates in back.

"Now hold on . . ." the hack man said.

Pulling a board off the top of one of the crates, Huck was looking at a bottle of Dom Pérignon, remembered it from the Ship, the first time he heard Dean O'Banion sing, took the first crate off the wagon, went and sat it on the passenger seat of the Dues, calling to the trucker, "You like champagne? Help yourself, courtesy of the Genna brothers."

The hack driver stood cursing as Huck and the trucker went and each took a case under an arm.

Huck saying to the hack man, "Remember what I told you about flogging that poor animal."

The hack man sat down in the road, smeared in horse shit, losing his delivery, the world of woes on him. Huck looked to the nag, wishing he could put her in back of the Dues and drive back to John D.'s ranch for fancy racehorses, tell the boss the story, see him do the right thing. Bending for the riding

crop, Huck stood in front of the man sitting in the street —
the truck driver hurrying past for another crate of champagne.

Huck saying, "You're gonna treat her right from here on.
You got me?"

The man looked up, gave a nod, reaching a hand up,
Huck not sure if he wanted the crop or wanted help getting
to his feet.

"I drive past here and see you again, you best have a carrot
in your hand, you get me?"

The hack man wiped at his mouth, wanted to say more,
but just nodded.

Huck turned to the Dues and tossed the whip onto the
seat, got in and drove off.

49

Huck took a seat in the outer office, but John D. wasn't waiting any longer, slipping off his gloves, going past the secretary's objection, opening the door, looking at the man across the grand oak desk, the plaque like the one on the outside of the door declaring William Emmett Dever, the new mayor. Huck thanking God that Big Bill hadn't run again, Dever, a wet democrat in spite of waging war against the bootleggers, had handed that Republican Lueder and Socialist Cunnea their asses on a platter. Word was this was a forthright man, aiming to clean up the city.

John D. hovered in the doorway, Huck guessing the new mayor was either hard of hearing or had nerves of steel, not looking up from the brief he was reading, William Emmet Dever flipping the page, eyebrows furrowed, giving the page his full attention.

Clearing his throat, John D. looked like he might throw a glove across the desk.

"Ah," the mayor said, giving a look of pleasant surprise, getting up, reaching out a hand, saying, "you'd be John Hertz, so good of you to come barging in." Ushering him to a chair, glad-handing, looking past him to his sentry of a secretary, who was quick getting up, looking apologetic as she hustled to close his office door. Huck hearing every word from the outer room, seeing John D. through the ribbed glass.

"So, to what do I owe the pleasure, Mr. Hertz? Or may I call you John?" The statesman likely showing some white teeth, saying, "Coffee, tea, vodka?"

"You know what I'd like, Mayor, I'd like a fair shake."

"And call me Will, what my friends call me. Feel like I know you, reading all the headlines you keep causing."

Huck heard him rustle the paper, reading from it.

"'Only a comic opera so far. Now it's a fight to the finish.' A quote by you, sir, a threat right above the fold, spewing your self-righteousness to the press. Sit, sit, please. Cigar?"

The sound of a drawer opening, Huck could make out the man pulling out a humidor and offering it.

Then he dropped some of the sugar-coating, saying, "You got something on your mind, let me guess — this about the bar your boys destroyed last week, landing six in hospital, a dozen arrests, or about the flipped taxi blocking traffic for an hour, or is it about the shootout at your livery, shot up the second time this year, that first one before my time, back when I was still on the bench?"

"It's about you putting a stop to Markin, that's what."

"A bomb thrown through the man's front window, blowing his wife and kids from the supper table." Dever not sounding so affable now.

"That's old news, and on account of his own union troubles. Look, Mayor, his boys start a fight they can't finish, and you sit reading about it — same way your predecessor did."

"You want to get on my bad side, Hertz, then you're saying all the right words." The mayor sounded like he was getting tired of the act. "My predecessor tried to get you boys in the same room to hash it out, but your thick heads won't hear it."

"Not some Rueben you're talking to, Mayor. I'm trying to decide if you're one to play favorites."

"You suggesting I take sides?" the mayor said.

"You talk like you're getting a handle on what's going on in your town. Meantime, Markin rolls my cabs in the street, shoots up my business, puts men in the hospital, others in the ground, and you've got no comment."

Huck could see John D. pointing a finger at the mayor. The mayor taking a cigar, making a show of using the cutters, likely looking at John D.'s pointing finger as he snipped. Taking a lighter, he puffed a cloud across the desk, saying, "Sure you won't join me?"

"Look around, Mayor, your town's gone to hell. You're new behind the desk, but time flies and four years, why it'll just go *pffff* — then you're thinking about re-election, wondering who your friends are."

Dever saying, "Almost sounds like a threat, sir."

"You think Markin's the only one who can hire gangsters?"

"I think you have the wrong idea about your present relationship with this office, and the very words coming from your mouth can haunt the man saying them."

"Then how about doing the right thing, revoke his license — pending an investigation into his affairs."

The mayor put his arms behind his head, leaned back into the leather, enjoying the cigar, saying, "You know what I'm doing, sir? I'm suffering a fool."

John D. sputtered, looked like he might jump across the desk and choke the pompous clod.

"I heard you out, Mr. Hertz. Now, if you don't mind, I've got a city to run."

"You didn't hear a word."

Dever leaned across the desk, his voice low. "You come here again with the same song, maybe I'll show you how many gangsters I know."

Watching John D. turn and storm through the outer office and down the marble hall, Huck getting up, nodding to the secretary, wishing her a nice day, following behind John D., knowing he'd be hearing about this all the way to Trout Valley.

50

"**H**ow's it work, this room service? Izzy asked, looking around this suite like he couldn't believe he got to live at the Drake, nine floors above the street where he once made his tips and plied his pickpocket skills, scrounging around back of the kitchen for scraps to eat.

"Guess you go on down and tell them what you want, and they send the waiter with it, silver tray and all," Huck said and gave Karla a look that warned this boy was likely to put them in the poor house, Izzy as tall and as wide as Huck in the hips and shoulders, with an appetite of something getting ready to hibernate.

Huck pointing out it had a kitchen all its own, showing him the fireplace.

"Where you figure they got a woodpile?"

"You order that too, comes dry and split."

Izzy going into the second bedroom, setting down his pack, and tossing himself backward on the real feather mattress.

Huck had been telling them more about New Orleans, what it was like, the kind of hotels he'd only seen but never stepped into: the Monteleone, Le Pavillon and the Bienville

House, places supposed to be as fine as the Drake, nothing like the kind of flea-joints he knew living down around the Quarter. Izzy always wanting to hear about the food, saying he'd like to go see it someday, dying to try some gumbo and alligator cheesecake, although he suspected Huck was pulling his leg on that one.

Karla liked hearing about the shopping and the sightseeing.

Huck telling them, "You drink your Sazerac, then you got your Old Sober to help you out the next day." Huck having to explain about Ya-Ka-Mein.

"How'll we get there?" Izzy asked.

"Well, the way to go's the Panama Limited on account of the Pullman cars." Smiling to himself, Huck thinking how he came north on top of a boxcar, riding the rails with the two brothers, trying to recall their names, and how he'd come into town a flat-busted drifter. Saying, "Or we go by car."

"In the Dues?"

Huck smiling at Karla, who was having none of that, opting for the train with its sleeper and fine dining car.

Later when they were alone, Izzy sleeping in his new bedroom, Huck sat in the armchair, reading the paper, about Jack Dempsey taking a break after his fight with Luis Firpo, Huck taking Izzy to the Polo Grounds in New York to see it, the Manassa Mauler versus the Wild Bull of the Pampas. Dempsey putting Firpo on the canvas seven times, and Firpo knocking Dempsey through the ropes — a hell of a scrap. Dempsey scoring a knockout at fifty-seven seconds in the second.

Sitting across from him on the sofa, Karla said out of the blue, "You put yourself in danger and we get a warm bed."

This again, Huck drawing a breath before saying, "Papers play up the danger, you know that."

"You want to make a life. I don't want to fear for yours." Trying to believe in his dream of building a place for them —

no picket fence around any dream she ever had in her life, she couldn't get the fear from her head, that if he kept working with those horrible men, one day he wouldn't come home. Then what good was all the money in town?

"I'll be done with it — soon."

She started to speak, then looked over at Izzy's door, then held it back, looking at Huck.

And he guessed what she was thinking — that soon enough could be too late.

"We been through it. Repeal's a matter of time, and I'm making hay so you don't need to dance for nickels, wear somebody's hand-me-downs. And Izzy goes to Northwestern like we talked about."

"Think we're well past hand-me-downs and nickel dancing." She glanced around the suite, the fine furnishings, living on top of the Drake, having this East Walton address, this place dubbed the Magnificent Mile.

"Living high costs high, and who knows about rainy days."

"We'll buy a business like we talked about, settle someplace and we'll do just fine. Have those kids we talked about, another girl around this place."

"Well, lady, that don't happen by talking."

"You always just go there, don't you?"

"Like you mind."

She couldn't help the smile, looking across at Izzy's closed door, no light showing under the crack.

"A girl that looks just like her momma — pretty as a picture."

"'Less it's a boy."

"Odds are even, but either's fine by me."

Karla came and sat on his lap, leaned against him, her head on his.

He was smiling, seeing it all working out. "And why not us?"

"The well-to-do don't like when folks like us go from dirt poor to moving next door."

"You want something, you reach and take it. Don't matter what they want."

"That what this is, you taking what you want?"

"You bet it is."

Her eyes were wet, and she shifted enough to put an arm under his head, drawing against him. "Just don't like what you have to do for it."

"Mostly I drive the boss of the windbags home in the evening, playing like his private security, that man with the weight of the world on him."

"Then running whiskey the rest of the night."

"Once or twice a week, and the route's safe enough, with cops who get paid to look the other way."

But she read about it in the dailies, how the Irish and Italians were going at it again, and cabbies were still shooting it out in the street.

"*Trib* makes it sound worse 'n it is — it's what sells their rags."

"All nice and good, except if you don't come back." She turned his face, looking in his eyes.

"I'm here now."

With that she got up, done with their talk, going to their bedroom, saying over her shoulder, "You say something about taking what you want?"

51

"**I**t's bad for business, that's why." Dean got the two sitting in the office up above Schofield's, the man in his florist's apron. Huck and Vincent Drucci sitting face to face. Gypsy Doyle keeping watch by the window, the Tommy gun on the side table next to him, looking out onto North State. Dean putting a man on watch since the trouble with Torrio and the Gennas had gone through the roof. A couple of South Side O'Donnells getting mowed down by a shooter Torrio brought in, the Fox claiming he had nothing to do with it, but the Irish knowing better.

Two days ago, Dean found out Torrio had climbed in bed with the Valley Gang, creating more allies for himself — all the while talking about another summit, wanting to limit the violence between the gangs and carve up the city like a holiday bird — again. Dean blew him off this time, told Torrio he was just another greaser working in the shadows, not worried about him making a move against the North Side. Since then, he kept a man on watch by the window.

"Bottle or a pot?" Dean asked the two at the table.

"Make it a pot," Vincent Drucci said. "I got a head you wouldn't believe."

"Put on a pot," Dean said to Doyle.

Leaving the Thompson by the window, Doyle went to fix coffee.

"All this shit's on account of you jumping the lift," Drucci said, accusing Huck.

"You wanted to know what I'd do if we got in a spot. You mouthed off to the cop and the spot showed up."

"So, you jumped the bridge like a big yellow bird," Dean said.

"Was nowhere else to go."

"Except the cop was as nuts as you," Drucci said.

"And if you kept your mouth shut . . ."

"The thing of it, you run off and leave me for the cops. What's that show me?"

"Shows you I ran the right way." Huck looked at him, deadpan.

Dean glanced from one to the other, looked like he might have to jump between them, saying to Drucci, "I got to admit, Vince, you asked what he'd do . . ."

"Who figured on cuckoo?" Drucci said.

"And pulling up and telling the cop you skipped bail, what's that, normal?" Dean said.

Drucci gave a shrug like he had him there.

When Doyle came with a tray, a coffee pot and four cups on top, he poured himself one and went back to the window.

"Where's the sugar?" Drucci said.

"I don't use sugar," Doyle told him.

Drucci shook his head, poured a cup, saying, "Every fuckin' man for himself."

"Okay, you tell the cop you skipped, and he jumps the bridge," Dean said. "Both swinging your dicks. You about done?"

"The point is, you don't run off and leave a man behind," Drucci said.

"Got you over the bridge, the rest was up to you," Huck said.

"The question I'm asking, can you two make this run without shooting each other?" Dean looked at Drucci, then at Huck, wanting Drucci going along on their runs, wanting the extra man in case of trouble, wanting it to be Drucci.

From somewhere a cop siren sounded, getting louder.

"Two O'Donnells down, and a raid on the blind pig last night, and we lost fifty crates. I got shit coming out of my ears, and you two acting like schoolkids," Dean said.

Huck sat quiet a moment, then looked at Dean, saying, "That true about you dressing like a priest that time, standing outside of St. Francis? Couple walks by and you tell the woman she's got a heavenly ass, making like you were soused." Huck looked to Drucci and said, "And you come along as he's pinching, and you put on a show of beating the priest up right in front of St. Francis. Hear it even made the papers."

"You heard that, huh?" The creases eased across Drucci's brow, the closest Huck had seen him come to smiling.

"That you acting like grown-ups?" Huck asked.

"We were kids."

"Sounds like you got a beef with the church."

"You kidding? The wife makes me go to mass every week and put ten bucks on the plate," Dean said.

Huck nodded, then said to Drucci, "And heard you walked in some garage, with Bugs and the Gusenbergs, the beer you were picking up being seized by two cops." Huck sipped some coffee and went on, "Told them you were feds, how they're messing up your investigation, had the brothers take their guns and handcuff the blue-boys to the radiator."

"Yeah well, a little fun on the job," Drucci said, lightening up some more. "Let me ask, how'd you know you'd make that jump?"

"I got this picture in my head, how it would look. Gunning it, seeing the bridge going up — best part was the look on your face."

And like that the tension was out of the room. Dean and Doyle laughing, even Drucci had to shake his head, grinning.

52

"**B**ut chauffeuring the man, it's embarrassing," Gypsy Doyle said, talking about Huck driving Hertz to his Trout Valley place. Playing bodyguard was one thing, but chauffeur? Lighting a smoke, he offered the pack, exhaling a blue cloud at the windshield.

There was no point explaining it again, Huck dropping him off out front of Schofield's, Doyle sounding relieved that the hard feelings with Drucci were done, dragging on the cigarette.

"You used to have a hook like a horseshoe and some moves too." Doyle rabbit-punching, his knuckles banging the dash, sparks flying off his cigarette.

"What do you mean, used to?"

"Think you'd a lasted a toe-to-toe with Jack Johnson? Not one round, brother, but for thugs in a barroom, you hold up just fine."

"That a pat on the back?"

"Any chump can steer a cab, work a mop over a killing floor, bust his hump, make a few bucks . . ."

Huck kept a hand on the wheel, the cigarette sticking up between two fingers, saying, "You mind getting to the point?"

"Smart money knows when to get out."

That surprised him, Huck looking at Doyle, the man sounding like Karla.

"This run to the bridge, don't think we're making a pick-up."

"Then what?"

"I don't know, but why's he coming on a run you and me been making for what, three years?" Doyle looked at the front of Schofield's like he might be overheard, pulled on his cigarette, saying, "Deanie and Bugs want to get at the Gennas."

"Wants him along cause this treaty ain't showing signs of sticking."

"How long you figure this one lasts? Deanie and Torrio can't look at each other, Deanie making dago jokes any time the man's around — how long you figure the Fox makes like it's all in fun."

Huck looked at him, letting him get to the point.

"You and me are talent in a town full of talent. I know plenty guys with it. Deanie's making flower arrangements for two of 'em right now."

Silence for a moment, Doyle going on, "Torrio's got shipments coming over, got his own deal with the Purples." Doyle looked at the front of the shop again. "Think it's why Drucci's coming along. Think we're going to hit the Gennas."

"With three guys?"

"Bugs and Two Gun left this morning, had a couple of Tommys on the backseat."

"Why tell us it's a run if we're jacking a load?"

"A need-to-know thing."

"Like they don't trust us."

"Unless we're bait." Doyle stubbed out his cigarette, opened the door and got out.

53

"You miss me yet?" Huck said, walking into the Drake suite. Taking in the view of the Oak Street Beach. Karla and Izzy in the front room, Karla knitting and Izzy reading a biology text, studying to make his grades.

"I'm trying." She tipped her head up for a kiss. Then told him she met the Lindberghs in the Palm Court that morning. Huck having no idea who that was, Karla explaining it to him, getting along with Anne like a house on fire, telling him they were getting together for tea tomorrow, Anne going to tell her what flying in a Ford, instead of driving one, was like, and how Huck ought to join them, maybe get some tips on aviating. Huck guessing she overheard him talking on the phone to Hertz, explaining about the taxi that flew over the bridge.

"Love to, but I know all you girls'll talk about are the three C's — cooking, cotton and kids." Huck winked at Izzy.

She shook her head at him, looked at Izzy, saying, "Thought you taught him to read?"

"Up to Grammar School Reader, Book Two, but you ever try teaching an old dog tricks?" Izzy was all smiles.

"Speaking of cooking, what's for supper?" Huck said.

"I could go for flapjacks, been a while," Izzy said, patting his stomach.

"A nice change from all the steak and oysters around this place," Huck said.

"You boys go on, I'm not peckish, and I want to get this sleeve done." Working the needles, she traded a glance with Izzy.

Izzy putting his nose back in his book.

"And since when do you sew?" Huck knowing something was up, these two playing a game on him.

"I'm not sewing, I'm knitting." Her eyes on what she was doing.

"Making me a sweater?"

"It's called a bunting."

"You sure you got the size right, and why's everything yellow?"

"Well, I can't go blue, and I can't go pink, though I've got a hunch it's blue."

Izzy closed his book and went to his room, said he'd get ready to go.

Huck tried to put it together, these two acting strange, then he stepped over to her, taking the knitting from her hands, easing her to her feet, saying, "You trying hard not to tell me something."

"Doctor at the Grant figures I'm about sixteen weeks."

He let it sink in, then held her close, Huck feeling her warm against him.

"Good thing we're past popping the question."

"Well, you popped something alright."

That night in their bed, with the light off, looking at each other in the near dark, Huck ran his fingers along her arm, her warm and smooth skin.

"Don't know what I was thinking back then." Her words in the dark, her head turned to him.

"Sounds like regret."

"Don't be pathetic. It's just I never saw me . . ."

"With a guy like me."

"Quit it. I mean getting out of that one-room place. I was pretty low back when I couldn't be a nurse."

"You and me on that sagging mattress." Huck drew her close, the silk of her long hair across his arm.

"That's what you remember?"

"Remember thinking if there's a God, sinner or not, I wanted to shake his hand."

"Why do you think it's a he?"

"Clear you never read the Good Book."

"This from a man still learning to read it." Putting a hand on his arm.

"Ask Izzy — the boy's been to church."

"Hiding in the basement of one doesn't count, but let's keep Izzy out of it."

"Izzy?" Huck called, loud enough to be heard down the hall, hearing him answer back, then asking, "God a man or woman?"

"Matter."

"Matters 'cause we got a ding-dong going here."

Karla was laughing, saying, "He's saying matter, you dope, like that's what God is."

"Well, why can't he just say it plain then?"

"You insisted he go to the best schools."

Huck could see the white of her teeth, liked seeing her happy. Guessing the Drake suite would be too small for four, he'd have to step up building them that place on a few acres like Trout Valley, Huck liking the quiet of the country, a place with a stream nearby.

"According to the Good Book, smarty, we started out sinning."

"Half of what's good, somebody calls it sinning."

"Well, you are a criminal."

315

"But with the best of intent."

"All the while sticking out your neck."

"You starting on that again?"

"I mean I was sinning right along, aiding and abetting."

"With a smile on your face and now a bun in the oven."

She play-slapped his arm. "You came knocking like temptation, standing at my door with your dance ticket in hand. What was a nice girl to do?"

"Was just glad you opened the door."

"Guess I am too."

"You ever dream of having all this, I mean back then?"

"Growing up was about getting by. Who could afford the silver lining?"

"All that's behind us, way behind."

And she cuddled closer. "How about you, you ever dream?"

"I remember dreaming of going against Jack Johnson, the champ who took out Jim Jeffries, guy they called the Boilermaker. Saw myself as a white kid with a good hook, and I wondered what it would be like. But that was like going to the movies, all make-believe. Still, a part of me saw myself making it. Now, look at me, I got all this, and the girl of my dreams."

She turned her head on the pillow, looking at him. "That what I am, a girl?"

"The grown-up kind."

"I think you figure you saved me from something, but I think I saved you too." She squeezed his arm, took a moment, then said, "That fella I told you about —"

"Jimmy the cheater?"

"Think he figured he was saving me too, ended taking his hand to me first time I showed him different. Then he was giving me sorry when I started packing, promising it won't happen again. Being dumb, I stayed. Next time he did it with a belt."

"Sure like to meet that fellow."

"It's what I thought when you told me you boxed — another one who likes hitting people." She ran her fingertips over his knuckles, still thick but not scarred anymore.

"It's not about hitting, more about not getting hit."

"Your eyes told me you're the kind that brings flowers to momma."

Huck thinking he'd like to go and lay some by his step-mother Bladie Mae's stone.

"Jimmy called me a vixen."

"Well, Jimmy didn't know much."

"You wouldn't do it, hit a girl."

"Pulled a pigtail once. But think I'd sooner give you my gun so you can shoot me."

"You still got a gun?"

"It's a figure of speech."

"But you still got the one under the seat?"

"Just in case of sinners." He guessed this was leading back to her saying she wanted him out of working for the taxi outfit and the gangsters, but in another minute she was asleep, Huck lying there, listening to her breathing, thinking of what heaven was like. His fingers moving across her belly.

54

Two men jumped from the side of the clapboard shack, dressed as city cops, aiming pistols in Huck's face as soon as he started to pull from the Belle Isle crossing, the load of whiskey taken off the skiff and put in the back of the truck. Huck looked at the burn-scarred face of the cop ordering him out, his pistol trained on Huck, and he didn't have a move.

"Back out!" Drucci was hissing through his teeth, but more men showed at the back of the truck, coming along both sides, shotguns aimed at the cab, these men not in uniform.

Huck seeing the man with the cap on the roof of the next shanty with what looked like a Lewis gun, its pan magazine set to spit rounds through the windshield. He put up his hands, giving Drucci and Doyle no choice but to give up too, letting the men have the truck.

Drucci got out, telling the cop with the scar, "Not going to forget you."

"You jack one of ours, we take one of yours, you mope."

"Still not going to forget it."

"I'm not hard to find." The burn-scarred cop chopped the pistol against Drucci's neck, causing him to stumble, but

Drucci stayed on his feet. Then the man gave them the choice of walking down Washington or getting planted where they were standing.

Taking a hold of Drucci's arm, Huck started moving, kept his free hand up, hoping not to get shot in the back, Doyle walking on the other side, steadying Drucci, wondering what happened to Bugs and Two Gun.

They had driven to Windsor, got a load, planning to meet up with Bugs and Two Gun to jack another one of Gennas' loads coming across at Belle Isle this time, getting jacked themselves, a truckload of Seagram's lost. The three of them walking ten blocks to the Blue Goose stop, waiting to catch a Hupmobile back to Chicago.

"Could've used some of your fancy driving tricks," Drucci said, touching the lump forming on the side of his head.

"What was he supposed to do?" Doyle said, looking like he wished The Schemer would lay off.

Huck didn't say anything, this thing between him and Drucci going back to being about him jumping the bridge.

Drucci saying, "The Purples crossed us, or could be the cops." Looking at Huck. "Or could be somebody else."

"You got something to say . . ." Huck looked at him, giving it back.

"You were quick putting up your hands."

Doyle got between them, Drucci looking like he might take a poke at Huck again. "Just walked off with our lives, now you two want to tear each other up." Doyle looking at Drucci, saying, "It's just a load of booze for Christ's sake."

"Fine, you tell that to Dean." Drucci shook him off and walked off, muttering to himself.

The three of them waited six hours to catch the Blue Goose back, taking them through Ann Arbor, Battle Creek, Kalamazoo, Benton Harbor, Michigan City, and Gary, rolling into Chicago at midnight. Drucci was convinced the Gennas were behind it, one of the Purples or a cop paid to give them up, spent the ride back talking about getting even.

Hymie Weiss picked them up from the depot, letting them know that Bugs and Two Gun were picked up by real city cops as soon as they drove into Detroit, the lawmen laying for them, holding them for questioning at 1300 Beaubien, but nobody came and said a word to either one, releasing them after ten hours in holding.

55

Huck let them out on Taylor Street, heart of Little Sicily, Vincent Drucci looking at him, saying, "Him and I could pass." He meant as Italians. "But you got the look of pure mick — and a look like you want to turn around." Telling him to pull up out front of Pop's and wait.

"He's good," Doyle said, getting out with Drucci.

And they stepped to the corner in front of Bello's Bake Shop as Huck drove the block and pulled up out front, getting out as Doyle and Drucci crossed the street. The three of them lit cigarettes, scanning the area and getting set. Drucci with the flat cap angled down and a sawed-down Browning on a sling under his coat. Doyle and Huck with pistols inside their jackets, both with newsboys pulled low, quiet for this time of evening.

Pulling on the door handle to the Gennas' speak going by Pop's Roadhouse, Doyle went in first, Drucci on his heels, Huck taking a last glance up the street, then back to the Yellow, borrowed from Moses at the livery. And in he went, dim and smoky like all these joints. The barman glancing as they came in, the place near empty, three men on stools along the bar, four more at a barrel, using it like a table, sitting by the only window in the place. Another lone old-timer at another barrel in the far corner, his head down, sleeping off whatever he'd been drinking, a half dozen empty tins in front of him.

Hands in his jacket pockets, revolver in one, brass knucks in the other, Huck moved to the middle of the room, waiting for Drucci to get the party started.

The barman, big and tired-looking, pulled a tap handle on a keg, pouring two glasses of beer, glancing at the three men coming in long enough to see they weren't cops. Huck guessing, like most prohibition barmen, he had his own sawed-off under the bar or against the wall at his back.

Another old-timer came in from the rear door, tugging on the rope belt holding up his trousers, a wad of chaw in his cheek, doing a jake-walk like the floor was a ship's deck in a gale, wagging a hand to the barman, calling him Tom and asking for another drink, looking like he'd been there since the joint opened, maybe longer. Staggering to the barrel table, his drinking buddy staying face down.

"You had your fill, Davey. You get on home now, and take that lump of friend with you," Tom called to him, setting the two glasses in front of two of the men at the bar.

"You ain't my mother." Davey spat tobacco juice at the floor, missing the spittoon.

"Get on before I plant my shoe in your butt." Tom telling the man in front of him that'd be a dime apiece.

"Just pissed a bucket's worth, filling your horse trough," Davey called back, his knees wobbling, but he wasn't done complaining. "Now you expect a man to go dry."

"Ain't exchanging views with you, Davey. Go drink yourself blind someplace else." Tom was starting to shed the good nature.

The scarred-up man at the near end of the bar said, "That old bugger even got a mother?"

The one next to him saying, "Stand me a drink, Tom, and I'll toss 'em out." The man rising, not as big as the scarred-up man, but still twice the size of the old-timer.

Tom wasn't paying attention, instead looking at Drucci stepping up and laying a hand on the bar, looking at the row of bottles and jugs on the crates behind Tom.

Doyle stepped behind the line of men, Huck in the middle of the floor, close to the table of men and the old-timers by the back door.

"What'll it be?" the barman asked Drucci.

"Way they test shine's, they put a match to it," Drucci said, looking over the bottles and jugs behind the bar.

"Well, we don't carry nothing like that, just quality stuff."

"The flame burns blue, means it's good for drinking," Drucci kept talking like he hadn't heard him.

The scarred one and the bigger man looking at him now.

"The flame burns yellow or red, then Jack, you're dead." Drucci turning his neck, looking at the scarred man next to him.

"Heard they pour it on a metal spoon," the scarred man said.

"You got one?" Drucci asked.

"Mister, I don't know your game . . ."

Putting a hand in his pocket, Drucci took a box of matches and set it on the bar, never took his eyes from the scarred man.

The man next to him touched his arm, trying to get him to see part of the sling and the shape under Drucci's coat.

"Comes in here like he's boss of the place." The scarred man stood, not letting it go.

Davey the old drunk was still going on, "Can be he don't know who he's talking to." Then looking at Huck standing in the middle of the room. "And what you looking at, bug-eye?"

Huck let it go, the old man going to the barrel table, his pal slumped on it, the old man raising an empty tin off the table as if in toast, saying, "To fuck with all ya." Dashing the tin down, stumbling and regaining his balance.

His buddy lifted his grizzled head off the barrel, took a fogged glance around, dropping his head back down.

Tom forgot the old-timers now, saying to Drucci, "Not a place you want to come acting like you're around the bend." His eyes going to the box of matches, then giving a sideways glance behind the stacked crates making up the bar, bottles and jugs lining the top.

"I'm looking for whiskey," Drucci said.

The barman looked at Huck and Doyle still standing behind the men at the bar, taking a half-step toward the bottles. Holding a rag in his hands like he was choking it.

Davey had run out of steam, sitting himself on the floor, looking dazed.

Drucci clapped his hands loud enough to get all eyes on him, looking at the shelf of bottles behind the barman like he was considering his pleasure.

Huck stepped closer to the four men at the table, all of them watching the scene at the bar.

Drucci saying to the barman, "You got Seagram's?"

"Old Time, V.O., some White Wheat, and Pure Rye. Just say what's your pleasure?"

Doyle shifted in behind the men on the stools.

"I'll take all you got," Drucci said, opening the coat and giving an almost lazy swing of the twin barrels, now aiming it at the barman's middle. He did it so slow he caught Tom the barman napping, now glancing behind the bar again.

The scarred man slid his hand down to his side, and Drucci swung the butt of the gun on its sling, catching the side of the man's head, stepping away and putting the barrels back on Tom. Tom reaching under the bar, then easing up and showing his hands.

The scarred man sputtered, spitting blood and a tooth, cursing.

"You were right, not hard to find at all," Drucci said it like he was passing the time of day. "You remember me now?" Drucci hit him again as the man's eyes widened, catching the scarred man on the side of the skull again, knocking him from the stool. Looking down and saying, "Vincent Drucci, 'case you don't see this as done, and I sure ain't hard to find either." His eyes never left the barman, saying to him, "Like I told you, all you got back there's mine."

The barman kept his hands up, saying, "Just expect to walk out of here with it, the three of you?"

The men on the stools were looking at each other, then over at their pals at the table. Likely wondering what the Gennas were going to say about ten men in the joint, letting three come in and walk out with their whiskey.

"This is Genna whiskey," Tom said like it mattered.

The man who'd been next to the scarred man said, "He can't get us all."

"Ones still standing after can give us a hand loading it up," Drucci said, picking up the box of matches, rolling it between his fingers, looking at the bottles behind the bar, guessing out loud there was double that in a back room. Not the whole shipment, but a good start.

"Why'd we do that?" the man said.

Doyle pulled his pistol, cocked it and fired.

The man was knocked spinning from the stool, clutching his upper arm, crying out, blood and meat flecking the bar and bottles on the shelf.

Past the ringing in his ears, Huck heard Doyle say, "That answer it?"

Drucci stood by the bar, hadn't moved from the spot, and watched the men carry crates and armloads of just the Seagram's out to the Yellow out front, filling the back seat and trunk. From the street it looked like a police raid, a confiscation of illegal booze, except it was all put in a taxi instead of being poured into the sewer.

All but Tom the barman and the scarred-up man were told to haul the drunks and the shot man out the back door and not come back. Drucci and Doyle were counting on them running straight to the Gennas, telling what just happened. All six brothers likely to arm up and come on the double.

Drucci had his coat off, set the sawed-down gun on the bar, reached Tom's single shot Powell & Clement from behind the bar and set it next to his, told Tom to just stand there. Getting a look at the scarred man, tall and wide like a cop, scar tissue under his eyes, looking like a prize fighter long past the end of his game, the burn-scar along the left side of his face making that eye look slanted and lazy, hair going gray at the temples, but still looking hard as oak.

"Told me you ain't hard to find," Drucci said.

"Guess I did."

"Where's the rest of it?"

"For that, you got to talk to Bloody Ang. Look, it was nothin' personal."

"Personal to me." Looking at Doyle, Drucci said, "Gypsy, how about you, you take it personal?"

Doyle nodded, saying, "Sure do."

"How about you Huck?"

"You bet."

"It settles it then — fight the man."

Huck just looked at him.

"Here's your chance, already softened him up for you," Drucci said, looking to the scarred man, pointing the shotgun at his chest.

"Can't be serious," the big man said, looking at Huck, then back to him.

"My boy here's the undisputed boxcar champ."

"I mop the floor with him, then what?"

"Then you walk out."

The scarred man looked at him, seeing he was serious, then at Tom, giving a shrug, then glancing over at Huck, and saying to Drucci, "I beat hell out of him, you two jump on me or back-shoot me."

"Like I said, it's your chance, but in case it don't go your way, what name you want scratched on your stone?"

"Newlan."

Shaking his head, Newlan exchanged a look with Tom the bartender.

Drucci was back to getting even for the jump over the river. Shrugging out of the jacket, not seeing a way around it, Huck set it on the barrel table, stepping to Doyle and handing him his pistol without a word, went to the center of the room, getting set. Watched Newlan slide his bulk off the stool, shedding his own jacket.

"Put up fifty, I'll give you three to one . . ." Drucci said to Doyle.

"Make it a hundred," Doyle said, then to Huck, "Don't let me down, son."

Surprised at first, Huck flexed his hands and shoulders, getting loose, letting the big man come to him.

And he did, coming straight in, Huck backing up, bumping the barrel, feinting and slipping a big right hand, countering and catching Newlan, smashing his fist against the man's ear, ringing his bell. Hitting him again, same spot, looking surprised when he didn't go down.

What he did, Newlan charged, giving him no room, plowing Huck into the wall, catching hold and kept him from ducking.

Landing an uppercut, Huck broke his grip. Newlan swung and clawed for a fistful of hair, crashing Huck's head against the end of the bar, glasses tipping and smashing. Twisting him around, still by the hair, grabbing hold of a busted glass, trying to stab it into Huck's face.

Huck sent a straight right between the rising hands, mashing the man's lips, Newlan stumbling into the bar, jabbing with the broken glass. Stepping back, Huck gave himself room, the big man threw the glass aside, coming and catching him solid, sending him tumbling to the wet floor. Newlan doubling his hands, raising them up, set to hammer them down, Huck on his knees, throwing a jacket-rabbit into the man's groin. And the big man's mouth went into a giant O, and he dropped like a felled tree, curling on the floor, cupping his groin and moaning.

Drucci was absorbed in the fight, but he caught Tom the barman pawing for the twelve gauge. Catching the Powell & Clement barrel and twisting it to the ceiling, Drucci drove the man back into the empty shelves. Tom not letting go of the barrel, cursing and kicking at him. Drucci butted with his head, blood splashing, ripping the gun from his grip, Tom sinking to the floor, holding his busted nose, groaning.

Cracking open the breach, Drucci tossed away the single shell and set the gun back on the bar. Bending and finding a bottle they missed under the counter.

Newlan was slow to his feet, his face bloody, he waved a hand at Huck, done with the fight, walking past the bar, grabbing his jacket. Ignoring Drucci and Doyle, he went for the door, puffing hard and took his chance on getting shot in the back.

"Want me to bring him down?" Drucci said to Huck.

Wiping at his mouth, Huck ignored him and dropped into the only chair that hadn't tipped, thinking he was going to throw up.

Putting both hands on the wood top, Drucci stood looking down at Tom behind the bar, saying to him, "You see me again, brother, best pin an address to your shirt, you understand me?" Then looked at Huck, smiling. "Looks like you could use one." Putting the bottle to his mouth, yanking out the cork, he took a mouthful and swished it around, then spat it out, looking at the bottle of Bertha's Revenge, making a face, but offering it to Huck, saying, "You want, I can find you a glass."

Huck shook his head, so did Doyle, and Drucci poured it out on the floor, then poured out a bottle of Old Hickory, one of Dillinger Pennsylvania Straight, Twenty Grand gin, and vegetable bitters, tossing the bottles behind the bar, all of them breaking.

"Let's go." Drucci pulled the shotgun sling over his head, took the box of matches, struck one and tossed it on the pooling booze, fire catching. Taking the single-shot, a shotgun in each hand.

A groan from the floor, and Tom the bartender rolled to his knees, pressing himself up, wincing at the pain, looking at Drucci, muttering under his breath.

Turning for the door, Drucci left the barman stomping at the flames, guessing the Gennas were on the way — wanting to pick a better time to be facing six pissed-off Sicilian brothers.

Letting Huck get the door, Drucci had a look out to the street, not wanting to walk into another ambush, saying to Huck, "Like the way you don't quit, didn't fight the man's fight. Starting to see what Doyle says about you."

"Fuck you," Huck said, going out past him to the driver's door, thinking what he was going to say to Karla, coming home looking like he could use a nurse.

Flames started to rise inside, the crackling sound as the bar caught flame.

"If you can chew — I could use a bite," Drucci said to Huck, getting in back of the taxi with the cases of whiskey. "Where's that flapjack joint from here? Can't go in the Fountain Court looking like that."

"And it's on me," Doyle said, getting in the passenger side, winking at Huck, "soon as he pays up the three hundred."

56

"**M**an says to get it done," Danny Stanton said, this half-Irish union racketeer looking at Gypsy Doyle and Huck, meeting them at the Chuck Wagon, the table over by the window. According to Doyle, he'd known Stanton for years, the two of them working their way up with Frank Ragen and Ralph Sheldon, both with ties to the Druggan-Lake crew, mixed up in everything from election fraud to bribery, Danny Stanton working these days with a yegg called Red Fawcett. Rumor had it, Stanton had been one of the guys who donned blackface and went burning a couple of Lugan homes on the South Side a few years back, stirring up retaliation against the Black Belt, some thinking it's what sparked off the riots in '19. These days, Stanton and Fawcett were working odd jobs for the South Side, meaning Torrio's people. Meaning they were so-called pals with the Gennas.

Danny Stanton telling them about his sit-down with Bloody Ang, the Genna boss putting a price on all the heads of the North Side, starting with the three guys who walked into Pop's Roadhouse, robbing him and showing disrespect. "Five hundred a man. Should'a seen the look when Genna found out — like the man was choking on a bone." Stanton shook his head, grinning at the reflection.

"Hits our trucks, and what — he figures we just stand around?" Doyle said.

"I start to tell him I got something in New York, but he still wants it done . . ."

Doyle looked at Huck, the two of them with a price on their heads.

"Reason I come to you — you and me go back," Stanton said to Doyle.

"And I'm obliged." Doyle knowing the man was sticking his neck out.

"Ang knows Drucci was one . . ." Danny picked up his beer, taking a sip. "And 'less I miss my guess, I'm looking at the other two. And if I figure it out, just a matter of time . . ."

Doyle shrugged like it didn't worry him.

"Then I had a thought. The man wants bodies, so why not give 'em to him," Danny said, waiting for Doyle to catch up.

Doyle looked at him like he needed it spelled out.

"You make it look good, like when they make flicks. What do they call 'em?"

"Stand-ins," Huck said.

"Yeah, somebody that don't matter takes your spot — and old Ang goes away an avenged man."

"You mean you get paid, and we lay low," Doyle said.

"And hoping you see the value of friendship . . ." Danny waiting.

Doyle creased his brow, thinking, then nodded and reached a roll in his pocket, counted off a few hundred and held it out.

Danny Stanton was quiet a moment, then took it, smiling before he said, "You remember them times with Yiddles?"

"Sure."

Huck wasn't liking the idea of somebody getting clipped, and if Bloody Ang Genna saw through it, next time it would be Capone taking care of it, hiring some talent off the boat, the kind that did these jobs one day, got back on the boat and went home the next.

And that's all that was said about it, Huck sitting across from Stanton, watching two old chums catching up, talking about the days of the Circulation Wars, when the *Examiner* and the *Trib* scrapped over the city's newsstands, just like Yellow and Checker were doing over the taxi stands, both papers paying Ragen's Colts to keep the other daily off the newsstands, Davy "Yiddles" Miller setting that one up. The two of them laughing about it, getting all nostalgic, throwing names around, guys they knew from back in the day: Lovin' Putty Anixter, Hinky Dink Kenna and Bathhouse John.

Danny Stanton recalling it was Dean O'Banion who shot Yiddles outside the opera, saying, "Man made a snub to Deanie and his date, something like, 'To like opera you got to be a bit of a Mary. Fact, for any man to sing . . .' Deanie brushes that off as a little ribbing, tells his date Yiddles is a hillbilly sister-diddler and what would he know about a thing like singing. Then Yiddles makes one crack too many, calling Dean a flower arranger, looking down and saying something about Dean wearing glass slippers, the reason he was as tall as his date. Deanie's date covers her mouth, smiling, and I guess it's the thing that set the man off. The fun was over for Deanie, and he pulls one of his pistols, promises him an arrangement and spoils the man's suit, right in the ticker — end of the line for old Yiddles."

Doyle and Stanton were quiet a minute, both sipping their beer.

Then Danny Stanton brightened, remembering something else, saying to Huck, "And to show what a small world we got, this Markin guy — you know the one — yeah, he calls me after his place got bombed, tells me how he got knocked from his supper table when it went off, lucky to be talking to me, all that, and goes on how he don't want Hertz touched on account he's a church-going man. But the bums who set the bomb, him thinking it's the same ones who been pushing his cabs in the drink — wanting me to set an example."

"He know who did it?" Huck said, thinking of working for Markin and the man never gave a hint that he knew Huck was with Doyle when he tossed the cocktail through Markin's window.

"Supposed to put the fear of God in anybody wanting to try again." Stanton was chuckling about it, going on, "This putz wants me reporting in, giving him a full account — wants to know what he's paying for. I put him straight on how it works and he says maybe he ought to get somebody else. So, I give him this look." Danny Stanton lifting one eyebrow, slanting the other one down.

"That's good," Doyle said.

"And I tell him just for wasting my time, he ought to get somebody standing on the ground floor, try and catch him when he flies out the window."

"Told the guy running Yellow something like that myself one time. And from the sound, I guess this Markin don't mind coming in second," Doyle said, laughing and clapping Danny on the back, motioning for Luka to bring another round of beer.

"Anyway, this Markin sits there, finishes sucking the air out of the room, mulling it over, says he'll let me know, then sticks out his hand — like shaking hands with a mackerel. And out I go."

"But he ain't called?" This from Doyle.

"Nope."

"Well, there you go," Doyle said.

"I'm telling you on account I want no misunderstanding," Danny Stanton turned to Huck. "'Case you hear something on the street."

Huck saying he appreciated the tip.

"So, back to these fall guys, what'd you call them, stand-ins?" Doyle said.

"Yeah, stand-ins, don't worry about it, Red and me'll take care of it — and it'll look good."

"You not worried about playing both ends, I mean with the Gennas?" Huck said.

"I collect and I'm gone, blowing town — know when I overstayed my welcome, same as you fellas ought to do."

57

"**Y**ou smell like smoke." Not the way she usually greeted him. Huck figured the change started around the time she got pregnant, but since the baby came, she seemed tired all the time, the baby keeping her up at night.

"You're smelling cigarettes." He came close, kissed her cheek, then brushed the top of Maudie's head, the baby asleep in her arms.

"Not that kind of smoke," Karla said.

"Could be I walked by somebody's bonfire."

Now the smile melted off, and Karla turned for the cookstove, warming a nursing bottle for Maudie, taking the pot of water off the burner.

"You don't want to tell me, Huck, just say so." Baby in one hand, she tested the temperature of the milk on her wrist.

"I just did tell you."

"You leave half the night, come back smelling of smoke, and I can't ask you about it." Giving Maudie the rubber nipple, the baby drinking.

"Was business is all."

"So, was it something or nothing?"

"I had a smoke, walked by a fire, was out on business — call it what you want. Why all this? You don't believe me now?"

"What's to believe, Huck, you haven't said anything."

"I don't tell you what you don't want to know. Isn't that how we've been doing this?"

"Let me ask, you think that brings us close?"

Huck walked to the dining table, saw the newspaper open the headline across the top calling it "The Hands of Death." Under it, a drawing of a strange clock face with three hands, one hand called *Moonshine*, another labeled *Guns*, and the third called *Autos*. The article talked about all the killings and deaths, blaming illegal booze and the turf wars. Huck closed the paper, saw on the front page Frank Capone had been gunned down by police. The headline "The Bloody Elections in Cicero."

"You read a thing like this and sure, it's an awful thing, a guy getting clipped like that, but it's got nothing to do with me." The shooting of Capone's brother, Frank, the man trying to strong-arm election results for incumbent Klenha at the Cicero polls, the South Side bringing in two hundred extra goons to make sure that citizens voted the right way. The goons clashing with seventy extra cops sent into the fray by Mayor Dever, the aftermath making the front page of every daily in the country. Huck saying, "Guess this Capone was backing a Republican."

"Somehow you think that's funny?"

"I think I know more than what the papers are telling."

"Well, it's not funny to me, Huck, none of it. Says it's likely to set off an investigation into dirty cops with gang ties, and the gangsters stirring it up. Does that mean you?"

"Told you, it's got nothing to do with me. Look, the papers blow everything out of shape. I know it, and you know it. I never even laid eyes on this Frank Capone. Seen his brother around, okay, but never even said a howdy-do."

"You play security for Yellow, drive that man to his ranch, I can live with that. I don't like it, but I can live with it, hoping this war'll blow itself out as you keep saying. But gangsters going around killing each other while Dean O'Banion's singing like he thinks he's Scrappy Lambert . . ."

"The man likes to sing."

"And makes pretty flower arrangements for their funerals — likely put half of them in the ground himself. How does that sound normal to you?"

"Okay, you want to know where I was, I made a run to Canada. Nothing to it but stay awake behind the wheel, unload the truck and collect the money — money so we live like this." Huck glanced around the place costing him a couple hundred a month. And he tried to soften things, saying, "Remember the drafts coming past the window in that dump? No heat, no hot water, sharing a water-closet down the hall, place always smelling."

"Beats O'Banion tossing roses on your box and singing 'Amazing Grace.'"

"You got an imagination on you, girl." Huck was trying to get her to smile, watching her feed the baby, thinking all this fretting couldn't be doing either one of them any good.

"It's not how I saw it, Huck, not a bit." Looking at him now like she might run off.

"Coolidge'll toss out the Eighteenth soon as he realizes all the tax bucks he's losing on the sales, letting guys like us scoop it all up. Folks love him, and he'll do the right thing. Then it's done."

"Listen to you — 'guys like us.'"

"I came here riding on top of a boxcar, hanging on for dear life, shivering in what passed for a coat. I leave, it's gonna be first class and in my own time."

"Or in a box."

"There's that bright side."

"We talked about you getting out, putting money into something legit."

"We got money in the yearlings, money in the stocks, money in the bank. What do you call that?"

"How about a flower shop?"

"I'm being serious."

"Got the piece of land, shovels ready to go in the ground, all of it legit." Their plan of building a ten-room ranch house on the twenty acres he bought in Schaumburg, six miles from the Hertz ranch.

"Don't think you're hearing me, Huck."

He looked at her like he wished he wasn't hearing her, stopped himself from saying so, Karla losing her smile around the time she found out she was expecting. Not that long since they went up the city hall steps, her in the white dress, him in a tux, Huck joking that he was making an honest woman of her. She had told him someday she'd like to make an honest man of him, too — hadn't guessed this was what she meant. And he didn't feel like explaining Dean O'Banion and his people weren't the kind you just walked away from, that and there was that price on his head, thinking that being associated with the North Side was a kind of shield from reprisal.

Not that he blamed her, spending too many days and nights alone, Izzy off attending St. Ignatius, making the grades to get into college, and Huck off making runs to Detroit, or up on the land, choosing the spot for their house, with the architect he hired, Louis Sullivan making a drawing of the prairie-style house with the hipped roof, overhanging eaves, cornices and wide porch with massive supports.

Heading for the door, not wanting his temper spilling out, not wanting to regret later what he felt like saying now. Telling her he'd be home late.

"Where are you going now — or is that too much to ask?"

But he had already closed the door behind him.

58

"**M**y place gets firebombed, it's the kind of thing that keeps me antsy," Morris Markin said, anger in his eyes, looking at Danny Stanton sitting across the desk. Stanton not introducing the man with him, standing by the door. Morris likely guessing that Gypsy Doyle was Red Fawcett, the partner Danny had mentioned the first time they met.

"Yeah, so you told me, why we're here, right?" Danny Stanton said, sitting across from him, waving a hand no, he didn't want a drink.

Doyle stayed looming by the door, watched the man's handshake, guessing on account it wasn't every day a couple of gangsters walked into his office.

"Surprised to see you. Told me you wouldn't be reporting in." Morris glanced at Doyle again, smiling, but getting nothing back, the man with a knife scar and cold dark eyes, a tooth missing from the middle of his mouth.

"Came by to see if you been reading the papers?"

"Sure."

"Then you put it together, the ones who pushed your ride in the river, a couple of South Side O'Donnells. Tragedy struck 'em in Back of the Yards."

"The two guys getting shot — the *Trib* said it was over a couple of beer trucks getting waylaid, Joliet I think, called them bootleggers."

"What it looked like." Stanton shrugged, the story of two of O'Donnells mid-level hoods being yanked out of one of the trucks, shoved into a car, their bodies dumped on a back road, found by some farmer coming to bring his tomatoes to market. "Look, Morris, we're here telling you the bare bones, the facts, so you see what's going on, but not enough that could lead to you having to testify, you get me?"

Morris Markin nodded but didn't look so sure.

Stanton had told Doyle he got wind Frank McErlane, head of the Saltis-McErlane gang, had been the real shooter. Didn't much matter who the two mutts were, Danny figuring the dead wouldn't mind having an extra crime pinned to their lapels.

"I never said I wanted anybody getting killed." Morris Markin looked concerned.

"Said you wanted an end to it."

"But I didn't mean . . ." Markin not sounding happy about it.

"What it means, Yellow'll be taking you serious from here on," Stanton said, looking at Doyle, Doyle holding his stare on Markin.

"How about that Huck fellow?"

"What you paid me to find out — who done it and disturbed your supper that time. Am I right?"

Morris nodded, not looking so sure, and he sipped from his glass, trying to mask his misgivings.

"Way it's looking, you're sucking the back tit, this war on the street. Got union troubles up the ying-yang on top. I don't know, guess some fellas don't mind coming in second."

Stanton looking at Doyle and giving a shrug. "For that, you sure don't need us." Putting on his cap, straightening it like he was getting set to go.

"So, you're saying that's it?" Markin said, leaning back in his chair.

"Well, for that you'd have to call up Hertz . . ." Stanton letting it hang, then, "On the other hand, things keep on, you know where to call."

"Sure, but I think —"

Stanton put up a hand, stopping Markin, putting on a look like an idea was sparking, saying, "Or, we put on a third man, to be on the safe side."

"A third man? How —"

Again the hand stopped him, Stanton saying, "Two guys walk up, catch your boys unaware, lay a beating on them, force them to dump their own cabs in the river. Papers made a joke of it, you a laughingstock."

"That was a long time ago."

"Yet the war goes on. You really want an end to it, something all-out so it don't happen again. For something like that, we'd be talking . . ." Stanton looking to the ceiling a moment, then back at Markin, saying, "Three hundred more a week'd get it done."

"More money!"

"Bring a swiftness to it." Stanton turned to Doyle, Doyle nodding that he agreed.

"I mean, sometimes you got to drive home the point, so to speak."

"I need to think about it."

"Yeah, you do that."

"Right. Well, I know where to —"

"Find me. Sure." Danny Stanton getting up, set to go.

"How about if Hertz plays it the same way, I mean, if he goes to, say, this O'Banion or that Capone, one whose brother was offed?"

"The racket we're in, what do you think, it's like calling up a cab?"

"I guess not."

"Me, you caught me between undertakings, if you get my drift," Stanton said. "So for now, we could help you out; another time — it'd be a different story. One thing you got going, word gets out you got us on board, others not so likely to work the other side, not wanting to step on each other's toes, you understand? Top of that, most of 'em are on the hop bringing in what you got in that glass." The first true word Danny Stanton had told him. "Moving forward, just keep an eye on the dailies, see how things are getting done, and have the three hundred ready end of every week. I'll send somebody by. And when it's done, another guy'll come to see you."

"But not you?"

Stanton shook his head, saying, "You'll know he's with me. He'll come talking about the brotherhood, the local IBT."

"Unions again? God, I avoid those people like the —"

The hand went up and stopped him, Stanton saying, "He sits in this chair, and you lend an ear, and you hear him out." It wasn't a question.

"And why on earth would I —"

"To keep the ear, for one." Stanton smiled, maybe he was kidding, but then he was out the door.

Doyle kept eyes on Markin a moment longer, then followed Stanton out.

59

Right after the new treaty between Torrio and O'Banion, Karla told him she needed a break.

Huck thinking it was a good time to slip away while there was peace, something they had talked about for a long while, saying, "Guess I can tell Hertz the old windbag to drive himself, talking to himself for a week. Yeah, a holiday's just the thing."

"I mean I'm moving out, Huck . . . till I . . . we get things sorted."

He looked dumbstruck, then saw the suitcases by the door, understanding she was serious, saying, "What's there to sort?"

"I been telling you . . . but you haven't been hearing me."

"It'll end, all the trouble, like I been saying . . . what we talked about."

She just shook her head, looking sad.

"I never wanted this . . ." Huck said, thinking of the house he was having built.

"I'm suffocating, Huck."

"Everything I do —"

She put up a hand. "I know you think that."

"Oh come on, moving where?"

"Wasn't going to tell you, but knowing you — and I do know you — you'd find out. Look, I don't want you showing up at the door, trying to change my mind, making light of it, standing there with a dumb dance ticket."

"You stay here, your home, Maudie's home. And I'll get —"

"No. It's done, Huck. I found a place — not far — I wrote it down." Pointing to the table, an envelope leaning on a candlestick.

"Well, you got it all worked out, all on your own." Biting back his anger, knowing letting it leak out would only make things worse. Seeing the determination in her eyes, he let out a long breath. "Saying it's my family or my livelihood. That it? Putting your foot down."

"Livelihood, Huck, means you to need to be living. What good is it otherwise?" She just shook her head, not how she wanted it.

Expecting him to just walk away from everything he built — a hundred thoughts crashing into each other, his head spinning. All he could come up with, "If you need anything . . ."

"Just need to be by myself . . . at least for a while." She was wiping at her tears.

He didn't understand it, but he nodded like he did, asking, "How about Maudie?"

"You can come by and see her anytime you want. I wouldn't take that from you — just call first."

Just call first, to see his own baby. He swallowed hard, saying, "Is there somebody else? Something I'm missing?" Knowing it was dumb to say it.

"Don't do that, Huck. You know me better . . ."

"And Izzy." Huck guessing it would just be him and Izzy, on their own again.

"I think we let Izzy make up his own mind."

Huck nodded, thinking Izzy would stay, and it would be just the two of them for a while, living on flapjacks and Leberkäse, same way it had been before they all moved in together. And it would be that way until — until what?

Turned out he was wrong on that score too, Izzy taking no time to make up his mind, looking sheepish and fighting back his own tears when Huck told him it was okay, saying his room would be waiting, in case he changed his mind. The young man hugging him like he never wanted to let go, asking when he'd see Huck. Huck telling him anytime, promised to take him to Luka's for flapjacks. All he had to do was call.

"This really what you want?" Huck said to her again at the door, trying hard not to let the anger show, reaching for the suitcases, but Izzy had them.

"Like I said, I don't know what I want, Huck, it's just the right thing for now." She held Maudie close, Maudie wrapping her hand round his finger. Huck kissing the top of her head, kissing Karla on the cheek, holding back from offering to help her down to the lobby, everybody at the Drake seeing her move out. Izzy set the suitcases back down, looked like he wasn't sure if he should offer his hand or give Huck a hug.

Giving him a hug and clapping him on the back, Huck stood at the door and watched them go to the elevator, this suite that had seemed like it was getting too small, knowing it was going to feel too big before the day was done. The elevator man opening the gate, and Huck gave a wave, and like that, they were gone.

60

It was either drop into a bottle or throw himself into his work. The night after Karla moved out, Huck went on a midnight run with Doyle and Drucci, the three of them driving the Hupmobile to Waterloo, parking behind the Seagram's plant on Erb Street, loading up with V.O., and driving back across the ice down by LaSalle.

Overslept in the morning, then he picked up Hertz at Trout Valley, the boss sitting in back, complaining about him being late, then telling him how he got wind that Markin had hired his own muscle, still thinking an attack against him could be coming, telling Huck he best stay sharp, looking at his bloodshot eyes, saying "What do you think?"

"Think it's a good time to hit you for a raise." Huck forced a smile.

"Should've seen that coming," John D. said.

Then Huck asked about the new yearlings that Fannie bought at an auction ring in Kentucky and was having them sent to Trout Valley. John D. excited at the prospects, telling how the woman just kept working her magic with the stock, taking on weanlings, yearlings, and two-year-olds, having a knack for picking them out. Some of the horses resold for profit long before their racing days, some they kept for stud. Fannie making a hell of a return on investment. Huck putting up another twenty grand, the money that should have gone toward construction of his Schaumburg house, Huck delaying it, wanting to wait to see what happened next, the ball in Karla's court.

That night he got a message from Gypsy Doyle and was told to come to the Green Mill, a joint on Lawrence, just to stand around with Doyle out by the cars, a show of force. The head of every gang worth mentioning was coming for another one of Torrio's sit-downs. The banquet hall being lined with tables, white tablecloths, the finest food and wine served to gangsters being treated like nobility, while the muscle stood outside shivering from whatever was howling in off Lake Michigan, about a dozen guys giving each other hard looks — all of them freezing their nuts off.

Following the meet, Dean invited his lads back to Schofield's, telling how Torrio stood at the head table, clinked a spoon against his wine glass and laid out his proposed treaty, carving up the city once again, calling it the holiday bird, as he was fond of saying. Little Italy south of the Loop stayed with the Gennas, a token piece handed to Diamond Joe and his crew. The Spike O'Donnells would control the Carey Patch, the Valley Gang the Near West, the Klondike O'Donnells the Far West, Joe Southers and Frank McClary gaining the Union Stockyards, the Touhys keeping the suburbs north of town, Torrio's outfit taking the Loop and most of the South Side, and O'Banion holding control of the North Side and the Gold Coast. Torrio harping to the room that sticking to the new peace meant they'd soon all be rubbing shoulders with the Fords and Rockefellers, saying how there was plenty to gain and nothing to lose, as long as they stuck with it this time.

Dean saying, "Man was looking at me the whole time he said it."

Dean had Huck and Doyle break out a few bottles of rye whiskey, talking about it and sounding like he meant to keep the peace this time, getting his lads to lay off hijacking any loads belonging to the Sicilians — for now. Then told them he'd be running the business from the office in back of Schofield's as usual, holding gang meetings upstairs once a week, playing it like a respectable chairman of the board, only with a lookout and a Tommy gun by a window, keeping watch out on North State, in case some other CEO breached the treaty. "We know how these greasers get," Dean said. "Never forget that."

When they drained the rye bottles, Gorilla Al proposed Dean sing for his supper. Which Dean was happy to oblige, asking what they wanted to hear, as if he didn't know, and he gave them that nice tenor rendition of "Danny Boy."

It was Huck with the Tommy gun keeping watch the day the black Cadillac rolled up, Johnny Torrio coming for another meet — this one just between him and Dean — two of his boys waiting by the car, Al Capone coming in with him and standing by the door, nobody checking either of them for firearms, a show of respect.

Coming in the upstairs office, hats in hand, Torrio and Capone greeted by Dean, wearing the apron over his suit pants, dropping the snippers in the pocket, the ones he used for trimming the chrysanthemums. Torrio held both arms out to him, the two men acting more like long-lost friends than stone killers on opposing sides. In spite of that, Dean ignored Capone, like he was there as window dressing, just another hired goon, Huck guessing Dean couldn't help but snub somebody, grinning and telling Torrio he really had a feeling maybe this time the peace would last.

Keeping an eye out the window, Huck couldn't help over-hearing Torrio say he came to drop in on a friend, and to ask for a favor, wanting some help with the clean-up from the mayoral election over in Cicero. The two sitting at the table across from each other.

"You want my advice?" Dean asked like he was surprised.

"You got a reputation, Dean, one that follows you like a shadow," Johnny Torrio said, putting warm behind the smile. "Everybody in town knows you swung the forty-second ward from one Crowe to another, Democrats to Republicans, could've done it in your sleep I hear tell."

"Yeah, well . . ." Dean acting humble, but taking the praise.

"That was some doing," Torrio said.

Huck thinking the doing was on account of the brace of pistols Dean carried at all times, three of them under his suit jacket, his tailor making special pockets — Dean's way of letting folks know he wasn't just the neighborhood florist. And if that didn't do it, then he had Moran, Drucci and Bugsy Siegel making a good argument standing around political rallies and the polls, letting voters know how they felt about it.

"Need me casting a ballot, John?" Dean reminding him that part of town now belonged to his man Capone there. He didn't look at Capone, just threw a thumb in his direction.

Torrio nodded, glanced over at Capone, saying the feds were keeping a tight lid on Al these days and anybody else with the name Capone, even followed the man's kid, Sonny, to school. "Guess you heard what happened to Frank?"

"Yeah, a real tragedy. How you people say it, *riposare in pace*." Murdering the Italian with no feeling behind the words.

Huck was watching Capone now, deep-set eyes that looked black, thick cheeks like he was squirreling zeppole in each one, the man standing with his hat in his hands, his eyes on Huck and the Tommy gun on the table by the window, in easy reach for Huck.

"A little help with the election is all I ask, and for that, I'm offering you a piece of the Ship," Torrio said. The Ship being the most lucrative gambling house over in Cicero, under Torrio's control, in fact it was the best joint in all of boozedom. Huck remembering the night Dean and the lads of Kilgubbin took him there after the stand-down fights.

"Yeah? How big's a piece these days? Me, I talk in percent — I call it plain English," O'Banion said, grinning, knowing Cicero was worth about three million a year just in illegal booze sales.

"A slice, you know, a nice piece." Torrio was smiling like was trying to keep it friendly.

"What are we talking, put a number to this piece, slice, whatever?"

Everything but the eyes were smiling, Torrio waving him off like he was kidding.

"A slice like the one you took, cutting up the city like that holiday bird you like talking about, pulling off both drumsticks, and the what-cha-call-its . . ." Dean snapped his fingers.

"Giblets," Huck said.

"Yeah, giblets." Dean turned a sour glance Huck's way, then looked back at Torrio, this old guinea they called the Fox.

"Let's say I sweeten it — a bagno, a nice one over in Blue Island — it's all yours. Just say the word."

"The word's *merda*, that how you say it? I mean, come on, John, you're talking about an out-of-the-way whorehouse. What's that, an outhouse." Dean meant to laugh, but it came out a snort, and he swiped a hand across his nose and mouth.

Torrio looked to be trying hard not to look insulted.

Dean going on, "One minute you offer a slice of the Ship, next minute an out-of-the-way cathouse, sixteen miles south of the Loop. I didn't know better, John, I'd figure you're trying to say something, coming here, offering me what you know I don't touch — whores — something I leave to you and the rest of the guineas, sorry, I mean Gennas." Dean having a strong rule against his crew getting mixed up in prostitution — something Torrio had to know.

"A man that doesn't branch out . . ." Torrio said, keeping his cool, waving a hand, looking to Capone, meaning he tried.

After the guinea crack, Huck angled from the window, more in position to cover Capone at the door, knowing the man was armed, that .45 Colt semi he liked to carry. Huck guessing any moment he might be seeing it, the tension filling the room.

"I ever want a whorehouse, John, I'll just reach out and take one, how about that?"

"Doesn't have to be this way," Torrio said, again with the arms out, trying to reason.

"And this peace of yours, last week some Genna zip sold my guys a load of rotgut. I didn't want to say anything, but there it is. Them people can't help but swindle, no offense, but could be it's in the blood — treaty or no treaty." Again, Dean making it a racial thing.

"You understand they're Sicilian, me, I'm from Irsina," Torrio said, giving another glance to Capone by the door, the man with his hands folded in front of him, his suit jacket open. "Al there's from Brooklyn, red, white and blue all the way."

Huck was wondering about his chance of grabbing the Tommy up, its stick magazine with twenty rounds. Being no kind of gunman likely didn't matter, how could he miss? If he had to do it, he sure hoped Dean would be quick diving for the floor if he had to spray the guy at the door. No idea what kind of kick one of these things had, having never fired one.

"And gambling joints . . . I want another one, I just go offer 'em a better deal than you."

"If you go against the treaty, you go against all of us," Torrio said, looking perplexed, trying one more time. "Come on, Dean, I come here hat in hand, making an offer . . ."

"Expecting me to stick my neck out and rig your election." Dean knowing Torrio had stirred up the crime commission, which was making rumblings about a crackdown, holding anti-crime conferences. Meaning this wasn't hat in hand as much as it could be a set-up.

"I say a thing, then it's so, and you can take it to the bank, I think you know that," Torrio said.

"I still ain't fixing your election."

With that, Johnny Torrio gave a kind of bow with his head, then a smile — no hug, no handshake — and he got up and turned to Capone, his man opening the door, not taking his eyes off Huck and the Tommy, backing out, shutting it and following Torrio down the stairs.

Hearing the car doors slam below, Huck turned from the window, Dean staring at him, taking the snippers from his pocket, shaking them at Huck, then without a word, turning and going out the door.

61

Two days later, in a show of good faith, Torrio worked a five-percent slice of the Ship in O'Banion's direction. Not to be topped, Dean sent the biggest arrangement of yellow and blue flowers he'd ever made over to Torrio's residence on 19th, instead of the gang's HQ on Wabash. Maybe sending it to his home was a gesture with a personal touch, maybe it was Dean's way of letting the outfit's boss know he had his address pinned on a map. He wrote on the card that yellow was a sign of friendship, and blue was for peace, then signed his name to it.

And it might have settled things down until word found its way to the street that the Gennas sold the North Siders a truckload of rotgut. Huck guessed it could have been Capone who leaked it. No way Torrio would do it and put his peace treaty in Dutch. Drucci pointing out that Huck had been the fourth man in the room the day of the meeting. And it sure didn't take long for word to come back that Bloody Ang Genna felt the sting of insult, denying his guys sold anybody rotgut, least of all the fucking micks.

Demanding an apology through Torrio, and not getting one, Bloody Ang had his crews driving their trucks through the North Side, disregarding the turf lines. O'Banion having one of the Genna trucks stopped by a couple of payroll cops, Dean getting Huck to drive, showing up as the officers held the driver and shotgun man against the side of the furniture truck at gunpoint. Huck and one of the cops opened the back, moving tables and dressers out of the way, finding crates of Canadian booze under tarps. Taking a bottle and uncorking it, Dean tipped it back and took a drink, saying as he splashed the rest on the road, "What d'you know, the real McCoy." Claiming the load in lieu of the rotgut his guys had been sold. Huck was told to drive off with the truck, the cops escorting the Genna men off the North Side, warning them about showing their faces again.

Next day, Hymie and Bugs told Huck to sit in that window upstairs with the Tommy gun, replaced the stick clip with a drum load and told him to keep a sharp eye on the coming and going from the shop. Huck was sitting there about midday when Torrio called and Dean got on the blower, the Fox not coming back in person this time, but still stressing the peace, and how they all stood to profit by putting their differences aside. Telling Dean he was forgetting the slice of the Ship.

"Can't forget your generosity, John, you keep telling me about it. But let's call the whole mess a misunderstanding, the Gennas selling my guys the wrong booze, driving their rigs through my turf. Oh, and speaking of the Ship, seeing I got a piece, a slice, whatever, I had a talk with management, then had my own bean-counter give the books the once-over — seeing how I got this piece or slice. Wanting to make sure the Ship ain't leaking, in all our interests, you understand." Dean winked at Huck.

"You went to see my books?" Huck hearing Torrio's raised voice over the line.

"The point being I see your pal Ang's got a thirty-G marker sitting there going ripe. But nothing to worry about, I took care of it . . ."

"You what?"

"Yeah, I sent him word, he walks in the place again, he better be coming to clear up the marker."

Silence on the line.

"Got to be trouble on the line, John, on account you keep breaking up — you not hearing so good. Anyway, I got word to him, nice and polite mind you, didn't call him a fat greaser, nothing like that, just told him nice he ought to clear it up."

Dean held the phone away from his ear, then said, "Yeah, it's got to be this line — tell you what, John, I'll try back another time." With that Dean hung up, looking pleased with himself. Saying to Huck, "You get all that?"

Huck not sure of the right answer, saying he wasn't really paying attention, wondering how he could help it when he was sitting twenty feet away.

"How you think that fat sausage-eating fuck's gonna take it?"

Huck not sure which fat sausage-eating fuck he meant, Torrio or Genna, saying, "I don't think it'll be sitting down."

"Goddamn right. Them two are gonna be on the ceiling." O'Banion was laughing like it made his day, saying, "Get Hymie and Bugs in here. The Schemer and Doyle too. It's time to get to work."

62

It was this code Torrio's outfit went by: You put a wrong on me or mine, and it gets settled — you'll know you wronged me, your whole family will know you wronged me, every son and daughter will feel it to the roots of the family tree. They will pay like they never paid for anything in their lives. There will be no confession, no day in court, no righting of this wrong. The debt will be settled and the upshot won't be in words — it'll come in blood.

And it hung over the North Side like a thick fog, and the peace was again dangling by a thread. Dean kept an eye on Torrio, having the man followed, the crime boss acting like a quiet man of simple means, going home to supper at his 19th Street flat, with an armed guard outside his door, another one in the lobby.

Coming up through the ranks of the Five Points Gang in New York, following Big Jim Colosimo to the midwest, John the Fox made his mark the day he got off the 20th Century Limited coming from Grand Central to LaSalle, the day before William McSwiggin, assistant state attorney, known to be blackmailing Big Jim, was gunned down in Cicero in broad daylight, a crime that had gone unsolved to the day.

To Dean, the Fox was no more than the king pimp, running his brothels and gambling dens, places looking like army barracks up in Burnham by the Indiana line — like his own square mile of vice-and-dice village, the Burnham and Arrowhead Inns, later the Roamer House over in Posen — the mayor and police force to a man doing his bidding. Torrio had become filthy rich, but the vice-and-dice was nothing compared to what came after Volstead, Torrio adding breweries and speaks to his landholdings. Illegal booze was flowing into all his joints, and he was making so much dough, he added the entire village of Stickney to his holdings. Torrio buying Texacos a mile or so from his brothels and dens, wiring them up with phone lines that allowed his boys to send a signal anytime an honest cop came asking questions, giving his joints a heads-up and time to clean up before a raid. After Stickney, he added Cicero, the fifth-largest locality in Cook County, a population of seventy thousand and home to Western Electric. Little by little meant bigger and bigger, and soon every speakeasy around was under his control, buying their booze from John "The Fox" Torrio. Any speak owner who didn't get on board worried about firebombings and worse. Just ask Dandy Joe Hogarty or Eddie Tancl about the worse part.

Dean didn't heed any of that. Having his tailor fashion pockets in every suit he owned to hide the arsenal. Didn't matter if he was walking into the Fountain Court or the new mayor's office, he went around town packed and loaded. Hymie and Bugs seeing he didn't go anyplace unescorted either, knowing the North Side boss had a bull's-eye middle of his back, another one on his forehead, pushing his Irish luck.

Huck seeing it as the man having a death wish, and not wanting to be standing too close to Dean when it happened, a chance of ending up as collateral damage, saying so to Gypsy Doyle, hinting again that he wanted out. He'd jumped in with both feet when Karla moved out, taking Maudie and Izzy with her. Now seeing that was a mistake.

"Man, you got to make up your mind." Doyle saying, "But do I have to explain again how it works? You're in, you're in — as in all the way, as in for life."

"Thought that was just the Italians."

"What'd you think this was, the Boys Club?"

63

Hardly slept that night, Karla sat on the divan by the window of the Belden. The baby, nearly a year old now, was sleeping against her breast. Looking out at Lincoln Park, the grounds white, snow swirling past the skeletons of trees to the south of the property, the park benches covered in white, the day just breaking. Wrapping the blanket round her shoulders, holding the cup in her hand, feeling its warmth. Grateful that Izzy had slept through the night, usually restless as well on nights since they'd moved out. Karla knowing the boy in him missed Huck, although he wouldn't talk much about it. Still feeling the bitch for doing it, she sipped her tea, saying a prayer she remembered from when she was a girl. Then added a few lines of her own.

"Protect that man from the trouble he gets in, and keep all the wicked from his soul. No matter he walks into it face first — and no matter how crackbrained he gets. You know what I'm talking about, Lord." Karla smiling to herself. "The man hasn't known much goodness or mercy in his life, and he's got no idea of heaven, and that's not all his own fault, the hard road you put under his feet, and the hard times you laid on his back too. But you know him, he's got a good heart under the scars. So, if you can see your way, send him an angel, maybe two if you can spare them."

"Who're you talking to?" Izzy was standing by his bedroom door, barefoot and wearing pajamas and rubbing an eye, looking around, almost looked disappointed that she was alone.

She looked up at him, thinking when did he get so tall — taller than Huck now. "Said a prayer if you must know."

"Thought maybe Huck came around."

"I'm sorry I woke you."

"Morning woke me." He took a moment, then a smirk crossed his face.

"What's funny?"

"Remember Huck asking if God was a man or woman?"

"And you said matter. Sure. And he says, 'Better question's how come we can't see him?'"

"You said it's on faith. That's what the priests talked about, faith, this church I went to a couple of times, mostly to get out of the cold," he said.

"You heard the sermons?"

"Remember the priest talking how you feel the heavenly host all around. Sure had my doubts about it at the time, being left on my own and all."

She smiled, then she held open the blanket, and he sat next to her, careful not to wake Maudie. She closed the blanket around the three of them, and he put his head against hers. And he told her what happened to his mother, how she went out to work one morning and never came back, getting caught coming home, a riot breaking, the police right on them, beating them with clubs. His mother falling victim, Izzy with no idea if it was the rioters or the police that did it.

"You ever go?" he asked, wiping his eye.

"Church?"

"Yeah."

"Some."

"And you talk to God."

"Sometimes it helps, 'least I think so."

"Huck ever do it?"

"If he did, he likely tried to work a deal."

"But he'd look out for Huck just the same."

"He?"

"Matter."

"Especially for Huck."

"On account he needs all the help he can get."

And they were both smiling, holding each other.

"And you and me have us," Karla said.

"The three of us safe right here."

"Right." She kissed the top of his head. And she was holding back her own tears.

"You and Huck ever getting back? I mean, there's the baby . . ." His voice cracking.

"Just needed to take a break — more me than him really."

Izzy nodded like he understood that, but this sure was a long break. "Think you'll move into that house he wants to build?"

"Someday — maybe."

Izzy liked hearing it, saying, "When do you think he'll come around?"

"Any day now."

"You could call him."

"I could."

And they were silent, looking out at the snow, coming down harder now.

64

Tapping on the door, he looked along the corridor, the building quiet this time of morning. This place he was paying the rent on, Karla, the baby and Izzy living on the eighth floor of the Belden, close to the Loop and not far from the Magnificent Mile. Somebody on staff at all hours, with a bakery on the lower level, something Izzy was sure to love. He was wondering how long she was going to play this, feeling like she kept slapping his hand away. But he wasn't going to start on that note.

A sound from inside, then he heard her voice.

"Who's there?"

"Room service." Huck thinking he should have had the operator try her suite first, instead of just dropping in.

The sound of the latch, then the knob turning, the door opening an inch, as far as the chain allowed. She looked out, then the door closed again. Stayed shut a moment, like maybe she was trying to decide. When it opened, she kept her hand on it, looking at him, giving him a smile, waiting on his line.

Huck held up his fingers, pretending he was holding a dance stub.

And she smiled, but just shook her head, trying to look stern, but she couldn't help the smile at the corners of her mouth.

"Been working on my Charleston moves." Glancing down at her bare feet. Then he gave it a try, right in the hall, a horrible attempt at the dance craze.

"Down on your heels, up on your toes — all the way up the stairs to my door, one step ahead of the paddy wagon, huh?"

He stopped, looking past her shoulder, hoping to catch sight of Maudie and Izzy.

"They're both asleep, and he's got school tomorrow." Karla glad Izzy had ducked back into his room, giving them time alone. Not wanting the neighbor snoop knowing her business, Karla widened the door, saying, "Well, you're here . . ." Pinching his sleeve and tugging him in.

"Glad I didn't wake you."

"Mean you're glad I opened the door." Rolling her eyes.

"Well, that too."

"Could've called, let me know . . ." Putting a hand to her hair.

"You look fine."

"Just fine?"

"Beautiful."

"Is everything alright?"

He nodded, saying, "Just couldn't stay away."

"I've been thinking of helping out at a hospital."

"Back to nursing?"

"Been thinking about working — not feeling obliged to does have its appeal."

"You don't owe me, and it's for them too."

"Yeah, I know. It's not about that. How about you, working, I mean?"

"It's complicated." Not wanting to get into it with her. She frowned.

"If you did go looking, any place'd take you — be crazy not to."

"With every unmarried woman in town lining up for nickels." She took the imaginary stub from his fingers, took his hands and got close, not wanting to get into it either.

"They say the cream rises," Huck said, shutting the door with his heel, taking in her scent as she rocked against him, the two of them swaying slow, the lamp on by the armchair across from the divan, her bedroom door open, the bed with its duvet and line of pillows, the night stand next to it. The double windows letting light spill in from the street, a nice city view, twinkling lights.

"Sure you didn't come by to check on me — peek under the bed . . ." Laying her head against his chest.

"Maybe I just came to dance."

"Could call up for something, you want something to eat?"

"The kitchen's closed — and just the dance is fine."

"Fine?"

"Beautiful."

"Come here with your sugar words, this early — how come I can't stay mad at you?"

"Was hoping you'd be glad to see me."

"Mister, I get a nickel a dance, that's all you need to know." Karla still swaying like there was music.

"Good enough for me." And he took her hands, Huck trying not to mess up the three-step.

"You think you've got me all figured?" She was looking up at him, still moving against him.

"Anytime I do, you surprise me." Huck remembering how he used to feel like he was on the wrong foot, too dumb to talk to her, and not much good at dancing. They slowed now, barely moving, close and holding each other. Thinking this is how they started out, back in that drafty, dim flat. A pantry shelf with a loaf of bread and a jar of something.

Her only change of clothes on a hanger on the closet door. Now they were living like this, not together, but a long way from where they started out, and he felt he was back to trying to get to know her.

"Izzy or the baby need anything?"

"He's still lousy about all this . . ." she said.

"I know, me too."

"But you're still with them?" She let go of him, pulling away, stepping to the window, looking out at the falling snow and twinkling lights.

Maybe it was a mistake coming here, not having something new to tell her, just wanting to see her, showing up at this sleepless hour.

"I don't want to open the door one day, have that Doyle, with that dumb missing tooth, telling me you won't be coming back. You understand that?"

He did understand that, kept himself from saying he was being careful, knowing that was lame. And he knew there was only so much being careful with Dean O'Banion going against both Torrio and the Gennas. And it wasn't fair, him coming over here like this. "Well, I thank you for the dance, lady."

"You hear me say I want you to go?" She turned and kept hold of his hand, and after a moment the smile returned, and she said, "Remember I let you drive me home, showed you where I lived."

"Showed me? God, you blindfolded me."

"You were peeking. Don't tell me you weren't."

"Not the whole way."

And her smile widened. "You were different then, maybe a little unsure, a little sad. I don't know . . ." She squeezed his fingers.

"Remember you saying 'Don't lie to me,' like somebody had done it before."

"Everybody gets lied to. Mostly, we lie to ourselves. And I learned early to look past the words. I just figured we could be more than that . . ."

"Was a time I thought you could read my mind, and that scared the hell out of me." Huck running his fingers lightly through her hair.

Leading him by the hand, she stepped to the divan, the two of them sitting.

"You ever think of leaving this place, I mean, far from this place?"

"The country's not far enough for you?" Huck thinking of the place he started to build in Schaumburg, hoping to continue soon.

She shrugged like it didn't matter. "Not much we can't do. Could go out west someplace, grow oranges."

"Hertz has a place out west." Huck thinking of the man's Amarillo Ranch, someplace in California called Woodland Hills.

"We can't run away from us."

"You mean from trouble?"

"I'll go anyplace with you, but I don't want you looking at me someday like I took something from you."

"What I don't want, is doing it with just a bindle on my shoulder. Never want to just slide by again. I go, then I want porters pulling our trunks."

"You've been looking out for us, and you still are . . ." Stopping herself, knowing they were just repeating the same lines.

"That's 'cause I'm as sure about you and me as eggs is eggs." Huck making a poor attempt at an English accent, putting his arm around her shoulder.

"You're thinking of food, aren't you?"

"You got me."

"Except the kitchen's closed."

"I'll ride it out."

"Well, why don't you stay till it opens?" She looked at him a moment, then she reached for the lamp, switching it off. Leaning against him, putting her mouth against his neck. And they stayed like that till Maudie started fussing.

65

Lifting his cup when the waiter came around with the pot, pouring more coffee, Huck looked around the Fountain Court, smiling across at her. Karla in a silk evening dress and the pearls he got her for her twenty-sixth birthday around her neck. Huck taking her to her favorite place for the occasion. Saying to her, "That fellow gave me an odd look."

"What fellow?" Karla looking around, then back to him, liked that they were back to playing, meaning things were good again between them. Huck vowing to back away from the North Side, and Karla moving back into the suite at the Drake. And he started thinking again about getting architect Louis Sullivan to make a couple changes and finalize the plans for the house in Schaumburg.

"That waiter," Huck said, pointing to a man in a tux, saying, "like he's wondering where we packed it all, coming in here and eating up all that chop suey, and drowning ourselves in coffee." Huck leaned back in his chair and clapped his stomach. "Was just thinking we could split a stack, that is if you got room?" He looked at their plates, the tea sandwiches and canapés they had ordered.

She just shook her head at him. "I'm stuffed, and I got to get up early." Pretending to stifle a yawn, then she lifted her cup proper, in one hand, the saucer in the other.

"You got no work since that dance joint burned down," he said.

"Well, sir, that means I've got to get up with the rooster and find some."

Waiting till the waiter in the tux returned, set down the silver tray with the check, thanked him, calling him Mr. Waller.

Huck making like he was getting an idea, then saying, "How about I get a cab from the livery, drive you any place you want, save you all that hoofing?"

"You mean save my poor tired feet?"

"That's right, lady, and save you plenty of time too. You find this job, then later, I know a spot by the lake . . ."

"Ain't it a little cold for Lake Shore Drive, sir?"

"Ahh, I've got this blanket and a spot by Flatfoot Lake, nice and warm, where the sun's always shining."

"That so?" Karla put her fingers to her mouth, stifling another yawn, saying, "Oh dear. This was real good, and you were right about it . . . what did you call them?"

"Flapjacks."

"Like pancakes, only different."

"That's right. It's all in the batter."

"That so?"

"Uh huh."

"Well, all this small talk's got me falling asleep." She closed her eyes, dropped her chin, and feigned a snore.

"Then I best walk you back." He tilted back in his chair, patted his pockets like he was checking for a wallet, pretending not to find it, looking alarmed.

"Still trying to pull that old trick?" she said.

"Was going to leave a nickel tip too."

"Well, I'm going to bed — and I mean to sleep."

"Just don't feel right, letting you walk on your own, this time of night, slippy ice and all."

"How you think I get around the rest of the time?"

"Just shows you need a man in your life — 'less you think I'm coming on too strong." Putting up his hands like he was ready to back off. Then reaching inside his jacket, taking his billfold, setting some bills on the tray, leaving a fat tip. The maître d' coming and getting her chair, saying it was good to see her again, calling her Mrs. Waller.

And she was smiling, saying to Huck when he left, "Well, you can walk me back, but no funny business, you understand?"

"I'll get you to your door, and I'll turn right around."

"Not even gonna try?" She let him help her with the mink stole, snugging it around her neck.

"Well . . . not 'less you want me to?"

"I'll let you figure it out." Then she reached his neck, loosened the Windsor knot, taking the tie from his collar, saying, "But first I need to blindfold you."

"Man, I just don't get women," Huck winked to the maître d'. Letting Karla fit the tie around his eyes.

Other patrons watching as Karla took his arm and led him through the Palm Court, getting their share of odd looks and smiles too, the waiter holding the door and thanking them, saying it was good to see them both again.

"Wish I could say the same, seeing how I'm blindfolded." Huck was led down the hall, saying, "Too cold a night for man or beast, and bet if I could see, there'd be a lead sky, promising to snow."

"Well, you'd be right."

"Be hell driving these city streets, and you trying to find work."

"Yes, I suppose so. Oh, what to do?"

"Think you best spend the night, my dear."

"Well . . . say, you sure you even got a taxi?"

"Sure, I do — a great big yellow one."

"Think I'll have to see it for myself." She took his arm and led him to the elevator.

"How about I show it to you first thing in the morning."

Later in bed, he looked at her next to him. "You sure are a bag of surprises, lady." Lying back, his head on the pillow, the scent of something sweet, a different scent than the one she used to wear, something he remembered from back home, lilac, he guessed.

"Not sure about being called a bag of anything." She turned her head, and in the fading dark he could see that smile, the light of morning starting to show itself past the drape.

"Well, you got a way of keeping me on my toes."

Her hand moving under the covers. "On your toes, huh?"

"You keep on, and I won't let you go." He arched his back, his teeth on his lip, trying not to make a sound. Pushing away thoughts of picking up John D. at Trout Valley in just a couple of hours.

"What makes you think I'm going?"

"Doorman'll see you sneaking off in the morning."

"You think he knows about us?"

"Young don't make him dumb."

"Well, I could just stay a little longer?"

"I think we ought to lay here and figure things out."

"You think I'm being difficult?" She stopped and looked at him, trying to read his thoughts.

"I think you're giving me a hard time." With that he took her hand in his, and he rolled on top, taking a wrist in each hand, and they were done talking.

66

Huck walked into the livery, nodded to Moses working on a Mogul up on the new rotary auto lift, the man's hair the color of snow now. He had the front wheels off, another taxi with its doors open, the rear seat pulled out. Snooky, the one-time apprentice, lay under it on a creeper, his boots sticking out.

The closet he once turned into a space for Izzy was stacked with crates of spare parts, a case of Sinclair Oil and a couple of toolboxes. Huck got an image of Izzy sitting on the cot reading a comic Snooky got him, handing him a sandwich bag he got from the Chuck Wagon.

He took the stairs to the office, tapping on the door and walking in.

Looking up from the paper across the big oak desk, John D. put red-rimmed eyes on him, a sign of his own late night. Huck expecting to catch hell for not picking him up at his ranch, making the man get himself into town.

"Somebody dump a Checker in the river?" Huck smiled.

"I wouldn't mind." John D. telling him Mayor Dever issued a warning to both outfits after three Yellows were bombarded with a hail of bricks from an overpass. A Checker driver held at gunpoint while his taxi was set on fire.

Huck sat down, looking at him in his fine leather chair, wondering if somebody else drove him here from his ranch.

John D. flapped his paper closed, looked like he was forming his thoughts. The man yawned, and Huck did too.

Giving him a minute, Huck felt how tired he was himself, saying, "Sorry I left you hanging."

"That for the time last week too?" Hertz said.

"Yeah, that one too. Couldn't be helped. Take it out of my pay."

"That the best you can do, take it out of your pay?"

"Said I was sorry." Huck wanted to swipe the paper off the man's desk. Not sure why he was getting angry.

"You either been drinking, or you could use one," John D. said, his voice calm, reaching the decanter on the bureau behind him, next to the gun case.

"It's a little early, no?"

"Nonsense." John D. swiveled his chair, reached a pair of glasses and started pouring, saying, "Hired a driver today."

"Another one quit?"

Huck watched him shake his head and fill the glasses, guessing what he had coming.

"Personal driver — and bodyguard."

Huck just nodded, feeling almost relieved.

"The finest — Old Forester." Sliding one across the desk, John D. left a sweaty trail on the oak.

"Hired a night watchman for the place too, a full-sized one."

Huck nodded again.

"Your head's not in the game, Huck, not for a while now."

"Not exactly going to be standing in a bread line, John. Don't worry about it." Huck smiled and picked up the glass and held it up.

Hertz clinked glasses, and the two of them sat quiet, sipping their drinks.

"That taxi you tipped in the river that time . . ." Shaking his head, thinking about it. "Only wish I'd seen it."

"Was three of them that time, a beaver dam of rusting tin in the Chicago." Huck smiling too, thinking back to when Dex Ayres first took him on. Then asked, "How about the horses?"

"The horses have nothing to do with it. You stay in that game as long as you want."

Huck nodded, his yearlings and breeding mares boarded at the Trout Valley ranch. Huck thinking of acquiring some adjoining acreage to his place and adding stables of his own, then saying, "Can you count on this new man?"

"Man raced Frontenacs with Louis Chevrolet one time, plus the man can shoot too, was a marksman in the Marine Corps. And shows up when I tell him."

"An unswerving man's something to respect." Huck wondering why he didn't run the new man by him first.

"Man shows that military kind of regard for authority — kind of refreshing." John D. eased back in the chair.

"Wears the cap and drives with you in back, a gun under the seat, in case he feels the need to shoot himself, hearing the same stories over and over."

"It's what the job calls for."

"Kind of a fighting, shooting, driving man."

"And shows up on time."

"Right, punchy and punctual. And not bucking the head muckety-muck." Huck raised his glass, smiling, the first time he thought of them as more than boss and driver.

"No bucking the muckety-mucks," John D. said.

"The man ask a fair wage?"

"Ten a day's what I offered."

"Man didn't dicker? Asked if the ten had a fiver for a friend?" Huck knowing unskilled labor was fetching about thirty cents an hour, twenty-five for non-whites and women.

"Seems fine with the ten."

"I'll give him a month," Huck said, sipping the fine bourbon.

67

Never totally sure how far he could trust Gypsy Doyle, Huck wondered why he felt that way, saying to him, "What you said about getting out of the life . . ."

"How's that?" Doyle looked at him, that knife scar angling down his face.

"You said once you're in, you're in."

"The way out's horizontal and feet first."

"Something like that."

"You making small talk or getting to a point? 'Cause if you're thinking that way . . ."

"I'm just asking."

"I were you, I'd keep that quizzical nature locked in the cellar." Fishing a pack of Camels from his pocket, then searching for matches, Doyle said, "Let's go, this thing ain't gonna drive itself." Lighting the cigarette, watching Huck put it in gear, driving the taxi he borrowed from the livery, Moses looking the other way.

Huck driving it to the North Side warehouse that got hit last night. From what the crew had gathered, the Gennas were lashing back for a truck the North Side had jacked the week before.

There'd likely never come a right time to tell Dean he wanted out, this war that kept reheating with Torrio and the Gennas. Doyle telling him Torrio's man Capone just shot one of the hijackers that had been working with Bugs. Caught up to the man at Heinie Jacobs's saloon on Wabash, Capone calling him out on account of the guy had assaulted Greasy Thumb Guzik, the Outfit's one-time accountant — what Torrio was calling his gang now, the Outfit. The hijacker told Capone that Guzik had it coming, then calling Capone just another low-life greaser, going for his pistol, Capone pulling first and capping the hijacker, spitting in his face as the man lay there coughing up blood. Doyle saw it as putting all of the North Side on notice, meaning now wasn't a time for talking retirement.

Pulling up to the Devon Avenue warehouse, they saw a cop car parked behind a couple of other sedans, the coppers standing there looking like they were at a funeral. Parking the Yellow, Huck saw Dean walking through the rubble, kicking a charred board, the man angry as a hornet, cursing to himself. Hymie Weiss and Vincent Drucci stood next to another sedan, surveying the wreckage, talking in low voices. The garage had been firebombed, burned to the ground, all the Seagram's gone. A stockpile of two hundred and fifty cases, some of what Doyle and Huck had just run in from Canada.

Huck stood breathing the acrid air, watching Dean pace, oblivious of his suit pants getting black below the knees. Every now and then kicking at something else, sending up more ash. Then he went and said something to the two cops, and they got in their cruiser and pulled away. Then he came over, saying to Doyle, "Go set up a meet. I want everybody there — make it tonight."

Dean nodded to Huck, meaning he wanted a word, telling him, "I want you with me." Then he handed Doyle the key to his own Cadillac.

Huck stood watching Doyle drive off, Dean looking at the wreckage another minute, then turned for the taxi, saying, "Okay, come on."

Huck back to being the driver.

In the front seat of the taxi, Dean said, "It's a message."

"Retaliation?"

"For what you did at Pop's — our joint till Torrio sliced up the town again, now it's the Gennas. Let's go." He pointed through the windshield.

Huck starting the Yellow.

"Doyle tell you, the Sicilians tried to put a hit on me?" Not waiting for an answer. "Only they couldn't get it past Merlo, you know who I mean?"

Huck nodded, knowing the name of Mike Merlo the fixer, head of the Unione Siciliana, a man wielding some weight in Democratic Party politics, not to mention the underworld, having ties to New York. Nothing Italian went on in this town without getting a nod from Merlo and his Unione.

"Genna's way of letting me know what he thinks of Merlo's rule — like a dago temper tantrum."

"Mind saying where we're going?" Huck wanting some directions.

Dean just pointed ahead, then pointed again when he wanted Huck to make a turn. Holding up a hand when he wanted him to stop outside the Four Deuces, a hangout for Capone's crew.

"Got a call from Duffy, the guy running this place," Dean said. "Wants out on account he knows the dagos are going down. Wants safe passage for some dirt on the dagos." Dean looked at Huck a moment, doing it like he wanted that to sink in. Then saying, "Only, dumb fuck Duffy goes home and tells his old lady they're pulling stakes and wants her packed in half an hour. So she starts giving him the business, how he can't just come in and tell her a thing like that, how they got family, kid's in school, yadda yadda. So he shows her the back of his hand, puts her in her place. So the little woman takes a lamp to his head like she's swinging for the fences — and goes Ty Cobb on him. So his bell got rung, head's bleeding from a busted chunk of lamp sticking in his skull, next she grabs the fry pan — she ain't done yet — but he ducks the swing and gets the upper hand and shoves her down, a pillow over her mouth, stops her from yelling blue murder so the whole neighborhood comes awake. Only, the dumb fuck's running hot and ends up snuffing her — you believe it, a guy that lamebrained?"

"His own wife?" Huck feeling the prickle on the back of his neck, getting a feeling Dean wanted him to help bury the poor woman.

"You look like you just dropped one in your pants." Dean seeing the look in his eyes, then laughing and saying, "So Duffy rings me back, wants another favor, a car and some cash, going to make a run for it tonight. Figures there's no way of explaining a thing like that to the cops — the first fucking thing he got right."

The bad feeling growing as Huck pulled up out front of the Four Deuces, this speak inside Genna turf. Huck wondering why they were meeting the guy here, and not on home ground. Then again, this was Dean O'Banion, Huck starting to think the man was becoming more unhinged by the day, that or he really had a death wish.

Another sedan pulled to the curb a half block up, its head-lights aiming their way, two men in the front, both with hats pulled low, engine running and the headlights switching off.

They sat quiet a few minutes till a lone man came walking the opposite way, coming from behind them. Dean seeing him in the sideview mirror, opening the passenger door, saying to Huck, "May as well stretch your legs. Gonna give him this car."

"This car?" That bad feeling jumping in size. The Yellow cab Moses let him use.

"And let the door hang open," Dean said, focusing on the man coming.

Middle of Genna turf and he wants to stretch his legs and let this guy have the taxi. Dean smiling at the approaching man like everything was roses, ignoring the two guys in the sedan, both of them looking this way, their engine still running.

Huck got out, reaching under the seat, dropping the Colt in a pocket, and he left the door hanging like he'd been told, watching the man approach, looking spooked, his skin sallow.

"You seen better days, Duffy," Dean said, stretching out his hand.

Duffy reached for the hand, saying, "This it, huh?" Looking at the taxi.

"This is it." Dean taking hold of his hand, gripping it tight, taking his left hand from his coat, sticking a pistol to the man's head and firing, still shaking the hand. Letting go as Duffy dropped, eyes rolling up. Then Dean shot him two more times where he fell, saying something to him, like he was explaining it.

The sedan's engine came to life, its tires rolling, the headlights still off, Huck grabbing for his pistol.

Dean hurrying to it, dropping the pistol in his pocket, calling to Huck, "Let's go!" Jumping into the back seat.

Forcing his feet to move, Huck got in back on the driver's side. Drucci was behind the wheel, Bugs Moran on the passenger side.

And the sedan pulled away, John Duffy lying on the sidewalk, at the door of the Four Deuces, a Yellow taxi with the doors hanging open right out front.

"Those fucking Gennas." Dean saying it with conviction, turning on the seat to get a better look out the back, the body on the ground, heads poking from doorways.

"The taxi . . ." Huck saying, trying to put it together.

"Told you I don't want you working with them," Dean said.

And the pieces fell together, Dean setting the scene: making it look like the Gennas clipped Duffy out front of his place. Huck wondering if Duffy had really suffocated his old lady and was going on the lam. Then wondering if Dean got word that Huck wanted out, showing him what happened to anybody who tried — something he could only have heard from Gypsy Doyle. If the Gennas connected him with the taxi, they'd likely come for him, meaning he wasn't walking away from this, Dean O'Banion seeing to it. One thing was sure, things were coming to a head between O'Banion's people and the Italians, Huck replaying what Doyle said, the only way out's horizontal and feet first.

68

Felt like he was in a vice, sitting by the upstairs window with the Thompson gun, Dean wanting him on watch. Two weeks since John Duffy had been killed out front of the Four Deuces. Dean back to snipping his flowers and filling orders, acting like it never happened.

Bugs Moran and Hymie Weiss sat at the long table, like it was the war room, talking the situation over, expecting the Gennas to lash back. Bugs telling Huck to take a break, go get himself a coffee, likely not wanting him to overhear what they were planning.

Going down the stairs, hearing Dean on the blower in the back of the shop, thinking he was taking an order, then getting what he was saying, offering to sell his end of the C&B. That being the brewery, one of the gang's biggest money-makers over the past years. Dean saying he'd take half a mill for his one-third interest, how he didn't want the bad blood going on. Then hanging up, smiling to himself, then seeing Huck picking up the coffee pot.

"You want a cup?" Huck asked.

Not answering, Dean just looked at him.

Feeling the chill, Huck took his cup and went out the front, stood under the striped awning, leaned against the bricks and stood looking at the traffic go past.

Next day Dean told a roomful of his core guys — Bugs, Hymie, Drucci, and Doyle — he'd sold their interest in the C&B, Torrio willing to buy him out for a half million, the money exchanging hands later in the week.

"Why we selling?" Hymie said, sounding surprised.

"You got a fish on the hook, you reel it in" is what Dean said, looking around at the long faces, saying, "Somebody else got something to say?" He opened his jacket, showing he wasn't carrying his three pistols, saying things were getting out of hand between the gangs, wanting them to just focus on bringing in the booze. Nobody saying what everybody in the room was thinking, how it was Dean who'd been stirring the pot since day one. Looks were exchanged, but nobody challenged him on it, leaving this weight hanging over the place.

A couple of days later, Dean was back to his joking nature, asking if Huck read the paper, taking a folded *Trib* from under his arm and swatting Huck on the backside with it. He took the paper from him and read: "Crime Boss Arrested." The story telling how John "The Fox" Torrio had been arrested along with ten others, caught with five truckloads holding a hundred and fifty barrels of beer at the C&B Brewery. Treasury agents confiscating a ledger of damning evidence, showing inventories and delivery locations, along with a line of speakeasies, and lists of politicians and prohibition agents receiving payoffs. One conviction for bootlegging already against him, John Torrio was staring at three years or more.

Huck looked up at Dean, understanding how he had set Torrio up, passing the paper to Gypsy Doyle as he came walking into the room with a tin, looking for coffee.

"You mess with the bull, and you get the horns," Dean said, taking a vase of flowers over to his work bench, taking single stems, and he started snipping off leaves, making a fresh arrangement.

Doyle didn't say anything, looking at Huck with dull eyes. Dean set Torrio up for a fall, something that was sure to come with South Side backlash.

Dean started humming "Danny Boy," in the best of spirits.

69

Danny Stanton took a chance on meeting with them, stepping into the Chuck Wagon, told them how it was, being there that time when Bloody Ang walked into Pop's Roadhouse, looking at the burned bar top and floor, the busted bottles — Vincent Drucci spilling the booze, trying to torch the place down in the middle of Genna turf.

"Figured he forgot about that — time flying by — the man having bigger things on his mind," Doyle said.

"Ang looks at the busted place, the bar smashed up, big fucking burn on the floor, the place looking like hell, and smelling like it too. Steps around busted glass, grabs Tom the barman by the neck, yelling he wants to know who tore up his place." Stanton looked at Huck, saying, "Barman fingers Drucci, and the guy you beat up fingers you, calls you by name. Bartender remembers Drucci calling you by name, so Ang has his boys ask around."

"They jack our load, and he acts surprised?" Doyle said.

"Except, turns out it wasn't the Gennas that jacked your load," Stanton said. "Ang swears he had nothing to do with it, figures it was the Purples, a double cross. Anyway, Torrio told him to lay off — this was then, mind you — still hanging onto his treaty, wanting it to work out. Now Torrio gets set up and hauled to jail — word is Bloody Ang wants to put hits on Dean, you two, and Drucci. That's just for starters."

Stanton looked at Huck. "Knows it was you drove Deanie when he popped the guy out front of the Deuces. Bloody Ang putting five hundred on your heads, ten grand on Deanie."

"That's it, I'm only five hundred?" Doyle said, smiling like it didn't bother him.

"And if he knew I was telling you, be five on me too," Stanton said.

Doyle nodded, knowing Stanton was sticking his neck out, clapped a hand on his shoulder, his way of saying thanks.

"Don't need to tell you, be a good time to take a holiday."

When Danny Stanton left, Doyle looked at Huck, saying, "Don't start that again."

Huck held back from slugging him, starting to come around to her way of thinking, that taking Karla and kids someplace else beat leaving a widow and orphans.

70

The copper pulled back the boarded-over door of the barroom called the Time-Out, Dean stepped into the nickel joint, Hymie Weiss and Vincent Drucci went to where the bar had been, Charlie the barman with them, looking unsure like he was going to take the blame for what happened last night: six men coming in, clearing out the place, then busting it up and setting torches to it, payback for what happened to Pop's.

Dean looked at him, saying, "Who did it?"

"One of 'em comes in now and then," Charlie said. "Dark hair, about yea tall, Slav maybe. Minds his own, takes a swallow and a swing on the floor, then goes."

"I'm not asking about his dance card."

"Don't got a name. Like I said, the guy just comes in, wets his throat, takes a trot around the floor, then goes. Don't hang around like most of them, looking for extras. From the gals, I mean."

Dean gave him a sharp look.

"I ain't no pimp, Deanie, understand that." Charlie knowing Dean's rule about running a brothel on North Side turf. "All

I can tell ya it was this guy comes back, five guys with him, all swinging axe handles. Whole place goes running for the door, these guys start tearing up the joint, with only me to stop them. So I'm outta business, thinking somebody owes me."

Dean looked at the cop.

"Place was busted to sticks by the time we got the call."

"And I'm still asking who pays for putting me out?" Charlie asked the cop.

"Illegal ain't it, a joint serving hootch?" the cop said to him, showing no pity.

"I'm on the street, looking at a bread line. I got kids, you know."

"The street beats jail, and sure as hell beats the morgue."

Dean put a hand in his pocket, pulling a wad of bills, handing some to Charlie, saying, "You need more come and see me. But when you come, come with a name."

Charlie nodded, promised he'd go around and find who it was, then added, "Like I said, I ain't no pimp. Just booze and a little dancing, that's it."

Dean looked to Hymie and Drucci, turning for the door.

Charlie waved a hand around the air, saying, "Gals in this place get paid a nickel a spin, other nickel's mine. They put out more, well, that's nothing to do with me. Like I said —"

"Yeah, you're no pimp," the cop said. "An upstanding citizen, right up there with the mayor." He spat on the floor.

"I'm out of it, 'least till I can get some lumber. You know a carpenter, a couple'a handy fellas?"

Dean stopped at the entrance, retraced his steps, stepping before the barman, Charlie looking scared now.

"I want to know who did this." Dean tapping the roll of bills the man still held in his hand. "Next thing coming out of your mouth best be a name."

Charlie looked at him, scared and nodding like he understood.

"You need me to, I can help jog your memory." The copper tapped his hickory stick along his leg.

"No need for that." It was Hymie nicking his head, wanting the cop to leave, waiting till he made his way through the ruined speak. Then saying to Charlie, "These cops sign up, get their stick and whistle and key to the call box. They forget what it's like."

The barman nodded, not looking so sure.

"You and me, we make our bread on the street — so, we look out for each other. You agree with that?"

"Yeah, sure, sure."

"Get us a name, and we make sure he don't come back, there's no next time."

71

Three days later they had their guy, Nicky DiSantis, one of Genna's dark-complected leg breakers, sometimes union agitator. Charlie the bartender fingering the man, giving them a nod from across the street, meaning this was the guy who torched the Time-Out, then he walked on. Dean wanting Doyle and Huck to take care of it. Huck feeling the more he wanted out, the deeper it got.

Now Gypsy Doyle crossed the street, pistol in his pocket, aiming at Nicky's back, had him walking across Michigan. Huck moved to the cab stand, tipping his collar up, cap down against the Hawk wind coming off the lake, hailing the driver who couldn't see his face, the Checker driver looking them over. The driver leaned back in his seat, parked at a Yellow stand. The same driver who once set Huck up with the three thugs in the Stutz, same driver who they relieved of his cab and left him at the side of the road, then dumped his taxi in the river.

Perfect, Huck thought. Forming an idea, not wanting any part of taking out Nicky DiSantis.

Huck tapping a corncob pipe out against the side of his door, the driver considered him. Huck getting in the front, now looking at the driver.

The man's eyes going round. "Aw shit!" Huck aiming his Colt at his belly, kept him from jumping out, Doyle pushing Nicky DiSantis in ahead of him in back.

Huck pointing through the windshield at the Yellow stand, the sign in plain view, saying, "Guess you don't learn nothing easy." Huck turned in the seat, saying to Doyle, "This the guy we ran out of town that time?"

Doyle grinned at him, saying, "Paid his money, took his chances."

"Look, I —"

"Never mind that," Doyle said. "Help us escort this eyetie out of town, ride him out on a rail, then we'll call it square."

"Look, I don't want trouble."

"Yet here you are sitting under a Yellow sign," Huck said.

The driver had nothing more to say, looked from one to the other.

"Drive," Huck told him.

And he drove down Michigan, turning at Roosevelt, Huck telling him where to turn, saying, "You want to show us some sights, the Wrigley Building, the Magnificent Mile, tell us the South Side's the dark side?"

"I got nothing to say."

Huck had him drive past Whiskey Row, over seventy bars crammed along a one-mile stretch on South Ashland, hundreds of miles of railway track criss-crossing Packingtown like mesh.

"Nothing but yiftos, Pomaks, and micks on the edge of the Black Belt. This part of town ought to come with a warning, that what you said?" Huck said.

"My people," Doyle said.

"Look, I changed my ways," the driver said.

"This fellow here's an eyetie, that what you call them?" Huck said. "We're running him out of town, and you're lending a hand."

Nicky DiSantis looking at them, Doyle's pistol pointed at him, Huck's aimed at the driver.

"Man called me a mick," Doyle said to Nicky, then said, "and he don't like eyeties, as you can tell. What do you do with a fellow like that?"

"Shoot him," Nicky said.

"That what you'd do?" Doyle said.

"Sure, shoot him." Nicky spat at the driver, called him *razzista*.

"So I give you my gun, and that's what you do, shoot him?"

"Sure. Give it to me."

"Now hold on," the driver said, panicking.

Aiming the pistol, Huck telling him to keep his eyes on the road.

Nicky saying, "I do it. We work something out, huh?"

That's when the driver jumped out, falling out on the road, rolling and scrambling up, more limping than running off, holding one arm with the other.

Jumping across, Huck grabbed hold of the wheel, the taxi bouncing up on the opposite curb, Huck bringing it to a stop. Looking back at the Checker driver limping off double speed.

Nicky grabbed for Doyle's pistol, the two of them struggling for it. Doyle using his size, grappling, Nicky clawing for it. The pistol going off, blasting a hole through the roof.

And Doyle hauled back and cracked the barrel across Nicky's forehead, knocking him back.

People on the street looking, some running, some ducking, Huck driving them out of there.

"Say we go someplace and get this done," Doyle said, knowing how Huck felt about it.

Nicky coming around, saying, "No, no, look I . . ."

"Yeah?" Doyle waiting.

"You kill me, and they come kill you. Why?"

"Well, it's what we do."

"I give you something, you let me go. How about that?"

"Give me something like what?"

Nicky thinking, saying, "I know they got a truck coming in, a full load, right now — today. I tell you where and when . . ."

"And I let you go?"

"Sure, sure."

"So go on and tell me."

"How do I know . . ."

"You don't." Doyle just shrugged like that wasn't his problem.

"I tell you and you shoot me?"

"On account that's what you'd do?"

"Me, no, I say a thing, I stick to it."

"You gonna tell me 'fore this thing just goes off?" Doyle waved the barrel, holding it on him.

And the man told them.

"Let's go see," Doyle said to Huck.

"How about the deal?" Nicky said.

"You're coming till we're sure."

"They see me, they kill me."

"Best keep your head down then," Doyle said.

Huck turned the Checker around and drove back toward the Loop, heading for Genna turf, not liking this at all.

Shaking a last smoke from the pack of ready-rolls, Gypsy Doyle lit it, looking out at the night sky, dark clouds blocking out the moon. They sat parked along the side of the factory, all three of them feeling the creeping cold, but nobody saying anything about it. Nicky saying the truck was late, but it had to be coming.

"Well, pardner, you best hope they show soon. We got sent to make a show of what happens to a guy who torched one of our places —"

"Soon, soon."

Huck sat behind the wheel, the snow starting to fleck the windshield, melting as it landed.

"What do you think?" Doyle said to Huck.

"I don't know."

"What I was saying before — about Deanie setting up Torrio."

Huck hesitated, saying, "This just you asking?"

"'Less you see somebody else, just me and Nicky here." Doyle glanced around the back seat, then saying, "And this mope sure ain't going to say anything, and unless you think I ratted to Deanie?"

Huck didn't answer.

"Well, do you?"

"Always figured you knew which side the butter goes on."

"Well, there we have it." Doyle shaking his head, saying to Nicky, "If you were to ask, I'd say the man, this is Deanie I'm talking about, he likes his kicks — sometimes more than he should."

Nicky looking like he had no idea what Doyle was talking about.

"All the time acting like he can't be touched," Doyle said. "Same way Big Jim was thinking, you know Big Jim?"

"Colosimo? Sure, sure I know."

"Thought he did too, till the bullet ripped out the back of the head."

And Nicky crossed himself.

Doyle going on, "He steps in and out of these treaties, this is Dean I'm saying, taking potshots at you Gennas, get you hitting back at us. Guess as long as Merlo and that Unione says they want no trouble, Torrio abides, meaning the Gennas keep in line, more or less — 'course, that's before Deanie set up Torrio . . . now, we got hits on all of us." Doyle blew out smoke.

Nicky looking confused.

Huck nodded, thinking all he wanted was out, and what he ended with was a price on his head.

"You ever figure on getting back in the ring?" Doyle said to Huck, dropping his smoke on the floor of the cab, stepping it out. "With the right trainer, who knows."

"You offering?"

"Me, I couldn't manage a spit bucket. I was a hack, a fixer, you know that." Then he said to Nicky, "Made some bucks off them fights, and had some laughs, but that's it."

Huck thinking back to the bout with Doyle, how he was supposed to take a dive in the first, only he didn't. The two of them slugging it out, Huck taking the win, but neither of them laughing that day. Walking away from the Doyle fight with a split knuckle that still bothered him any time it rained, Huck wondered yet who jumped him that night after the Mulligan fight, laid him out in the alley and took his measly winnings.

"Maybe one time you could've done alright," Doyle said.

"Out back of some boxcars, but in the big ring . . . naw."

"That's the thing, you never know . . ." Doyle sat quiet a while, then said, "How are things with your gal — met her nickel dancing, right?"

"Been hitched a couple years now."

"Yeah, had a kid, remember you telling me. What, a year old?"

Huck wondering why Doyle was bringing it up. Never talked much about their personal lives on those long drives. Huck realizing he knew little about Doyle's.

Doyle nodded, saying, "Things've gone our way, we made piles of dough — and you figure on getting out."

"I'm not saying —"

"It's written all over you — but don't worry about it, you ain't alone. Bet Nicky here wishes he was out right about now. That right, Nicky?"

"Sure. I want out so bad, you got no idea."

Huck looked back at the two of them, then he saw headlights of a truck coming across 22nd, making out two guys inside.

"That's the one," Nicky said, getting excited.

Doyle looked at his pistol and checked the load.

Huck reaching under the seat.

72

Looking from Nicky to the pistol pointing in his face, the driver considered his chances, then lifted his hands off the wheel.

Doyle shoved Nicky aside.

Huck held his pistol on the shotgun man, telling him to get out, Doyle getting the driver from behind the wheel.

"Open the back. Anything but cases in there, you die first," Doyle told the driver, walking him and Nicky around the back.

Not saying a word, the driver gave Nicky a dirty look, unlatched the back, then swung the door open, Doyle looking in, then telling the three men to unload it and pack the cases into the Checker.

The plan was to take the truck to a warehouse past the Loop, unload it and leave it along the side of a back road in Cicero. Then drive the Checker to the North Side and dump it in the river, for old times' sake. But steam was rising from under the truck's hood, the engine knocking, and Doyle changed the plan, had the driver get up in back and pass the crates to Nicky and the shotgun man, getting the whiskey into the trunk of the Checker, the rest onto the rear floor and back seat, a few more on the floor in front. A half dozen crates wouldn't fit. Huck looking at the weight, not sure the springs would hold nearly fifty cases.

"Now dump it in the slop," Doyle told the driver, meaning he wanted him to drive his truck into Bubbly Creek, an arm of the Chicago River used by the slaughter yards for their run-off, large pipes flowing sludge into the stream, turning it into an open sewer, huge bubbles of chemicals and grease, the banks plastered with hair from slaughtered animals.

"That's my own truck." The man stitched his brows, looking miserable about it, but he got behind the wheel, Doyle watching him while Huck held the pistol on the others, the snow still falling in thick flakes.

Huck saw it first, a sedan rolling this way, coming fast past the stockyards, headlights on, looked like four men inside.

The driver of the truck saw it too, and he veered from the river, the wheels slipping and sliding, started to turn toward the sedan.

Doyle fired at the truck, then fired at the oncoming sedan.

Nicky and the second man saw their chance and ran, Huck aiming, but not shooting. The shotgun man running for the sedan, Nicky chasing after the truck. Doyle held out his arm and fired, and the shotgun man dropped. Nicky kept running.

The sedan pulled up and the four men got out, two with rifles, one with a Tommy gun. At the truck now, Nicky was yelling and pointing to the four men coming.

Huck got the taxi in gear as the men opened up, a blast from the Tommy shattering windows and bottles, tearing into the Checker.

Getting to the driver's side, using the taxi like a shield, Doyle returned fire as Huck got behind the wheel and tried to drive out of there, the chassis bottoming out, the wheels spinning in the muck, more bullets striking the passenger side. Huck having to back up and roll forward. More glass burst in back — the smell of gin — then the rear window exploded, glass flying inside. The four men spreading out, two trying to flank them, the one with the Tommy walking straight at them, ready to let loose.

"Let's go!" Doyle was running for the river, away from the truck, drawing fire.

Jumping out, Huck chased after him, going as fast as his legs would take him, auto fire ringing behind him. Huck pointing his pistol out behind him, firing a couple of rounds as he ran. Seeing Doyle stumble, grabbing his arm, but he kept running past the stock pens, Huck catching up, the two of them ducking along the pens, moving as fast as they could.

The shooting stopped behind him, and he chanced a look back. Two of the men getting in the sedan, the others coming on foot, Nicky and the one in the truck joining them.

Doyle's sleeve was bloody, Huck leading him along between the pens, the gagging stench of the hog pens and the slaughter yard beyond it. Huck not sure of his direction, just had to get them out of there, hoping he was heading back toward the Loop, guessing they were a half dozen blocks from the Chuck Wagon. If they made it, they could call Schofield's and get some help, but he'd be bringing all this down on Luka. Not seeing an option, he led Doyle past hundreds of pens, like being in a maze of pig shit.

Out past the side of the slaughterhouse, he looked for the sedan and the pursuing men, couldn't see anybody now, the snow falling like a veil. They were leaving tracks and a blood trail in the snow, Doyle's sleeve dripping, the man looking pale, holding the arm tight to his body. Huck helped him around the building, got them out to the street, moving along. A car drove past, Huck trying to flag it to stop, but the car kept driving, an old man inside, knowing trouble when he saw it.

"Come on." Taking Doyle by his good arm, leading him.

Doyle not complaining, but he was slowing, his jaws clenched against the pain. Wouldn't be able to keep moving for long. Huck getting them into an alley, thinking they were close to Luka's now, keeping off the main streets. Huck having to guess which back door to bang on.

"Hell of a time for pancakes," Doyle said, shaking from the cold.

Banging on a door, Huck called Luka's name, banging again, saying who he was. Getting the feeling he had the wrong door or the man had better sense than to open up.

Then he heard the voice from inside, "Who's that?"

Huck saying his name again, that he needed some help.

And Luka cracked the door, the goose gun's barrel sticking out, recognizing him and seeing Doyle was injured, he pulled the door back, letting them in, then locking it behind them. Huck needing to use his telephone, getting the operator to make the call. It was Two Gun Alterie picking up at Schofield's, hearing him out. Alterie saying he was on his way.

Huck going to the front, Luka setting his ten-gauge on the table, settling Doyle on the floor, propped against the wall, getting his coat off, a towel tying off the arm, staunching the bleeding.

Then Luka went and got a box of shells, and he laid his cleaver next to the box. Huck keeping watch out the front.

"Think we lost them?" Doyle said, his voice strained, looking at the cleaver like maybe this mad Hunkie was thinking of performing amputation.

"Sure." Huck nodded, looking at Luka, doubting that they had, not with the tracks and blood trail leading to the back door. Telling him Alterie was on his way, bringing help and a sawbones. Thinking of Alterie coming with his ten-gallon hat, cowboy boots outside his pants, and his criss-crossing holsters, coming like the cavalry.

Luka kept the lights off, took his goose gun and he moved low, looking out the front window. Looking at Huck, showing two fingers, meaning two were coming along the front. Huck hearing something in back, guessing the others were trying the rear door. Checking the four rounds in the magazine, knowing they couldn't hold them off for long.

Then Luka waved to him again, saying it was cops.

Huck moved to get a look, seeing the patrol car out front, two coppers getting out, both holding pistols, both looking around, then coming to the front door, knocking on it.

"Yeah?" Huck called.

"Open the door." Then after a moment, "Alterie sent us."

Huck nodded to Luka, watching him unlatch the door, letting the cops in. Huck recognizing Lieutenant Grady from the time they switched the Genna cases, whiskey for water. Grady saying he had a sawbones from Cook County waiting at Schofield's, a house call off the books. The two cops helped Doyle to the patrol car, and they left for the flower shop. A couple of minutes later, Alterie showed up with the Gusenbergs, leaving brother Frank to keep watch on the Chuck Wagon, making sure the Genna men didn't come back that night.

Alterie taking Huck back to Schofield's, Dean and Hymie Weiss wanting to hear what went wrong.

73

"**T**he buffoon with the white hat's the goddamn chief of police," John D. pointed out Charlie Fitzmorris, telling Huck as the two of them sat in the mayor's outer office. Huck there as a favor, John D. wanting to throw a little intimidation around, Mayor Dever granting him another sit-down. Hertz telling him to dress down, more like a thug than a guy who owned a place in the country and drove around in a Duesenberg.

Watching the two men through the ribbed glass, they could overhear them through the closed door, the mayor and the top cop talking about bass fishing, what kind of bait to use, one thinking night crawlers, the other swearing by wobblers, keeping John D. and his thug waiting in the outer office. The secretary clanking on her typewriter, making like she didn't hear a word. Likely went home with a load of supper-table talk every night of the week, bending her husband's ear.

Hertz told Huck that Mayor Willie was a new breed of pencil-pushing son of a bitch, unlike his shyster predecessor, Big Bill Hale. "Two of them in there talking like we can't hear them. You know what I think?" John D. raised his voice, "Willie walks down lover's lane holding his own hand — the son of a bitch."

The secretary's lips tightened, and she kept clanking on her keys, Huck thinking she was picking up speed, typing faster, like maybe she was getting mad — or scared.

The two officials in the office were keeping them waiting, letting Hertz know his place. Spinning the homburg in his lap, John D. sat fidgeting like he was in a rocking chair, which he wasn't — like he couldn't get comfortable, peering in through the ribbed glass again, describing the scene, how the mayor was putting on a show, and the chief was lapping it up. Wondering if Morris Markin had come to see the new mayor, selling his side of the story.

The secretary was intent on stacking papers now, had hardly even glanced at them since they came in and announced themselves, nearly a quarter hour ago. John D. saying, "You know me, Miss?"

"Pardon, sir." She practically jumped, like she did forget they were there.

"I said do you know me?"

"You told me, and yes sir, I did advise his mayorship."

"I'm John D. Hertz, in case you forgot who sends the Christmas hams around." He made a show of putting two fingers into his watch pocket, checking the time, leaning back to better see the dial, saying, "Likely be next Christmas before these two get done."

"I did let him know, sir. I assure —" The woman's voice coming in a squeak.

His hand went up to stop her, John D. saying, "I put in the first traffic light this city's ever seen. Did you know that, miss?"

"Yes, you've told me, the last time you were here, sir." Tapping the ends of the stacked papers on the desk, she set them down, looking about her desk for another duty needing to be done.

John D. was back to peering through the ribbed glass, saying to her, "Ought to be thankful we're not getting all the government we're paying for. You know who said that?" He stood and stretched, stamped a foot, claiming his circulation was leaving his limbs.

"No, sir." The woman looked like she might crawl under the desk. Now she glanced toward the ribbed glass, likely praying for the meeting to end.

"Will Rogers, that's who."

"I'll remember that, sir."

Huck sat back and picked the morning *Trib* from the table, the photo for the lead story sending a chill. He read the headline: Unione Siciliana president Mike Merlo succumbs to cancer, dead at forty-four. Huck stared at it, then at the wall, the news sinking in. The man who tried to foster peace between the gangs, not wanting the bloodshed — the man who had likely been keeping Dean O'Banion alive — had just died.

"Invites me down, then has me sit and wait while he jaws on with the chief — a goddamn quarter hour. Thinks he's putting me in my place, does he?" Raising his voice, John D. got up again, looking like he wanted to throw the woman's typewriter through the ribbed glass, saying, "Wasting my time while he talks about fish and bait." With that he set his hat on his head, tilted it just so, asked the woman to forgive his profanity, and he walked out.

The slam of the door brought Huck around from reading the article. The secretary looking at him from behind the desk. John D. Hertz was gone, done with waiting on the mayor.

"Looks like something came up." With that, Huck followed him out, hearing John D. ahead by the elevator, talking to the operator.

"That man wants my support — I'd sooner set flame to this goddamn den of bureaucracy."

"Yes, sir." The operator waited for Huck to get on, then closed the door, operating the rheostat lever, taking them down.

74

Huck was wishing he'd never said anything to Gypsy Doyle about Hertz trying to see the tight-assed mayor, the Yellow boss storming out of there, back to talking like taxis were tanks after the latest altercation, retribution hailed on the Yellow livery after a Checker cab was stolen and used in some booze heist.

"That fuckin' mayor, the son of a bitch and his crackdown," Gypsy Doyle said. "Papers calling us the driest city in the country. You believe that shit?"

Driving Doyle from Schofield's back to the Drake after the meeting Dean had called. Doyle coming off a long night, his arm in a sling, in pain and cranky about getting called to Schofield's, having to leave a pretty blonde between the hotel sheets. The smell of her stale perfume coming off his wrinkled suit.

"We had a good run, but it's playing out different now," Doyle said.

Huck feeling the same way. Instead of coming into Schofield's, sitting by the window with the Tommy gun, Bugs Moran had sent him to pick up Gorilla Al Weinshank and Vincent Drucci from an all-night card game at the Ship, then had him pick up Doyle from the Drake. Huck back to playing chauffeur in his Duesenberg, then was told to sit by the window of the flower shop, not part of the meeting, but on guard, keeping an eye out the window, the Tommy with the drum mag next to him.

Twenty of the North Side associates had gathered. Some Huck hadn't met before: Jack Zuta, Adam Heyer, Handsome Dan McCarthy, along with Maxie Eisen, the shooter standing just over five feet and going about two hundred pounds. Two Gun Alterie in his cowboy get-up, Frank and Peter Gusenberg stood by the door, looking like something Mary Shelley might have drawn up. Dean coming in dressed in his apron, looking unconcerned about the death of Mike Merlo, patting Heyer's Alsatian dog lying on the floor.

Standing before them, next to a dour-looking Bugs Moran, it was Hymie Weiss who told the room that with Merlo gone, the so-called peace with the Italians was gone too, the gloves were off. The word was that Bloody Angelo Genna was taking over as head of the Unione Siciliana. Meaning they were on full alert, needing to double on the armed escorts when making runs from Canada, extra guards on their warehouses and on Schofield's.

After the meeting, Huck was driving up Michigan, Doyle looking over at him, saying, "Should've packed and gone on that holiday."

Huck nodded, saying, "Got a feeling you're not talking about Wisconsin Dells."

"More like booking one of them Pullmans, get out to the Grand Canyon, someplace far enough on a one-way ticket. Or better yet, get on a liner to Paris."

"Hymie wants me sitting watch on the place," Huck said. "He wasn't asking."

"Gonna need a hard bark for what's coming."

"And a thick head."

"And you do it on account you got a woman wants you coming home nights — plus the kid, Maudie, right?"

Huck nodded, surprised he remembered her name.

"Don't mean to play mother." Doyle waved a hand like he wanted to forget it, reaching for his smokes.

"Well, mother, you don't need to worry about me."

"They want us making a run," Doyle said, not looking at him.

"When?" Huck not liking it.

"Likely a day or two. Wants to make it look like it's business as usual, not like we're running scared."

75

"**L**istened a while and heard nothing, looking in the front window like a peeper — nothing." Doyle replaying the attack on Morris Markin's house back in '23. His way of breaking the tension, him and Huck making the run to Detroit with the armed escort, the Gusenbergs following them along U.S. 12 in the Ford. "Picked up the bottle with the rag shoved in, checked up and down the street, turned back to the car, make sure you didn't take off." Doyle grinning. "Lit it and tossed it, right through the window, hitting something inside, and the whole thing goes up — *whoosh* — drapes catching right off. Should've seen your face."

Huck remembered roaring out of there, thinking Doyle was leaving the bottle with a note, what they had agreed on, warning Markin what would happen next time.

"Imagine the man's passing the peas, gets blown from the table," Doyle said, laughing about it now, sure wasn't laughing then.

"Yeah well, worked out in the end . . . the man packed house," Huck said.

"Moved all the way to Kalamazoo in full retreat, just what your man Hertz wanted, am I right?"

Huck knowing it only made things worse but didn't say so.

"Sent chills through every Checker man," Doyle said. "Bet some quit and some shit. Yet Hertz only hires you on. Never got that part."

"My boyish looks versus your criminal element. What's to figure out?"

"Jesus, listen to you, son."

"Way Hertz saw it then, it gained Checker public sympathy, making Yellow look the villain."

"Well, his pansy in the purple chair wanted things done, and they got done. Told you from the start, I got my own way, you recall that?"

"Believe you said you did things with a bang."

"Guess I lean to the theatric — could've been on the stage. What do you think?"

"With that mug?"

Doyle giving him the gap-tooth smile, Huck checking the side mirror, looking at the Gusenbergs in the Ford, right behind them.

"You ever see either of them crack a smile?" Huck asked, seeing the sign, coming up on Ypsilanti, the skiff set to cross at Walkerville this time.

Doyle watched an approaching vehicle until it passed. "Took action like your man Hertz wanted, sent Markin packing, made you look like you weren't sitting on your thumbs. You're welcome."

"Some alderman wanted to yank every cab off city streets till the whole mess got sorted." Huck knowing he should leave it alone, but he kept talking, "Got the police chief making a show of cracking down, his boys pulling everybody over, Yellow and Checker both, searching for weapons. If Big Bill was still on the job, it might've gone different, but with that Dever . . ."

Doyle looked out at Ann Arbor in the distance, settled himself, the shotgun leaning on the seat between them, saying, "Papers blow all that shit out of proportion, and it don't matter which clown's at city hall, making it look like he knows which way's up." He waved a hand. "Like I told you back then, it'll blow over — and it did."

Huck remembering how John D. paced his office, kept a couple of the guns loaded in the case with the sign *In case of sinners*, fearing retribution — would have fired Huck on the spot if he knew he had a hand in it.

"That was then, now's now," Doyle said, looking out. "You got your head in the game?"

"Yuh."

And they were quiet a while, Huck giving a careful look ahead as they pulled into Detroit, the river about to come into view. The last time he made a run, they crossed on the ice back in March. Huck switching off the headlights now, slowing down on the lower road. Seeing the signal man ahead, his lantern in hand.

On that last run they got wind that one of two Genna trucks got mired in the ice, dropping a wheel through, crippling the overloaded truck as cops from the Detroit side drove out and busted the two men and seized the shipment. A second patrol car gave chase, going after the other truck, getting into a gun battle and wounding two more Genna men before they gave up, both trucks seized, several hundred cases on board. So much for paying off the cops and the Purples.

"I seen this raid last week," Doyle said. Looking for the signal man who would be flashing his lantern light across, meaning the truck was here, giving the all-clear, the man on the Canadian side wagging his lantern back, getting set to ride the power skiff across, bringing the load, the best way they had of getting it across until the river became ice again in four or five months. Huck hearing about this proposed bridge that was to span across to the Canadian side, like a bootlegger's dream come true, unless reform kicked in before construction on the bridge got started.

"You still with me?" Doyle looked at him.

"Yeah, go on, this raid . . ."

"One of Druggan's places, the third floor of some storage joint on Wabash. Anyway, cops got wind, some windbag on the second floor, typing away, complained about beer dripping through the ceiling, spoiling the report she was typing. Cops go kicking down the door and find the office above full of barrels of the stuff, one of them dripping, causing the leak. Was a wonder they didn't all bust through the floor, all that fuckin' weight. Shame of it, the cops couldn't see themselves getting the barrels down the stairs. So, what'd they do? They poured it out the window, every fucking drop. That secretary saying the cops were up there a while, her suspecting they were drinking their fill, coming up with their plan, how to get it out of there. Should'a seen it, looked like a goddamn river flowing out the windows — and the smell. Enough to make a man weep."

Huck swung the truck around, backing it to the spot, the signal man wagging his lantern again, getting an all-clear back, meaning the rum runner was set to cross. They both got out of the truck, the Gusenbergs taking positions, keeping watch as they readied to unload the boat, with the trouble with Torrio and the Gennas, no idea where they stood with the Purples, all of them eager to get it done and get out of there.

76

Bugs, Hymie, The Schemer, and Doyle sat at the table, all of them looking dour, the Fountain Court busy this time of day, the afternoon tea crowd. The Gusenbergs stood by the door, expressionless. Huck being called down from his suite, figuring they wanted him to pick somebody up — Huck the driver.

Huck asking, "What's up?" Looking at the faces looking back at him. Nobody asking him to sit.

Doyle kept his voice down, telling him Deanie had been counting up the week's legit take, Schofield's doing alright. "Making a bundle off the Merlo funeral."

Huck nodded, getting the sense from looking from face to face something was wrong.

"Scalise and Anselmi stepped in, along with Yale . . ."

All of them looking at Huck. Huck not getting it, thinking there was nothing unusual in that. John Scalise and Albert Anselmi were part of the crew, and Frankie Yale got hired on to do the odd job.

"Bell over the door gets Deanie stepping out front. No sign of Two Gun," the man supposed to be upstairs keeping watch.

"Deanie must've figured they were coming for an arrangement," Doyle said. "So he's feeling easy with two of his own with this Yale guy who sticks out his hand, asking how Deanie's doing, Scalise and Anselmi on either side, smiling like they're all pals. Deanie asks who the flowers are for, and Yale grabs hold of his hand and won't let go, saying they were for him, pulls his pistol with his left, Scalise and Anselmi too, all of them firing, hitting Deanie seven times, then walked the fuck out, their car running out on Superior."

"He's dead!" Huck saying it too loud, a couple of tea drinkers turning and looking to their table.

Everybody looking at him.

It was Hymie who said, "Two Gun was supposed to be upstairs, except he says he called in sick, says he talked to you . . ."

"Me?" Huck was shaking his head.

"Told you to spell him."

Huck kept shaking his head, looking from one to the other. "I got no call. Was up in Schaumburg all morning." Huck talking to his architect and builder, a work crew clearing the site on his acreage.

The four men just looked at him.

"Look, if somebody called, I'd've been there — same as always." Huck getting this was like a trial, a nice public place, downstairs of where his family was living.

"Scalise and Anselmi switched teams, from the look. But what I want to know . . ." Hymie said. "What side you're on?"

"Lou asked me nothing. Put me and him in a room —"

"Lou took out more of the Outfit and Genna crews than I can count. That sound like a guy who'd cross us?"

"I know who he is, and you know the man's half nuts and half flakes, and we've all seen him get things squirreled up under that cowboy hat." Huck feeling the anger gaining, knowing there was a way to talk to these guys, and this wasn't it.

"Maybe you'll get your chance," Hymie said. "But right now . . . Lou's out of town, and I'm asking you . . ."

Huck looked around the table, then to Doyle, this guy supposed to be his friend.

"Lou called out Deanie's killers, wanted a shootout right on State Street, O.K. Corral–style," Drucci said. "Big balls for a squirrel. Or maybe that sounds like a rat to you?"

"We sent Two Gun out to Colorado," Doyle said. "Shooting tin cans at his ranch till we call him back."

"That doesn't clear it up," Huck said, knowing how these guys played, worried for Karla and Izzy and the baby.

"Deanie had Crutchfield sweeping out front when they came in, talking about ordering flowers," Vincent said. "Heard the whole thing and got under a table when they shot Deanie. According to Crutchfield, Lou called first thing, said he won't be in on account he was under the weather. Man said Lou sounded awful, at death's door, how he put it, but never said anything about you coming in."

Feeling relief wash over him, Huck looked from one to the next, saying, "So, what more do you want?" The anger rising again, like these guys were toying with him.

"We'll let you know," Drucci said through his sorrow, looking like he enjoyed watching Huck squirm.

It took a moment, Huck seeing the meeting was over. Feeling the shock of hearing about Dean, he walked past the Gusenbergs at the door, relieved to get out of there. Any luck at all, they wouldn't trust him now, leaving him out of their business going forward. Huck had salted away enough for a couple of lifetimes, invested well in the yearlings, and had built a tidy stock portfolio paying him fat dividends, Huck financially secure and feeling long past the need of sticking his neck out.

77

Hymie Weiss took over the top spot on Christmas Eve, same time John "The Fox" Torrio was rumored to be planning an exit for Hot Springs, showing gray around the edges and handing over control of the South Side to Capone, all of them knowing it was Torrio and Capone that called the hit on Deanie.

Showing the North Side was still a dog with bite, the lads of Kilgubbin held an elaborate funeral for their boss, double the size of the one held for Mike Merlo just the day before, Dean's coffin costing ten grand, silver and bronze walls, lined in satin, and put in back of a hearse, leading a mile-long procession, twenty-six cars and trucks just to carry the flowers, rolling past fifteen thousand mourners — the North Side sending Charles Dean O'Banion off in style. The archdiocese denying him burial in consecrated ground, but an old priest who had known Dean since he was a boy recited the Lord's Prayer, then said three Hail Marys in his memory. His resting place: the unconsecrated ground at Mount Carmel Cemetery in Hillside, just west of town.

The day after the funeral, an announcement appeared in every major daily declaring that in respect to their fallen leader, the new board of governors for the North Side would run the organization as equals, and it was going to be business as usual — a veiled threat to Torrio and Capone, putting them on notice, the North Side was coming for them.

And within the week they held true to it, hijacking a pair of Genna trucks, and another belonging to the Outfit. Same time, Frankie Yale was detained by police while boarding the New York Central, trying to duck out of town. He was released after questioning, but the message was sent, the North Side knew he was one of the three, meaning they knew Anselmi and Scalise were the other two.

The second Monday in January, Doyle told Huck to drive him and Drucci to Palermo Restaurant, Huck telling him no.

"Like I told you, there's one way out," Doyle said.

"With the change of management, seems they don't want me around."

"Who says so?" Then Doyle eased up, telling him they were just going for veal and antipasto as far as he knew, meeting a guy, then he held out the key to a Packard.

No idea who owned the car, Huck took it from him, not believing a word. Drucci and Doyle sitting quiet on the ride, Drucci in back, making Huck feel uneasy. Huck wondering if they were back to thinking he had something to do with the hit on Dean.

Drucci told him to pull to the curb a half block from Palermo's, reaching the floor of the back seat, pulling a pair of Tommy guns with stick clips, handing one forward to Doyle.

"Got to kill the veal calf first?" Huck looked at Doyle.

Drucci telling him to shut up. Huck not saying anything as they waited in silence until a Cadillac pulled up to Palermo's door. Drucci telling Huck to roll up, slow and steady.

Doing like he was told, Huck saw three men climb from the back of the sedan, Drucci and Doyle rolling down their windows, sticking the barrels out. The Cadillac's driver spotting the gun barrels, started yelling, then diving under the dash. One man dropping to the floor well of the Cadillac, the others for the sidewalk, Doyle and Drucci emptying their clips, shooting up the Cadillac and the entire front of Palermo's. Huck tearing away when they were done, weaving through traffic. Drucci whooping in back, saying they just got that fucker Capone, Doyle turning in the seat, looking back. Finding out later, they only wounded the driver and one of the others, Capone unhurt, but busy ordering up some armor-plating for a new Caddy.

Wasn't two weeks later, Doyle showed up at Huck's door at the Drake, telling him Torrio and his wife, Anna, returned home from shopping in the Loop, Anna going inside their place on South Clyde, Torrio helping the driver with the shopping bags, looking up as he heard a car door shut, seeing Hymie and Bugs coming at him, Hymie with a shotgun, Bugs reaching inside his coat. Hymie blasted the driver, and Bugs shot Torrio as he turned to run, dropping him on the steps of his house, then standing over him, aiming at his head, the pistol misfiring. Drucci in the sedan started honking the horn, wanting to get the fuck out of there. Torrio a bloody mess on the ground, his wife screaming from inside the house. Seeing neighbors start to appear, Hymie left the Outfit's boss for dead, running to the car, Drucci rolling them the hell out of there.

Doyle convinced him the North Side knew he had nothing to do with setting up Dean, wanting him to come with him to Schofield's, a show of good faith, the North Side finding out Torrio was hanging on, part of his jawbone torn away, but the Fox refused to speak to the cops, only saying it would get taken care of — told them not to worry about it.

They walked into the flower shop as Hymie and Bugs were saying if it wasn't for Drucci honking and panicking, Torrio would be dead now.

Drucci sat sullen, looking at Huck, saying, "Guess you'd'a done better, huh?"

Huck looked out the window, thinking yeah, he would have done better, guessing everybody in the room knew it too. He was thinking back to the day he jumped the bridge, Drucci sitting next to him, nearly shitting his pants — forcing himself not to smile as he looked out, seeing a cop car pulling up out front. The two cops coming in the door were on North Side payroll, coming up the stairs and asking Bugs to go in for questioning about the shooting, told him the detectives had an eyewitness.

Refusing to press charges — what Torrio called a misunderstanding among friends — they had nothing to hold Bugs on, witness or no witness. Torrio's refusal meaning this would be settled in the old ways, and by some shooter they'd bring in. On his release from hospital, the police moved Torrio to the Cook County lockup to serve nine months for violation of the Volstead Act after the raid on the Sieben brewery a few months earlier, the cops busting Torrio's trucks all loaded with beer barrels, John "The Fox" outfoxed, one of the last things Dean O'Banion had been behind.

Every day of Torrio's sentence a newspaper arrived at his cell, courtesy of the North Side. A note attached that read: *So you can see what comes next.*

The May 27th, 1925, edition of the *Trib* told how Bloody Angelo Genna drove from his Belmont Harbor home, heading his coupe south on Sheridan, turning at Ogden, then toward Lincoln Park, unaware of a sedan following, pulling up alongside as he stopped at Hudson. Bloody Ang looking over as two men on the passenger side opened up with shotguns, blasting him and causing him to crash into a lamppost. The sedan speeding off.

The witness to the shooting remained nameless — most folks eyeballing a situation in that neighborhood knew better than to talk to police. The way the locals looked at it, if the law wanted to know who did it, all they had to do was wait until the next gangster got killed, then they'd know.

John the Fox was left to pace in his cell, brooding about what he read over the battles of boozedom. On June 13th, the lead story told how Mike "The Devil" Genna was in a car with Albert Anselmi and John Scalise, two of O'Banion's assassins, the headline reading: "The Day of the Sixty Shots." Reporting how the three men were chased by a bureau car gonging and flashing its lights, four coppers inside, pursuing them up Western, doing more than seventy, ending at 59th after Genna's car jumped the curb, slamming into a lamp post, the police car narrowly missing his bumper. Everybody getting out and exchanging fire. Two of the cops were killed on the spot, a third wounded, the fourth pursuing the fleeing men solo into a garage where more shots were fired. Mike Genna smashed out a basement window and tried to hide as more officers arrived on the scene, the cops claiming they found Genna shot to pieces, dying on the basement floor, nothing they could do for him. Scalise and Anselmi were spotted and arrested as they got on a Western Avenue car. A fourth man was never identified.

July 8th Vincent Drucci came to the Drake, knocked on Huck's door, tossed him a car key when he opened, telling him they were taking a spin to Grand and Curtis, looking at him like he was hoping Huck would object. Huck went quietly, not wanting Karla alarmed more than necessary.

Out front of the hotel, Tony "Cavalero" Spano got in the front seat of the black sedan, Drucci and Moran climbing in back. Huck knowing better than to ask, just drove where he was told, pulling over a block from the intersection, Spano getting out, saying he was going to meet an old pal. Drucci told Huck to keep it running, and he watched as Drucci and Moran got out too and crossed the street. Huck seeing Spano greeting a man out front of the grocery, extending his hand, the other man with his back to the street. Huck watched Moran and Drucci run across between passing cars, both pulling pistols, Spano holding on to the man's hand, the same way they had done it to Dean O'Banion. Moran and Drucci shooting the man four times, middle of a crowded city street. Huck already rolling the sedan when the three men came running and jumped back in. Stepping on the gas and driving them out of there.

"That's three down, and three to go," Drucci said, the man elated, clapping Huck on the shoulder, saying, "That slob bleeding his guts, know who it is?"

Huck shook his head.

"Tony the Gent, that's who." Drucci leaned forward, laughing and clapping Spano on the back, another Genna gone, saying, "This man's got a killer handshake."

"If that don't get the rest of the Genna mopes running, nothing will," Spano said.

"Going to plant all of them fucks — get 'em a family discount on some nice plots," Drucci said, laughing some more.

They found out later that Tony "The Gent" Genna was rushed to Cook County, the man living long enough to tell his brother Sam that it was Spano who set him up. But with three of the brothers dead, Sam, Pietro and Vincenzo saw there would be no avenging the dead; they could only join them. So they packed it in and the last of the Gennas got out of town, none of them attending brother Tony's funeral, the same Cardinal refusing any of the brothers Catholic funeral rites.

That left their territory up for grabs, and before the North Side could take over the Loop, the Aiello brothers capped Spano for what they called past transgressions. Then they came knocking, making peace and forming an alliance with

Hymie Weiss and the North Side crew, bringing with them some powerful ties to the Castellammarese clan out of New York. All of them focused and wanting to be rid of Capone and his Outfit once and for all.

78

"**C**an you say daddy?" Huck playing with Maudie, the little girl on her momma's lap, hiding her eyes with her fingers. "Dadd–dee." Huck stretching it out, getting a gurgled laugh back.

"Daddy Huck. She can't believe your momma pinned that on you." Looking at Maudie, Karla said to her, "Just try to imagine naming a sweet bundle that — Huckabee. Not so bad when you clip it down to Huck, like in the kid's book."

"And a fine book it is," Huck said to Maudie. "One I'll read you some day."

"Well look at you. Could hardly read your own name back when we met. Just a poor country bumpkin, rode in on a rail, and laying bad lines on me."

"And now look at us — got this fine place, a bunch of fine suits, and a shiny car, but I still got a name like something that ought to come with a cork in it — Old Huckabee, aged in Bogalusa." He made a face and the baby belly-laughed, poking a wet finger, taking hold of his cheek and lip, pulling on it, giggling all the more.

"Well, truth be told, I've come to love it. It's got a ring to it. Huck-a-bee with the hard bark, showing me his sweet side."

"Still gonna take you to see it someday, Bogalusa, I mean."

"Not sure if that's a promise or a threat, one you keep making."

"The home of the Frogmore boil, where we pinch the head and suck the tail. But if you'd rather have Paris, you just got to say so."

"Are you talking about the two of us packing up a trunk?" She made a face at the baby, saying, "Why can't he just say so?"

That got a toothless smile and a bubble on the baby's lip.

"Washington Parish, a stone's throw from the 'Sipp, where we fais-do-do and got the gris-gris too."

"Down where the good folk like to swing anybody they don't like from a sweet gum tree."

"Speaking of swinging . . ." Huck holding out his arms again, and Maudie tucked her head away again. "We got the Mardi Gras and Krewe of Zulu, a good mix of frog, Cajun and a touch of Haitian Creole, you name it, we got it, cher."

"Compared to all the Paris fashion and style, and Gertrude Stein's place, and Maurice Chevalier and Josephine Baker, and Picasso and Matisse."

"Don't know that rabble, but if you love it, then I'll love it. Sounds like Paris here we come." Looking at her sweet face, the round eyes, the smooth skin, looking like the day he met her.

"You mean it?"

"I wouldn't say so if I didn't."

"You will love it, I promise you that."

"I know I will, and for the record, I never saw anybody swinging from a sweet gum." Then he made a face, causing a belly laugh from Maudie's depths, causing them both to laugh too.

"Maybe with you out of work, I'll be shed of these worry lines and gray hair too."

He nodded, knowing she was right, wanting nothing more than getting out of it, feeling it all coming to a head, remembering her tending to his scarred knuckles, dabbing on the liniment. Taking his hand in the night, kissing the tops and saying she'd like to see him pick up a six-string and hear him play, something he talked about back then.

"Always said you and me, we're like chalk and cheese, remember?" she said.

"Chalk and cheese that never felt wrong."

"Just 'cause something doesn't feel wrong, doesn't make it right."

He bent his head against her neck, putting his lips to the smooth skin, feeling her warmth, his fingertip running along her collar bone, Karla letting him do it. He took her hand, eased her to her feet, hands going to her hips, drawing her against him, the baby between them.

She nuzzled her head against his chest, hearing his heartbeat. Putting her fingers on his shoulders, she swayed against him like the three of them were dancing.

"Laissez les bon temps rouler." He closed his eyes, laid his hands on her shoulders, and they were swaying.

"Not sure what it means, but it's nice," she said, and they moved to the unheard music.

79

The Gennas were gone, and Torrio was out of the game, the North Side aiming to sweep up Capone and the Outfit. Clear the board and it would be all theirs, the other gangs sure to fall in line.

After the trip to Paris, taking in much of Île-de-France, Huck stayed away from Schofield's, spending time at the new ranch house, taking Maudie to see the yearlings and keeping house with Karla, talking about growing the family, having a couple more kids. Karla busying herself with a flower garden that surrounded the house, Maudie following with the watering can, the little girl like her shadow, Izzy with his nose in his books, his sights on Northwestern and the Kellogg School of Management.

Sitting with the six-string on the wide steps of their rancher, Huck was watching them in the garden, and he tried to put together the old tunes, "Crazy Blues," "Memphis Blues," and "St. Louis Blues" — ones he heard Mance Lipscomb play back in the Quarter. Mance was short for Emancipation, a sharecropper hailing from Texas, working cotton in Tennessee before ending up in the Quarter. About sixteen then, Huck listened to him porch-playing that raw sound, what the man called ragtime blues. Told Mance he wanted to learn it, and Mance showed him some Jelly Roll tunes, tried teaching him some picking and progressions before going on the run from the husband of a wife he'd been visiting at Faubourg Lafayette. Escaping what he called convention, Mance jumped out an upstairs window, rolled off that roof and kept on right out of town, stopping long enough to pass Huck his hand-me-down guitar, told him he couldn't take it where he was going, not saying where that was. Huck guessing he'd gone back to Texas.

Huck recalling those old tunes, wanting to learn some Vernon Dalhart and Ukelele Ike numbers. He tried fretting the strings, doing a bass line while picking, thinking it was like getting Maudie to rub her head and tummy at the same time. A long way to go before sounding halfway like old Mance. And he was wondering where that old guitar of Mance's ended up, Huck having to leave it behind when he went on the run.

One thing he felt sure about, with Dean gone, he was out of bootlegging, meaning Karla wouldn't be praying every time he went out the door, wondering if it would be the last time.

But Hymie Weiss wasn't letting him just walk out. Huck driving into town, parking his Duesenberg outside the Chuck Wagon, taking Izzy for flapjacks, keeping up the tradition anytime Izzy was home from school, Huck wanting to hear about life at the college, Izzy making the junior football squad. Luka greeting them like family, the man's hair receding in a V, calling them his best customers, claiming nobody downed his Pfannkuchen like Izzy. Izzy ordering a double stack.

Sitting in his usual spot, the table by the window, Huck saw the sedan pull up out front of the new office building going up across the street, where the rummy dive had been. Vincent Drucci parking behind his Dues, coming in with Frank Gusenberg, Vincent drawing up a chair and sitting down at the table, with Frank standing by the door, that frozen look on his face.

Vincent saying, "Hey, kid. All grown up, huh?" Smiling at Izzy.

Izzy telling him he grew two inches since his birthday.

"It's the pancakes," Drucci said. Then to Huck, "We got something to talk about."

"You can see I'm eating," Huck said.

"Well, you don't come by so much, so when's a good time?"

"I told Hymie, I'm out."

"And here I am — asking a favor."

Huck sighed, looked at Izzy, Izzy putting down his napkin, saying he was going to the can, that it was good to see Vincent again, leaving the table, going through the curtains in back.

"I'm out," Huck said.

Vincent just looked at him, giving a slow nod, saying, "Then I best get you a gold watch, huh?"

Huck drew the watch chain from his pocket, the one he took from Bubbling-Over, all those years back, letting it dangle, showing it to him.

"Get that in Cracker Jack?"

"Took it off a guy I shot."

"You shot a guy, huh? Just one?"

"Just one." And he stopped himself from asking, "That time I jumped the Oak Street Bridge, you really shit your pants?"

Drucci looked over at Frank Gusenberg, got up and didn't say another word, turned and walked out the door. Gusenberg shot Huck a look, then followed Drucci out. Huck having to force down the last of his flapjacks, making like everything was okay when Izzy returned, the two of them back to talking about his school.

Word came back that Drucci and Frank Guesenberg drove to a barbershop on Roosevelt, Samoots Ammatuna sitting in a chair, getting the hot towel put on his face. Ammantuna being the guy who walked into the Unione Sicilane after Bloody Angelo was killed back in May, Samoots trying to move in on part of the Gennas' operations and the Unione too, just like that. A thing that pissed off Capone and Hymie Weiss in equal measure. Meaning that man's ticket was going to get punched, just a question of who got to him first.

Getting a shave and a little off the top, Ammantuna was planning an evening at the Auditorium Theater, attending *Aida*, a four-act opera, with his sweetheart. His two bodyguards not showing up that day, Samoots thinking nothing of it. The barber seeing the two men coming in pulling pistols, ducking behind his barber's chair, Drucci and Gusenberg stepping in and blasting Ammantuna with the towel still on his face. Drucci saying as the man lay on the floor dying that he just spared Samoots from having to spend a night hearing that awful opera shit, sounding like cats getting stepped on. Then looking at the barber peeking in terror from behind his chair, saying to him, "You see what happened?"

The man shook his head, no, no, he didn't see a thing, unable to speak.

"Amnesia just saved your life, pal. Let's hope it sticks." He reached down, felt around in Samoots's pockets, found the opera tickets, saying to the barber, "You like opera?"

Speechless, the man just nodded.

"Knock yourself out." Drucci handing him the tickets, a little blood on the one.

With that, Drucci and Gusenberg walked out and drove off.

He could picture it going down, Huck guessing he was meant to be the driver, waiting out front while Drucci and Gusenberg clipped Samoots. The North Side cleaning up.

80

The wind rippled the leaves of the tall oaks, Huck sitting on the porch as the sun was peeking over the treetops to the east, the tips of his fingers sore from playing the flattop. Karla stepping out, a cup of tea in hand, the housecoat pulled to her neck, her feet bare, the diamond on her finger. The woman never taking it off.

"Starting to sound like something." Meaning his guitar playing. She sat next to him on the steps.

"A few chords, but finding my way." He set the neck of the Orville Gibson against the post, told her he was thinking about driving over to Trout Valley to look at the new yearling stock Fannie Hertz had brought in. Was going to leave her a note by the bed, knowing she still liked to add to her worry lines anytime he went out the door, still thinking his past was trying to catch up. She had met Drucci and Weiss and Doyle at the Fountain Court years ago, and she saw past the manners, fine suits and slicked hair, and it always worried her. Who could blame her?

"Maudie's going to have me facing the day any time now." She yawned around the smile, the little girl with enough energy for any two kids. "I scramble you an egg?"

"I brung fritters, hot off the press." What Huck called donuts, told her he picked them up at Fenz's, the local general store.

"Know what Izzy's trying to get her to eat?" she said.

"Flapjacks?"

"Wants to know why I can't make 'em like Luka."

"That boy's got a craving — one I got him started on."

"Comes yesterday and brings pork chops. I look at them and he says these aren't cooked. I say, 'I can see that,' and he says, 'Drop butter in a pan and slide them in.' 'That why you come around,' I asked, and he just grins at me. I say, 'You want me to fetch your slippers, anything else I can do?' He tells me come to think of it he's got a tote full of laundry, a week's worth of underpants and football jerseys."

Izzy came to the screen door behind them, more man than boy and several inches taller than Huck now, a textbook in his hand.

"I'm not the slipper type. Think you'd know that about me," he said, winking at Huck, holding a fritter in his hand, taking a bite. "I told her I'd cook them up."

"Like you know how?" And she was back to smiling, slinging her arm around Huck's shoulder.

"She points to the stove and tells me, 'This I got to see.'"

"Least you didn't burn the place down," Huck said. "Did you?"

Karla turned to look at Izzy, saying, "Sets the skillet on the hob and asks me, 'You got butter?' And I say, 'You see a churn?' I tell him, 'There's lard, but smell it first.' Next he says, 'You got onions?' And I say, 'You see onions?' Same thing with the salt. I figure with all this fuss, I may as well just cook them myself."

Huck was smiling.

"Boy's just the same as you, a chip off the old block," she said. "Thinks with his stomach."

"These are good, by the way," Izzy said to Huck. "This all there is?"

"There's six in the bag," Huck said.

"Oh." Taking a bite, saying, "Afraid 'was' is the proper tense." Izzy licked sugar from his fingers. "Oh, that the baby crying?" Then he was gone, going back to his studies, appetite taken care of.

81

D riving the winding back roads from Schaumburg to Trout Valley, stirring up dust, gravel pinging the underside of the Dues. Soon he'd be seeing the stone gate of the Hertz place up ahead, the long drive between the trees leading to the manor house with the thirty-five rooms on nine hundred and forty acres, Huck coming to see the new yearling stock, Fannie Hertz suggesting Huck sell a couple of two-year-olds and acquire a couple more brood mares from the Hurricana Stock Farm in Amsterdam, New York, she had her eye on. Huck going with her advice, the woman knowing her horseflesh.

That's when the bullet punched the windshield. Instinct kicking in, Huck slammed on the brake, dropping his head, losing sight of the road, reaching under the seat for the pistol that wasn't there, the one he stopped carrying when he was done working for Hertz. The Duesenberg rolling down the shoulder and stopping at the edge of the meadow.

Waiting in the quiet, then easing up enough to see two men step into the road, out past the ugly hole in the wind-shield, one with a rifle, one with a pistol, both coming this way.

The one with the rifle had taken the shot from the tree line west of the Hertz property, about two hundred yards at a moving target, no doubt the man could shoot. Holding the rifle loose in one hand, down at his side, the other one with the pistol down along his leg, the two of them walked like they were taking a stroll.

He tried to back onto the road, but the back bumper was caught on a rock or in the muck of the ditch, the back wheel spinning, getting no traction. Crawling to the passenger side, Huck pushed the door open, staying low to the floor. Could have another shooter on this side just waiting for him to make a move and finish the job.

"Huck! You still with us, son?"

Huck trying to put a name to the voice, a familiar one.

"It's your old pal Danny Stanton."

Not calling back, trying to figure out a move.

Danny Stanton back to working for Capone's Outfit, meaning the one with the pistol was likely Red Fawcett.

Taking a quick look up from the ditch, wanting to get their position. Less than a hundred yards off now.

"That's far enough," Huck called, trying to stall.

And it did stop them a moment. Likely guessing if he was going to shoot, they were already in range.

"I'm out of this," Huck called, looking around, the nearest trees fifty yards behind him, meaning he was a sitting duck.

"Not how they see it."

Down on the ground, Huck looked out from under the chassis, seeing both walking the center of the road, about sixty yards off. He was seeing Karla's eyes, thinking of Izzy and Maudie, how he wouldn't be around for her next birthday. Then remembering the lighter, reaching in the pocket. Peeling off his jacket, taking off the gas cap, shoving the sleeve down the filler, hoping to soak it. Something he learned watching Gypsy Doyle that time out front of Morris Markin's place.

"Come out and I'll make it quick," Stanton called. Thirty yards now.

Huck waited, holding the lighter. Looking under the chassis again, only one of them standing in the road now, twenty yards off and waiting. Huck moved to get a better look, seeing it was Red Fawcett in the road. Looking at the pastureland behind him. Meaning Stanton had gone off the road and was likely coming along the opposite ditch, trying to flank him, just in case he was armed.

He got in a crouch, looking around again, and he flicked the lighter several times, getting it to spark, the sleeve slow in catching.

"It ain't personal — want you to know it," Stanton called, just across the road from the Dues now. Huck was lying on his back, as flat to the ground as he could get, watching the sleeve catch, hoping Stanton couldn't see it. The flame licking the fabric and up to the filler hole, Huck with no idea how much time he had. Rolling from the Dues, not sure where Stanton or Red Fawcett were when he jumped and started to run, zigging for the tree line. Catching sight of two more men coming across the pasture, both of them armed. Meaning Huck was cut off, with no chance of making the trees, practically running right at them.

The two men out in the pasture both raised their rifles and both were firing. Hearing shots from behind him too, Huck felt the burn on his arm as he dove for the ground, the two men in the pasture both firing again.

Then it was quiet, Huck on his back, looking up at clouds rolling, somebody calling his name. Huck realizing it was Hertz in the pasture. His foreman Angus with him, the two of them firing at Stanton and Fawcett, had them both retreating.

A couple more men showed at the tree line from the north, in the direction of the riding pen. Both of them taking shots,

Danny Stanton and Red Fawcett returned fire, running to the trees, going the way they had come, veering off at a run.

The fuel tank exploded, sending shrapnel in all directions. Huck knocked to the ground, holding his bleeding arm, the breath gone from his lungs.

John D. was calling his name again.

Flat on the ground, Huck rose enough to see them, and he raised an arm in a wave, meaning he was alright, staying where he was until the two hands coming from the north walked from the trees. They had found footprints and a tire track, along with an expelled .303 cartridge in the muck, guessing Stanton or Fawcett had fired the first round from the edge of the trees, putting one through the windshield. Then coming to finish it.

"Heard the shot at the ranch and figured it was early for hunting, some poachers that needed running off. Should've figured it had to be you, trouble always right behind," Hertz said. Not to mention the old trouble with Morris Markin was still in play.

The foreman cleared his throat.

"Well, Wayne here heard it, came and got me straight away," Hertz said.

Wayne nodding.

Thanking Wayne, Huck looked at his sleeve where the bullet grazed the arm, tearing his jacket sleeve, a stinging groove along his forearm. His auto a smoking wreck behind him on the edge of the road.

Hertz pointed a finger at it, saying, "See you wrecked your own car this time."

82

"**H**e put hits on all of us. With the Gennas done, he figures it's him or us," Gypsy Doyle said.

Gorilla Al had taken a couple of guys and had gone after Danny Stanton, laid an ambush, was sure they winged him as they ran him out of town. Still on the lookout for Red Fawcett, but thinking he was long gone too.

Huck had called Doyle, asking to meet at the Chuck Wagon. Doyle coming with Two Gun Alterie, the madman back in town, none of them going out alone these days. Alterie not saying anything about Huck not showing to replace him the day Dean was killed.

Doyle told Huck how Bugs and The Schemer had been fired on, middle of the day, driving down Congress, lucky to get out of there. And how he and Drucci got in a shootout with a couple more of the Outfit, putting both of them down. Next thing, The Schemer and Hymie were bushwhacked out front of Standard Oil, having to shoot their way out.

"So Hymie puts a full-on assault on Capone's joint in Cicero, six cars with a dozen Thompsons tearing past, burping over a thousand rounds into the place — tore the fuckin' place to hell. Should've seen it."

"You get him?"

"Guy's got a rabbit foot shoved up tight. Must've rattled him, though — next thing he's calling for another ceasefire, waving a white flag and offering up all the bootlegging north of Madison. As ceasefires go, you know how that's worked out. So, Hymie says, 'No fuckin' deal.' Vowing to wipe every dago off the map. Saying it just like that. Right now, putting a plan together — a no-fuckin'-fail-this-time plan."

Two Gun called from the door, pulling both his six shooters, quick-draw style, as a Cadillac stopped out front. Gorilla Al getting out with Frank Gusenberg behind the wheel, Al coming this way, looking like hell was following.

Pulling open the door, shaken up, he came to the table, saying, "The fuckers just got Hymie."

83

Capone had put two snipers across from the flower shop. Hymie, his bodyguard, his lawyer, a couple of other guys cut down as soon as they pulled up out front and stepped on the sidewalk.

It was Drucci who called them all in, telling how the shooters hid in the upstairs window across the street, blasting the four men with Thompsons. Hymie and Murray dead on the spot, the investigator Hymie had just hired, along with his bodyguard, wounded.

"Going to be a hell of a payday." Making a fist and slamming the wall, he looked around at them, what was left of the gang nodding.

They sat quiet for a minute, Huck at the back of the room, not wanting to be there.

Drucci walked to the window, looking across to where the shooters had been. Then said, "Fuckers even hit the cornerstone of the cathedral." The Holy Name right across the street. Could hear Deanie saying it looks good on the spongers, after they refused to allow him to be buried in their consecrated ground.

Bugs Moran saying, "'Least they refused to bury the Gennas."

"Those fucks don't belong in the same dirt."

Drucci getting the room nodding.

"This fuck Capone wants our turf," Drucci said, his voice rising, "I'm asking, are we gonna let him take it?"

"Fuck no!"

"Fuck no is right, lads. We're gonna stand our ground, Terry Druggan and the Valley boys are with us, gonna help take 'em out."

What good's it going to do if you end up dead? Huck was thinking it, no doubt he'd get pitched down the stairs if he said it aloud. And it dawned on him, there would be no walking out with Drucci leading them — the man declaring all-out war.

"I never got on with Druggan much — figured the man for a snake. But he's stepping up, same as all of us got to do," Bugs Moran said, looking around the room, standing next to Drucci, making it plain the two of them were taking the reins after Hymie. "Anybody ain't got the stones for it, now's the time . . ."

Nobody saying a word, all of them looking around at each other, some eyes stopping at Huck.

Huck knowing Drucci was begging him to say something. With the meet over, he stepped out the back, Doyle coming and standing next to him, lighting a cigarette, offering the pack, saying, "You still think you're walking out, then you ain't paying attention."

Huck nodded, exhaling a stream of smoke.

"I been in it since the shit with the dailies. Was with Deanie and Hymie through thick and thin. Me, I feel I owe them, you get that?"

Huck nodded, he did get it.

"We cap Capone, and it'll feel good and put an end to it."

"You think that'll be an end to it?" Huck said, looking at him.

"When they come, it won't matter if you figure you're in or out. Plus, they already tried, right?"

Huck understood that too, wondering how to keep any of it from Karla.

"Drucci wants us making a run . . ."

"Detroit?"

"Mannheim, on the Canadian side, our guys jacked one of Capone's. Wants us bringing it back."

"Means I'd be leaving Karla and the baby." Huck thinking of them alone in that house, with Izzy off at school.

"Even those animals don't go at women and children, that code they got."

Huck thought about it, knowing that Drucci wasn't asking, and Doyle did go after Stanton and Fawcett, showing whose side he was on, so at least he owed Doyle, saying to him, "When?"

"Tomorrow night." Doyle told him it was a load of scotch stashed in some abandoned house. "The stuff meant to end up as Capone's private stock, the way it was told to me. Labels on the bottles got a royal seal. Alexander and MacSomebody, House of Lords, something like that."

"The Schemer wants to raise a glass in one hand, hold his dick in the other, piss on the box they put Capone in, all the lads of Kilgubbin drinking to Deanie and Hymie."

Still talking like it was some boys' club. Huck thinking in the end it was going to be every man for himself.

84

Starting the eight-hour run the next night in the truck Doyle stole off some truck yard, the old Winton complaining the whole way, Huck sure they couldn't outrun anybody in this heap. A dozen miles from Kalamazoo and the motor was clanking and pinging like it was set to spit up a piston. Thinking they wouldn't make it to the crossing, Huck kept an eye on the rearview mirror, a couple of times seeing headlights behind them for long stretches, considering they might have a tail. Doyle called it Huck's delusions, but no doubt they needed a better set of wheels.

Huck parking in an alley out back of a two-bit hotel called the Mulberry, south side of Ann Arbor, signing the register as Hiram and Johnnie Walker, then walking to the corner diner, a trucker place near the highway, nothing fancy. Both chowing down on what passed as Irish stew, Doyle betting they scraped whatever got run over off the two-lane. "Tossed it in the pot with carrots, potatoes, and onions, and voilà, you got the daily special, fit for any of these truckers."

Karla had been fierce about him not making this trip, threatened to leave him again, and he was explaining and

441

promising all over, and he had trouble falling asleep in the room, on top of which Doyle sawed logs all night. Huck wanting to throw a shoe at him, but figured he'd likely get shot for it.

Early the next morning, he took a walk and got in an old Haynes parked out back of a shoe repair on the main drag, the key left in it. Picking up Doyle standing with their bags out front of the Mulberry, he drove the stretch to Detroit in falling snow, the lack of visibility not allowing much of a look behind them, crossing the ice to the Canadian side at Walkerville, getting to Mannheim by mid-afternoon, what tried to pass as a town just west of Waterloo, parking in the lane behind the old bungalow, fronting on Willard.

The two of them walking around the block, looking at the place from the front, theirs being the only tracks in the snow. Going around back, Doyle drew the .45 from his cross-draw, putting the key in the lock, looking at Huck, turning the knob. Stepping in, Doyle put his back to the wall, Huck coming in behind him, the Colt Doyle got him in his hand, listening for anything in the silence.

Pulling off his coat, Doyle went around, keeping away from the windows, no drapes or blinds on any of them. From the look of the place, nobody had lived here for years, cobwebs holding it together, and the air was foul. A ratty armchair and a table with three legs, a split log serving as the fourth leg, the only furniture in the front room, a mattress covered in stains and dust on the floor of the bedroom in back.

In the bedroom, Doyle slid the old mattress aside, pulled up a piece of floorboard, looking down at the cases of the fine scotch in the crawl space under the house. Druggan's boys had hit the Outfit's shipment, shot it out with the driver and shotgun man, drove them off, and hid the load here, fearing another run-in with the Outfit when they got to the border.

It was snowing hard enough to make Huck and Doyle abandon thoughts of driving back that day. They'd wait to see what the next morning looked like, not chancing a fire in the potbelly and a smoking chimney, Doyle not fully trusting Druggan and their new allies. No way to get the place warm, the temperature dropping as day gave way to evening.

Sitting by the window with his coat wrapped around him, Huck looked from the corner of the window, not seeing much through the falling snow, about fifty feet of visibility into the alley past the grill of the Haynes. They ate chicken and ham sandwiches and a couple of apples they brought from the Kalamazoo diner, then Doyle went and tried to catch some sleep on the sway-back mattress. Huck settled in the armchair in the parlor, dust rising up and making him cough. Seeing his breath, he pulled the crippled table close and laid the Colt on it, and he caught a fitful hour of sleep.

Something woke him — a sound that didn't fit. Could be his mind playing tricks, the sleepless nights working against him, likely the rafters creaking from the weight of the gathering snow. Clearing away the remnants of sleep, he listened in the dark, not sure what time it was. Not the scrabbling in the walls or the rafters that he'd heard earlier. Listening in the darkness, he heard it again, a creak coming from outside. He reached for the table, his finger curling around the trigger of the Colt, the steel cold in his hand. Sitting up, he waited, then went in a crouch to the window, staying to the side and peering out.

Doyle stepped from the bedroom, pulling his suspenders up, getting into his coat, looking over at Huck.

The scraping came again from the back of the place — then a creak, Huck thinking a porch board. His heart was pumping, fully awake now, he put his back to the wall, watching Doyle move along the hallway, motioning for Huck to take the front, Doyle in view of the back door, the kitchen to his right.

The crash sent the back door flying open, bashing against the plaster. Somebody calling, "Police!"

Doyle fired twice and threw himself to the floor, somebody returning fire, the front window shattering. Same time, the front door flew in, Huck firing as a man in one of those Biltmore hats showed, the man going down. Another window smashing somewhere.

Getting down behind the armchair, waiting with the ringing in his ears. No idea how many were there. Thinking the one he hit wouldn't be getting up, no idea if they were lawmen, meaning Mounties on this side of the border. He could make out Doyle lying on the floor, not sure if he'd been hit or how bad. Moving along the wall, Huck edged toward the front, the cold coming in the open door. Hearing more glass break somewhere through the ringing in his ears. Past the potbelly stove he could see the shape on the floor, the man he shot lying face down. Huck moved close and took the pistol from the dead man's hand. No uniform, just the hat like he'd seen Mounties wear. Huck stayed low and shoved the front door closed with his foot.

Doyle crawled along the back hall, got the back door shut, then went to the threshold of the kitchen. The window had been shot out, and if anybody had got in, they'd be on the far side of the icebox.

Flattening to the floor again, Doyle slid into the galley, the counter on his left, the icebox at the end, the broom closet beyond that. Huck moved along the wall so he had a watch on both doors, able to cover the kitchen from where he crouched. In the dim, he could see Doyle moving along the counter. Waiting at the side of the icebox, then he dove to the floor, turning as he landed, the pistol in both hands. Huck seeing the movement, a man swinging something. And Doyle fired up twice, the muzzle-flashing, the man spinning backward into the icebox and against the wall. Dropping whatever he was holding, the man groped for the counter, trying to keep himself from going down, and Doyle shot him again.

Huck kept the two pistols on the doors, guessing the gunshots would bring the real cops.

Doyle hurried to the bedroom, shoved the mattress aside, pulled away the floorboard, reached down and pulled up a case of the scotch, a dozen of the bottles, coming out with it, shifting it under one arm, the pistol in the other, signaled for Huck to follow, then went for the back door, setting the case down.

"Go!" Doyle yanked the back door and nodded his head for Huck to follow. A shotgun blast knocking Doyle backward, the case dropping and bottles shattering.

The man out on the porch was late seeing Huck along the wall.

Huck firing both pistols and the man disappearing.

Kicking the door shut, Huck went to Doyle, looking at the mess of the wound, his shirt blood-soaked.

Doyle stared up at him, then he coughed up blood, tried to speak, and he was gone.

Huck looked at him a moment, closed Doyle's eyes with his fingers, fired a shot through the back door's window, the shotgun firing back, taking the door off the hinges.

Going to the front, Huck stayed low, stepping past the bodies, opening the door and jumping off the porch and running around the side, the man with the shotgun swung on him, cutting him off from the car in the lane. Firing at him.

Returning a wild shot, Huck tore across the dirt road, past another garage on the opposite side. Another shotgun blast, buckshot striking the clapboard behind him. Huck jumped a fence at the end of the property, the rotting boards collapsing under him. He scrambled up and kept going.

Somewhere a dog barked like crazy. Huck making his way into a thicket of trees, tumbling down into a ravine, striking his arm on a rock, then crashing against a fallen log, his face scraped by brambles. He lay there at the bottom, catching his wind, then he was moving again, cradling the arm, not sure if it was busted. Damn snow meant he was leaving footprints, making him easy to track as soon as it got light enough.

He came to another house that looked abandoned, cutting across its yard, moving along the side of the place, trying to get a look back at the house, Huck thinking he could have gotten turned around when he took the tumble. Looking out from the side of the house, he caught the shape of a man standing by a sedan, its engine running. Not in a Mountie uniform, the man stood on the near side of the Ford, his back to Huck, smoking a cigarette, looking in the direction of the house.

Stepping up behind the man, Huck stuck the barrel of the Colt into his back, saying, "How many others?"

The man froze, then lifted his hands slow, saying, "Three."

Huck poked him with the barrel.

"Four," the man said.

"Three ain't coming back."

The man gave a nod.

Telling him to take his pistol out slow and drop it, Huck said, "You want to drive or die?"

"Let's go with drive."

"Don't mind leaving one behind?"

The man shook his head — no, he didn't mind.

The man got behind the wheel, and Huck got in the back, dropped the second pistol in his pocket, keeping the Colt trained into the seat, saying, "First dumb move, you get one in the spine."

The man nodded, moving slow, then driving nice and easy.

"Name?"

"Ralph."

Recognizing the man from one of Torrio's peace talks, used to head the Sheldon Gang, before going with Capone's Outfit. Huck saying, "Ralph Sheldon?"

"Yeah."

"Trying to figure how you tailed us."

"Got a tip, I don't know."

"Other thing I got to figure's where to drop you — like a ditch."

"Best you don't shoot when I'm driving." Sheldon sounding at ease.

"Can see how you'd think that."

"Maybe I can help you out . . ."

"You just try to kill me?"

"It was Doyle we came for. Don't even know you."

"I'm nobody."

"And I'm just the driver."

"Ralph Sheldon's telling me he's just the driver."

"How am I doing?"

"You're still breathing."

"Like to keep right on doing it."

"And give you another crack at me."

"Like I said —"

"Yeah, you're just the driver." Huck knowing something about Sheldon, running his own gang for years, hijacking and bootlegging, feuding over turf with "Polack Joe" Saltis in Back of the Yards, before siding with Capone's Outfit.

"Like I said, we came for Doyle, and getting some booze back."

"The cops for real?"

Sheldon shook his head. "Just figured to take you that way."

"How many at the border?"

"Got eyes at Walkerville and Belle Isle."

"Those guys back there all Capones?"

"Two, other two are local — well, were local."

Huck betting the three in the house were dead. The one with the shotgun still back there. Flexing his left hand, he was thinking his left arm was banged up, but not busted.

"Where do we cross?" Ralph said.

"Why don't you tell me?"

"There's a place called Sandwich, you know it?"

"I see anybody . . ."

"And I get it first."

Huck nodded. Not sure what to do with Ralph Sheldon, knowing what Drucci and Moran would do if Huck showed up with him.

"Maybe you jumped me, and I didn't get a good look at you," Sheldon said like he was trying to help out. "Like I said, I got no idea who you are."

"Just drive." Huck guessed Sheldon knew exactly who he was.

"I go back, tell 'em I got told to drive with a gun in my back. Nothing I could do. Bad enough going back to Capone with no crew and no booze, maybe with him thinking I got caught napping . . ."

"A chance he'll shoot you."

"There is that." Waiting for a minute, then Sheldon said, "So, what do you think?"

"Think about what?"

"The not-shooting-me part."

"Just drive."

85

Huck stepped into Smithfield's, Schaumburg's one and only butcher shop. Hanger steaks, suckling pig, chickens and ducks, links of sausages, all of it hanging or in racks in the window. Signs claiming *We smoke our own* and *Pickled Tongues, Pig Feet & Home Rendered Lard.* He stepped over the fresh raked sawdust, his arm in a sling, the doctor at Mercy Hospital calling it a bad sprain.

Finished with dispatching a chicken, the counter woman greeted him and took the bird by its feet, immersing it in the scalding bucket, holding it like that, and asking what happened to his arm.

"Did a slip and fall."

"Got to watch your step these days."

"Now you tell me." Huck passed the time talking the weather, the woman taking the chicken from the bucket, laying it on the counter. Huck asked about pork chops, showing with his thumb and finger how thick he wanted them, waiting while she put them on the scale, wrapping them up. Handing her the four dollars, barely given any change back. Huck thinking back to when that mattered.

She blew at a bang, wiping her hands on her bloodied apron, saying like she was apologizing, "Cost of everything's going through the roof these days."

Huck smiled, thinking what Gypsy Doyle had said about it being easier to weigh the money than to count it.

"Ought to see my rent bill." She rolled her eyes, then noticed his new Dues outside, frowning, then saying, "Guess some of us don't got to worry so much."

Smiling and telling her he practically stole the car, he thanked her and walked over the sawdust, saw two men coming to the door, one on the left was taller with blond hair, the other one wider and darker, wearing a cap pulled down. First thought, they had badges under the coats, and not coming in for meat. Second thought, the pistol he was back to carrying was under the seat and these were a couple of Capone's — Ralph Sheldon giving him up after all. The fear going through him like a jolt.

The one in the cap pulled the handle and stepped in past him, the bigger one stepped in front of him at the door — one in front, one behind him. Shifting the package to his injured hand, he turned so he could see them both, eyes down enough to see the brogue shoes not belonging on coppers. Huck smelling the Clubman on the guy in front.

"You that fella?" The blond man was Irish, pointing a thick finger at him, standing flat-footed.

"Think you got me wrong," Huck said, ready to take a swing.

"Sure, I seen you Back of the Yards one time . . ." Letting the door shut out the cold, nodding his head to his pal, the first one was smiling, trying to come up with a name, saying, "What's that place?"

"Irish rules," the man in the cap said, snapping his fingers, not coming up with the place either.

"If you're not that fighter, then you're his twin. Man, the way you did it, toeing the line and slugging the bejesus out of some big ape, don't remember names so good, but you were tenderizing the beef that day."

"Bet against you on account the ape had the muscle and the mouth to go with it, fists like hams," the second man said. "Tore a piece off him like you didn't stop to notice, hitting him like you was chopping wood."

"Wrecking Bill." Huck nodded, easing some.

"That's it, Wrecking Bill. Took him in the second as I recall, don't think old Bill landed one worth talking about," the blond man said. "Cost me ten bucks that day." The man in the cap being good natured about it.

"Sorry for your bad judgment," Huck said, letting out a breath, smiling now.

"Can't judge a book by the cover's what they say." The second man clapped him on the back.

Huck agreed, that's what they say.

"Ain't seen you lately," the first man said.

"Retired."

"You get busted up?" Looking concerned, eyeing the sling.

"Maybe I got some sense knocked in me. These days I got trouble just slipping on the ice."

Leaving them looking disappointed, Huck walked into the street, getting in the Duesenberg, this one a Model J, silver and black with a straight eight, what the salesman called the fastest, top-of-the-line set of wheels on the market, driving toward his ranch. Feeling finally done with the gang life, and wishing it was done with him. Hearing through the grapevine that Vincent Drucci was bent out of shape, finding out Huck didn't take out Ralph Sheldon when he had the chance, the man in on the killing of Gypsy Doyle. Huck taking a ride back to Chicago with Sheldon, the gangster dropping him off at Mercy.

Drucci sent him word that he didn't want a Benedict Arnold like Huck around, and if Drucci saw him on the street, Huck best tuck tail and run like the yellow dog he was. Drucci sending West Side gunman Joe Saltis and a couple of other hitters to clip Sheldon.

Finding out there was a contract on Sheldon, Capone sent his own hitters after Saltis. Huck thinking it wouldn't end till they all planted each other — leaving the world a better place. Always enough for everybody, more money than any of them could count, but these guys just kept squabbling over the bones.

Could be Drucci would send somebody after him anyway, even things up for the time Huck jumped the Oak Street bridge.

86

"**M**ilk to go with that?" Karla asked, teasing Izzy, who was going by Isaac these days.

"No thank you, ma'am." Drinking his coffee black, same way he always had.

"Help you grow tall."

Huck was looking up from the paper, glad the sling was off his arm, smiling at Isaac, still thinking of him as Izzy. The young man excited about being accepted at Northwestern and longing to get on the football squad, telling them how the Wildcats were heading for the championship this year.

"Flapjacks is what did it," Huck said, smiling and looking back to the paper, scanning a piece on the recession, how Henry Ford was shutting down all his factories, the company switching from the Model T to the new Model A. Fifteen million Model Ts out there, and old Henry Ford was making the switch, making stockholders like Huck nervous as hell.

The Dow Jones had been kind to Huck these past years, his broker advising he shift significant money into energy, everybody wanting to own a radio and an electric icebox, plug-in irons, vacuum cleaners, and all the modern gadgets that saved on manual labor. He was closing the paper, nearly missed the article on the second page. Vincent "The Schemer" Drucci shot dead by police.

Reading how Drucci had been arrested after trashing the office of Dorsey Crowe, the alderman of the forty-second ward and a backer of Mayor Dever. Drucci went in smashing out windows, tossing over file cabinets and beating up the secretary, the man having the tantrums of a two-year-old. According to the police statement, it took two cops to put him in the back of their patrol car. On the way to the station, The Schemer reached over the seat and tried to wrestle the gun off Detective Dan Healy, the cop claiming he was given no choice, shooting Drucci four times and calling it self-defense. Huck having trouble with the story, knowing the cops would have handcuffed a madman like Drucci before putting him in the back of the car. Huck also knew that Healy was a Capone-friendly cop, had been on their payroll for years.

What he felt was a kind of relief that Drucci was gone. Meaning the North Side now fell into the hands of Bugs Moran, the last of the lads of Kilgubbin. Huck having no grief with the man, long past wanting anything more to do with any of it.

"Can you stand some good news?" Karla sat down next to him, seeing he was smiling.

"Huck's just looking at the pictures again," Isaac said, looking across the table.

"Wiseacre." Rolling up the paper like he was going to swat him, Huck was happy to close it, not wanting Karla to see the piece. She had met Drucci at the Fountain Court and knew who he was, the man sending a chill down her spine.

"Oil and electric's up," Huck said. "And I'm thinking of buying a Ford when Henry's fancy Model A comes out."

"What about your whatchamacallit?" Karla said.

"The Duesenberg stays, and the Ford's not for me."

They both looked at him.

"Not getting me behind the wheel of one of those," she said, never drove in her life.

"For a certain college boy." Huck saying it like he was asking somebody to pass the salt.

"You mean it?" Isaac practically spit his coffee.

It turned out Huck had a knack for turning his money into more money. Cleaning some of it through Schofield's back when O'Banion's widow, Viola, still owned the shop. Diversifying, dealing through a broker Gorilla Al had put him onto, putting some in stocks, then some in land, and Huck put a bundle into yearlings and two-year-olds, letting Fannie Hertz put her good eye for thoroughbreds to work. Huck had taken substantial gains from the sale of shares in Yellow Cab Manufacturing back when Hertz sold that operation to General Motors in '26, Huck practically doubling his money. Loaned out some as venture capital through an investment firm Hertz set up, acquired the adjoining forty acres to his property, and put the rest into gold — more money than Huck could spend in a lifetime. And being out of the liquor trade, he had a chance for a long one, watching Maudie grow, and Isaac turning into a fine young man with all the potential in the world to make something of himself — a long way from the street urchin stealing fruit off a grocer's cart and dipping his fingers in other people's pockets.

"You said you had some news," he said, looking at Karla.

She just took his hand, put it on her belly, looking into his eyes, letting him figure it out.

87

Huck stepped to the front of the stands, looking over the rail at the oval dog track in Riverside, eight dogs all muzzled and chasing the automatic rabbit on its own track. The thin crowd was cheering and excited.

It had been nearly two years since Vincent Drucci had been killed, two years since The Schemer wanted to clip Huck for sparing Ralph Sheldon. Surprised when Gorilla Al rang him up, saying he and Bugs wanted to meet, quick to say it had nothing to do with the old business. Huck hesitated, but Al asked him to do it for old times' sake. One thing was sure, it had something to do with the old business, but he still figured he needed to stay on the right side of these guys.

He couldn't help but smile when he saw them coming past the rows of seats, Bugs and Gorilla Al both in navy suits, looking like they could be brothers. Huck thinking of a book Izzy had read all those years ago, one about the Bobbsey twins. And he remembered the three of them — Gorilla Al, Gypsy Doyle and Nails Morton — walking toward him on that rail line after the fight he refused to throw, feeling the doom as they came toward him.

Gorilla Al walked up now, his hand extended, clapping Huck on the arm, the way they had done when they clipped Dean O'Banion.

Bugs Moran looking around like somebody might jump from the bushes, then shaking Huck's hand too, saying, "How long's it been, Huck?" And "Yeah, time flies."

Huck spotted the Gusenberg brothers, Frank and Peter, up in the stands — a good surveillance spot at the top row — with Peter, the one they called "Goosey," keeping an eye on the boss, the trouble with Scarface not over, not ever going to be over, till one of the outfits was wiped completely from the map.

"So, why am I here?" Huck was looking to the dog track, the eight dogs tearing past.

"Like I said, nothing to do with the old business — 'less you want it to be." Gorilla Al was joking with him. On the blower, he'd called it a lucrative investment opportunity, what Gorilla Al heard Huck was into now, cleaning all that whiskey money. Huck's instinct was to decline and say no, he wanted to scream it over the phone line, but he'd hear them out, then do it with the right amount of thought, and do it politely, then walk away without feeling like he had to watch over his shoulder.

"Different than the old days, huh?" Gorilla Al looked at the dog track, the race over now, the stands half full. "Beats standing behind a boxcar and banging hell out of some poor slob, you refusing to take a dive, keeping us from making our nickels and dimes, what we figured was easy money back then."

"Was you fellas making the easy money. Me, I was taking some hard licks." Hardly believing he was ever that dumb and desperate, standing toe to toe and slugging it out, taking all comers, with a bunch of drunks circling around, cursing and shoving at his back, drinking from the barrel of free beer, Gorilla Al refereeing, and Gypsy Doyle and a couple of the North Side lads moving through the circle, taking bets, keeping an eye on the money.

Huck looked at the oval track now, the greyhounds being led away, finished tearing up the turf, the automatic rabbit stopped on its track. Glancing to the half-full stands, nothing like a stakes race — and nothing about dog racing being legal in this state.

"Remember that chop suey guy, the old man chasing you?" Gorilla Al said.

"You setting me up to fight what you called his kid, and didn't tell me the guy was ranked. Sure I remember."

"Wanted to keep it real — more like theater."

"Except the old man was Chinese, the kid not even close."

"Crowd too sloshed to notice a thing like that."

"Remember he hit like he had bricks tied to his hands."

Gorilla Al clapped his shoulder again, saying, "Yeah, good times."

His one-time busted knuckle still troubled him sometimes when it rained. Huck remembering the blows he took to his ribs and jaw, getting the wind knocked out of him, trying to give better than he took, the circle of men shoving him forward, keeping him from falling, his fists dropping like they were weights. Hands passing dollars all around him, and tins of beer going down. The odds changing by degrees, round one odds giving way to round two odds, then it was all down to who would be standing by the end. Blood and pain and fists landing into flesh.

"People bet good money on this, huh?" Huck said, looking back at the track, keeping it good-natured, steering away from the good old times. Seeing the four-inch knife scar along Bugs Moran's neck, a souvenir from the man's own rough life, the twisted middle finger that had been busted and never healed right showing as he fumbled a cigarette from a pack, offering the pack around.

"Downsized from the racehorses you been raising . . ." Moran said.

"But the money's as good — well, the potential's there," Gorilla Al threw in, meaning they knew where he'd been sticking his money. "And purely legit. Well, we're working on that."

Huck nodded, knowing that Moran owned a couple of these tracks, one in Southern Illinois that'd had its stands torched to the ground shortly after the Hawthorne track, the one that Capone owned, met the same fate.

"Going to buy a dozen more tracks, a couple here and some prime spots around the country. Thinking of our own nest egg for later on — and all by the book," Gorilla Al said.

Wondering what book, Huck nodded, thinking these two wanted him to believe they were looking to settle down and go legit, Moran with the bulge of two pistols under the tailored suit, looking over his shoulder every minute, even with the Gusenbergs at his back, keeping a watch. Huck with enough contact with the old crew, knowing Bugs Moran was behind the attempt on Tony Lombardo, don of the Unione Siciliane and a pal of Capone's, the link Capone needed to the union, Capone being second-generation Neapolitan, not Sicilian, meaning he could never be a ranking member of the union.

"How much you looking for?" Huck said.

"It's a sliding scale thing," Moran said. "Depends how far you want to be in."

"Right now, I got a lot tied up."

"Got yourself some new ponies, way I hear it. Still hanging around with Hertz, the guy really rubbing off on you."

"I've done alright by him."

"You got a knack, kid, knowing who to rub up against," Moran said, just enough edge to his voice. "What's that one he's got, Reigh Count? The Kentucky Derby, was it? Maybe I read about it."

Huck nodded, this guy showing he kept tabs on Huck, making it sound friendly.

"You got a piece of that action?"

Huck shook his head, saying to Moran, "I'm mostly into yearlings and some two-year-olds, buying and selling, some mares, some stud horses."

"All that from cabs and booze, huh?"

"A little this, a little that."

"Well, tell you what, you don't sound too keen, but how about I go through the motions, give you some numbers, then I leave you to mull it over? Leave it up to you," Moran said. "Meantime, let's you and me get some breakfast. They do decent eggs in the clubhouse."

"Got that other meet," Gorilla Al reminded him.

"Right now I'm having eggs. You go on. And take them with you." Moran nodding toward the Gusenbergs.

Gorilla Al looking like he was going to object, then nodded, shaking Huck's hand again, saying it was good to see him again, telling him not to be a stranger.

Moran saying to Huck, "You drop me off after?"

"Sure." Huck having to shift his plans, driving into the city first instead of back to Schaumburg, Karla promising to take Maudie for chocolate soda at Margie's Candies later.

They got up, Huck seeing Gorilla Al walk through the stands, the brothers going with him.

Moran led the way to the clubhouse, saying, "You still got that fancy ride?"

"The Dues. Yeah."

"Me, I been a Cadillac man since short pants, but I been thinking of giving it up for Lent, switching to Daimler or could be a Dues. What do you think?"

"Think you can't go wrong either way. But the Dues has the straight eight, two hundred and sixty-five horses. Does a hundred at the top end."

"You and your ponies." Moran smiled, giving him good-natured, treating Huck to breakfast in the trackside restaurant, white tablecloths, waiters in uniform, a table by the window offering a view of the racing dogs — this guy who'd never had the time of day for him.

Huck knowing this would get back around to pumping money into the dog tracks, something he had a poor feeling about, not the dog racing, but getting back in bed with Bugs Moran or any of the North Side lads. Ordering eggs over easy, and feeling he was walking on a patch with land mines.

88

"**F**olks bet on anything, this being the latest, meaning there's money to be made." Moran made a joke about his money going to the dogs. Telling Huck how it started in California about ten years back and was spreading across the southern states, and already big in Florida.

"How much you looking for?" Huck asked, in his mind he was coming up with a list of reasons his cash was tied up, but admitting it sounded bankable — once it became legal.

"Half a million on a track, the grounds, the stands, a couple of savvy investors and we set these up across the country. Thought you'd see it — but sounds like you got the brakes on, already made up your mind. Getting set to tell me you'll call me . . ." Moran grinned, leaving it like that, not what Huck expected.

Moran looked around, the waiter coming to ask if he wanted anything else, Moran saying, "We're done here." Getting up, dropping a few bucks on the table, asking Huck, "Sure you got time to drop me off? That or I call one of them cabs, take my chances."

"Happy to drop you." Huck wanting to get out of there, thinking he'd drop him off at this garage the North Side had been using, then stop by Schofield's, the place under new management these days, buy a couple dozen roses for Karla, likely surprise her that he hadn't forgot about Valentine's Day. Then take her and Maudie for those sodas. He'd already made reservations at the Drake, going to take them for afternoon tea at the Fountain Court, still Karla's favorite place, then for some dancing after. Just the two of them, Karla leaving baby Emma with the nanny, and Maudie spending the night at a friend's, calling it a pajama party.

The two of them walked out, Moran making observations about the Dues, saying, "This the Roadster, huh?"

"Yeah, the Model J."

Moran going on about liking the straight eight and heard how these babies could burn up the road, always felt right having a fast set of wheels under him. "Get you out of trouble as fast as you got in."

Huck offering him the key, saying, "Why don't you find out, be my guest."

"Can't say no to that." Moran catching the key as Huck tossed it.

Getting in the passenger side, Huck eased back as Moran put his foot on the accelerator, letting the Dues loose all the way into town, the man smiling, loving the power, sold on getting himself one, shaking his head as he pulled to the curb, the only parking spot up the street from the garage, a sign in its window *S-M-C Cartage*.

"Well, you think about going to the dogs, just don't take too long. These things got a way of taking off, then you're left behind, smacking your forehead, saying, 'What was I thinking?'"

"I know what you mean," Huck said.

Bugs Moran looking ahead, seeing Ted Newbury wave to him, standing by his own car, holding his hands out, wondering what was going on.

"These guys . . ." Shrugging like what can you do, Moran said, "Got some old business to take care of — Canadian booze that fell off the back of a truck, the same old story, huh?" And he got out, gave Huck a wave and started walking, calling to Newbury to keep his shirt on.

Huck slid across the seat, the engine still running, putting it in gear and pulling out and rolling along North Clark. Seeing the police wagon ahead, right out front of the garage. Turning his head, wanting to warn Moran about what could be a raid, but Moran and Newbury had seen it and were turning and walking the other way, Huck driving past, wanting nothing to do with old gang business.

At the end of the block, he heard the shots, knowing the sound of Tommy guns, a lot of rounds, knowing it came from inside the garage, then the boom of a shotgun — not the sounds of a police raid. Looking back over the seat, he saw Moran and Newbury were running the other way. And Huck pushed the pedal down, getting out of there.

89

Dailies across the country painted the picture, how witnesses spotted two uniformed cops leading the two shooters from the garage. One witness receiving a letter after giving her statement to police, the letter advising her to keep her mouth shut. The woman leaving town without another word, and without leaving a forwarding address.

Seven men had been gunned down, Gorilla Al Weinshank among them, Capone's spotter across the street getting it wrong on account of Al and Moran having the Bobbsey twin looks. Among the dead were Bugs Moran's second-in-command Albert Kachellek, who went by Jim Clark, along with Adam Heyer and both Gusenbergs. Five of the gang, and then Schwimmer, an optometrist with gambling problems who liked hanging out with the gang, and John May, the gang's mechanic. All of them made to stand facing the wall, likely seeing it as a police raid, nothing new to the gang, all of them cut down by Tommy guns. Highball, Adam Heyer's Alsatian dog, the only survivor, left chained to the axle of a truck.

Huck got a call at his ranch the next day, Bugs Moran talking in a quiet voice, found out Capone was in Florida at the time of the shooting, giving himself an alibi, hiring Jack McGurn to set it up. McGurn putting spotters in the upstairs windows across from the warehouse, two cops coming in the front, one with a shotgun, two men in plain clothes coming in the back, the two armed with Thompsons. Moran guessing McGurn imported the shooters, mistaking Gorilla Al for himself, not a mistake any of the local Outfit would have made.

"You and me, we take care of this, these fuckin' Sicilians."

"It's done," Huck said, so many of the North Side dead in that garage.

"Maybe you can forget what they done," Moran sounding angry now, like Huck was back to betraying them. "You and Al go back. And the Goose, and Frank."

"Heard it's payback for the Lolordo hit." What Huck picked up through the grapevine. Kachellek, aka Clark, and the Gusenbergs had capped Capone's man Lolordo, along with the man's wife. Just two months back, and so it went, somebody avenging somebody else.

"They asked Frank, the man hit fourteen times, who shot him. Frank says 'Nobody shot me.' You ask me, now there's a man."

Huck not saying what he was thinking: yeah, loyal to the end, and a lot of good it did him.

"And to think I was going to let you in on the dog track thing . . ."

"And I appreciate it . . ." Not the way Huck saw it, Moran looking for financial backing, the only reason he gave Huck the time of day.

"Tell you what, forget it."

Looking at the handset, the line disconnected, he set it in the cradle. Thinking Moran ought to change his name and looks and leave town, do it fast, or he'd end up the same way. And for the first time, Huck realized Capone's spotters likely made him out driving past the warehouse, putting him back in league with the North Side. Meaning he could end up right back in the crosshairs.

Still thinking about it when he got in his car and drove back into the city, not telling Karla where he was going, not wanting her to worry. Pulling the Dues up out front of the entrance of the Lexington, 22nd and Michigan, Huck sitting in his car with his hands on the wheel, not wanting Capone's people getting the wrong idea, knowing there were already eyes on him.

It was Frankie Rio who came from a side door, walking slow and looking around, coming to the driver's side, tapping on the glass, leaning and looking in as Huck rolled down the window.

"Your compass get scrambled?" Frankie looking in at Huck.

"Want to talk to your boss. He don't have time now, I can come back."

"You got something to say, say it to me."

"No offense, Frankie, you're not the mouthpiece type. What I got to say, it's going to be one on one."

"Funny place to be giving orders."

"Do me a favor, go tell your boss I said please — just like a moment of his time."

"'Cause if this is about another fuckin' truce, or you turning Benedict Arnold, it's a bit late for that, in case you ain't been paying attention."

"You going to tell him or keep flapping your mouth?"

Frankie Rio looked at him a moment longer, rolled his eyes like he had a hundred better things to do, rapping his knuckles on the roof of the Dues, leaving Huck sitting there with the motor running.

Something inside told him to mash the pedal and get the hell out of there, away from this place where he stood a chance of ending up a stain on the sidewalk.

When Frankie Rio came back out, another goon stood by the door. Frankie waving for Huck to come.

Getting out, Huck kept his hands away from his sides and walked up the sidewalk.

Frankie leading the way to the telegraph office along the side of the building, opening the door. The goon walking behind Huck. The three of them stepping into the darkness, Huck told to stop once inside. Frankie patting him down, saying, "You got stones down your pants, or they just in your head?"

The goon's name was Enzo, the big man snorting.

Huck was led to a staircase and up they trudged to an office on the fourth floor. Huck told to go inside and take a chair. Sitting there alone about ten minutes. An inner door opened and Enzo stood holding it, giving Huck a hard look. Huck getting up slow, stepping past him into the office.

Al Capone sat behind the desk, not looking up, a cigar between his thick lips, reading a ledger or something like that, Huck just standing there.

Finally he looked at Huck, saying, "Who the fuck are you?"

"North Side."

"Yeah, I remember . . ." Capone almost smiling, recalling the time he came with Torrio to the flower shop, him and Huck eye-fucking each other, Huck with the Tommy gun by the window. "You the taxi guy — put them in the river."

"That's right."

"First time I got busted, got so juiced driving my Caddy, ran right into the ass end of a taxi, the damn thing parked, bright fuckin' yellow. You picture how juiced a guy's got to be to drive into something like that. Good thing it wasn't you behind the wheel."

Huck nodded, hearing Enzo chuckle behind him.

"You want coffee, tea, last rites?" Capone grinned.

"I'm good."

"So, how can I help? And throw in why I don't have Enzo give you a wire tie."

"And chance wrecking your nice rug? Persian, 'less I miss my guess," Huck said.

"Good point." Capone looking at Enzo, saying, "Do it outside."

"Look . . ." Huck not sure if he should call him Al or Mr. Capone. "I've been out of it going on two years. All that's behind me."

"Yet here you are."

"Just want to be clear."

Looking at the goon, Capone said, "Hey Enz, maybe I can use that on the stand, 'All that's behind me.' What d'you think?" Then back to Huck. "Got me subpoenaed to testify in front of the grand jury, 'case you ain't heard."

"Think I read about it."

"Bunch of merciless fucks — and me with bronchial pneumonia."

Huck just stood and listened.

"Hauled a sick man up from Miami, you believe it?" Puffing on his Hav-A-Tampa cigar, shaking his head. "They make some Supreme Court ruling, how money I make by breaking the law's all of a sudden taxable. How's a thing like that make sense, money by ill-gotten gains all of a sudden taxable — paying on something that ain't legit in the first place? Just a bunch of greedy fucks if you ask me."

"Bet you got the kind of lawyers can chew up the charges and spit it out."

"The suits call it a strong case, but I got a couple of nurses can swear I been in bed a month, but why am I telling you?" Closing the ledger, his eyes losing the friendly glint. "Tell me again . . ." Pointing his finger at Huck.

Huck repeated his name.

"Sound more hick than mick."

"I did some driving for them, from time to time. Whiskey from Canada mostly."

"You the one jumped the bridge, with what's his name . . ."

"Drucci," Enzo said.

"Yeah, that fuck. Showing him how to shake the cops, huh? In a yellow car."

"I was making a point, seeing how he'd take it."

"Did more 'n that, my friend, plenty more. How many of my loads you jack, shooting it out with my guys?"

"Like I said, I been out of it two years."

"You come here playing Mary Sunshine, take a chance on getting the bum's rush out the window — or worse."

Huck nodded, saying, "Hoping to go out the door, same way I come in, have supper with the wife and kids — tonight, tomorrow, and going forward."

"Where's Moran?"

"I got no idea. Heading out of town if he's smart."

Capone nodded, saying, "You got any idea how many times Johnny and me tried making peace with you micks? A bunch of hotheads, always taking a crap on our good thing. So, now it's done." Then he looked thoughtful, saying, "Huck Waller, why else I know that name?" And he looked to Enzo, the big man standing by the door, his arms hanging down as close to his sides as his arms could get.

Enzo saying, "The guy with Gypsy Doyle, one that got the drop on Sheldon."

Capone nodded, saying, "You didn't clip him."

"Needed him to drive."

"Could've done it after."

"I'm no killer."

"Out of it till you got spotted with Moran . . ."

"Got invited to his dog track, and he needed a lift. Talking about getting me to invest. That's it." Huck seeing how this was a bad idea, hardly buying his own story. Hoping Capone didn't know he was the driver that time the lads tried to rub him out walking into his favorite restaurant.

Capone sucked on the cigar, his eyes never leaving him.

"So I let you go, then what?"

"You never hear from me again."

"Any idea how many of my guys are in the ground?"

Huck didn't answer, the two of them eyeing each other.

"Me neither." Another draw on the cigar, then Capone said, "How much you figure you cost me?"

Huck shrugged.

"Can't bring back the dead — but you can repay the dough."

Huck waited.

"I let you walk, and you show up any place near them fucks . . . what do they call them, Kill— . . ."

"Kilgubbin," Enzo said.

"Got the kill part right. Get seen with what's left, and you join 'em, and it's not just you, you understand? I give it to the moolies, them that got no trouble with letting you see it happen, your family one at a time, then you. Not how we do things, this oath we got, but the Irish . . . them you can't reason with."

"I just want out." Huck put up his hands.

"But you've done alright, taking money from my pockets over the years. Got enough to retire on, invest in horses, fancy place in the country, now talking about dog tracks." Capone looked at Huck's tailored suit. "Enz here tells me you got a nice ride downstairs, better than mine, he says."

Huck nodded, getting an idea where this was going.

"Horses, cars, what else?"

"You want a list?"

"Yeah, now you mention it." Capone looked at him, waiting.

"Money in a couple businesses, second mortgages, stocks, bonds, land."

"Land's good, gives you a place to bury the bodies, but stocks — those fast-talking hustlers — just another racket, all that up one day, down the next, nobody knowing for sure. Ain't got the stomach for that."

Huck waited now, didn't say how he'd quadrupled his money over the past decade, living like a king off the dividends, meaning his money had been scrubbed clean.

"You pay it back, what you took, and you walk. How's that sound?"

Huck sat a moment before saying, "Didn't exactly count it."

"Then let's think in round numbers . . . and don't leave nothing out."

Huck wasn't expecting that.

Glancing to the ceiling, Capone worked the cigar, puffing a cloud to the ceiling, saying, "Let's call it a mill, ought to be close. What do you think?" He wasn't asking, and he definitely wasn't talking terms.

"It matter what I think?"

"Not so much."

Huck speculating how to raise that much cash, just paid the architect and builder the final installment on the house and barns, paid Fannie Hertz for more yearlings and two-year-olds he bought, thinking there was no way, not without liquidating just about everything, but nodding like it was no trouble.

"Recompense is what the feds call it," Capone said. "Less you got bones about making good?"

"I got no problem." Seeing Capone glance up at Enzo. Huck saying, "Going to need some time . . ."

"Take the time you need, call it a month, but know it ain't over till you come in with it. Meantime I'm thinking if I made the right choice, you get me?"

"Yeah."

"Then why you still here?" With that, Capone reopened the ledger, turning to a page, writing something down.

Huck rising out of the chair.

Enzo opened the door, making a kissing gesture with his fat lips as Huck walked through the door.

90

Selling some of the yearling stock back to Fannie Hertz, giving up ten points on the sale, cashing all his bonds and selling off his General Electric and U.S. Steel, half the General Motors and most of the Sears Roebuck. Took him two weeks to do it, losing plenty on the sale, racking up a hell of a tax bill. Sold his Duesenberg and picked up a used Model A, older than the Ford he'd bought Izzy.

He scraped up most of the money, and with a pistol under his jacket and bulging suitcase in his hand, he walked back into the Lexington, lugged the suitcase, guessing it weighed thirty pounds, up to the fourth floor, looking to pay the son of a bitch, this gangster worth about thirty million.

What he found was the place crawling with Treasury agents, Capone not in his office, a pinched-looking man glanced up from behind his spectacles, sitting behind Capone's desk, inspecting the same ledger Capone had written in. The man telling him he was Treasury agent Frank Wilson, asking, "Who in hell are you?"

"Think I got off on the wrong floor." Huck wiping his brow, saying he was sorry, taking the suitcase and getting out of there, not seeing any of Capone's Outfit hanging around, only the man's secretary in the outer office. Leaving word with her, wanting Capone to know he had shown up. Taking the suitcase before some treasury guy asked what he had there, Huck walked back down and got in the Ford and drove back to Schaumburg. Expecting to hear from Capone, letting Huck know where to drop the money.

In his mind, he had considered borrowing from the First Chicago Bank, thinking he might have to leverage his property too, not enough in dividends left coming in. He could sell the remaining yearling stock, hoping for a better price at auction than he'd get from Fannie Hertz.

Not a word from Capone or his people. Huck considering what to do with the money till they came. He could put it in a bank, but he'd have to explain it, and the idea of an amount like that sitting in an account didn't feel right, not with the number of bank failures happening over the past year.

Standing with Karla on their front porch, he told her things would be tight for a while, Karla knowing about him selling off everything to make the payment to Capone. Standing next to him, an arm around him, head on his shoulder, saying, "Not worried about the money, never was. But if you are, I can always go back to nickel hopping."

"That still a thing?"

"You want me to find out?"

"We'll be alright." Huck hugged her close, the two of them looking out at the pastures and fence line, the row of trees beyond that — all he had worked for.

"Sure we will. But if not in a bank, what are you gonna do, hide it under the mattress?"

91

The first edition told how Capone, along with one of his bodyguards, had been picked up in Philadelphia, carrying concealed weapons and getting sentenced to a year each. Capone already on bail on a contempt of court charge, the feds had been closing in on him, set to sink their teeth in. It had been weeks, Huck wondering why he hadn't heard from Capone's people, when the operator rang the phone in the parlor. Taking a breath before he picked up.

It was Fannie Hertz, the woman distressed, telling him they'd had a fire at Trout Valley. Crying, she told him somebody torched the stables, killing eleven of their prize horses, the police looking into arson. John D. beside himself, and she asked Huck if he could come, and he was on his way.

Driving the last crest of hill, past the copse of trees where Stanton had fired from, he gripped the wheel tighter and kept driving, then he was looking at the manor, men moving behind the house as he pulled up the long drive, the falling leaves blowing up behind him.

The stables out back were a smoldering ruin. Huck pulling the Ford to a stop, getting out, that acrid smell hanging in the air, a full day after the fire. Some of the horses were in a corral, others had been moved to another barn. A bay reared up, a ranch hand hanging onto its lead, dodging its hooves, trying to calm the horse.

And he saw Fannie, going to her, her face streaked with soot, her hair wild, and he was hugging her, not knowing what to tell her. The woman looked like she hadn't slept since the fire.

"Eleven of them gone." She pointed to where the carcasses were still laid out, each hulk covered in a blanket.

He wanted her to tell him what happened.

"Heard somebody yell, and I woke, saw the flames and I ran out . . ." She pointed over to the where the stables had been. "Everybody trying get the horses out, but . . ." And she was sobbing into his shoulder.

Her maid came and took her by the arm, getting her into the house, telling her she needed to get some rest.

And there was John D., standing by the ashes, barking orders. Seeing Huck, he stormed toward him, anger flashing in his eyes, practically yelling, "The hell do I pay you for?"

Huck just looked at him — hadn't worked for the man in over a year.

John D. collected himself, told him he was sorry, the man looking broken.

His foreman came and stood next to him, nodding at Huck, telling John D. the press would be arriving soon.

John D. nodded, collecting himself, telling the foreman to get them gathered on the lawn at the side of the house, giving them a view of the burned stables and the line of dead horses. Saying to Huck, "Come with me — please."

"Damn sorry about this, John."

"Guess we all knew it could come — this damn taxi business." And he stood silent, looking to the scorched remains. Finally saying, "Hear you got troubles of your own."

"Depends what you heard."

"Those bootleggers getting gunned down have something to do with you selling off your yearlings, something I know you'd never do."

"Call it the price of getting out." And he told John D. about the rest of it, making the payment to Capone.

"How much?"

"A million."

John D. didn't say anything more, then the foreman waved from the side yard, and Huck followed him across the lawn to where the group of reporters waited, their photographers setting up the cameras on wood tripods.

John D. Hertz stood before them, now a composed man — the *American*, *Daily News*, *Evening Post*, *Herald-Examiner*, *Journal*, and the *Tribune*, all the newshawks standing at the side of the manor house, the burned stalls at John D.'s back. Eleven of his prized horses dead, now being winched and hoisted one by one into the back of a flatbed, another truck waiting. Photographers held up their light meters, getting the settings right, flashing their bulbs.

The reporter from the *Trib* got it started, asking what set it off, asking Hertz to tell it in his own words.

"Who else's words would you suppose?" John D. had found a new calm and was steady now, speaking about the tragic loss, calling it a savage attack by cowards, those with a checkered past.

"Are you saying this has something to do with the taxi war, Mr. Hertz?"

"For that, you best ask the detectives."

"Do you suspect Morris Markin's behind this?"

"When I see a son of a bitch of low morals with a complete lack of principles, and not a spot of decency, yes, I suppose I might look that son of a bitch's way."

"To be clear, sir, by 'son of a bitch,' you're referring to Mr. Markin?"

"If you recall the time my livery was bombed, three good men injured. Or the time a line of Checker cabs went tearing past in broad daylight, a killing caravan, everyone filled with murder and treachery, assassins emptying their weapons into my walls, one of my men gunned in his prime, dozens of my fleet shot up."

"But, to clarify, by 'a son of a bitch' —" The *Examiner*'s man was cut off.

"Was Reigh Count among the dead?" The reporter from the American interrupted.

"Reigh Count's in England, thank God, winning the Coronation Cup, finishing second in the Ascot Gold Cup."

The *Journal*'s man waved his hand, getting Hertz looking his way. "Let me ask, sir, are you satisfied with the police chief's efforts?"

"What city are you living in, son?"

Getting the reporters chuckling and nodding.

"You're asking me to speculate, gentlemen. Do I think palms are being greased, officials looking the other way while wild men shoot up this town, keeping honest men from making a living?"

"You make it sound like you've had no part in it, Mr. Hertz, this war?" It was the reporter from the *Tribune*.

Hertz looked at him a moment, then said, "Do you know the difference between instigating and retaliating, son? An honest businessman ought to rely on the powers that be, and should see a prompt stop to lawlessness. I ask you, have you seen any stop to it?" Pointing behind him to the scene, another carcass being winched onto the flatbed.

"So, you're alleging there's corruption?" the *Trib*'s man pushed for an answer.

One of the reporters joking that re-elected Mayor Big Bill Thompson was the poster child of corruption.

"The good mayor and the chief will tell us they're doing all they can. Me, I say show me, don't tell me when the results do not line up."

"To clarify, are you saying you haven't had a hand in it, the taxi war?" This from the *Daily News'* man.

"My credentials speak for themselves, sir. Need I remind you, I put in the traffic light, the first one our fair city's seen, keeping folks safe, putting in taxi stands for their convenience. Employing six thousand drivers, creating the largest taxi business in the world."

"So to be clear, you suspect arson as the cause here, Mr. Hertz?"

"Suspect! A child can tell you the cause, son. Let me ask you, have you ever heard a horse screaming its last — burning to death?" His voice broke here, John D. shaking his head, then saying, "If it wasn't for my loyal people here, Anita Peabody would be gone too. God bless them one and all for their swift action. No doubt, Anita Peabody and Reigh Count were the targets of these cowards, the finest racehorses in the world. For those ignorant of the sport of kings, Anita Peabody is our American champion two-year-old filly, winner of the Belmont Futurity Stakes. Reigh Count the winner of six races last season, including the Kentucky Derby. This year shipped to England, cleaning up over there, winning the Coronation Cup as I've said, coming second in the Gold Cup at Royal Ascot. Coming back to America, I was just offered a million dollars for him."

"What kind of man would offer a million dollars, Mr. Hertz?" This from the *Post's* man.

"Better yet, what kind of man would turn it down?" John D. said. "Question you should be asking is what kind of man would want to destroy something like that? Eleven of my innocent beauties taken from us, meeting a terrible end, a screaming sound I'll never get from my head — and me, unable to save them."

"I'm sure we're all very sorry for your loss, Mr. Hertz, but can you give us an idea of the total damage here?" the *Journal*'s man asked.

"You're asking me to put a price on the priceless, son."

The *Journal*'s man apologized, then said, "Where do you go from here, sir?"

"Well, gentlemen, since law and order's in short supply, it's with a heavy heart that I am announcing I'm going to sell." Hertz let that hang.

"Sell the horses?"

"I'm selling Yellow."

"You're getting out of the business?"

"You heard me right." John D. looking from face to face, judging their reactions, like a man already seeing the headlines.

"Do you have a buyer in mind, sir?" Some doubt in the newsman's voice, this from the *Herald-Examiner*.

"I'll keep that under wraps for now, gentlemen. We'll let the smoke clear and the ink dry, then I'll have more to say."

"Hard to believe you're getting out of the taxi business, Mr. Hertz?" The man from the *Post*, sounding skeptical.

"It used to be, I said a thing, and you boys gobbled it up and scribbled it down. Never a doubt in your minds. I don't know what might have changed that."

"Well sir, some of us fellas got to know you." The man from the *Examiner* grinned, showing they were all friends here.

"Well, you got me there, boys."

The *Trib* man called, "You really planning on retiring, Mr. Hertz? Come on, now."

"At forty-nine, I hardly think so. But I can tell you I'm heading for greener pastures, something bigger and better, as always."

"How about the horses, you staying in that game?"

"It's in my blood, boys. Wild horses couldn't drag me away."

There was more chuckling, pencils scribbling.

"There are stakes races to be won yet, gentlemen."

"How about your cars, and other interests."

"All I'll say . . ." And he let his eyes go from man to man. "You haven't seen the last of John D. Hertz — to put it plain, I'm just getting to the start line." The smile had a sly edge, Hertz holding it as the photographer flipped the hood over his head, holding up the flash.

"Now what?" Huck said to him after, the two sitting on the porch, John D. letting go of the facade he'd put on for the press. The man looked near exhaustion as he took the decanter, pouring them each a couple of fingers of scotch. He'd sold a majority share of the company to GM back in '26, sat on GM's board, and had his fingers in the pies of several other companies.

"Now, I turn the page and see what life's got in store."

"You really selling?"

"Lock, stock and spoked wheels. Between me and you, Huck, I've already lined up the interested party."

Huck thought a moment, then looked at him. "Not going to tell me it's Markin?"

"The man sees himself merging the two companies." John D. didn't meet his eyes, just looking out over his pastures.

"Always figured you'd sooner firebomb your own livery than sell to that man."

"Let's say we've all got our price, my boy. I won't exactly be giving it to him. Besides, times are changing. I see tough times ahead, and people thinking twice before paying cab fares."

"You've got an idea, don't you?" Huck shook his head, John D. Hertz always thinking a step ahead, not a man to be counted out.

"As a matter of fact, I do. And I'm prepared to let you in on it."

"You know I'm pretty much busted."

"What I know is you sold some yearlings, some stocks and assets, and you're set to pay this gangster almost everything you've got, the money he says you owe him. Have I got that right?"

"Pretty much."

"And correct me if I'm wrong, but he's currently a guest of the state for possession of a weapon, with the feds sifting through his books as we speak, looking for witnesses and evidence to build their case, making it look like the man's fate is sealed."

"That man's got a way of slipping out of jams."

"Not this time."

Huck looked at him, but John D. didn't say more.

They sat quiet, sipping their drinks, the evening coming, a chill starting to settle in.

"So, this new idea . . ." Huck broke the silence.

"In a while I'm going to pick up some cars cheap, then I'm going to rent them. Let folks drive themselves around."

"You think they'll go for that?"

"Why else would I do it?"

Huck nodded.

"And when Capone doesn't come collecting . . ." John D. said.

"Could put it in a bank, or back in stocks, collect interest and dividends till he shows up."

John D. nodded, then said, "You heard what goes up is bound to come down."

"You're trying to tell me something, John?"

"That market you're talking about . . ."

"Yeah?"

"It's about to go bust."

"How do you figure?"

Hertz held up the fingers of one hand, counting off. "You've got stock prices wildly inflated, unemployment going through the roof, the Fed cutting off easy credit with an aim to slow runaway prices." He curled the fourth finger down, saying, "On top of that, you've got rising interest rates." The fifth finger. "And you've got so-called savvy traders buying on margin. The whole mess unsustainable."

Huck looked out to the trees, letting that sink in.

"I'm saying if I'm right, then that mess is about to slide off. Meaning there's a reversal coming — all the signs are staring us in the face."

"You sound pretty sure."

"You ever know me not to be? Look, here's the rule, you buy when everyone else is selling, and you hold on and sell when everyone's buying."

"What you're really saying is I ought to throw in with you instead?"

John D. smiled.

92

Huck stepped onto his porch, a cool breeze this morning, a far cry from the heat wave earlier in the month. Reaching down for the paper, he glanced at the headline as he started to step back in. It caught his breath.

Black Monday. The lead story telling how Wall Street was echoing the avalanche of sliding stock prices — the Dow tanking twelve points from the opening bell. The caption under a line drawing: "Can the thud of bodies be far behind?" Will Rogers in his syndicated column was calling it a tailspin, how you had to get in line to find a window to jump from.

Huck read about the panicked sell-offs following last week's Black Thursday. The piece speculating that Tuesday was promising to get even darker than the Monday, market analysts claiming there was nothing to stop the slide.

Pulling the old watch chain, the one he took from that pimp Bubbling-Over all those years ago, he saw it had stopped. Winding it and putting it to his ear.

He stood there looking out across the peaceful land — his land — not sure how long he stood there, then the phone was ringing inside, pulling him from his thoughts, and Karla was calling to him, saying John D. was on the line, wanting a word.

Acknowledgments

A big thank you to publisher Jack David — always generous of his time and spirit, and for affording me creative freedom. I also appreciate his tales from the trenches, his sense of humor, and the articles he sends on occasion, some of which have sparked ideas that have made their way into my novels, including this one.

Thanks again to the ECW team for their continued enthusiasm, professionalism and united efforts. They all do an excellent job. Additionally, I'd like to commend Samantha Chin, the managing and production editor, for wearing many hats and remaining one step ahead of everything — always a delight to deal with. And a nod to creative director Jess Albert for her efforts in seeing that this cover design landed just right.

I greatly enjoyed working with editor Lesley Erickson for the first time. And I appreciated her careful notes, as well as her support.

Thank you to copy editor Peter Norman. I always feel reassured once he's gone through my manuscripts, done the fact-checking and pointed out any of my grammar violations. Nothing gets past Peter. Nothing.

Kelly Laycock brought her outstanding proofreading skills to this one, and I am grateful for her contribution.

I'd like to acknowledge David A. Gee, who not only designed the *Dirty Little War* cover but also the one for my very first novel many years ago. It's nice to see that he hasn't lost his touch. Well done.

As always, I feel truly blessed to have the support of my loving family, Andie and Xander. I'm all the better for having them in my life.

Entertainment. Writing. Culture. ──────────

ECW is a proudly independent, Canadian-owned book publisher. We know great writing can improve people's lives, and we're passionate about sharing original, exciting, and insightful writing across genres.

──────────────── **Thanks for reading along!**

We want our books not just to sustain our imaginations, but to help construct a healthier, more just world, and so we've become a certified B Corporation, meaning we meet a high standard of social and environmental responsibility — and we're going to keep aiming higher. We believe books can drive change, but the way we make them can too.

Certified

Corporation

Being a B Corp means that the act of publishing this book should be a force for good — for the planet, for our communities, and for the people that worked to make this book. For example, everyone who worked on this book was paid at least a living wage. You can learn more at the Ontario Living Wage Network.

This book is also available as a Global Certified Accessible™ (GCA) ebook. ECW Press's ebooks are screen reader friendly and are built to meet the needs of those who are unable to read standard print due to blindness, low vision, dyslexia, or a physical disability.

The interior of this book is printed on Sustana EnviroBook™, which is made from 100% recycled fibres and processed chlorine-free.

FSC
www.fsc.org
MIX
Paper | Supporting
responsible forestry
FSC® C016245

ECW's office is situated on land that was the traditional territory of many nations, including the Wendat, the Anishnaabeg, Haudenosaunee, Chippewa, Métis, and current treaty holders the Mississaugas of the Credit. In the 1880s, the land was developed as part of a growing community around St. Matthew's Anglican and other churches. Starting in the 1950s, our neighbourhood was transformed by immigrants fleeing the Vietnam War and Chinese Canadians dispossessed by the building of Nathan Phillips Square and the subsequent rise in real estate value in other Chinatowns. We are grateful to those who cared for the land before us and are proud to be working amidst this mix of cultures.

ecwpress.com